The Rules

(Summer Nights Series book 2)

LAUREN H. MAE

First paperback edition July 2020

Interior formatting by Streetlight Graphics
www.streetlightgraphics.com

Character illustration by Leni Kauffman
www.lenikauffman.com

www.laurenhmae.com

To The Chat.

"A life without love is like a year without summer."

—*Swedish Proverb*

One

*D*ANI PETRILLO HAD ONE RULE for the day: Do. Not. Cry.

It wasn't that weddings themselves made her teary. At twenty-nine, she'd been to plenty of them and not once had she felt even the hint of a tingle in the back of her nose. In fact, she'd been *not crying* at weddings as long as she could remember. When she was nine years old, her mother dressed her in a canary yellow gown that clashed hideously with her white-blonde hair, and made her a junior bridesmaid at her second wedding. Bruce—the man who'd lived next door to them for Dani's entire life until he'd moved in and become her step-father—was a nice enough guy, but the moment didn't exactly move her.

Her father had remarried a year later. He started a new family with a woman named Hannah who'd come with two daughters, already adults. Dani had been dressed and dolled and trotted out for both of their weddings before they'd become strangers to her again. Step-siblings, cousins, co-workers—she'd seen plenty of friends get married, and she'd been perfectly happy for them, but she'd never been that girl who heard "Pachelbel's Canon" and worried about her eye makeup holding up.

Neither had Cat, her best friend since age eleven, and the one wearing the white dress today. In all the hours they'd spent in Cat's bedroom, trying on Cat's sisters' makeup and old prom dresses, it hadn't occurred to them to dress up as brides. They both seemed to be missing that gene that wrapped all little girls' fantasies in white lace and fairytale love. It was why they got along so well.

But earlier that evening, in a stone chapel filled with fresh-cut peonies and lit with hundreds of white votives, when the four-piece mariachi band dressed all in white had played "Ava Maria" and she'd caught Cat blinking back tears, Dani had been glad the makeup artist had chosen waterproof mascara for the bridal party.

And now, on the brick patio in the courtyard of a fancy boutique hotel downtown, beneath hundreds of white globe string-lights twinkling in the night sky, watching her best friend smile adoringly at her new husband, Dani's throat felt as tight as a champagne bottle ready to pop.

Except instead of booze, it was a good ugly cry that was dying to escape.

"Time's up," she said, waving her hand in Cat's face to separate it from Josh's. (Despite that little wave of emotion, they were a lot.) "Pick your poison."

"Noooo," Cat whined. "That's against the rules."

"Sorry, Cat. 'No Shots' rule is boring. Choose."

"Just one," Josh said. At least someone was willing to have some fun. He gazed down at Cat, twisting a lock of her black-brown hair around his fingers. He looked different today without his usual surfer-dude stubble and backward base-ball cap. Older. Maybe it was the navy blue tux or the fact that your wedding day is sort of the pinnacle of adulthood, but something about him seemed fundamentally changed. The whole night did. Which was why they needed shots.

"Fine." Cat's scowl softened, and Dani felt a jolt of victory. They didn't call Josh The Cat Whisperer for nothing.

"This did not go well the last time," Sonya reminded them with a judgy sip of champagne. She was referring to Josh's thirty-fifth birthday party a few weeks back, when Cat had decided she could match Dani drink for drink and ended up swimming in the Chesapeake in cut-off shorts and her UVA hoodie. Dani wasn't going to take the blame for that one, though. Who forgets their phone is in their pocket when they jump in the water? Although, she probably didn't need to laugh so hard over it.

"Enough dodging. If Cat doesn't pick, I do." Dylan Pierce—the best man and vocal opponent of the "No Shots" rule. He slung an arm around Dani's shoulders, his expensive cologne wafting into her space as he shot her the kind of smile that made good girls want to be bad. It was his trademark, that smile. In the two years she'd known Dylan, she'd never seen him wear any other expression. It was the kind of smile that said whatever bullshit is going on around him, he neither noticed nor cared. *Oh, the world is ending? Here, let me make you a drink, sweetheart.*

He was the perfect ally.

"Have a little fun, Kit Cat," he went on, poking her arm. Dangerous tactic given the way Cat glared at him, but Dylan got away with stuff like that. With Cat it was because he was Josh's best friend, but with most women, it was that face. Dylan could say whatever he wanted as long as he looked at you with his big puppy-dog eyes. They were this soft, mossy-green color that looked entirely subdued in the midst of his other striking features: thick, chocolate-colored hair, meticulously-shaped stubble beard, dimples that looked like they were chiseled into his cheeks. That broad, prominent nose that ended in an unexpected, impish little upturn. On any other man, it might look too big. On Dylan, it looked bold and confident... like him.

But then there were those eyes.

Dani turned back to Cat, annoyed at how

long she'd been looking at him. "What's it going to be?"

Cat bared her teeth and growled at Dani like one of those tiny toy dogs that thinks it's intimidating. She was adorable.

"Tequila," she relented.

"Excellent choice." Dani turned to the poor waiter who'd been standing silently by while they hashed this out, and he hurried off to the bar. Moments later, he was passing out five little glasses of brown liquor.

"Body shots?" Dylan asked.

Dani rolled her eyes and held up her glass. "Nice try." She turned to the newlyweds. "A toast. To Catia and Joshua, may your love sicken us all for years to come."

"Here, here," Sonya said.

Cat waited until Dani had tipped the shot to her mouth, then quickly shoved hers into Josh's hand, grinning triumphantly when he downed it for her.

Wuss.

Breaking the "No Shots" rule was decidedly Dani's best move of the night.

She'd managed to pry Cat away from Josh by flirting with the DJ and coaxing him into some old-school music—Cat was an absolute fool for Shakira. Cat did a little pirouette on the dance floor, showing off the half-moon stains under her arms, and Sonya snorted into her champagne glass.

"How do you feel, Mrs. Rideout?" Dani shouted over the music to the bride.

"I feel like this day couldn't have been more perfect."

Sonya beamed. "Aww. Young love."

Cat caught Josh's eye across the courtyard and blew him a kiss, one satin peep-toe heel kicked back behind her and a cheesy grin on her face.

She looked like a vintage movie star in that dress, the way it hugged her curves like she'd been dipped in Spanish lace. The back plunged dramatically, right down to her waist, and her dark hair fell in big, bombshell curls over both shoulders. She'd worn an old-fashioned mantilla veil for the ceremony but she'd paired it with a red lip and a subtle cat-eye liner because she would never completely submit to any tradition.

Classy, fierce Catia.

Lovesick, googly-eyed Catia.

The thought came to Dani unbidden and her neck heated, embarrassed at the whiny, unsupportive little voice inside her head. It was just that she'd known Cat most of her life and she'd never known there was another version of her that some cute guy she met in a bar would unlock—one who walked around with hearts in her eyes and blew kisses. But when Cat met Josh,

Prince fucking Charming, her best friend became *that girl*.

The one who'd suddenly gone misty-eyed. Again. *For God's sake.*

"Kit Cat!"

Cat sniffed and dabbed at the corner of her eye. "I know. God, I feel like Emma. I'm so emotional."

As if she'd been summoned by the wedding gods, Emma pushed into their circle, holding four plates of cake in a move only someone who'd waitressed through college could pull off. She passed them out while belting out the lyrics to Jagged Edge's "Let's Get Married."

Emma was in her glory. While Sonya bossed everyone around, and Dani kept them all plied with champagne, Emma soaked in the ceremony of it all.

Emma's had been the last big wedding—a vintage bed and breakfast with a harp and a Cinderella-style dress, her college sweetheart for a groom. She'd cried pretty much the entire day. But they'd known this about Emma from the start. Cat was a surprise.

Dani filled her mouth with cake to keep from saying anything snarky about Cat's waterworks. "I'm glad Josh didn't smoosh this in your face," she said, though she wasn't really. That was one of her favorite wedding traditions.

Cat laughed, her tears magically abated by sugar. "He made me promise not to do it to him."

"No way! And you agreed?"

"I left him guessing until the last minute."

Sonya shook her head. "You two are something else."

Dani smoothed her tea-length, navy blue dress, watching her feet wobble on her heels from the tequila. Was she missing something here? How was it that all of her friends had found these perfect guys and she was still bobbing from sinking ship to sinking ship? Her last three boyfriends had worn out their welcome in a matter of weeks.

Truthfully, she hadn't given much thought to the idea of settling down like this—looking at the same face day in and day out, listening to the same person's jokes, sex with the same person. Forever. She hadn't even had the same hairstyle for more than a few months.

And yet here was Cat, practically glowing at the idea of forever.

Dani scooped up more cake with her fork. "Don't you ever worry that, I don't know, you'll get bored?"

Emma made a noise like she was genuinely offended on behalf of love.

"Is that what you think? Josh is boring?" Cat gave her an evil grin. "I know you guys think he's some sort of Prince Charming, but he's not always." She lowered her voice and leaned in. "He has the dirtiest mouth."

"Oh my God. TMI," Sonya said.

Dani rushed to swallow her bite of cake, her finger in the air. "Hold up. I'm going to need you to expand on that statement."

Cat giggled, her cheeks glowing red. "I'm just saying, people have so many layers. You could live with someone for fifty years and probably never discover them all. You'll only get bored if you decide you've seen enough and stop peeling them back." She scooped some frosting off of her plate with her finger and licked it off. "Besides, if bored is the worst thing that happens between us, I'll join a book club. I've had enough turmoil in my love life. So has Josh. It feels good to have someone who I know will always be there."

"You had us, though," Dani said.

"Okay, someone who is always there and who also looks mad fine in his underwear."

Dani snorted. "Oh my God. Who knew getting married would turn you into a little horndog?"

Cat tipped her head onto Dani's shoulder, knocking the white orchid she had fastened askew. "Layers."

Dani pressed her thumb into the corner of her eye, blotting her mascara back into place. Back to keeping things light. Moments like this— teary, loaded moments—they made Dani itch. She fished her phone out of the top of her dress and angled it toward Cat just as she put more cake into her mouth. The flash startled her, and her beautifully done-up face twisted awkwardly around her fork.

"Oh my God! Why?" That sappy look in Cat's eyes was replaced by the spitfire Dani recognized.

"For the album!"

Sonya laughed. "I hope you're sharing that."

Dani had been keeping a file of horribly-timed photos of all of her friends for years. They came in handy for birthdays, anniversaries, basically any event you didn't want ruined with a slide-show of embarrassing candids. Sonya only found it amusing because she never seemed to take a bad picture. Her skin was dark enough to hide any imperfections and she was a total gym rat so she didn't have an ounce of hidden flab for anyone to document.

"Don't worry," Dani said. "I'll post it while she's lying on a beach in Hawaii and tag Josh."

Cat stuck her tongue out. "I hate you."

Mood officially lifted.

"Take a real one, Dani," Emma said. She took everyone's plates and set them on the nearest table.

"No." Cat scowled.

"Come on, Kit Cat," Dani said, maneuvering them into a half-circle. "We need one of all of us!"

Sonya and Emma squeezed in, and Dani came around to Cat's other side. She threw her arm around Cat's neck, avoiding all of the curls and lace and fresh-cut flowers. "You're my best-est friend in the whole wide world, Kit Cat," she whispered, stretching her arm out to get them all in the photo. "Always remember you loved me first."

Cat snort-laughed, Emma opened her mouth to say something, and Sonya put on a super-model grin. Dani snapped the photo.

"Ugh! Dani!"

Jagged Edge faded out and, in a testament to the skill of DJ Hotty Mcfly, blended seamlessly into the first notes of "At Last."

Dani pushed Cat with her elbow. "You should go find your husband."

"I should." Cat squeezed her around the waist. "Love you, Dani."

"Love you more."

Dani watched Cat cross the dance floor to her husband. Josh met her in the middle, cupping her face in both of his hands, and kissed her like she'd been gone for years.

When Dani turned back around, Emma and Sonya had both beelined toward their dates. *Great.* She could feel her good mood waning as the lyrics got more and more romantic and she stood there alone.

She swung her eyes around the courtyard for someone to talk to and spotted Dylan waiting at the bar. He hadn't brought a date, which was un-like him. She couldn't remember an event where Dylan didn't have a new woman on his arm. Last summer, she'd tagged along with Cat to a charity softball game that Josh and Dylan's architecture firm had sponsored. Dylan spent the entire time either on the field or in the dugout, but by the time it was over, he'd somehow snagged three women's phone numbers.

At a softball game.

His dating success wasn't a mystery. Dylan was six feet of lean muscle and had that deadly combination of a boyish smile and a tattooed chest. It made it easy to overlook his overgrown frat-boy persona.

She had to admit, he looked especially tall, dark, and handsome in that suit. The blue tie made his mossy eyes look sort of emerald actually, and she'd never found a reason to complain about the way a nicely-pressed dress shirt showed off his narrow waist. She allowed herself the indulgence of checking out his ass as he leaned his elbows on the bar.

But when she dragged her eyes back up his body, he was staring back.

Oops.

Dylan cocked his head to the side, his smile smug. Heat slapped her cheeks. No doubt about it, she'd been caught. There was nothing left to do but own it. Besides, flirting with Dylan might be just the thing she needed to get her out of this sentimental mood she'd found herself in.

Now if she could just walk over there without swaying.

"Hey," she said, bumping Dylan's upper thigh with her hip. He had a good five inches on her even in her heels. "Order me one, will you?"

Dylan's lips curved into a grin. "Sure thing."

He held up two fingers to the bartender and the kid pulled out a matching glass. Dylan turned back to her, his eyes dancing as he swiped a thumb over her cheek. He held it up, and her face flushed again.

Frosting. Great. So much for owning it.

He licked the frosting off of his thumb, watching her closely. "You sure you need another drink, Dani-pie?"

"Yes, *Dylan*. And don't call me that."

"It's your Instagram name."

"Stop stalking me on Instagram."

"Never." The bartender slid two shots across the bar. Dylan tossed a few bills into the tip jar and balanced them both in one hand. "Trade you yours for a dance," he said. "Unless you're afraid you might turn to mush when I get my hands on you."

"I'm not sure you can keep up with me on the dance floor," she said, ignoring the fact that she knew he could. She also knew she was pleasantly buzzed and feeling more than a little emotional. Bad combination when you're thinking about pressing yourself to another warm body. Especially a hard one like Dylan's.

Dylan's chest puffed predictably. "I guess I have something to prove then."

"Fine." She held out her hand and he placed one of the shots in it. She could behave herself for a dance.

"So here we are," she said, wrapping one arm around his neck, the other clutching her shot. "Officially the last ones on the singles cruise."

Dylan's hand landed on her waist. "We knew it was coming."

"We did."

"You remember the first night we all met?" he asked, his voice uncharacteristically nostalgic.

"I do."

"It's weird, right? One minute you're on vacation trying to get laid, and the next your best friend meets his future wife. Sappy fucker."

Dani laughed, nearly spitting out her tequila. She wiped at her lips, then took a proper sip. "Don't act like you don't love your boy."

"I love him," he said, looking over the top of her head. "Everyone does."

She caught something in Dylan's tone that surprised her. Not envy, but a comparison nonetheless. She followed his gaze across the dance floor, seeing Josh and Cat still cuddled up. "They are a little sickening," she said.

"Right?"

"Don't forget I was there for that magical moment. You'd have thought the heavens had just opened up and choirs of angels were singing." Dani batted her eyes and swooned in her best Cat and Josh impression.

Dylan laughed into his tequila. "Foolishness."

"Gag-worthy."

His arm tightened around her, turning them,

and another whiff of that cologne, salty and fresh, swarmed her senses. He smelled delicious. She imagined running her tongue along the razor edge of his facial hair, and then mentally slapped herself for it. So much for behaving.

She gulped the rest of her shot and was about to suggest another when a petite woman with greying black hair and olive skin tapped Dylan on the shoulder. He turned, the tips of his ears going red.

"Dylan, sweetie, I'm going to head out. I'm exhausted." The woman turned to Dani, flashing a pair of familiar green eyes. "Hi, I'm Irene. Dylan's mom."

Oh wow. He was the spitting image. This was priceless.

"You're Cat's best friend, right?"

"Dani. Nice to meet you."

"Oh, you too!" Irene's eyes dropped to Dylan's hand on Dani's waist and her grin pulled wider. "Well, I just love Cat. She's darling. Have you known each other long?"

Dani glanced at Dylan and winked. He was hating this. "We've known each other since we were kids."

"Just like Dylan and Josh."

"Even younger," Dani said. "We met in middle school."

Irene clasped a hand over her heart as if that were some sort of sign from God, and Dylan's eyes closed like he was praying for strength.

"Oh! Well, that's just adorable," Irene cooed.

"Okay, Mom. I'll see you later. You sure you're okay to drive home?"

"Yes, of course, Dylan. I've been drinking coffee all evening. I'm going to say goodbye to the newlyweds. I love you. Call me this week."

"Bye, Ma. Love you too."

She tapped his cheek and floated off in a cloud of Chanel.

Dani's lips twisted from holding in a laugh. "Such a momma's boy," she teased. "I never would have thought."

"Yeah, yeah." He tugged her wrist until she was looking at him again. "I think I deserve another dance since she interrupted us."

"No. My feet hurt. Let's take a walk."

"Even better."

They ditched their empty shot glasses and wove through the white tablecloths to the far end of the courtyard. Dani wrapped her arms around her bare shoulders. It was June in D.C., and at least eighty degrees, but a sudden chill swept over her skin when they lost the heat of the crowd.

"Why didn't you bring a date tonight?" Dylan asked. He slipped an arm around her as they walked, rubbing her goosebumps away. It was a friendly gesture, but she found herself leaning into the touch, the comfort of skin on skin.

"Why try to make some new guy feel comfortable with all of you jerks all night?"

"No time for that."

Dylan gestured to a stone bench between two topiaries covered in lights and Dani sat, crossing her legs and letting her shoe slip off of her heel. The relief was instant.

"I'd rather just have fun and enjoy being with everyone," she said. The thought of entertaining a date all night had daunted her. She hadn't even considered it. "How about you?"

Dylan's eyes swept over her bare legs, far from discreetly. "How was I going to get my dance with you if I had a date?"

"So smooth, Dylan." He was on top of his game tonight, and the way he flirted never failed to send sparks to her bloodstream. The baser parts of her had always been intrigued by the guy with the good hair, dressed way too fancy for every situation. Dylan never hid his own interest either. Being the only two single ones in the wedding party, it may have occurred to her that the two of them could make a mutually beneficial bad decision. The kind she'd avoided due to how complicated it could get with their group of friends. Besides, after that conversation with Cat, sleeping with someone because she was alone with them and buzzed felt a little like putting on a dress she'd grown out of.

Then again, the thought of going back to her hotel room alone when everyone else was coupled up didn't feel great either. Just that little contact of his hands on her arms made her want to lean in and soak up the connection. *Imagine the way his whole body would feel.*

Dani heard the opening notes of the song Cat had chosen to round out the night, and another wave of emotion tickled the back of her throat. The party was over. In more ways than one.

Shawn, the other groomsman, went rushing by, his ginger-bearded cheeks blotchy and red from the booze. He snickered like a kid sneaking out of the house, pulling his wife behind him as she tried to keep up in her heels. "After-party at the hotel bar," he said, tipping his head in that direction.

Dylan raised his eyebrow at Dani. "You in?"

"You didn't think I was turning in early, did you?" She should totally turn in early.

"Not for a second." Dylan's eyes did a little zig-zag over her face, and a shock of heat pooled in her belly. Suddenly he was much closer and she couldn't remember which one of them had moved.

"Maybe I can get another dance at the after-party then," he said, running his tongue over his lip. She wanted to bite it.

She tipped her chin, matching his flirty expression. "Maybe I should stop at my room and change first." Oh, God. Her voice had gone all breathy against her will. Was she really doing this?

"Okay." Dylan's mouth quirked in confusion.

Slow on the uptake, this one. It was now or

never. She pulled her lip between her teeth and wrapped her fingers around his wrist. "Maybe you should come with me."

Dylan's whole body went stiff for a fraction of a second, but he quickly recovered. His dark eyes swept over her, sizing her up like he was trying to decide if he could consume her whole or if he'd have to take her piece by piece.

Just when her cheeks started to burn under the weight of his stare and what she'd just proposed, a smile spread across his face, pulling hers with it. Then he went in for the kill.

He dipped his head, his breath warm on her ear. "My room has booze."

Hey, Bad Decision, it's Dani Petrillo. Nice to see you again.

Two

*H*OLY SHIT. DYLAN TRIED TO keep the shock from his face as he led them up the stairs to his room, but the possibility that Dani Petrillo had just propositioned him banged around in his brain making his steps unsteady. He'd been fantasizing about Dani for two years now. All of Cat's friends were cool, but Dani was the kind of woman he'd always had a hard-on for—classy as hell but with a wild streak she didn't even try to hide.

Could he honestly have gotten this lucky? Not that he wasn't confident in the Dylan Pierce effect, but Dani had always seemed to be immune. When he'd given her his classic "let's move this party to my room" line, he'd expected her to laugh in his face. He'd steal at least one more peek at her in that dress, and he'd wake up the next day with balls as blue as the sky.

But she was still holding his arm, still rubbing her thumb along the inside of his wrist, making his skin burn with that tiny bit of contact. She had to know what she was doing.

Dylan slid his key card into the reader and held the door open, watching as she crossed into his room. He flicked on the small bedside lamp, letting the rest of the room stay dim.

"You ever think about doing this whole song and dance?" she asked, trailing her finger along the nightstand as she floated over to the king-sized bed in the middle of the room. She dropped her heels and took a seat on the edge. "You know, the chapel and the caterers and the centerpieces?"

"I don't know if this is really my style."

"That's right. You're more the love 'em and leave 'em type."

"Hey, now. You've got me all wrong, Dani-pie," he said with a grin. He loosened his tie and went to the credenza where he'd set up a makeshift bar—top-shelf liquor, a set of engraved tumblers he'd bought for the occasion. He plucked a bottle of Patrón from the flock and she nodded.

"Come on, Dylan. We've spent a lot of weekends together since Cat and Josh bonded us all for life. You haven't brought a single girl to more than one event."

It was a harsh assessment, but it wasn't far from the truth. He had a little bit of a reputation for getting in and out when it came to women, but wasn't it better than leading them on, wasting their time? Ingratiating them to the people he cared about just so they could say goodbye shortly after?

He poured the liquor and thought of Josh and Cat wrapped around each other on the dance floor, all shiny-eyed and hopeful for their future. That was never going to be him. Why pretend?

Though, there was something about the way Cat looked at Josh that made Dylan's chest feel warm and tight.

And right on the heels of all that warm tightness, was the overwhelming desire to get completely trashed. He handed Dani one of the shots he'd poured, taking a safe seat in the armchair while he waited to see how this was going to play out.

She sipped her shot, hissing at the burn. "How's your mom feel about your lone wolf schtick?"

His mom. For the captain of team Why Don't You Find Yourself A Woman, Irene Pierce had an impeccable sense of when to interfere. And the way she'd inspected Dani like a horse at market was *exactly* why he hadn't called any of the women in his contact list to accompany him to this event. Dani took it like a champ, though. She hadn't even flinched.

"I never said I was a lone wolf. I like company." He winked, and Dani rolled her eyes. "I just don't like the idea of tying my ship to one dock."

"I'm glad you didn't put that in your best man speech."

He let his eyes wander up her bare legs, crossed at the ankle. The skirt on her brides-

22

maid's dress rode up to mid-thigh and he imagined what her skin would feel like under the pads of his fingers. Probably like silk. It probably tasted even better.

"What about you?" he asked, his voice thick. "I've seen the constant revolving door of men you ruin." He meant it. She'd probably ruined every single one.

"Hey, I like company too." She sucked in a weary breath and stared out the window where they could hear the staff cleaning up after the reception. "I guess I've just never really thought about it before. *Forever*. Maybe if I found the right guy."

He studied her face, the way her brows pulled together and she chewed her bottom lip. Dani seemed like she was in a contemplative mood tonight. Weddings did that to people, he found. There were two moods at weddings: recapturing your youth or examining your future. He wasn't sure which one he was in yet. He'd see where this conversation took him.

"And how will you know?" he asked. "Will it be like those two?" He jutted his chin in the general direction of the reception. "Lightning and angels singing?"

"God, please. Not like that." She finished her shot and set the glass on the nightstand. "I don't see it going like that for me."

He nearly laughed. He may not be the forever type, but even he could see that any guy who was would give their left nut to come home to a woman like Dani Petrillo. All that blonde hair and tan skin, plus she was a firecracker. Smart, gorgeous, and a little intimidating. Just enough to keep you on your toes without being untouchable. The homecoming queen with the girl next door smile.

The perfect woman if you were the type to look for something like that.

"Why's that, Dani-pie?"

Dani waved his question away, but something in her voice changed. She shrugged, playing it off. "Let's just say, I don't tend to go for the kind of guys who angels sing for. But Cat is my favorite person in the world, and Josh, well, anyone who's that good to her has a special place in my heart." She raised her glass again. "To other people's sappy, obnoxious love. Better them than us."

Dylan smiled, downing the rest of his shot. *Cheers to that.*

When he looked back, Dani's expression had changed. Her mouth tipped into a flirty grin and she slowly uncrossed her legs, letting one dangle off the edge of the bed.

His hand tightened around the empty glass. He had half a mind to check his pulse, see if he'd passed over to his own private heaven, because this could not be real. But when she licked her lips and dragged her eyes to his mouth, any question he had as to why they were alone in his hotel room vanished. Fire erupted on his skin. He wanted to touch her like he wanted the breath in his lungs.

"Come here," he whispered.

Dani set her glass on the nightstand and crawled to the edge of the bed, standing in the small space beside the window. The city lights beamed a glowing circle onto the floor and she stepped into it like she was stepping on stage. Without a word, she unhooked the halter of her dress, letting it fall.

All of the words he knew quit on the spot and he sat there slack-jawed. It was probably for the best; nothing he could say could make this moment any better.

He reached out a cautious hand, resting it on her hip to pull her closer. Her pink painted toes squished into the hotel carpet as she stepped out of the pool of fabric, standing there in just a strip of white lace.

He gave himself to the count of five and then he was on her.

"Is this real?" he asked, tugging her onto his lap. She fell onto him with a giggle that rushed his veins. He dragged his tongue up the soft skin of her neck while she undid his belt with one hand.

"You're awake, if that's what you're asking."

He knew he was by the sting of her nails on his skin. She'd pulled his shirt free and shoved

her hands down the back of his pants, squeezing.

Oh, this is going to be fun.

"How did we get here?" he asked into the
hollow of her throat. It was salty and damp, her
reaction egging him on.

"You sure do have a lot of questions."

"I just want to make sure I can find my way
back."

"Let's take this one trip at a time."

He stood with Dani's legs wrapped around
his waist and stumbled the three steps until they
fell onto the bed. "I can do that," he said. "But
I'm taking the scenic route." He crawled forward,
pushing her back into the mattress, and planted
his hands on either side of her head. "Let me
look at you."

Never shy, Dani met his request with a smol-
dering expression that made him rethink how
long he was going to be able to do this. Dani
looked amazing in everything she wore, that
dress she'd just removed was no exception, but
seeing her naked—the gentle curve of her hips,
the way she was barely more than a handful on
top, but so perky and round—it was unmatched.

He watched as she flicked open the buttons
on his shirt, shoving it off his shoulders. When
she moved to his fly, all the air left his lungs.

"Let me get a condom," he said.

"I was hoping you would say that. I didn't
exactly come prepared."

"Well, you know me. I'm a fucking Boy Scout." He winked at her in the dark and her poker face washed with charmed amusement. Whenever Dani let her tough-girl exterior crack, it did things to him.

He dug through the duffle bag spilling onto the chest of drawers, mentally pumping a fist when he found the little gold packet. He looked over his shoulder as he stepped out of his pants and rolled it on, watching her run her foot over the hotel duvet.

"You were good today, Dylan," she said. "I mean, not that you had a tough job or anything, but you pulled off the best man thing pretty well."

"Aw. Thanks, Dani-pie. I'm swooning." He climbed back onto the bed, hovering over her, nipping at her chin. "Couldn't have done it without you." He balanced on one arm and lifted his hand to give her a high five. "Enough back-patting for now. I'll let you keep telling me how great I am when we're done."

"Don't make me regret this."

"That won't be a problem," he said, kissing her again. He was going to make sure of that. That was always his goal, to make sure a woman enjoyed herself and maybe thought about him a few times after they parted ways. But if he was going to get a shot with Dani, he didn't just want her to remember him, he wanted her to forget everyone but him. For tonight, at least.

He yanked her panties off, dragging his fingers between her legs, making sure she was ready, but she wasn't interested in taking their time. "Now," she ordered.

He tried to keep the smirk from his face at the way her eyes had gone wild. "You okay there, Dani-pie?"

"Dylan!"

God, she was gorgeous. He kissed her again, then tossed her leg over his shoulder and finally fulfilled his biggest dream of the last two years.

Just like in all of his fantasies, Dani met him halfway.

Don't do it. Don't do it. Don't do it.

"Oh my *God*," Dani moaned. Shit. She was awful at listening to her brain. She really hadn't intended to give Dylan any more ammo for his enormous ego, but she'd have to give him this one, because Oh. My. God.

Dylan smiled against her mouth, clearly pleased with her reaction. Not that she'd spent much time wondering how this might play out between them, what he'd be like—sure, she'd let it cross her mind once or twice, he wasn't exactly subtle—but she had to admit, in the small amount of brain space she'd assigned him, she'd severely underestimated him.

Dylan let her leg fall, leaning forward and

grabbing her hips to pull her underneath him. Now she could reach his back and ass, and she couldn't get enough exploring. His body was new and familiar at the same time. She'd seen him in a swimsuit a hundred times, scoped out the visual contours of his body, but she hadn't imagined how good all this smooth muscle would feel flexing under her palms. How firm and warm his skin would be.

"You taste like candy," he said, curling his back to run his tongue between her breasts.

"That's a line if I ever heard one." But she wasn't opposed to lines at the moment. Lines were fucking working.

"How about this, then? You're gorgeous and a dream come true."

"That's better." She let herself giggle at the ceiling while Dylan moved up her neck, pressing a soft, tickling kiss to the skin below her ear. She pushed her fingers into his thick, dark hair and felt him buck inside her. She'd been thinking about touching that hair for as long as she'd known him, pulling it, messing it out of its perfect style.

"Shit, Dani. You feel so good," he said, his lips exploring her body like he was committing it to memory. The way he seemed almost giddy, a smile on the edge of every kiss, surprised her. If she didn't know him better, she might have believed that "dream come true" line. Still, she could let herself revel in a little ego-boosting for the night.

He pressed again—a deep, rolling hip-flex that stole her breath.

Her mouth dropped open, but no sound came out.

"Right there?" he asked.

She nodded her head. "Don't stop."

His mouth crashed into hers, hungrier, but still edged in a grin. She felt herself inching closer and closer to the headboard with every perfect thrust, but just before she hit, Dylan reached behind her without breaking their kiss and tugged a pillow behind her head.

For some reason that did it. She cried out and he met her eyes in the dark, watching as she broke around him, quick and intense, like a series of fireworks exploding one after another and driving her hips into his.

He was only seconds behind her, his fingers tightening on her waist as he emptied and shook. "Holy shit, Dani-pie." His weight dropped onto her and he groaned into her neck, hot humid air pricking her overly-sensitive skin.

Holy shit was right. This was her best worst idea ever.

He sucked in a breath, his chest pressing into hers with every pant. "Can you breathe?"

"Barely." She didn't mind, though. After all of that tequila and physical exertion, the marathon day, his weight was like a warm, heavy blanket.

She could close her eyes and pass out right there, probably sleep like a baby.

But she shouldn't.

Eventually, Dylan peeled himself up and she heard him close the bathroom door.

She flipped into her belly, the cool sheets caressing her front. "I'm going back to my room," she slurred into the pillow.

A minute later, Dylan hopped onto the bed beside her and pulled the duvet up over them. "Sure you are."

"In five minutes."

She heard him laugh and if she wasn't so damn comfortable, she would have retaliated. As it was though, a smart answer was far too much exertion. Her limbs were liquid and she was pretty sure her mouth was hanging open.

Dylan rolled toward her, hooking his leg over hers and trapping her in place. "Wake me up when you go," he whispered.

She didn't reply. Something deep inside her brain waved its hands and shouted at her but she imagined it sinking into the plush mattress, its voice muffled and muted.

Dylan flicked off the lamp on the bedside table. "That's what I thought."

Three

DYLAN RUBBED AT HIS EYES, shielding his retinas with his hand as he forced them open. Painfully bright light streamed in through the curtains. *Jesus*—it had to be mid-morning, the sun was so bright. It had been a long time since he'd slept in this late. He sat up to read the clock and his eye caught on a mess of blonde curls buried in the pillow beside him.

Right. That's why he hadn't woken up with the sun. He'd been up half the night with Dani fucking Petrillo. What the hell had he said to her last night to end up here? He had no idea, but he wished he could go back in time and give last night Dylan a high five.

Dani made a little sleep sound, burying her face deeper into the pillow. His lower half stirred. The curve of her back, her golden skin contrasting against the bright white hotel sheets—could he handle naked Dani fully sober? Maybe not, but there was only one way to find out.

He trailed his finger between her shoulder blades, hoping to entice her into one more round before they had to be at brunch downstairs. She whined adorably, then tossed onto her back, throwing an arm over her eyes.

Perfect. He rolled onto his side and snaked his hand under the sheet, walking his fingers down her soft stomach, but when he got to her hip, she bolted upright.

"What time is it?"

"Ten-thirty," he answered, pressing his lips to her arm. She smelled like the flowers from the chapel and the frosting from the cake. Delicious.

"Shit." She rolled to her left, jumping out of the bed and yanking the sheet with her.

"Where are you going?"

"Shit. Shit. Shit!" Dani scrambled around the room tossing pillows and searching the floor frantically. Dylan grabbed a pillow, dragging it over his lap. No sense in letting her see how he'd assumed the morning was going to go. "We're supposed to be downstairs."

"So? We can show up a few minutes late."

"*We* can't show up anywhere, Dylan. Now I have to figure out how to get back to my room without anyone seeing me in the middle of the breakfast rush." She sat down on the bed and pulled her panties on under the sheet. "Damn it! What the hell was I thinking?"

"Jesus, Dani. Way to make a guy feel good in the morning."

"Sorry." She paused her redressing to look him in the eye. "I didn't mean that. This was...

33

fun. But I don't want it to be everyone else's business, okay? Especially Emma and Sonya and, oh my God, Cat."

Dani's mascara had smudged under her eyes and her hair was a little on the wild side. Maybe she had a point about the optics of the whole thing.

"Look, I'll check the hallway for you and you can make a run for it. Like you're escaping a serial killer or something."

"Don't be like that, Dylan." She hooked her bra behind her back and let the sheet fall away as she crawled over the bed. Heat burned down his neck when she knelt beside him. "It's Cat's wedding. I don't want us getting caught in a compromising position to be the memory everyone takes away from the weekend. We should just chalk it up to a fun night and make sure it doesn't happen again."

She had a look like pity in her eyes and it rubbed him the wrong way. It wasn't like he was planning to make something out of this. Sure, it was fun, but he didn't do a lot of second meet-ups. Not even for a woman like Dani. Usually he was the one who got to break that news, though. Today he was on the flip side, and he didn't entirely like the way it felt.

He rolled out of bed and found his boxers on the floor, yanking them on. "Yeah, all right, Dani-pie. I'm not really too psyched about Josh finding out either. Or Shawn. I get enough shit from those two about this type of thing. You being Cat's friend and all would probably piss Josh off, so let's not mention it."

"Dylan." Dani sighed and came to stand in front of him. He'd never seen her like this. She was usually done up in heels and cleavage-baring tops whenever they were together. Here, barefoot and in her underwear, her hair sticking up in the back, she looked soft. Cute instead of like she was about to bite your neck and slap your ass. And he'd been right about that, for the record. She put her hand on his forearm, squeezing. "I'm not just Cat's friend," she said. "We're friends too, right?"

"Yeah," he muttered, a little bit like a child. She raised her eyebrows expectantly, and he shook off the pissy mood his ego had put him in, reaching down to give her a hug. "Friends."

"Good." She picked her dress up off the floor where it was still crumpled and stepped in, quickly fastening the halter behind her back. "Now, look out in the hall and give me the all-clear."

Dylan gestured for her to wait behind the door. He patted his hair back into place before peeking his head out into the hall.

Where he came face to face with Shawn's wife, Minnie.

"Hey, Dylan! I was just about to knock. Where did you run off to last night?"

"Um..." He glanced back at Dani, then

35

stepped into the doorway, shielding Minnie's view of the sheets strewn around his hotel room. "I was beat. Long day... golfing, and ya know..."

"Are you coming downstairs?"

"Yeah. In a few. Where are the newlyweds?" He scanned the hall again and saw Cat's sister coming out of her room, then Shawn meandering toward them looking like he might have slept in the outfit he had on.

"I don't know," Minnie answered. "I didn't dare knock on their door."

Shawn cocked his head, his bushy orange eyebrows slanting inward. "You doing okay, buddy?"

"Yeah. Didn't sleep too well. Too much tequi-la." Dylan waved at Cat's sister as she passed, and smiled at another woman who must have been a relative of the bride's. She had about a hundred. Dani was right about it being rush hour. "Well, I'll see you two down there."

"Okay. We'll save you a—"

He closed the door in Minnie's face and gave Dani a shrug. "There's a lot of people out there."

"Shit!" She looked frantic again.

"Look, just wait here while I shower and get dressed, then I'll head down and text you when it looks like everyone is already down there."

"Okay," she said, her crazy curls bouncing as she nodded. A vision of them squeezed between his fingers flashed before him.

He grabbed his t-shirt from the bed and

headed toward the bathroom, then paused when he thought of one more solution. "You could join me. Save yourself some time getting ready."

"Dylan!"

"It was worth a shot," he said, slinging a towel over his shoulder.

Damn, she was cute when she was mad.

When Dylan walked into the hotel dining room, Cat jumped up from her seat and waved him over to a round table. Her parents and Josh were there, all of them with overflowing plates.

"Dylan," she said. "Over here." There were two chairs left empty, and he assumed the other was for the maid of honor.

"I can just grab a seat with Shawn." He didn't feel like sharing breakfast with Dani at the moment, childish as it was.

"Don't be silly," Cat said. "Sit."

Josh stood to greet him, followed by Cat's father Carlos.

"The best man," Carlos boomed, shaking his hand much harder than necessary. The guy was huge.

"That'd be me."

Dani had mentioned once that Carlos was like a second father to her. Her parents moved out of state once she left home, and Dani spent a lot of college breaks with Cat's family. Suddenly

Carlos' presence felt really awkward, like meeting your date's dad before prom night when you knew exactly where that dress he'd paid for was going to end up.

Dylan cleared his throat, flipping his phone around in the pocket of his sweatshirt. He really needed to text Dani, but now it might be obvious.

"You gonna get some food, man?" Josh asked, amused.

Cat caught Josh's tone and looked up at Dylan from her eggs. "Why are you acting weird? Are you hungover?"

"No. I'm fine. Let me grab a plate and I'll be right back."

He stepped away and headed toward the buffet table, sneaking his phone out on the way.

What the hell was wrong with him? Why was he acting like a criminal? This was Dani's secret, not his. He didn't care if Josh or Cat or Carlos knew what he and Dani had been up to. They were grown adults. If she wanted to be all weird about it, she could, but he certainly didn't have to feel guilty.

Dylan: Everyone is here. You can come out of hiding.

He was piling bacon onto his plate when she replied with an eye-roll emoji.

Dylan: BTW we're sitting together. With Cat and Josh and her parents.

A few moments went by this time. Enough time to finish loading his plate and pour himself some coffee.

Dani: Who picked those seats?

Really? What, did she think he was looking to make this awkward-as-hell morning after into a romantic brunch date? He set his coffee down, balancing his plate, and typed with one hand.

Dylan: The bride. Guess you should have brought that date after all.

He felt guilty as soon as he said it. Dani was right: this was Josh's wedding brunch thing, and here he was making it about his bruised ego. He gathered his things and headed back to the table, determined to get himself straightened out before Dani arrived.

He took the seat closest to Josh, reaching over him to tap his mimosa to the bride's. "You look gorgeous this morning, Kit Cat," he said with his sweetest grin. Everyone called Cat "Kit Cat." Everyone except Josh who called her Catia, butchering her beautiful name with his New England accent. She ate that shit up, though. *Love.*

"Thank you, Dylan. That's sweet of you to say."

Josh slid his arm around her, beaming. Fuck, his best friend was sprung. And Cat was just as bad. They say your wedding day is the best day of your life and he was pretty sure that was spot on for Josh. Dylan hoped for Josh's sake things would stay that way, but everything shines when it's new. Give it time and all that lovey-dovey shit turns to resentment. Hell, Josh should know that. He'd been married once before and it hadn't turned out well. But Josh's parents had died when he was a kid, before they had a chance to get divorced, so he had this warped vision of how things could have been. He'd been looking his whole life for it.

Josh deserved all of that, he did, but the very thought of it made Dylan's skin itch. There's only one person you can truly count on, and that's yourself. Dylan's own parents had done a bang-up job teaching him that lesson. He chuckled to himself at the thought. Dead or alive, parents will find a way to fuck you up one way or another.

"Catia," Carlos said correctly. "Where is Danica?"

Danica? Dylan almost choked on his eggs. *Is Dani's name Danica?* He'd known her for two years and he'd always assumed she was a Dani-elle. He was pretty sure he'd called her that at some point.

While he was trying to remember a specific incident, and hoping it wasn't last night, Dani walked into the dining room. She'd showered and let her hair dry in waves that looked like she'd just come from the beach, and she had on a pair of tight jeans and a blood-red blouse. She was also back in heels and makeup— regular Dani. Or...*Danica.*

"Good morning, everyone," she said, leaning over to kiss Cat's mother on the cheek. Carlos and Josh both stood to give her a hug.

Dylan contemplated whether he should too. Would not hugging her make it obvious he had just seen her naked in his bed an hour ago? But he had seen her last night, and it wasn't his special occasion, so why would they hug? No, he should stay seated and stop acting ridiculous.

Dani pulled the chair out beside him and took a seat.

"Aren't you going to eat?" Cat asked. "Why does everyone have to be reminded to eat? This isn't like any of you."

"Right," Dani said. "Sorry. In a minute. I just woke up."

Dylan couldn't help the snort that came from him at her lie, and she sent him an icy glare in return.

He turned his attention to Josh and Cat. "So, you two are headed off tonight, right?"

Cat smiled and turned to Josh in that way she had where she let him answer stuff, then stared at him like he was reciting poetry.

He shot an eye roll at Dani, but she wasn't playing along.

"Yup," Josh said around his sip of coffee.

"Seven days. You've got everything under control at work?"

A little over five years ago, Josh was the lead architect at a boutique firm in the city, and Dylan had a job selling construction materials to contractors. When Josh's boss wanted to sell the firm, they'd taken a huge gamble and invested every dollar they'd ever saved to go into business together. They were both barely thirty years old at the time, and had zero experience running a business, but Dylan had the connections, and Josh had the drive. Best decision they'd ever made.

He gave Josh his *closer* smile. "You got it, partner."

"We have a lot of irons in the fire right now and we need them all," Josh said. He had his glasses on instead of his usual contacts, and instead of sweats like Dylan, he'd put on a real shirt. He didn't look the least bit hungover. Dylan suddenly felt like he was rushing into class ten minutes late and being questioned by the professor on his homework.

"I'm aware, man," he said, irrationally irritated at the reminder. "I'm the one who put the irons there."

Josh smiled and picked up his coffee cup, the brand new ring on his left hand glinting. "Good. I shouldn't need to hear from you for a whole week then."

"Looking forward to it."

He glanced beside him at Dani. She smiled as a waiter filled a glass of water for her. With Cat and Josh out of town, he wouldn't have to worry about seeing Dani either. They could consider the whole thing forgotten.

Dani pressed her fingers to her temples as the bright sun taunted her hangover. Her rolling suitcase caught on the door of the hotel, and she had to tug it with both hands, nearly toppling over from the exertion. She pulled her sunglasses onto her face and bit back a wave of nausea. She really should have eaten something at brunch, but she was too busy lamenting her latest act of self-sabotage.

How could she have possibly thought sleeping with Dylan because she was feeling sorry for herself was a good idea? Hadn't she been standing on the dance floor pondering her lot in life moments before? She supposed she had her answer as to why she was the only one who hadn't found any sort of meaningful connection. And to top it off, sitting at that table with their best friends, pretending she and Dylan hadn't woken up together was torture. Now every time she and Dylan saw each other, that's how it would be.

And she was about to experience it again.

She stepped into the valet area to find Dylan packing his bags into the trunk of his Audi.

Ugh, she was too hungover for a repeat of their awkward morning. She needed to clear the air, though, before they both went their separate ways and ended up at some group event in the near future with this weird tension still simmering.

"Dylan," she called, dragging her suitcase over the curb with a thud. "Hey."

He looked her up and down as she approached, but his expression was flat, like he was looking at a stranger. Maybe he was just hungover too.

"Hey, Dani."

Something soured in her stomach at the sound of her real name. From him it felt formal. Off. Where was Dani-pie?

"Listen, about earlier. I meant what I said about us being friends. Can we just go back to the way things were?"

Dylan licked his bottom lip and smiled thinly. "Of course."

"Oh." He'd said that awfully quickly, but she supposed she didn't have a right to claim a bruised ego. She knew exactly who she was dealing with. "Okay. Well, good. I was worried."

"Hey, we're grown-ups. We've both done this before. If you don't want anything to change, then nothing will change."

If she didn't want it to? What exactly did that mean? She opened her mouth to question him, but he was giving her a look like the conversation was over. Maybe it wasn't worth it. Expounding on loaded sentences like that were what drama was made of, and drama was why you didn't drown your sorrows by sleeping with your best friend's husband's best friend.

"Great," she said. "Glad we cleared that up. Again."

"Yup. Me too." He gave her a salute, then slammed his trunk, heading for the driver's side. "I'll see you around, Dani."

"Okay." Her head started to pound just thinking about it.

Four

"So this is Cat's boyfriend-now-husband's best friend?" Benji asked.

"That's the one."

"You little fiend! Does Cat know?"

Benji had never met Cat, or Josh or Dylan for that matter, but they'd been sharing an office at Root Media long enough that he knew all the characters in her stories. Just like she knew that his boyfriend Ronnie was in Northern California for the weekend for his old roommate's fortieth birthday, and Benji was pretending he wasn't jealous but secretly he was stalking them all on Instagram like Hipster Sherlock Holmes.

"Cat does not know, but she's in Hawaii for a week. It will be old news by the time she gets back. No need to share."

"Would she be upset?"

"Of course not. I don't think."

Benji rolled his office chair over to Dani's desk and propped his elbows on the edge, resting his neatly-bearded chin in his hand. One of his unruly, rust-colored curls fell across his forehead and he blew it aside. "Show me a picture."

"Ugh. Fine." This was part of the game they'd been playing for years. Benji would pretend to beg for gossip and Dani would pretend to be put out, but honestly, it was refreshing to have someone outside of their inner circle to talk to *about* the inner circle.

She turned her laptop toward him and opened a few pictures she had uploaded from the wedding. She'd intended to use the photo-editing software her office owned to spruce them up and give them to Cat when she got home from her honeymoon. Even without touching up, though, everyone looked great. Especially Dylan. Maybe she was showing off a little.

"Here you go."

Benji leaned forward, peering through his wire-rimmed glasses. "Oh, I remember him. The charity 5k your friend made you do. You showed me pictures and you talked about his ass in those shorts for days afterward."

She rolled her eyes at the hyperbole. *It was maybe like one day.* "Do you write down every-thing I say?"

Benji pointed at her. "This has been brewing for some time."

"That's an overstatement. Dylan and I have a certain flirty chemistry and maybe it was bound to happen eventually, but now it did, and I'm over it."

Benji crossed his arms and frowned. "And why exactly are we over Mr. Adorable Smile?"

She shot him a look. "Because maybe I want more than just an adorable smile. Look at this picture." She clicked again to enlarge a candid of the whole group. She'd been studying it for two days, lamenting. It was right after the official pictures had been taken, when everyone's dates had rejoined them. Shawn and Minnie leaned against the chapel wall, chatting. Sonya and Marcus hugged, probably counting down the minutes until it was their turn. And then there was Cat and Josh—their foreheads pressed together, beaming at each other as if the photographer had posed them that way. He hadn't.

And there she was, third-wheeling it with Emma and her husband.

Cat's wedding had been like being flown around by some ghost from a Christmas movie. *Look at what you could have had, Danica. But now you're alone. Muhahaha.*

She clicked away the photo and pressed her eyes closed. "I guess maybe it's cliché, but Cat getting married just has me thinking that maybe I want someone too. I mean, for God's sake. I slept with *Dylan* because I was feeling sorry for myself. If that isn't a warning to get my life together, I don't know what is."

Benji's eyes went wide. "Wow. Could this be the end of an era? Dani Petrillo hangs up her single-life badge and settles down?"

"I'm just tired, Benj. Dating isn't easy and it's a lot less easy when you're the last one in the game. It used to be all of us girls going out on the weekends, taking road trips, and now it's just... me. I guess staying at home on the couch and eating take out with a good guy doesn't sound so bad anymore."

Benji laughed. Dani had been rolling her eyes at his Netflix and Chill weekends for a while now. She supposed she deserved his amusement.

"A friend of Ronnie's just tried this dating site," he said. "He's one of the guys on this boys weekend. He had to go and get himself coupled up leaving Ron and the birthday boy the only ones going stag on this trip. Anyway, I digress. The point is, last time we saw him, he was singing from the rooftops about it. We didn't even know he was looking and then boom. Magic. They're talking about moving in. And he's cute!"

"How cute?" she asked suspiciously. Benji was a little more forgiving when it came to men's grooming habits. The two of them rarely agreed.

"Adorable!" He pulled out his phone and started scrolling. "The site is called Eight Dates to Your Soulmate."

Dani held a hand up. "Stop. I've heard enough."

"Don't judge. We work in the business. We know catchy slogans sell. It doesn't mean it isn't the real deal. Ah! Here it is." He held up his phone to show a dark-haired man with thick scruff and chocolate brown eyes.

"Okay," she said. "He's cute."

"And a good guy. Smart, funny, owns a dog."

"A dog?"

Benji shrugged. "Studies show a man with a dog is more likely to be marriage material."

She snorted. "All of these slogans and studies, how can this not work?"

"Well, maybe start by toning down the snark. Just think about it. You know what Oprah says: 'If you want something you've never had before, you have to do something you've never done before.'"

"Quoting Oprah in regards to my dating life is a sure-fire way to get me to end this conversation."

"We'll see." Benji shoved off the side of her desk with his feet and his chair went sailing back to his desk. "I'm going to grab lunch at Carter's. You want to split an order of fries?"

"Of course I do."

"Milkshake to dip?"

"Why can't you just date me, Benji?"

"All the good ones are taken, love."

He blew her a kiss and slipped out the door, closing it conspicuously behind him. They never closed their door which meant he thought he was being slick giving her some privacy so she could check that site out. Which she wasn't going to do.

She turned back to her laptop and opened up a brochure for a museum she'd commissioned a logo for. The color wasn't exactly right and she needed to email the designer for a redo, but before she could load her email, her group chat chimed.

A message from Sonya. Attached was another picture from the wedding—Josh dipping Cat dramatically on the dance floor, Shawn and Minnie singing into their beer bottles. She caught a glimpse of herself in the background, sitting alone at the bar, chatting with the old man pouring shots, and groaned.

She clicked the attachment away and went back to her logo but her web browser icon taunted her. "Oh, fine." It wouldn't hurt to just look at the home page. She knew a shoddy website when she saw one. If it looked at all cheesy, she'd forget the whole thing and pride herself on her savvy consumerism.

Unfortunately, when she typed the site into her search bar, it was stunning. The design was young and modern. The testimonials sounded real instead of like scripted sales pitches. The entire aesthetic said: Trust us. We're way better at this than you.

Damn it. Okay, she'd just click on one.

"I was at the point in my life where all of my friends were married off. The single life was great while it lasted, but I started to want more. Eight

Dates matched me with eight really fun dates, and one of them happened to be exactly who I'd been looking for. Now I have someone to enjoy life with instead of sitting on the sidelines."

Okay, the first half of that could have been lifted from her diary. She clicked another.

"I've never believed in the concept of soulmates. My friend suggested this site to help weed out all of the terrible dates I was meeting out in town. I didn't have any expectations, but through Eight Dates To Your Soulmate, I met my fiancé and I couldn't be happier to leave the single life behind for true love."

She looked up from her laptop suspiciously. Did Benji hack into this website and write testimonials to mimic her life exactly? It wouldn't be outside of his skill set. She navigated to the sign-up page, just to explore. There were about a million questions, which she supposed meant the process was thorough. Way more thorough than her own vetting process, if she were being honest.

She scrolled through pages of pictures of happy, smiling couples until she got to a section called "The Rules" and her cynic's heart laughed. This could not be for real.

She was still chuckling when Benji came

back in with their food and an *I caught you* look on his face.

"I knew it," he taunted.

"Don't get excited. Did you read the fine print here?"

"What fine print?"

She narrowed her eyes. "This isn't just a dating site where they match you up by twenty-one unique personality traits and you swipe right—"

"I think you're confusing a couple of different apps, baby girl."

"Anyway, there are rules. It's like a dating boot camp."

Benji turned away and unpacked his take out bag. "Of course there are rules," he said, his eyes on his fries. "There are always controls in an experiment, and if they're promising your soulmate in that short of time, they have to control the environment."

"So you have read it."

"I skimmed it."

She pursed her lips. "Does Ronnie know that?"

"Oh my God. Stop. We looked at it together. We do have single friends, you know." He pointed at her with a fry. "Case in point."

"Well, then you know it clearly states that you aren't allowed to sleep with any of your matches until you've gone out with all of them."

"Yes."

Dani scoffed. "And you thought I'd be interested in that kind of restriction? How exactly are you supposed to know which one is your soulmate if you're not sleeping with them?"

"This is your problem, Dani." He fell into his chair with his milkshake and rolled over to her desk. "Listen to what you just said. Now think about what you've told me time and again. 'He's between jobs, but the sex is great,' or 'Sure, he was rude to the waiter, but oh my God his tongue.'"

"Those sentences sound vaguely familiar, but—"

"No buts. You deserve the whole package. Someone who is worth your time in *and* out of the bedroom. This way you make a clear decision. You're not dickmatized into thinking you should cut a guy some slack on his behavior because he's got other talents."

"Okay, well there's another problem."

Benji huffed out a sigh. "What is it?"

"With my schedule, it could take months to go on eight dates!"

"So?"

"So, months without sex? Benj, I don't think I've gone months plural since college."

Benji's mouth dropped. "Are you serious? Where do you..." He rolled his hand like he couldn't bring himself to say it.

She shrugged. "I've had a lot of short-term serious boyfriends." And let's face it, she'd been getting male attention since she was fifteen. She knew what it was that drew guys to her, and it wasn't her business degree or her epic fashion sense. Not that she wasn't on board, or was doing it only for their benefit. She liked sex just as much as they did and most of the time she was fine with however long it lasted. She was just starting to wonder why it *never* lasted.

"God," Benji said. "Before Ronnie, I think it was a year for me."

"I know."

He reached for a fry and popped it in his mouth. "You're blowing my mind right now."

"So the point is, I hate starting something I can't finish."

"Okay, so think of it like going on a diet before a big trip, or staying off the internet so you don't see spoilers for *The Bachelor*. It's just a couple of months."

Dani tugged his milkshake toward her and dipped a fry. "I'm on a diet right now," she said. "See my self-control."

"Well, love," Benji said, his patience clearly winding away. "I've seen the results first hand. I guess you just have to decide what you want more, the D or the HEA."

"The what?"

"Happily Ever After."

Some unused cells in her brain started to flicker to life at the thought. For the first time she could remember, she thought she might actually want the H E... whatever he said.

Five

*D*YLAN HADN'T HAD A TWO-DAY hangover since February 2010. He remembered it distinctly because Shawn and Minnie had just gotten married, and he was so sick that he had to book another night at the hotel and sleep it off before he could physically drive himself home. He'd paid an outrageous fee for not returning the tux on time, and when he'd made it out into the sunlight the next day, he'd barely recognized his own face. Anyway, the point was weddings were clearly bad for his health, and he was glad that with Josh and Cat finally wedded in matrimonial bliss, he could hang up his groomsman hat for the foreseeable future.

He found his car in the municipal parking garage and tossed his bag in the back before starting it up and letting the air conditioning blow some relief onto his face. He'd been off his game today. Three cold calls to developers and a bid drop off, and he didn't feel great about any of them. On top of the specter of too much tequila he'd been carrying around, he was just in an all-around piss ass mood. Since sales was a good ninety-percent about being charming, it hadn't been a great day.

Once the car had cooled down, he pulled out of the garage for the long drive back to the peninsula where he lived, which at the moment was an inconvenience of epic proportions. The late-day sun felt like an interrogation lamp. *What's your fucking problem, man?* it screamed. *Get it together.*

He knew it wasn't just the booze that was lingering from the weekend. He'd been pissy since Dani had run screaming from his hotel room. At first, he thought he just didn't like the feeling of being blown off that way, but something else nagged behind his wounded ego. That fuck-up feeling he hadn't had in a while, when one of his do-what-feels-good decisions came back to haunt him. He was always very clear in his relations with women, but occasionally they heard what they wanted to hear instead of what he said. It happened and it sucked. That wasn't the case with Dani, though. It was the opposite; she was fine, eager to forget the whole thing. Yet he couldn't shake the feeling he'd set something off-kilter.

Twenty minutes into the drive, he spotted a liquor store and steered his Audi into the parking lot. He turned off his engine and listened to the click, click, click of the car cooling. The temperature on the dash said ninety-four degrees even with the impending sunset. If Josh was in town, Dylan would have convinced him to head to the beach to catch a few waves to round out the workday. But Josh was in Hawaii, so some cold beer and central air conditioning would have to do.

He was halfway across the parking lot when his phone buzzed in his pocket. He swiped the ringing phone and held it to his ear. "Shawn. I'm just picking up some beer. I'll be home in thirty."

"Bad news, buddy," Shawn said. "I can't make it for the game."

"Why the hell not?"

"Mattie's got a fever and Min's running late from work. I can't ditch out on her tonight."

"But you can ditch out on me?"

Shawn guffawed. "Bear me a kid and I'll move you to the top of the line."

"Josh would never do this to me."

"Josh would absolutely do this to you."

"You're right," Dylan said, scowling at his phone. "You both suck."

"Sorry, Dylan. Next time, I promise."

Well, that was just fucking great. He looked down at his watch. He was already in the city and dressed to impress if he did say so himself. He had no reason to go home now. He pulled up his contact list labeled "downtown" and swiped his thumb quickly up the screen, setting the numbers scrolling like the big prize wheel on *The Price Is Right*. It stopped somewhere in the "M" listings and he tapped the name most likely to be in his proximity.

The line rang and a smokey voice that had a few fun memories attached to it answered. "Dylan Peirce."

"Mia. I knew you still had my number saved."

"It's been a while. Is this work or pleasure?"

"Always a pleasure with you. I'm in town. You up for a drink?" *And maybe a little more to get me out of this mood.*

Mia didn't miss a beat. "Tell me where."

And just like that, his night turned around.

On Monday nights, Dani met Cat after work at the little pub that was halfway between their offices. It was her favorite part of the week. They would drink margaritas and eat fried food and vent about work and family and—on the rare occasion when Josh wasn't being an angel—men.

But this week, Cat was in Hawaii and Dani had a date. Nick Elway was the brother of a junior consultant at Root. Jean had been dying to set them up, and last week Dani had done a little social media stalking and decided Nick had a cute smile and looked damn fine wearing board shorts and no shirt on the back of his friend's boat. Jean and Instagram had been a little vague on what it was Nick actually did for a living, but Dani was sure it was something... something.

"Thanks for meeting me," Nick said, pulling out the chair for her at the table for two he'd booked at Arabella Steak House in the West End. The small high-top was in the center of a bay window looking out onto the busy downtown street. A single candle flickered from the center of the table, reflecting in the glass around them and keeping the space from being too dark.

"Of course. I came from work anyway."

Nick took his own seat, running a hand through his intentionally messy black hair. He had great hair. Another point in his favor.

The thing with dating in the city was it was sort of like high school. There were all these boxes guys could fit into and there were very few who straddled more than one. There were the corporate-types who tended to have sticks so far up their asses that they couldn't sit straight. Then there were the starving artists who were always a blast, but there was only so much she could take of the thirty-something-still-lives-with-mom lifestyle. It was rare to find a guy who didn't take himself too seriously but could also afford dinner. Nick had potential, though.

"So my sister says you're a partner at Root," Nick said.

"I am. I was promoted a couple of years ago when one of the owners retired. Big office, staff of my own. That's about the gist."

"Branding must be fun." He waved a hand in

front of her, gesturing to her dress. "If your own look is any indication, I'd say you're good at it."

"Oh yeah?" she said, leaning across the table. She already liked his particular style of flirting. "And what image am I portraying right now?"

Nick's lips curled upward revealing straight, white teeth and comma-shaped dimples. His eyes ran the length of her. "Let's see. Sky-high heels," he said. "Power statement. You can handle anything."

"Astute."

"But that dress." He hissed through his teeth and she felt her cheeks flush. "That dress says you're no stiff suit. I'd say fun is high on your list of priorities."

Dani sipped from the glass of water in front of her, returning Nick's appraising look. "And what is it you do, Nick? And don't tell me you're a psychic because I will *so* believe you."

Nick laughed, a low rumble that came from his broad chest. "I'm, ah, in pharmaceuticals."

"Oh. Sales?"

"Mm-hmm." Nick drank his water too. Gulped it actually. Odd, but back to that face. Were his eyes ocean blue or navy?

"I've always heard that's a stressful profession."

"It is."

"Have you been doing it long?"

"You know," Nick said, picking up a menu

and glancing around for the waitress. "Work is boring. What do you do for fun?"

Dani lifted her menu as well, but before she could answer, the waitress came for their drink orders. Nick ordered a beer and Dani went for a mid-shelf wine. Something that said classy, but not snobby. She really was good at her job.

When she returned, Nick lifted his pint, touching it to Dani's wine glass. "So you were saying?"

"What do I do for fun?" Dani tapped her nail on her lower lip. What was the sexiest sounding hobby she had? "I do yoga," she said. Very rarely and only when guilted into it by Emma, but he didn't need to know that.

Nick ran his tongue along his teeth. "I'd like to see that."

"How about you?"

Nick opened his mouth to answer but his phone buzzing caught his attention. He reached into the inside pocket of his leather jacket and glanced at the screen. "I'm sorry," he said. "I need to take this."

"Sure. No problem."

Dani watched him go, then picked up a piece of crusty bread from the basket on the table, trying not to moan out loud as she popped it in her mouth. This was an impressive choice for dinner. She probably didn't need to worry about Nick living with his mother. She took another bite and turned to the street view. A couple walked by holding hands, whispering to each other in that intimate way lovers did when they thought no one was looking. She felt a smile pulling at her cheeks. *Huh.* It seemed that going on a date with a cute, stable guy had put her in an entirely different state of mind about public displays of affection. Who would have thought?

But as the happy couple passed, she spotted Nick on the sidewalk too. He was leaning on the window of a black SUV idling on the street, decidedly not on his phone. She couldn't see the driver, as much as she craned her neck, but their conversation carried on. Finally, Nick straightened, reaching into his inner jacket pocket and pulling out a small package that she also couldn't get a good look at. The driver of the car handed him something back and then drove away.

That was sort of weird, but no need to jump to any conclusions. Maybe he forgot something at work and a co-worker brought it to him. Or maybe he just happened to run into someone he knew while he was taking an entirely separate phone call.

Ugh. The twisting feeling in her stomach disagreed, the one that'd been honed to announce a coming disaster. She'd experienced enough of them that she was like a cow sensing a thunderstorm. Twisty stomach: check. Tingling scalp: check.

She pictured a bubble bursting overhead, soggy, wet confetti dropping onto her head.

Goddamn it.

She clicked into her messaging app and found Sonya. Sonya's fiancé was a commercial airline pilot and out of town a lot, so she was usually free for a quick second opinion. Or an impromptu rescue mission when it came to that. And quite often it did.

> **Dani: So... I'm on a date with a guy who said he's in pharmaceuticals and he just stepped outside to exchange a package with some guy in an SUV.**
>
> **Sonya: hahahahahahaha**
>
> **Dani: ???**
>
> **Sonya: Only you.**

Wasn't that the truth.

> **Dani: Whatever. What are you doing? Marcus gone this week?**
>
> **Sonya: He is. I get off in half an hour, then heating up leftovers and watching Breaking Bad.**
>
> **Dani: Meet me out instead. I need to cut this date short. I'll buy you a burger somewhere.**

Sonya: Deal. Bruno's. See you at 8.

Great. Another date ending with the old "My friend has an emergency" line. She couldn't wait to tell Benji about this one. He'd never drop the dating app thing after this.

Outside, Nick paced on the sidewalk with his phone to his ear, so she popped her phone back in her clutch and went for her wine. She was at least getting a buzz out of this. But just as the Moscato started to warm her cheeks, something else caught her eye over her stemmed glass.

Actually, someone. The absolute worst someone for this particular situation. Her teeth clenched and she struggled to swallow the fruity sip.

You've got to be kidding me. Was this some kind of hidden camera prank?

First, she was quite possibly an accessory to a crime, and now, across the room with his hand on some woman's ass, was the poster boy for how desperate she'd let herself get.

Fuck. Dylan stopped himself from saying the word out loud—barely—but seriously, fuuuuck.

Just as he leaned in to whisper his closing line into Mia's ear, he caught a pair of blue eyes gaping at him from a seat by the window. Blue eyes he'd recently become intimately acquainted with. Including the way they looked clenched shut in pleasure.

Except now they were wide open, watching him cop a feel. Could this day get any worse?

He yanked his hand away from Mia, then gave Dani a smile and a head nod. She was alone, but there was a beer at the place setting across from her and a man's coat hung on the back of the chair.

He swallowed hard, something bitter stinging the back of his throat. Was she on a date? Maybe she was just with a coworker, a business meeting.

No. This wasn't a business meeting type of place. Not that any of that mattered to him.

"Dylan?" Mia looked up at him with big brown bedroom eyes, her lip between her teeth.

"Sorry, what?"

"I asked if you want to get a car." She trailed a finger down the buttons of his shirt.

This was his cue, but for some reason his answer stuck to his tongue, his previous line disappearing into thin air.

What the hell? Of course he wanted to get a car. That's why he was there, but he also had a cat-killing curiosity about whose jacket that was on the stool across from Dani. And he should probably go say hello, right? Any other time he would go say hello. "Yeah," he said, giving Mia a smile and a wink. "Just give me a minute. I see a friend I want to say hi to."

"Ok. I'll come with you."

Fuck. "Great."

He zig-zagged through the crowd, Mia at his heels, until he got to Dani's table. She looked spectacular—tight dress, knockout heels. A memory of her in those little lace boy shorts, her hair loose and wild, flashed in his brain, making his mouth go dry.

"Dani-pie." He leaned in for a hug, pressing his lips to her forehead, then shoved his hands in his pockets so Mia wouldn't get any ideas about holding his. God, he was a dick.

"Hi, Dylan." Dani's eyes flicked to his date.

He cleared his throat. "This is Mia."

Dani gave Mia a smile that was entirely disingenuous, and a little thrill slid down his spine. Then he mentally kicked himself for it.

"Nice to meet you, Mia."

"You here with a date?" he asked, glancing at the jacket.

"Um. Yeah." She gestured to the street. "He just had to step outside."

Dylan's jaw clenched. As hypocritical as it was, given the woman standing beside him ordering them up an Uber, hearing about Dani's dating life after he'd seen her naked was intolerable.

Mia seemed to pick up on the tension. She looked between them suspiciously. "How do you two know each other?"

"Uh, my best friend married Dani's best friend," Dylan said safely.

Dani's fake smile fell. "Yup, *Josh* and I are old friends." She looked pointedly at him and he winced. For God's sake, he knew how to run into a woman he'd slept with. It happened more than he liked to admit. But for some reason, this time felt different.

Mia's gaze drifted to the crowd as she seemingly tired of this awkward little dance playing out in front of her. "I'm going to head to the ladies room," she said. "Dylan, I'll meet you at the door."

Dani watched her go, then turned a tight smile in his direction. Tension whipped and crackled between them, making his palms sweat. Why should this be uncomfortable? He knew he was going to see Dani again, obviously. And seeing her with another guy was perfectly normal. But when he'd kissed her forehead, and she'd wrapped those surprisingly strong arms around his back, that coat and beer across from her had taunted him, sucking all of the enjoyment out of it. Normal was weird now and he fucking hated weird.

"All right, Dani-pie. This is a little uncomfortable, right?"

She smiled. "I don't know what you're talking about."

He glanced after Mia, glad when he didn't spot her. "You're the one who said you wanted things to go back to normal." *Unless you changed your mind and you want to go back to you and me in that hotel room.*

"This is normal."

"Totally. I just wanted to make sure you thought so."

"Well, I guess we're all good, then."

She crossed her arms to end it there but he wasn't letting her off that easy. "Are you coming to my Fourth of July party?"

Dani's lips parted and she stuttered at the quick subject change. "No."

"Why the hell not?" She'd been there last year, just like he'd been to Emma's Christmas Cocktails get together, and he'd run in that charity 5K Sonya's hospital sponsored. Josh and Cat's relationship meant they all spent holidays and stuff together. It had been that way for two years now.

Dani leaned back in her stool. "Dylan..."

"Bring your date if you want." His hand curled into a fist at his side at the thought, but whatever got her there. This new dynamic was unsustainable and they both knew it. Dani had said she wanted things to go back to the way they were, and her coming to his party was the way they were, goddamnit.

She chewed her lip. "Are you inviting Mia?"

"Nah, she's more of a 'when I'm in town' type of friend."

Dani rolled her eyes and took a sip of her

wine, letting him dangle. It was working. Moisture formed on the back of his neck as he waited. He could hear his heart beat like a loud clock ticking in a silent room. For whatever reason, he really wanted her to come.

"It's a little late to find a date," she finally said.

"Or come alone." He shrugged. "You know you'll have a good time."

Her pretty lips pursed and all of his blood rushed downward.

"Fine. I'll come."

His breath whooshed out, and he mentally pumped a fist in the air. He'd count that as a win.

Six

ANI OPTED TO WALK TO Bruno's, though she'd spent the entire seven blocks looking over her shoulder for dark SUVs. Sonya was right—only her. After Dylan had left with Mia, and Nick had returned, giving her some story about it being his mother on the phone, she'd pulled out one of her ready-made excuses and left him with a full beer and the basket of bread to himself.

How the hell had she let herself get set up with a drug kingpin? That was probably romanticizing it. For all she knew, Nick was just selling weed to high school kids.

Oh my God. This was her life! She'd just tried to quantify her date's status in the hierarchy of drug dealers!

And of fucking course Dylan would be there to witness it all. Him and *Mia*. When she'd spotted them it was like every bad decision she'd ever made had manifested into physical form and found a date to attend a live showing of her humiliation.

When she reached the door to her favorite bar, she took her hair down and ditched her jacket, reaching down to massage her calves. Her "sky-high" heels were feeling less power statement and more unnecessary torture devices now that she was clicking across a beer-soaked wooden floor. By the time Sonya showed up, still in her scrubs from work, Dani was perched on a stool at the bar, obliterating a strong mixed drink.

"Dressed a little fancy for this place," Sonya said, hugging her then hopping onto the stool beside her. "Where did this drug dealer take you?"

"Some expensive steakhouse a few blocks from here."

Sonya held up a hand to the bartender and he waved. "Guess he can afford it, given his line of work."

"Shut up."

Sonya giggled and took a menu from the bartender. She ordered a margarita and nachos, and Dani signaled a refill on her cocktail.

"I'm starving," Sonya said. "I could go for a steak dinner right about now."

"Well, order up. I'm getting the brownie sundae."

"Wow, dessert for dinner, huh? You've had bad dates before. What was it about this one?"

"Besides the felony?" Dani sighed. She might as well admit what was really bothering her.

Somewhere on the walk there, she'd realized that any other night she would have been live-tweeting the hilarious tale of her date-gone-wrong. A date with a kingpin (he was definitely a kingpin) might have gone viral. She would have laughed about it for days, then leveraged the attention to plug some business for her company.

But instead of turning her lemons into lemonade, she felt like someone was squeezing those lemons into an open wound.

And she knew exactly what was rubbing her raw.

"I was supposed to be having drinks with Cat tonight," she blurted, "but instead I'm on another dead-end date, and she's on her honeymoon. It's just starting to feel like the beginning of a new era."

Sonya's perfectly-arched brows slashed inward and she crossed her arms over her purple scrub top. "Is this some weird knee-jerk reaction to Cat's wedding, like when Emma bought her house and you decided you needed a bigger kitchen so you had four quotes by the following weekend?"

"And then I realized I never cook so I called the whole thing off?" She thought for a minute. "Maybe." She did have a habit of not knowing what she wanted until it was shoved in her face. She gulped the last of her drink and dropped her head into her hands, letting out a low whine.

"Look at you," Sonya said. "You're practically

in mourning. Why are you acting like she's dead? Cat and Josh have been attached at the hip for years now."

"Yeah but before it was Cat and her boyfriend. Now it's Cat and her *husband.* It just feels like everyone's joining this club that I'm not invited to. You're all married or engaged, and I'm a lifer at the single's table, destined to bring one bad date after another to all of your weddings."

Oh my God. She was Dylan. The tequila in her belly burned at the implication.

"You're not a lifer. Shut up. You're an idiot."

A smile cracked her face unexpectedly and she snorted. Tough love was Sonya's forte. Dani had a feeling it was what made her a good nurse. Sonya gave it to you straight. It might hurt, but there was a certain comfort in knowing she felt you were strong enough to hear it. "Fine," she said. "Maybe I'm not a lifer. I just didn't expect to be so far behind."

"To be fair, this is sort of a new concern for you."

"What do you mean?"

"The morning Emma got married, you crawled out of some guy's bed and met us late and hungover at the hair salon."

She chewed her straw. "Emma got married years ago. Doesn't count."

"Okay, but when Marcus and I got engaged *two months ago*, you sent me a condolence card."

"That was a joke. I'm very happy for you."

"I know. I'm just saying, this is the first I've even heard you mention the idea of settling down. Like Cat getting married flipped some switch in your pretty blonde head."

Sonya was right. All four of them were tight, but she'd known Cat since middle school. They'd even picked the same college so they didn't have to be apart. When Sonya and Emma were assigned to the dorm room across the hall, their circle was complete, but it had kind of always been Dani and Cat, and Sonya and Emma. Now it was Sonya and Emma, and Cat and Josh, and she was fresh off of a one night stand with Dylan and a date with a drug dealer.

"I don't know," she groaned. "I guess it occurred to me that if a nutcase like Cat can find someone, then maybe I can too. And maybe I'm afraid to be so far behind."

Sonya slurped the last sip of her margarita. "Dani, you're not behind. You've done great things with your career. You partied hard, but you also worked your ass off. Maybe this is the year you finally find the right guy and actually have the time to spend with him."

"Maybe." She pictured Nick exchanging packages with the driver of a black SUV. Left to her own devices, she wasn't off to a great start.

There's always Benji's website.

"Look," Sonya continued, "with the exception of Emma, none of us were looking for love when we found it. I was getting my masters when I met

Marcus and it was the worst possible time to have a boyfriend, and we all know how hard Cat fought the idea of falling for Josh when they first met. Once you start trying to find love the way you think it's supposed to look, you set yourself up for disappointment."

She had a point. Maybe that was part of what was holding her back on Benji's idea. It wasn't that she had an issue with meeting men online. Like every woman of a certain age bracket, she'd spent some time on Tinder, but she definitely wasn't there to find her soulmate. This app seemed like a real endeavor. A commitment to find commitment. It cost a hundred bucks to join, for God's sake. There had to be a higher tier of engagement there. Which was what she wanted, of course. That was the whole point, but there was that one little problem in the description. Something she definitely hadn't imagined when she pictured finding the right guy. What was the point if she couldn't follow the rules?

"My friend Benji suggested something," she hedged. "It's a dating site."

"Since when do you need a website to meet guys? You have plans every weekend."

"It's not to meet guys. It's to meet a good guy."

Sonya's brow furrowed in thought. "Okay. What's the site called?"

"It's called Eight Dates to Your Soulmate."

Sonya made the exact face Dani had given Benji.

"I know, I know, but you have to admit it sounds interesting. It's based on some scientific algorithm. Probably the same one that knows what kind of sheets I buy and wine I drink so it can plaster ads all over my browser. That algorithm knows me better than my parents."

"So did you make a profile?"

"I thought about it."

"Okay..."

She looked at Sonya over her glass. Benji hadn't understood her problem with the fine print. Cat and Emma would have been mortified if she'd said it out loud in their presence, but Sonya would get it. They had a few things in common.

"See, the rules are you can't sleep with any of them—the matches."

Sonya scrunched her nose.

"I know."

"How are you supposed to know if someone is your soulmate without sleeping with them?" Sonya asked. "What if you're completely incompatible?"

"I guess the point is by taking that off the table, you're more likely to, I don't know, bond elsewhere first." Dani shrugged. It made sense on paper but—

"So you're supposed to go out with all these great guys while becoming a born again virgin for, like, months?"

"Mm-hmm."

Sonya made a low whistle. "That's going to be tough."

"I know. It's like sitting in front of a dessert buffet trying to eat a salad. *All* I'm going to think about is the dessert. I'll be too tense to focus on any redeeming qualities."

Sonya chewed on her straw, then flipped her braid to her other shoulder. "Okay, so you can't sleep with the soulmates. What you need is a freebie, then. While you do this."

"A what?"

"A freebie." She took a bite of a chip, crunching loudly. "Like the extra snacks you eat during the day but don't record on your calorie tracker."

"That's not a thing."

"Yes it is. What you need is a guy to keep around just for the sex. To tide you over."

Dani threw her hands up. "I thought that was the problem. I've had a lot of those."

"Yeah, but those were guys who disappointed you and ended up being in that category by default. I'm saying maybe you pick one guy on the side to keep you, you know, satisfied, while you put in the time finding a good one. Someone with no expectations and no potential."

"Hmm." That technically wouldn't be cheating. She could pay her hundred-dollar subscription for cake and eat it too. She understood the reason behind the rule—you weren't supposed to be thinking about having sex with the guy before you checked some of the other boxes—but what better way to not be thinking about sex than to be having sex with someone else? If she was satisfying the part of her brain that was leading her astray, sending her toward all of the wrong guys, then she would be more inclined to seek out the good ones. Ones that had more to offer. Same destination, different route. It really was about the spirit of the law, right?

"I think this could work," Dani said, her mood turning brighter.

"Of course it can. You just have to be ultra clear with yourself as to what it is so you don't get confused. And be clear with the guy too. Call up one of your old stand-bys and set some rules."

"Right," she said, already writing her profile in her head.

Sonya pointed at Dani with a tortilla chip. "And most importantly, pick someone whose feelings won't get hurt when you cut them loose. You can't be taking someone else down on the way to your soulmate. The karma alone would kill any chance of it working out."

"Right. Of course." So find a hot, emotionless guy with no expectations or desire for anything more than sex.

She just might know a guy like that.

It was nearly midnight when Dani dropped onto

her couch with her laptop and a glass of wine. She'd had to take an Uber home after drowning her sorrows in tequila and Sonya Advice, now she was in her pajamas, no makeup, the television on for company. Basically a "before" picture for Benji's website.

She let her laptop boot up, considering all of the pros and cons. Sonya's plan would work, and she was serious about wanting to take control of her life, push it in a more stable direction. A picture of Josh and Cat laughing together at some secret joke flashed inside her head, then one of Shawn and Minnie hijacking the microphone at the hotel bar at the rehearsal dinner, singing off-key while giggling like kids.

She wanted that. Did it make her a little less badass? Maybe. But everyone grows up.

Here goes nothing.

After the hundred-question form that she was surprised didn't include a saliva sample, she got to the free-form section titled: *What I'm looking for.*

She let herself picture the type of relationship she could see herself in. What type of guy she could stand to look at day in and day out. Then she took another sip of wine and started typing.

I'm not looking for long walks on the beach or even flowers on Valentine's Day. You don't need to look at me with stars in your

eyes—in fact, I'd prefer you didn't. It's creepy. I just want to find a guy who likes to have fun but has all of the adulting down too. Care about your job, care about your friends, love your mom. Stay out late drinking wine with me until we have to sleep the morning away, but also know when it's time to go home or get up. Most importantly, please don't make me regret this.

Seven

ANI'S WEDGE SANDALS WOBBLED ON the crushed stone as she stepped out of the car into Dylan's driveway. Nick hadn't been wrong about the power statement thing. She'd always found it easier to deal with the male species, especially ones who'd seen her naked, when she could look them in the eye. At five-four, she needed the assist.

And if she was going to use this party as a chance to talk to Dylan about being her freebie, she'd take that little bit of extra confidence.

She'd rescinded her RSVP to his Fourth of July party five times in her head over the last week. Once for every time she'd pictured their last run-in—her date in the middle of a drug deal and his hand on some chick's ass—but Dylan was the perfect solution to her problem. Sonya said to find a guy with no expectations and no chance of getting confused, and if there was one person she could be sure fit that description, it was him. Besides, despite kicking herself for it in the morning, the night they'd spent together had been pretty hot. Now she had the chance to turn it into an opportunity. She just needed to man-up and ask him. *Hey, remember that thing we did at Cat's wedding, Dylan? Let's do it again. On the regular. No strings.* In what world would Dylan turn that down? She'd make sure she had a moment alone with him and lay the offer on the table.

Unless he'd invited someone.

That thought stopped her dead. He'd said he wasn't inviting Mia, but he hadn't said whether he'd have another woman on his arm today. That would ruin her whole plan.

She looked down at the store-bought cup-cakes she'd brought, melting in their plastic container, and blew out a breath. Too late now.

The front door was propped open by a rock—typical—and she slipped around it into the living room. Dylan's house didn't scream bachelor pad, but it was heavily implied. Instead of art on the walls, there was a vintage beer sign from Camden Yards hanging over a bar cart in one corner. The other walls were mostly covered by floor-to-ceiling bookshelves, sparsely populated and organized in no particular way. His furniture was all high-end, though. Too bad he couldn't be bothered to spruce it up with some decor.

"Dani!" a voice called as she stepped through the back slider, out onto the patio. Cat sat on the edge of Dylan's kidney-shaped pool in a white bandeau bikini, her hair tucked through the back of one of Josh's baseball caps. She jumped up and crossed the grass to greet her.

"Hey, Kit Cat." Dani leaned in for a hug, but Cat pinched the inside of her elbow with her short, sherbert-colored nails.

"Ow! What was that for?"

"That picture you posted of me in the bridal suite, swishing mouthwash and digging under my dress for my garter."

Oh, yeah. She'd forgotten about that. That post got over a thousand likes. She'd captioned it: *Bridezilla #nofilter.*

"I was commemorating my best friend's wedding day," she said. "It was artsy."

"Whatever. I hate you but I'm glad you're here." Cat hooked her arm through Dani's and dragged her to a couple of empty lounge chairs. She plopped onto one of them and picked up a plastic tumbler of iced tea.

Josh and Shawn waved to her from the pool, and she waved back, wondering where Dylan was. She'd like to get the awkward hello out of the way and work on pretending things were normal before she made them complicated again.

Dani heard a splash and looked up to see Josh hoisting himself out of the water. He skipped a towel, instead walking straight to Cat's chair and wrapping her in a soggy, full-body hug. Cat squealed and swatted at him as he soaked her. It was their usual nausea-inspiring adorableness, but then Josh whispered something in Cat's ear that Dani couldn't hear, and Cat's shoulders fell.

"I'm fine," she whispered back, less stealthily than Josh had.

Dani's Spidey-senses flared. *That was weird.* There was an edge to Cat's voice Dani hadn't heard directed at Josh before.

She studied her nails, pretending not to be intrigued by that little interaction.

Josh kissed Cat on the forehead and stood. "I'm going to get a drink. Dani, you need one? Shawn's mixing."

"Absolutely." For a big, Irish, ginger-headed dude, Shawn made an unrivaled margarita. It was all they drank when he was around. She was surprised Cat wasn't double-fisting them.

"What was that all about with Josh?" Dani asked when he was out of hearing range.

"Nothing." Cat's eyes flickered with guilt. She should never play poker. "I wasn't feeling well this morning. You know how he is."

Obsessed with her every breath? Yeah, they all knew. But Cat usually liked that. She certainly never snapped at him over it. Dani studied her friend a little closer. For having just returned from her honeymoon, Cat didn't look at all sun and sexed-out. She looked more like she'd just returned from a grueling trip up a mountain on horseback.

"You don't look great."

"Thanks."

"No, I'm serious." That pink glow in Cat's cheeks that had popped so beautifully in all of her wedding pictures was gone, and she had bags under her eyes like she hadn't slept in a month. "Is everything okay in Josh Land?"

Cat's nose wrinkled. "Of course."

Stupid question—things were always okay in Josh Land. But what else would have her stressed out?

"Anything new going on at work you want to talk about?" Cat was a victim's advocate attorney. She worked long hours and saw depressing shit every single day, but Cat never missed an opportunity to prove how tough she was. Still, doing that kind of work could wear on anyone.

Cat wiped her forehead with the back of her hand. "No. No. I'm just... tired. It's been a long month."

"Sure," Dani said, letting it drop.

She was about to bite the bullet and ask where Dylan was, when she felt a familiar tug on her ponytail. She steeled herself to turn around and see her plan shot to hell by a busty brunette or a blonde swimsuit model beside him, but when he rounded her shoulder and took a seat on Cat's lounge chair, he was alone.

He was also shirtless in bright red swim trunks and he had a pair of Oakleys pushed into his hair. Pool water, or maybe sweat, beaded on his bare chest and glistened in the deep ab lines across his stomach. Dirty memories made her mouth water.

"Dani-pie," he said, his eyes glowing in the sunlight. "Glad you could make it."

"Me too. Thanks for the invite."

"Open invitation," he said. "You know that." Something secret sparked between them as they pretended her attendance here hadn't been pre-negotiated. It fizzled just as quickly when he reached over and poked Cat's arm, needling her over her drink choice. This was fine. It was just *Dylan*. Sure, the last time she'd seen him she'd been at the bottom of a hill, but today she was a warrior with a plan. She just needed to invite him along.

"So, how was Hawaii, guys?" Minnie asked Josh and Cat. She climbed onto the picnic bench beside Shawn and clinked her glass on his.

Cat sighed and snuggled under Josh's arm on the lounge chair they'd decided to share despite it being a hundred degrees. "It was amazing. It was so hard to come back."

"I bet," Dylan said. "Did Josh get you on the board?"

Josh laughed into his beer.

Dani already knew the answer to that. Cat was no daredevil, nor was she particularly out-doorsy. One time in college, she and Sonya had tried to talk Cat into taking a rock climbing class with them. Sonya was into it for the full-body workout, and Dani had checked out the website and found a page full of hot instructors who she decided she didn't mind being harnessed to. They'd forced Cat to come, and she'd made it about ten feet off the ground before she curled into a ball and made the instructor carry her dead weight back to the ground.

"Do I look like I have a wetsuit tan line?" Cat asked.

Dani snorted. "You look like you spent the whole week in the position you're in right now."

Dylan tossed her a mischievous wink. "I bet there were a couple of other positions involved."

"Good point. I'm sure she spent some time on her back."

"Probably some on her hands and knees."

"Alright," Josh said, but even he was smiling at Cat's mortified expression. She was so easy.

"You two are rude," Cat said. "How was your date, Dani? With the guy your co-worker set you up with."

Ugh. She'd almost banished Nick from her mind. Leave it to Cat to remember. "We... didn't have a lot in common," she said, ignoring the way Dylan's eyes stayed on her. "I called Sonya to rescue me."

"You didn't even use him for a night on the town? Must have been bad."

Understatement. But it didn't matter. She was done with guys like Nick.

Her new dating adventure rushed to Dani's tongue, but something reached up and pulled the words back. If she did tell Cat, she'd have to leave out the whole chastity clause and how she planned to get around it. Especially since he was sitting right there. She flicked her eyes to Dylan, and he turned back to inspecting the pool water.

"I actually have another one lined up for next weekend," she said, leaving it at that.

Cat tapped her iced tea to Dani's drink. "Nice."

"What are you on some post-honeymoon diet?" Dani pointed at Cat's barely-touched plate from lunch. "You barely touched your food."

She shook her head. "It's too hot to eat."

"How about a frosty margarita?" Shawn asked, slurping his straw.

Before Cat could answer, Josh squeezed her shoulder, standing. "Come swim, Catia."

Cat got up to follow him, holding his hand for the ten-foot walk to the pool. Something was definitely off with them, but it clearly wasn't having any effect on their penchant for PDA.

"It's like they're still on their honeymoon," Minnie said.

Shawn chuckled. "It's been like that since they met."

"I think they're just adorable." Minnie put her chin in her hands and sighed dreamily.

Dylan snorted a mocking laugh and sipped his beer.

"Stop it, Dylan," Minnie said. "They're happy. It makes me happy."

"Christ. You're such a romantic, Min. You know, love is just a chemical reaction in the brain to get the human race to procreate. It's an illusion—like when your heart stops and you see your dead grandma telling you it's not your time. All that lovey-dovey shit is just survival instinct."

Dani narrowed her eyes. That was despondent even for him.

Minnie kicked him underneath the table. "Why are you such a spoilsport?"

Shawn laughed. "He just misses Josh."

"Fuck off," Dylan said mildly, but he did look a little forlorn.

Dani never could understand Dylan and Josh's close friendship. They were such different people. Josh had a quietness about him like he was always contemplating something existential. Not that he wasn't fun. He was laid back and laughed a lot and was the perfect counterbalance to Cat's tightly-wound personality, but he took life seriously.

Dylan, on the other hand, was born to be a salesman, always talking, joking—he took being the life of the party seriously.

Whatever it was that fueled their Odd Couple friendship, Dani could relate to Dylan's plight. When Cat and Josh were together it was like they were in this little bubble that no one else could breach. They genuinely wanted to be looking at, talking to, sitting next to each other no matter who else was in the room. And when you were the other person in the room, well, sometimes that sucked.

"Dylan's right," she said, sipping her fresh drink. "They're Team Too Much."

Minnie nudged her with her elbow. "You don't really mean that."

She looked over her shoulder to the pool. Cat had her arms around Josh's neck, looking at the sky while the pool water sloshed around them. Josh was looking at Cat. He was always looking at Cat, watching her move with a permanent grin.

"I love them but at some point you have to wonder how long this obsession with each other can last."

Dylan bumped her fist from across the table. "See, Dani-pie gets it."

Shawn looked between the two of them, his eyes narrowed. "Maybe you two should spend less time together. Your negativity burns so much brighter side by side."

Dylan laughed, but Dani felt her cheeks flush. Had they been spending a noticeable amount of time together? Was their exit from the reception more obvious than she thought? If so, that was going to make what she was going to propose a lot more dangerous. The others could never know about this arrangement if Dylan agreed.

She opened her mouth to dispute it, but the music changed and Shawn started drumming a solo on the wood of the picnic table, making Minnie laugh.

Dylan caught her eye and they shared a commiserating look. Maybe she'd imagined the whole thing.

Eight

SOMETIME AFTER ELEVEN, JOSH STRETCHED his arms above his head in an exaggerated *well, that's it for me, guys* stretch. "I should take Sleeping Beauty here home," he said, running his fingers through Cat's ponytail and smiling at the side of her face. She'd been passed out in his lap since their private swim.

Dani caught Dylan's gaze over Josh's head, and he rolled his eyes. She rolled hers back then took out her phone and snapped a picture of Cat's face smooshed against Josh's thigh to post the next day.

"What'd you do to her, Josh?" Dylan said. "Kit Cat used to be fun before you married her up."

Josh got himself out from under Cat and slapped his palm against Dylan's. "I'll come by in the morning and help you clean all this stuff up," he said.

The tables were still covered with plates and napkins. Beer bottles lined the fence around the yard. The kitchen wasn't much better—there were enough leftovers for an army covering every surface. It was a mess. And a perfect opportunity.

"I'll stay and help him pick up," Dani said.

"Dani taking one for the team," Shawn said. "Dylan, it's been real, man. Another Fourth on the books."

After Josh had roused Cat and they all hugged their goodbyes, Dylan went to the stereo and turned up the volume. "What do you think? Can we make the cleaning party better than the actual party?"

"Considering people were falling asleep at the actual party."

Dylan looked wounded. "Cat fell asleep. She's your friend."

She shrugged. "And she married your friend."

"There's no accounting for taste."

They each grabbed an armful of trash and moved into the house. "Did you mean what you said earlier?" she asked, making room on the counter. "About love being an illusion?"

He raised an eyebrow. "Is that a surprise?"

She supposed it wasn't. That was why she was here, after all. Hot emotionless guy, right? But he didn't seem emotionless earlier. He seemed angry. She moved to the sink and started rinsing plates. "I just hate to think of you being bitter about something. You're such a happy guy."

"I make myself happy."

"And humble. Also a humble guy."

He laughed, grabbing a dish towel to dry. "I

just mean that's where people go wrong. They start putting their happiness in other people's hands, then when the other person doesn't give it the attention they'd hoped for, the resentment starts. It's always the same."

"Wow. I never knew you were such a romantic."

"Your date next week the romantic type?"

She froze. So he *was* listening. "Why do you care?"

He shrugged and gave her that grin of his that reminded her of a wolf, all bared teeth and hungry eyes.

"I don't know," she said. "First date, so I guess we'll see."

"How'd you meet him?"

There was her opening. She turned away and started packing cookies into Tupperware. "Um. I haven't actually met him yet."

"Blind date?"

"Dating app."

He laughed. "You're kidding."

She huffed a sigh. "Why does everyone keep saying that? Plenty of people use online dating."

"Sure. But you're Dani. You walk in a room and men stop talking to stare. You could just spin and point and take one home."

"That's what I'm trying to stop doing."

Dylan abandoned the dishes and came to stand across from her. "Look, I'm just saying you can't be that hard up."

"I'm not 'hard up' but you wouldn't understand. You don't know what it's like. All you're looking for is a good time." Dylan was a summer night—hot, fun, fleeting. She didn't want to be that anymore.

"And what are you looking for?" He cocked his head and crossed his arms over his chest. "Something like Josh and Cat?"

"Not like that," she said quickly. Though, after her conversation with Benji, she wasn't sure what she was looking for. Apparently she'd been leading herself astray for years, and now she needed an app to get her love life sorted for her. "Maybe I'm turning over a new leaf."

Dylan studied her. That wolf look was gone and his smile tipped curiously. The thing with Dylan was even when he was spinning lines in her ear, his big green eyes always had an innocence to them that sucked you in. Like he was born with the perfect disguise. She was never sure which one was the real Dylan: the one who had a new woman every week, or the one who'd looked genuinely hurt when she'd insinuated sleeping with him had been a mistake. If she looked at him just the right way, she was almost inclined to find out.

Now wasn't the time to explore whatever lurked under Dylan's outward facade, though. She had a proposition to make and it had nothing to do with his emotional nuances.

"This dating site," she said, "it has... rules."

"Sounds like a blast."

"Shush. The rules are simple. Eight matches, you schedule your dates when you can. But the thing is, you're not allowed to sleep with any of them until you've gone on all the dates."

"So you're giving up sex for however long it takes you to go on eight different dates? Have fun with that."

She grinned. "Actually, the rules say no sex with the matches... not no sex."

His mouth turned up at the corner. "I see."

"I just thought, maybe, since we've already been there..."

Now both corners were creeping upward, his pointy canine teeth peeking out from beneath his upper lip. He looked so dangerous sometimes. "Are you suggesting a little arrangement between me and you?"

"Limited time only deal," she rushed. "It would be over when the eight dates are up. That has to be clear." She blew out a breath and squared her shoulders. "What do you say, Dylan? You up for some benefits with this friendship?"

Dylan leaned back against the counter, crossing his arms over his chest. His arms bulged, and her tastebuds flooded. She couldn't read his face, though, and it was making her nervous.

"Let me get this straight," he said. "You practically ran out of my hotel room a few weeks ago, and now you want to use me for my sexual prowess while you go on some dating pilgrimage to find the love of your life? Do I sneak out in the night, like you did the morning after the wedding?"

Dani winced. It sounded really harsh when he framed it that way. "It's not that..." she started. Her stomach twisted. She never would have asked him if she thought for a second that he was going to be anything other than one hundred percent game. "I don't want to use you, Dylan. I swear that's not what I meant."

His cheek twitched. Then his eyes crinkled and he started to laugh. "I'm kidding, Dani-pie. Use me. Hell, you're the one who has to date these guys after being with me. Honestly, I think it's going to put a sort of pall over the whole thing. But that's the price you pay."

Her lungs deflated in relief. She was afraid for a minute that she'd accidentally stumbled upon a secret living chamber in Dylan Pierce's heart of stone. "Okay, well. I guess your feelings are intact," she said. "So, do we have a deal?"

"Maybe."

"Maybe?"

"I think I need a preview on my new investment." He dropped his eyes down her front and dragged them slowly back up.

Goosebumps flared on her skin. "We've done this before," she said. "You know exactly what you're getting."

"True, but that was old Dani. This is newleaf Dani. How do I know the features haven't changed?"

"Fine," she said. "You want a test drive?" She leaned the inches she needed to close the distance between them. Now that he'd said yes to her proposal he was hers to flirt with.

Dylan swiped his hand over the countertop, pushing aside Tupperware and platters of cookies, then hoisted her onto it. Her heart hammered in her chest, his rough touch sending lightning bolts through her skin.

He used that rough touch to push her legs apart so he could stand in between them, then he placed his palm on her knee, running it slowly upward. She had skinny legs—toothpicks. She'd always been self-conscious about it, but with Dylan's big hand wrapped around the back of her thigh, they felt like just the right size.

"God, you're sexy," he whispered.

"Don't use lines on me, Dylan. If we're going to do this, give me some credit."

"I'm not. I mean it. You—" he cut himself off, with a whisper-soft kiss to her bottom lip, his breath shuddering when he pulled away.

Dani's belly flipped, catching her off guard and making her face burn. It was a reflex to being kissed that way. Could have happened with anyone.

Though, they were still staring at each other.

The room went silent suddenly, Dylan's playlist coming to an end, and she looked over his shoulder at the clock on his microwave.

"Stay," he said, reading her mind. "It's late."

"Not tonight." She slid off the counter. "If we're going to do this, let's not complicate it."

He scoffed, his eyes dropping to the floor. "It's not like we haven't shared a bed before, Dani."

Not your bed. Something about that felt like a whole other thing—getting undressed together, climbing under his covers that probably smelled like that cologne she remembered from the wedding. No. She wasn't muddying the waters already. "Josh said he'd come over in the morning," she said. "I'm not going to be here when he does, and I'm not sneaking out of here like a criminal."

"Like you did last time?"

Her cheeks warmed. "Right," she said. "So, let's avoid that."

Dylan stood silently in the kitchen, his eyes like hot coals raking over her skin while she gathered her bag and fixed her ponytail. He finally snapped-to when she headed for the door.

"Okay, Dani-pie," he said. "Thanks for coming. Party's always more fun with you."

She smiled, his compliment hitting her in that same reflex place in her gut. "Bye, Dylan."

She reached for the knob, but he caught her hand and tugged her back against his chest. He kissed her again, a weird mixture of lingering lust and something warmer. *Friendship.* They were friends. Another reason why this worked.

"See you soon," he said, releasing her.

"See you soon, Dylan."

If there was one thing that was certain about this arrangement, it was that.

Nine

"DYLAN, YOU'RE GETTING SAND ALL over my floor," Irene said, swatting him with a dish towel as he entered her kitchen.

If he'd heard that once, he'd heard it a million times. Since Dani had helped him clean up after the party, he'd decided to spend the last day of his holiday weekend surfing and getting a home-made meal at his mother's house. He tried to do it at least twice a month, but work had been busy and he hadn't seen her since Josh's wedding. He'd pay for that today with a list of chores she needed done, but it was worth it. Her farfalle and sausage was a lot better than whatever cold cuts he had in his fridge.

"I told you I was coming from the beach, Ma." He leaned down to hug her, her five-foot-nothing, pear-shaped frame disappearing into his embrace. The smell of marinara sauce wafted from her apron, making his stomach growl.

"Yes, I just thought you might leave some of the beach there."

He released her and dropped into a kitchen

chair, setting his feet on another. She swatted him again and he set them on the floor. A visit to his mother wasn't complete without a few welts. She was like an overzealous coach in the locker room. Those towel flicks actually hurt.

"How's the car?" he asked, rubbing his arm. "I wish you'd let me get you a new one."

His mother had been driving a beat-up station wagon since she'd moved from the home Dylan grew up in to a small ranch closer to where he lived now. It cost her more to live here and she was on a fixed income, working part-time at a small grocery store that cut her hours every winter when the tourists left town. Whenever he parked his sports car next to her car in her driveway, guilt kicked at him.

"It goes," she said, waving him off. "I want you to pass on my compliments to Josh on the beautiful wedding. It's good to see him so happy. I've been praying for him for a long time." She crossed herself and kissed her fingertips, pressing them to the sky.

Irene Pierce had taken it upon herself to be the official fusser and fawner over Josh when Dylan had brought his new parentless roommate home for a good meal one weekend freshman year in college. Seventeen years later, she hadn't stopped.

"I'll let him know," he said, knowing exactly what was coming next.

Three, two, one...

"That will be you someday, Dylan. I'm holding my breath. I'm turning blue." She padded in her slippers over to the stove, stirring something in a pot. "You didn't even bring a date to Josh's wedding. Couldn't you find one nice girl to invite?"

Oh, he'd had plenty of options—just none who wouldn't misinterpret being introduced to his mother. And, besides, that decision had turned out pretty well for him. He thought of his new arrangement with Dani, all because he hadn't brought a date to Josh's wedding, and had to bite his cheek to keep from smirking.

This was all part of appeasing his mother, though. Pretending someday he'd show up there with a wife and kids. That was why he usually invited Josh along for these visits.

In college, Irene would pepper Josh with questions about studying and girls, and he always had a respectable answer. With her inquisition satisfied, Dylan could get away with being more vague about how he was spending his undergrad days—shitfaced and working his way through the freshman girls' dorms. Now she could grill Josh about Cat, and smile and swoon over his happy, domestic life. She could get it out of her system because that was never going to be him.

"I was the best man, Ma," he said. "I was in charge of the party."

"Mm-hmm."

"Besides, I didn't want to split my time between a date and my mother. Whoever I brought would be sorely disappointed."

She shook her head but her cheeks turned red. "You're flattering me because you want food."

He stood and wrapped an arm around her shoulder, kissing her temple. "I can get food anywhere. I want *your* food."

That was enough to put a smile on her face and she went back to humming at the stove. Doing a quick check of his clothes for sand, he went to her living room to find the television on.

"Ma, what the hell is this?" he asked, falling onto the couch and searching the cushions for the remote.

"Don't you dare switch that station, Dylan." Irene came rushing into the living room, wiping her hands on her apron. "I've been waiting all day to see what happens with Felicia's husband when he finds out she married someone else while he was in a coma."

"Huh?" He held up a hand, thinking better of asking for an explanation. "Can't you wait another hour or so?"

"You want to be fed, you'll leave my television alone."

"Fine, but I don't get why you watch this romance crap," he teased. "It's nonsense."

"You sound just like your father," she said with a sappy smile.

His smile fell. *Here we go.*

This was the other thing he could count on when he came here for a meal. The chores and the towel he could take, but why his mother thought it was a compliment to compare him to his drunk, serial cheater of an old man was beyond Dylan.

"You know I hate it when you say that, Ma."

"Oh, Dylan." She dropped into the chair across from him and brushed invisible lint from her pants. "You know, when I was pregnant with you, I would look forward to this show coming on so that I could sit and put my feet up for an hour and just get lost in the story. We didn't have DVR then, so I had to get all of my house work done and get Katie down for her nap in time for it to start. You've been watching it as long as I have."

"Maybe Dad could have been home more," Dylan said. "Helped you out a little."

"Dylan, not everyone owns their own business and makes their own schedule."

He huffed out a laugh, forcing himself to let it go. She'd been doing this since he was a kid—making excuses, bending the truth to make it more palatable. His mother wasn't crazy and she sure as hell wasn't stupid, but when it came to his father, she was the definition of out of her mind. If it weren't for his sister, Katie, Dylan might have thought he was the crazy one, but they both remembered the way his old man had dropped them all like a hobby he'd gotten bored of, even if his mother liked to remember it differently.

The truth was that a lot of his dad's "long days at work" were sick-days turned seedy hotel room meetups with women he met at bars. And yet, for some reason, twenty-two years after he'd taken off with one of them, his mother was still making excuses for the bastard. And still tossing out comparisons between his father and him, while willfully ignoring the way they cut at him.

Unlike Vinnie Pierce, Dylan had never paid for sex. He'd had his fair share of women, sure, but he'd *never* cheated, and he didn't spend whole paychecks on swill from a can. Still, vices were vices whether you poured them from the top shelf or the well. What was the likelihood that he'd be raised by a man like Vinnie Pierce and not inherit an inclination to fall victim to them? He didn't need the reminder of the damage his genes carried.

He studied his mother, hands folded in her lap, her olive skin permanently lined from a life of hard work and disappointment. That's what marriage was really about, making excuses for hurting someone or lying to yourself about how much someone hurt you until you were so worn down you couldn't tell the difference between love and pain. And he wanted none of it.

He opened his mouth to say so, but his gut twisted, and he reminded himself not to make things harder on her now by arguing about the past. "You're right," he said. "Sorry, Ma. Lunch smells amazing, by the way. Thanks for cooking."

Her face brightened. "You're welcome, sweety."

He stood and walked to her chair, dropping a kiss on her forehead. "You have anything you want me to take care of while I'm here?"

"Oh, yes." She pulled herself to her feet and headed toward the back door, rattling off a list with a smile on her face.

There. See? He was absolutely *nothing* like his father.

Ten

DYLAN FELT A VAGUE SENSE of crankiness inching over him as he waited in a line of evening traffic. Beside him, Josh tapped his fingers on the notebook on his lap, staring out the window. He'd been frustratingly quiet all day, and Dylan was starting to take it personally. Not that he needed to chit-chat the whole ride, but a little acknowledgment that he was sitting there might be nice.

Dylan reached up to loosen his tie, then turned the knob to get more cold air. The car crept another couple of feet, then red. Another pointless horn sounded.

It had been thirty minutes of this: beep, brake lights, tap, tap, tap.

"Dude."

Josh's hand stilled. "Sorry."

"What's your deal? You look like you're waiting for a stay of execution."

"Just want to get home."

And Dylan wanted to get back across town to Dani's place. Tomorrow night was her first soulmate date or whatever it was called, and she'd invited him over. He'd woken up that morning hard as a rock, using all of his self-control not to handle the situation himself in the shower. Add in the commute from hell, and he was a little antsy too.

But now he'd finished his last meeting of the day, and all that stood between him and Dani's bed was a ride across town to drop Josh at his Jeep. A vision of the night in his hotel room played in Dylan's head, and he shifted uncomfortably in the seat. The replays were almost as hot as the original.

He thought about the first night he'd met Dani—summer night, sweltering even on the coast. Josh had found himself surrounded by a group of women at a bar. It happened all the time, not that Josh ever appreciated it, but this time, when Dylan tracked him down, instead of wearing his usual bored expression, Josh was staring at this little Latina woman who barely came up to his shoulder like he was having a religious experience.

Dylan had noticed Dani right away. Her red lipstick and little black dress stood out in a bar full of bathing suit cover-ups, the same way his dress shirt and slacks probably had. He'd have shot his shot right then, but it was clear his buddy was already half in love with Cat. He'd figured it was better not to interfere. Then, once Josh and Cat's relationship turned down the forever direction, it became obvious that Cat's best friend was not going anywhere, and that she was completely off-limits.

But the thing he'd discounted was how much he and Dani shared a disdain for limits. It also seemed that for all of her "let's forget it happened" talk, she'd come running right back. Continuing to sleep together was Dani's idea. Whatever happened from here, he was blameless, and that was his favorite place to be.

Second favorite. Between Dani's legs was his new favorite.

"Let's talk about the Jansen bid," Josh said, frowning down at his phone. He ran his thumb over his brow, smoothing the line that had been there all day.

Dylan's latest Dani thought-bubble popped. "What about it?"

"What's the status?"

"Um. Got a meeting Wednesday, I think. I don't have my calendar memorized, but it's moving."

"You need me there?"

"Not yet. Gotta hook him first."

Josh leaned back on the headrest and closed his eyes. "Building like that's a lead on a lot of other big-money buildings."

They both knew Josh didn't have to tell Dylan that. Fredrick Jansen and his wife Juliette were philanthropic developers—a rare breed. What made them different from the typical profit-mongers was that they had a sort of grandiose idea about their buildings and their place in the community. Among other things, that included using green materials to revitalize some of the eco-monstrosities downtown, and hand-picking a select team of professionals with a similar "vision" for the city. Money flowed out of these two like a river, and they were looking to part ways with their current design team.

Competition was stiff, though. The Jansens had carved out a niche of renowned socially responsible projects that every firm in town wanted their names associated with—including Josh.

Josh got off on all that preservation work, and he was the one designing the plans. Dylan didn't care what Josh drew as long as the commission was high. This building wasn't huge money, but the potential to be Jansen's go-to firm for other projects meant consistent revenue and name-recognition. Josh knew as well as he did, that was the key to longevity for a small business.

"I'm gonna bag 'em for you, bro." Dylan popped a piece of gum in his mouth and tossed the wrapper at Josh. "Think of it as my wedding present since I didn't get you one."

Josh didn't laugh. "We need to focus our attention on these long-term deals. Recurring business. It's the only way to keep our bottom-line secure."

Dylan rolled to yet another stop light and eyed his friend. Apparently this was more than just project chit-chat. "For a guy who just spent a week in Hawaii surfing and getting laid, you're awfully stressed. Something I don't know?"

"Course not. Just..." Josh tossed his phone on the dash and pushed his fingers into his hair again. "Thinking about the future is all."

Whatever it was worrying Josh, Dylan wasn't taking it on today. He needed to drop Josh at his Jeep and try out the new slideshow of Dani he'd made in his head while he drove to her place. He gave Josh a salute, choosing to ignore the worry lines creasing his friend's forehead. "Count on me, man," he said, and left it at that.

Eleven

"SO HOW DOES THIS WORK?" Dylan asked.

Dani handed him a glass of wine and took the seat beside him on her couch. "If you're asking that, maybe I picked the wrong person for this."

"I think you know that's not true."

She definitely did. When he'd shown up at her door in a white dress shirt and grey trousers, his jaw covered in dark, evening stubble, she'd thought that she'd picked quite perfectly.

Tomorrow night was her first official date with match number one. Christian, a lawyer from a prestigious firm in Dupont Circle. They'd matched at ninety-two percent and had both clicked "yes" to accept each other as one of the magic eight. It felt like a huge step, but for some reason, it was *this* that had her stomach in knots: Dylan in her condo for the first time for pre-date number one. She found her palms were damp, and a tiny butterfly had taken up residence in her belly since she'd left the office.

Chill, Dani. You've done this before.

She swung her leg over Dylan's lap, strad-
dling him, and watched as his stomach muscles
tightened under his shirt. She needed to get back
a little control, remind herself what her goal was,
and why Dylan was here. The way his lip curled
up told her she was headed in the right direction. "Should we set some ground rules?" she
asked, flattening her palm on his chest.

"You mean like safe words?"

"Um. No." Her confidence shifted again. She
wasn't sure if he was kidding, but she let that
drop. "I mean like no sleeping over."

"Okay."

"No cuddling afterward."

Dylan laughed from his belly, then wrapped
his arms around her and hugged her to him
while she squirmed. "Veto. I like cuddling."

"Dylan," she said, pushing off of his chest.
"The point is to keep a nice clear line. We already
spend a lot of time together. It could get confusing."

"Are you worried about me or yourself? Because you're not the only one who has a date
tomorrow night."

A flash of his hand on Mia's ass at the restaurant a few weeks ago played in her mind leaving
a bitter taste in her mouth. "Oh yeah? Who's the
lucky lady?"

"Uh uh." Dylan wagged a finger, then pressed
it to her lip. "Rule number three: no jealousy."

"Jealous?" She laughed but it came out a

little too high-pitched. "That's ridiculous. But, since we're on the subject, no sleeping with other people while we're doing this."

"Woah." Dylan released his grip on her thighs like they'd turned to molten lava. "You're the one who's beholden to your boot camp rules. I'm not out here looking for a soulmate."

"Stop saying it like that."

"That's the name of the app."

She groaned. He was exhausting. "Dylan, be honest, are you in the habit of getting laid at the frequency I'm proposing?"

His jaw twitched as he sucked on his tongue. "That's an awfully personal question."

"I'm offering you a sure thing. Consistent sex for months. You want to give that up for the work it takes to *possibly* sleep with someone else?"

Dylan huffed a breath and scratched at his brow. "So we do this until you find the love of your life?"

"Eight dates. A few months. Or maybe you meet someone special—"

He cut her off with a throaty laugh.

"Stranger things have happened. If you do, we call it off. But until then, this is it."

Dylan's lips flattened into a pensive line. She tried not to fidget while she waited for him to decide the fate of her entire plan.

"Okay, Dani-pie," he said finally. He tapped her butt, then squeezed. "No sex with anyone else. Now let's stop the chit chat and get down to business."

"Okay."

He didn't move.

"What?" Blood rushed to her cheeks. He was still looking at her, half-amused. This was supposed to be easy, why did she feel like a virgin on prom night?

"Do you need me to seduce you, Dani? Cause I thought it was pretty clear why I was here."

"No, I don't need you to seduce me." *Ughhhh.*

He threw his arms wide and cocked his head, his eyes glittering. "All right, then. Come and get it."

Her mouth dropped open, then she burst out laughing. *Exhausting!* But also kind of adorable. She took a deep breath and reached for the buttons on his shirt, flicking the top one open. She'd been looking forward to getting her hands on all of that smooth muscle again. Two years was a long time to look but not touch when it came to Dylan Pierce. She deserved a reward.

When she'd opened his dress shirt, he shrugged it off of his shoulders, then reached for the hem of his undershirt, pulling it over his head and tossing it behind him. She ran her palms over his bare chest, biting her lip to keep from moaning.

Dylan had always meticulously removed any chest hair he might sport, and given his dark coloring, she was willing to bet it was a lot. But he had a tattoo on his left pec that she assumed he didn't want covered—a nautical compass that he'd once told her represented freedom. She had a little bird at the nape of her neck that signified finding her own way. She'd always found it interesting that they'd chosen such similar symbolism. Though, freedom meant something entirely different to Dylan, which was why he was perfect for this.

Dylan watched her touch him, his eyes tracking her skin on his skin, his hands patiently on her waist. When she traced the circle of the compass with her nail, his stomach muscles tightened and his fingers squeezed her flesh. She laughed under her breath, knowing she'd found a secret spot. He'd already found all of hers. It was only fair.

The laughter died on her tongue, though, when his hands dove into her hair and he crashed into her mouth, sucking her bottom lip between his teeth. He tilted his head, replacing the bite with just the heat of his open mouth and the soft brush of his lips, sharing her air in some sort of tantric makeout technique that had her heart slamming in her chest. Finally his self-control snapped and he thrust his tongue against hers. The sound he made when he tasted her was pure guttural relief and it echoed through every bone in her body.

He pulled away and smiled, leaving her jaw unhinged as she gaped at him. The edges of her

memory of the last time were smudged with tequila, but she didn't remember *that*.

"Kiss me like that again," she breathed.

He blinked, a hint of surprise in his eyes,
then one side of his mouth pulled higher and
he wrapped her waist with his arm, flipping her
onto her back. Her eyes widened, then her toes
curled into her sofa. With all these nerves, she'd
almost forgotten how fun this was going to be.
He stretched out over her, all hardness and heat
and did what she asked, no less hungry than the
first time.

He moved to her neck, pushing his palms up
the outside of her thighs and taking the hem of
her pencil dress higher. Then before she'd even
registered the loss of his body heat on her belly,
he dove downward and pressed one firm kiss between her legs. Her sharp inhale sliced through
the quiet of the room. She gripped the edge of
the couch until it felt like her fingers were going
to break off. Christ, he'd barely touched her.

"So sensitive," he said, nipping the inside of
her thigh as he pulled her panties off.

"Please stop talking."

Dylan laughed against her skin and the vibra-
tion of it tore through her, arching her back. He
pressed a hand to the inside of her knee, holding
her still while he went to work with his tongue.
Each long delicate stroke was a mile, pushing
her toward her peak in record time. She hadn't
felt this close so quickly since the last time they

did this. Before that, maybe ever. Hell, that kiss had her halfway there.

He switched the direction of his tongue abruptly, and her muscles clenched, her legs shaking. "Okay, okay," she begged. She wasn't going to last a minute like this and she really wanted to see his face when she went over the edge. The last time he'd watched her so intensely, his eyes going black, eating up her every move. He'd looked so proud of himself, and—though she'd take this secret to her grave—she might have thought about that expression a few times since.

She tugged on his hair, and he looked up at her, grinning. Then he dragged the back of his hand slowly across his mouth. *Gawd.*

"Get up here."

"You say uncle awful easy, Dani."

A flash of self-consciousness hit her cheeks, but his smile erased it. "Shut up. Take these off."

He kissed her hard, all tongue and teeth while he undid his belt, shoving his pants down over his hips, then pulling a condom from his wallet. She pressed her teeth into her lower lip in anticipation as he placed himself exactly where she needed him. But just before that first thrust, his eyes went soft, the corners crinkling. His growling, grunting scowl turned upward into the kind of smile that made her heart jump.

She didn't have much time to analyze it. He rolled his hips, grinding them into hers, and her vision blurred. A desperate sound she'd never heard herself make tumbled from her mouth, and she buried her face in his neck to muffle it.

"Fuck." She felt the word roll out of his throat from beneath her teeth. His other hand palmed her ass, and he yanked her hips to just the right angle. The one he'd found so easily the first time. Apparently Dylan didn't need to be taught something twice.

"Dylan—" He was relentless, and the end of her sentence trailed off into a slur.

"I'm right behind you, Dans." He tugged her hair until her head fell back and kissed her again. This time they were chaste little pecks, one after another, on her top lip then her bottom. There was no growling, just coaxing, smiling. She didn't need much, and that pushed her over the edge.

She dug her nails into his back, holding on while her body convulsed beyond her control. "Shit. Shit. God."

Dylan snorted a laugh through tightly clenched teeth. It was a bad habit. She cursed like a sailor when she came, but he was no better a moment later. He pushed forward and rested a hand on the armrest, giving himself the leverage he needed to go faster, deeper. "Fuck, Dani. You are such a fucking goddess."

She huffed her own laugh through her uneven breaths. What was it they say? Drunk and orgasming men tell no lies? She'd take it.

Dylan collapsed and she held his head in the crook of her elbow while he panted against her chest. She hadn't even taken her dress off. "You okay there, killer?"

He reached down and hiked his pants back up, leaving them open and sitting low on his hips as he helped her pull her skirt back into place. "So, what do you think?" he said. "It was worth a second time, right?"

She laughed. He wasn't looking for validation—his cocky grin told her he was just pointing out that he'd been right. "Yeah, Dylan. Second time was definitely worth it."

"You know what they say?"

She sunk into the cushion and draped an arm over her forehead, still catching her breath. "What do they say?"

"It's the third one that's the charm."

She giggled and shoved his arm. She'd just have to see about that. As for tonight, she'd gotten exactly what she needed. Tomorrow, she would take the first step in finding what she needed for her life.

Twelve

ATE NUMBER ONE ON THE road to Dani's soulmate was not off to a good start.

Christian Graham, a criminal defense attorney at a prestigious firm in Dupont Circle, was her very first match on Eight Dates To Your Soulmate. The way it worked was the site gave you access to the basic details of the profiles you matched with. If you liked one, you clicked a little heart button (*gag*) and if they clicked it too, voilá! They became one of your chosen eight.

She'd clicked Christian's because he was tall with good hair and the kind of blue eyes that made women want to pay for your sperm. She'd thought his almost instantaneous reply was a hint at their potential chemistry, but in person, his whole vibe screamed stuffy corporate type. She found that despite the fact that she was one too (minus the stuffy) she didn't really like corporate types. They were too... calculating. But this entire thing was supposed to bring her men with more potential, and maybe that sort of shrewdness translated well in a relationship.

She'd never really stuck around long enough to find out.

"So yeah, youngest in my firm to hit that benchmark," he was saying. "The rest is history."

She nodded and smiled. She'd missed the climax of the story, too busy wondering if he was the type who would share a plate of buffalo chicken nachos or turn out to be a steak-medium-rare guy. She'd put her money on the latter.

"Red or white?" he asked. He'd turned his attention to the wine menu. Hopefully not because he'd realized she wasn't listening.

"Oh. I was thinking of getting a cocktail."

"I like a good gin." He flipped over the menu. The place he'd chosen was uber pretentious, with quirky names for all the cocktails like "Ginger Bailey" and "Widow's Walk".

"I'm feeling tequila. Think they can make a frozen margarita?" She knew they couldn't. She was just testing him.

Christian squirmed a little in his seat, running a finger under his collar. Ha! If he was this uptight about happy hour drinks, imagine him in bed. Though, she wasn't supposed to.

She sort of got it now, the whole meaning behind the rule. Say Christian was a cunnilingus genius. She might be inclined to stick around to hear the second part of that boring story. Then who knows how long she'd waste on him?

Wow. Way to self-sabotage, Dani.

It was possible she wasn't putting in enough

effort here. She'd been judging Christian from the minute he showed up in his cherry-red Beamer, tearing his sunglasses off like he was Maverick from *Top Gun*. If she was going to put the time and effort into this app, she needed to be more open, let the science have a shot.

"So, Christian, what made you sign up for this whole dating app thing? I have to admit it's my first time."

He sipped his water and licked the moisture off of his lip, somehow making that gesture look entirely unappealing. Sort of like that little lizard on TV that sells car insurance. "Now that I've made partner," he said, "the others sort of expect the whole family man image. I need to make a good impression."

She batted her lashes to keep from rolling her eyes. Find a soulmate to further your career—*how romantic.* And from someone who found romance a little sickening, that was a telling thought. "I see. Well, that's certainly one way to go about it."

"What is it you do again?" he asked. "Marketing?"

"I'm a branding consultant."

"Same thing."

"Um, *no.*" She took a centering breath. "I started out in marketing, actually, but I found branding more interesting. It's helping clients figure out who they are, defining their image, their story. It's more creative than just selling a product."

Christian's gaze drifted over her shoulder as she spoke. She couldn't really claim indignance though, since she'd just done the same.

Okay. New tactic. She was not going to bail on this before they'd eaten.

The waiter came and Christian ordered the salmon. Almost as predictable as the steak. She ordered a burger and fries. He pretended not to be appalled.

After a few wordless bites, his phone buzzed from the pocket of his suit coat, and he reached for it. "Sorry," he said. "I'll just be a minute." She expected him to get up and leave her alone, but he lifted it to his ear right at the table. At least the drug dealer had the courtesy to step away so she didn't have to listen to his conversation. She slurped a big gulp of water, wishing it was a margarita, as she watched him take the call.

Okay, so maybe it wasn't the same algorithm that knew her wine. She could pick this poorly on her own. Why was she always finding herself in these situations? The guys she met were either a thrill ride and one step from homeless, or great on paper but required a stimulant to have a conversation with. Was there no happy medium? Didn't any fun men have jobs, stability? It was exhausting, really, and the optimism she'd started the night with was starting to disintegrate.

She couldn't get discouraged yet, though. This was only one date. She had eight. There were bound to be some kinks in the plan. Maybe she'd filled a question out wrong along the way.

Christian spoke loudly now, gesturing with his hands and drawing the attention of some of the other diners. She briefly hoped whatever it was was important enough that he might get called away, but she knew it was more likely he just thought of himself as important enough to be rude. Finally, he ended the call with a "Cheers" and her eyes nearly rolled back into her skull.

She looked at her watch wondering how long it would take them to make that burger. "So, I have a thing at nine," she lied.

Christian didn't look disappointed.

Dylan held the door, letting his date slip past him into the dark club. Chivalry, he decided as he stole a look at the back of her mile-long bare legs, should never die. Kendra was the hairdresser to their part-time receptionist. When she'd stopped by last week to deliver some hot oil treatment to Sari, Dylan happened to be in the office. It was lust at first sight, and now he had her on a Saturday night, dressed in a body-con number that barely covered her ass, leading him down the stairs to a basement bar that he was about a decade too old to be in. Lucky for him, you could barely see a thing in this place besides strobe lights and artificial smoke.

Kendra pulled him by the wrist until they'd wedged into a pack of bar patrons. She slid in front of him, boldly pushing her ass into his crotch as she leaned over the bar. He chuckled under his breath. Twenty-somethings were almost too easy these days. Pick them up in a car that you paid for yourself and had a full tank of gas, and they were putty in your hands. The fact that they were so easily impressed by self-sufficiency probably said more about the state of the economy than it did his own worthiness, but he'd take it.

Kendra ordered something he couldn't hear, and he threw his credit card down on the bar, circling his finger to tell the bartender to keep a tab open. Minutes later, they each had a glass of something blue and were pressed against each other, and about a hundred other people, on the dance floor.

"So you design buildings?" she shouted over the bass. Kendra had immigrated here from the UK and her accent made everything she said sound like Mary Poppins, even while she ran her fingers over the buckle of his belt, her hips swaying. The dichotomy was sexy as hell.

"No," he shouted back. "I get the business, convince developers to hire our firm to design the buildings."

She offered him something like a confused pout but dropped it. "I want to own my own business someday. I've been a stylist for years, but it's something else to do it for yourself."

"Sure."

"How did you get started on your own?"

Dylan drank his Blue Curacao, his self-respect wincing with each sip. "My partner actually had the idea to go into business for ourselves. And, you know, he planned it all out. He handles the details."

Way to impress her, Dylan.

It wasn't like he didn't participate. He and Josh each had their own strengths. That's why they worked so well together. It just happened that responsibility for running a business was one of Josh's strengths, and making them a lot of money was Dylan's. Still, the comparisons kicked at him.

"Maybe I can talk to him some time," Kendra said. "Your friend. Pick his brain. I can cut his hair in exchange." She smiled, separating from his hold long enough to pull a business card out of her clutch. She tucked it in the hand that had just been halfway to its goal of cupping her ass.

"Yeah, sure." Dylan held up the card and forced a grin before shoving it in his pocket. When he did, he felt his cell buzz and pulled it out. He barely had enough elbow room to angle the screen to his face, but when he saw the text, his grin stretched.

Dani: No soulmate tonight. Guess you're stuck with me for a few more weeks.

Dylan gestured with his head and Kendra followed him off the dance floor. "I have to hit the men's room," he said. He lifted her hand and kissed her knuckles. "I'll be right back, sweetheart."

He rounded the corner to the hallway where the bathrooms were, setting his drink on top of a condom dispenser.

Dylan: Can't say I'm disappointed.

Dani: And here I thought you were the supportive type.

Dylan: I fully support a long and thorough journey for you to find The One, Dani-pie.

Dani: Since it looks like you might get your wish, should we say next weekend? Same time, same place?

Dylan: It's a date, but I'll see you before then. Thursday? Minnie's party.

Three little dots appeared, then disappeared, and for some reason his heart had traveled to his throat to wait for her response.

Dani: Right. Two dates then. See you Thursday.

Dylan: See you Thursday, Dani-pie.

When he pushed out of the men's room, Kendra was waiting for him. "This place is kind of loud," he said, cringing at the way he'd suddenly become his mother. "You wanna go somewhere else?"

Kendra licked the gloss on her lips and smiled. "How about my place?"

Dylan was about to drop his drink on the nearest table and remote start his car when the weight of his phone in his pocket stopped him.

Right. The rules.

"Sorry, sweetheart. I have an early morning so I have to sleep at home tonight. I was thinking more like another bar."

Kendra gave him a *what the fuck* look and he almost agreed with her. He couldn't believe the words that were coming out of his mouth. But eight dates with Dani? He'd be an idiot to give that up.

"Suit yourself," she said, turning on her stiletto.

He really hoped that's what he was doing.

Thirteen

"YOU LOOK PRETTY." CAT LEANED over her ginger-ale, touching the sleeve of Dani's blouse.

It was Thursday night and they were squeezed into a shiplap booth at The Swell—a trendy seaside bar with exposed-brick walls and wavy glass windows. Shawn had rented the entire upstairs lounge for Minnie's birthday party.

"Thanks," Dani said. "You look cute too." Cat had on a white sundress and gold sandals. Her hair was in a huge bun on top of her head. She looked more alive than she had on the Fourth. Or at least she didn't look like she was about to pass out. Her cheeks were still pale though, and she was still sipping soda and picking at her food. So much so that Josh had gone back to the buffet to try and find her something else she might like better. He seemed to be doting on her more than usual. Since when could she not get her own food at a party? It was weird.

He came back with a plate of crackers and cheese and slid in beside Cat. Cat snuggled into his side, practically in his lap, and Dani had a vision of her teenage years—sitting at dinner across from her mother and her step-father, scrolling through her texts while they ignored her.

She pulled out her phone now, figuring it was a good opportunity to add to her embarrassing photo collection. The party was in its second hour. People would be getting messy. Shawn was already on the dance floor wearing a pink party hat and a t-shirt that said "It's my party and I'll puke if I want to."

Perfect.

She snapped a picture and saved it just as a text came in.

Dylan: Hey, gorgeous. Come here often?

Dani smiled and looked around the room for him. He'd been bouncing from table to table since he'd arrived forty-five minutes late, in a pair of jeans that did him all sorts of favors and a white t-shirt that she was sure had a designer label stitched on the inside despite the casual look.

Now, she spotted him in line for booze. He had his elbows propped on the long wood and brass bar, his head tilted to one side. She could just picture the smile he was wearing—one side of his mouth tugged higher than the other, dimples popping, teeth bared.

Dani was feeling amused at how well she knew him, until a busty redhead appeared from behind the bar, setting down a pint glass in front of him and batting her eyes. She popped the cap off a bottle and poured it like someone was tucking dollar bills in her thong. *Kind of unprofessional.* This was a family event. Shawn and Minnie's son was here.

"I'll be back," she said. She crossed the dance floor and slid up next to Dylan, letting her arm brush his. "Can I get a vodka cranberry, please?" she asked the bartender.

"Put it on my tab," Dylan said, his eyes sufficiently refocused.

"That's kind," Dani said. "Unless maybe you're just remembering the last time you got me a drink."

"I remember that often." Dylan's eyes dropped down her front, then raked back up. "And now here you are, flirting with me in broad daylight."

"I'm not flirting. I'm just ordering a drink."

The bartender slid Dani's drink across the bar and went to help someone else.

Dylan inched closer. "Let's dance," he said, his smile wicked.

"Thought you were talking to the pretty girl behind the bar. I don't want to step on your game."

"You know I only have eyes for you."

That comment had her belly reflexively flipping, and she cursed herself for being so easy.

Somehow, sleeping with Dylan hadn't eased that constant push and pull between them. Which was alarming.

"What did I tell you about lines?" she asked, turning away.

"Gimme that dance and I'll only speak the truth."

Dani glanced around the room at the audience of all of their mutual friends, and her flirtatious mood slipped. "You don't think that might be suspicious?"

He leaned in, letting his breath tickle her ear. "First truth: I don't think anyone will suspect we're fucking because of a slow dance."

Dani felt her nostrils flare. "You're such a poet, Dylan."

"You said no lines." He smiled his Good Boy smile, the one where he looked all innocent and cute.

"Okay," she said, sufficiently exhausted by his verbal gymnastics. "One dance, but again, this is feeling awfully familiar and I don't want you to get the wrong idea."

"That's the best part about this thing," he said, leading her out to the dance floor. He took her hand and let his other fall safely on her hip. "It's familiar. Easy."

Wait. Was that true? She'd always assumed Dylan preferred the thrill of new things, given his track record of a different face for every occasion. In fact, it had crossed Dani's mind that he may get bored of this arrangement before she finished her eight dates. Lands already conquered and all that. But there was nothing disinterested about the way he slipped his thumb under the hem of her shirt when he turned her.

"Careful," she whispered. He moved his fingers to a more innocuous place on her lower back, his eyes dancing with amusement, and another thought jumped up and waved its hands. It was the secret thing. That was why he was so into this. He was getting off on the thrill of hiding.

Whatever. Dylan's motivations didn't really matter. They were each getting their due.

But when Dylan spun her again, Cat and Josh stared back at them, wearing matching perplexed expressions.

"So if they don't suspect a thing," she said, nodding in the direction of their friends. "What do you think those looks are for?"

"Who cares? Everyone is drinking."

"Cat's not. She's drinking ginger-ale, and she's watching us."

"Let her look." He leaned in, his breath warming her ear. "You want me to kiss you right here, make her eyes bug out?"

Dani's cheeks flamed. "Don't you dare. Maybe we need more rules regarding public appearances. I sort of thought they were obvious."

"No letting on that I have intimate knowledge of that pretty little face you make when you—"

"Dylan!" She slapped a palm on his chest, fighting the urge to leave it there and explore the firm ridges of his pecs.

"Chill, Dani." He laughed. "Look, they're back to staring at each other."

Okay, they were. Maybe she was overreacting. It wasn't like she and Dylan didn't have enough history to take a casual turn on the dance floor with each other. She'd danced with Josh at the wedding, Shawn on the booze cruise they took last spring. She'd served as Emma's husband's official dance partner at the three weddings and two birthday parties they'd attended while Emma was pregnant. Why should dancing with Dylan be any different?

Because Josh, Shawn, and Adam didn't undress her with their eyes on every turn, and they certainly didn't talk about her O face.

"How was your date the other night?" she asked, suddenly obsessed with picturing Dylan with some other woman.

Dylan's eyes danced. "I forget now, wasn't there a rule about this?"

"What?"

"Asking about dates."

Dani thought back to the original agreement. It had gone off track, but she didn't remember a gag order in place. She was too nosy to agree to something like that. "I don't think so."

"I'm thinking I might propose one," he said, spinning her too fast.

Her drink sloshed onto her fingers and she wiped them on his jeans. "I'm thinking I might veto that proposal."

He laughed. "Why's that?"

"We should be comfortable enough with the arrangement that talking about dates with other people shouldn't affect us. We're friends. Friends talk."

"What if I don't want to talk about it?"

She huffed a breath. "Well, then, I think you should consider what that means in terms of—"

Dylan stopped her with a finger to her lips. His eyes narrowed and a tiny muscle in his jaw twitched. "New proposition," he said. "You, me, let's get out of here."

"What? Where?"

"Follow me." He was tugging on her wrist before she even had a chance to answer, her sparkly peep-toe heels wobbling as she rushed to keep pace.

The Swell had a long, narrow hallway where the bathrooms were located, but Dylan went for a third door, unmarked and at the end of the row.

"What is this?"

"Closet." He spun her around until she was inside the small room, and closed the door.

"Why are we in it?"

"Because you're turning me on with all your rules talk. I needed to do this." He took her face in his hands and kissed her hard, smiling as he pulled away.

"This isn't part of the deal," she whispered sharply, her heart pounding.

Dylan trailed a finger down the side of her throat, then tipped her chin with his thumb. Electricity zinged in her belly and she tipped her head to the side, letting him suck at the skin beneath her ear.

"So what?" he said, breathing the words against her ear.

"This is stupid," she hissed. "We're going to get caught, Dylan!"

God, she sounded like a schoolmarm. When did she become so rigid? This whole soulmate journey was already dulling her edge. Or maybe it was just that she was stuck in a closet with the one person who'd always had her beat.

Dylan smiled against her lips, taking the bottom one between his teeth. "Caught by who, and who cares?"

"I don't know, any one of our friends?" But she was already pressed against him, her neck and chest damp from the lack of air conditioning and breathing room. If anyone walked in now, they'd be caught before he even touched her. And too late for that, since he'd already hiked her leg up around his waist.

"No one is gonna know, Dani-pie." He reached between them and flicked open the button on her jeans.

"You're serious?" She couldn't help her giggle when she thought about stuffy Christian Graham balking at a frozen cocktail last weekend. Now look at her.

"I am if you are," Dylan said.

Screw it. She'd never been good at being the adult in the room. She dove her fingers into his thick messy hair and pulled his face back to hers while Dylan reached for his wallet.

She could just picture Cat's face if she caught them. In high school, when Dani had confessed to Cat that she'd had sex with Jimmy Hamill under the bleachers after the championship football game, Cat had been appalled. She'd stood there against their lockers, her arms full of A.P textbooks, gaping at Dani. *"You're going to end up pregnant!"* she'd cried. *"And then what, Dani? You won't be doing keg stands on the weekends, that's for sure."*

"Oh my God!"

Dylan's head shot up, alarmed. "What?"

"Do you think Cat's pregnant?"

"What?" he repeated, more forcefully.

"Is that why she looks like she's been run over by a truck?" Details sorted themselves out in her brain. "She wasn't drinking on the Fourth and she slept through half the party. She's not drinking today either!"

"Jesus, Dani." He glanced between them, his fly hanging open, his voice a little out of breath.

"Sorry. Mood killer. I didn't mean to—it just popped into my head."

"Well, pop it back out." He dove back into her neck, then paused. "You're on the pill, right?"

"Yes."

"Okay."

Dylan tugged her camisole free from her jeans but her mind had reversed to the previous exit. That had to be it, right? Was Cat really pregnant? For God's sake, she'd been married a month. Sonya would be next. Emma already had one and was working on a second, and here she was doubling up on birth control to— "Christ, Dylan."

"Told you the third time's a charm."

Fourteen

"WHAT DO YOU MEAN YOU think she's pregnant?" Sonya asked. Emma squealed at the same time, and a woman passing by her on the street jumped, then shot Dani a haughty look. Dani quickly adjusted the volume on the video call.

"I mean she hasn't had a drink since she got back from the honeymoon, and she's been uncharacteristically emotional. She cried through her whole wedding!"

Emma looked confused. "It was her wedding!"

"Wouldn't she tell us if she was?" Sonya asked. "Or Josh would. I don't see him keeping this secret."

Dani shrugged as her heels clicked down the sidewalk to her office. She'd been in off-site meetings the entire morning, texting Sonya and Emma beneath conference room tables to try and schedule this call while they were all out for lunch.

"Maybe it was the honeymoon," Emma said,

clapping her hands at her desk. "That is so romantic."

Dani shook her head. "If it was the honeymoon, she wouldn't have known on the Fourth, and she was definitely alcohol free that whole day."

"Hmm." Sonya tapped a fingernail to her bottom lip. "Maybe Prince Charming knocked up his very Catholic wife before they got married. That's why she doesn't want to tell us."

Emma gasped. "Oh, can you imagine? Carlos will have Josh's head."

Sonya gave an evil laugh, and Dani tried to imagine her own dad caring about something so silly. He and her step-mom used to let her high school boyfriend stay over in her room. Her mother bought her condoms when she was sixteen. Growing up alongside Cat and her traditional Catholic family was eye-opening. Though, she had to admit there were times when Carlos's firm hand felt a lot more like love than the "freedom to grow" her parents gave her. It drove Cat crazy, but her parents were never too busy to find out exactly what she was up to. Which was why she was never up to anything.

"It's sort of Romeo and Juliet romantic, though," Emma said.

Sonya rolled her eyes. "How?"

"Romantic or not," Dani said, "why is she keeping it from me?"

"Why don't you just ask her?" Sonya said. "Let's add her to the call right now."

"No! If she doesn't want to tell me, I'll just have to get used to not being her confidante anymore."

"If Cat were here, she would say you were being *sooo* dramatic," Sonya reminded her.

Emma's giddy smile fell. "Maybe she has her reasons, Dani."

Dani shook her head, an ache worming its way into her chest. "What reason could she possibly have to lie?

Twenty-four hours after Minnie's party, Dylan was back at Dani's condo. Her cheek was squished against his bare chest, his hand resting comfortably on the back of her head. She laid there, trying to pretend they weren't cuddling, and thinking about the conversation she'd had with Sonya and Emma.

Having Dylan there had been a good distraction. She certainly hadn't been thinking about Cat while she was propped on the edge of her kitchen island, her chin bouncing on his shoulder. They'd ended on the couch, and now, with just the sound of Dylan's heavy breathing in the otherwise silent room, her mind was spinning again.

"You want a beer?"

He groaned, sitting them both up. "Sure," he said, dropping a kiss on her cheek.

She went to her bedroom for a t-shirt, then padded the few feet to her kitchen. Her condo was cozy, which was a nice way of saying tiny, but the hardwood floors and stainless steel appliances were brand new when she'd bought it. The living room had a whole wall full of windows and she had an extra bedroom which was a rare amenity in these older buildings.

"So what were you in town for today?" Dani asked.

Dylan answered over his shoulder as he found his way to her bathroom. "I'm trying to close the deal on this historic renovation in the West End," he said. "Old fuddy-duddy owner. I should have taken Josh with me, they could have talked golf."

She lazily perused his ass while he took care of the condom. Two matching dimples poked his lower back and he had a line across his hips where the skin below was about ten shades lighter. The hazards of spending half your life in swim trunks. It was a nice view.

He turned, and she quickly darted her eyes to the beer.

"I'm sure you smooth-talked him." She popped the caps off of two bottles of Heineken, meeting him back at the couch.

"I am pretty smooth," he said, thanking her for the beer with a quick kiss. "But I don't think this guy was charmed. Might need a new tactic." He blew out a breath then took a long pull of his beer. "Josh wants this job. Lately, every conversation with him is like an interrogation. I get it—he wants to do more historic rennos, and the Jansens have a big budget. This one connection could fund the expansion we've been planning, but his stress is getting to my head."

Dani turned to face him, pulling her legs underneath her and studying a line on his brow that she'd never seen before. The worry in his tone was completely off-brand, like he'd let a secret slip. "But you're still in it?" she asked.

"Yeah." He scrubbed a hand over his chin, staring at a spot on the floor. "I guess I'm just used to it coming a little easier. I'll get him, though."

"I have full faith you will." Hell, she'd been closed by Dylan Pierce more than once. "And I think it's pretty clear Josh trusts you to do your thing, so don't psych yourself out about it."

Dylan cocked his head, looking her up and down, and his lips tilted into a smile. "Thanks."

She squeezed his shoulder. "Speaking of Josh, has he said anything to you about Cat?"

"Like what?"

"About her being pregnant."

Dylan raised an eyebrow. "You're still on this? Why don't you just ask her?"

That was the second time she'd been asked that today. Didn't anyone understand that the point wasn't whether she knew, it was whether Cat wasn't telling her? Everyone was acting like it was no big deal that she was out of the loop, but it hurt.

"I'm not still *on* it," she said with a little more aggression than she'd meant to. She sunk into the couch cushions, a combination of embarrassment and irritation mixing in her chest. Of course Dylan wouldn't get it. He'd probably never had a hurt feeling in his life. "Forget it," she said. "I was just wondering."

Dylan looked hard at her, his eyes sweeping around her face in a way that made heat paint her cheeks. Like he could see every insecurity she was trying to hide, and she wasn't sure she liked it. But then he surprised her. He nudged her with his elbow, his cheeks rounding into a boyish grin.

"I'll find out for you, Dani-pie," he said.

"Yeah?"

"Yeah. Count me in." He winked. "Secret mission."

Out of nowhere, a laugh bubbled up in her chest, squashing the tension that had been building all day. "Okay," she said. "Secret mission."

Dylan squeezed her bare knee, then reached over her lap and grabbed the remote control, pointing it at her television.

"Are you staying?" she asked, her voice jumping an octave.

He shrugged, his shoulder muscles popping. "You just gave me a full beer."

She took a sip of hers, watching him carefully as he flipped through her channels. This was new. The last time he'd pretty much zipped his fly and flew. Which was what they'd agreed on. This, though. This could be okay too. She crossed her bare feet on the coffee table. "No sports."

One side of his mouth lifted in reply, but he was focused on the screen. Finally, he stopped scrolling and clicked a title, turning up the volume.

"Old school," she said when the theme song to *The Office* came on.

"Classic."

"Agreed." She watched his profile as he stared at the screen, the way little lines appeared at the corners of his eyes when he found something amusing. It was sort of cute.

Shit. Should she be thinking stuff like that? She'd let herself enjoy Dylan's face before all of this, but now it felt dangerous to let a fond thought like that slip through. Although, wasn't that why she chose him for this? She was fond of him in a way. If she'd despised his company, this never would have worked.

"Relax, Dani," he said when she'd been staring too long. "It's a long drive back to my place. I'm just procrastinating."

"I'm relaxed."

Dylan rolled his lips inward and turned his head to squint at her.

"What? I am!"

"Do you want me to leave? It just seemed like you were in for the night, but if you have plans or you want me to go, just say so."

Maybe she should tell him to go, keep things simple, but she sort of liked having someone to veg out with. Her condo felt too quiet sometimes, lonely even, and tomorrow night she was going to have to dress up and act all proper and pretty for date number two. It was nice to be herself. Nice to be with a friend. Especially when her friendship with Cat felt so... off.

She took another sip and rubbed her suddenly damp palms on her legs. "I don't want you to go."

"You're sure?"

"I'm sure. I just assumed you'd have somewhere else to be on a Friday night."

He turned back to the television, settling into her couch. "Nope."

"Well, I'm starving. You want to order some takeout?"

Dylan paused mid-sip, his beer resting on his bottom lip.

"Relax," she said, needling him back. "I'm not suggesting a dinner date. We have to eat and you're already here."

He tipped his bottle, taking a long swallow

that she watched travel down his throat. Then he grinned. "I'm totally relaxed," he said. "Pizza?"

"Chinese."

"Thai?"

"Deal."

It wasn't a dinner date, but Dylan still insisted on paying for the takeout. Women didn't pay around him; friend or date or... whatever Dani was. While they'd been waiting for the delivery, and Dani had been lounging around in a t-shirt and panties, looking fucking adorable, he'd started to wonder if maybe she was right to question why he'd decided to hang around tonight. It wasn't exactly his M.O. (he'd certainly never ordered takeout after a night with Mia) but he hadn't had a great day and hanging out with Dani had turned his whole mood around.

They were friends. They could share a meal.

"So tell me about your date tomorrow," Dylan said, arranging the food containers on Dani's coffee table.

"Um." Her eyes darted nervously. "Why?"

"You're the one who said we should be able to talk about that stuff," he said. Though his jaw tightened involuntarily when he said it. That was just a reflex, he told himself. Caveman shit. No sense in analyzing that.

"Okay, his name is Michael. He's a journalist.

Freelance. Sports." She sighed. "Fine, you were right. This is uncomfortable."

He pulled a spring roll apart and popped half in his mouth, secretly pleased that he was making her squirm the way he had when she'd asked about Kendra. He rolled his hand for her to continue. "Where are y'all going?"

"To a concert. On the waterfront."

"Romantic." He chewed the other half, then took a swig of beer. "Like you wanted, right?"

"I suppose so." She stabbed her Pad Thai and filled her mouth.

"Let's see a picture."

Dani's ice-blue eyes popped, her dark lashes blinking rapidly. *Beautiful.* He couldn't help but think it. Even with that horrified expression on her face, she was gorgeous. Mike was a lucky guy.

"No way," she said.

"Why not, Dani-pie?"

"This is all sorts of weird, Dylan. I'm not showing you a picture of my date while your belt and tie are slung over my arm chair and we're eating shirtless takeout. That's not what I meant when I said we should be able to talk about it."

He looked down at his bare chest. Technically he was the only one shirtless, but he didn't think clarifying would help his cause. "I really didn't peg you for a prude, Dani," he said. "This is an arrangement you came up with—"

She shook her head and finished her bite. "Sonya came up with it, actually."

A splash of beer went down the wrong tube and he sputtered, coughing into his elbow. "Wait, so Sonya knows about this? Does Cat?" He blinked at her, his eyes streaming from his near-choking experience.

"No. Only Sonya and Benji know. And neither of them know it's you."

"Who's Benji?" He wasn't sure why he was getting defensive. What did he care who knew he was sleeping with Dani? She was a badge any guy would be proud to wear.

But maybe that was it. He didn't like some guy named Benji thinking that he was treating Dani in some way he wasn't—like a piece of ass or a trophy bang. He never would have suggested some hook-up arrangement with Dani Petrillo. She was a goddess—gorgeous, smart, out of his league if he were honest. Sure, he'd made a few half-hearted passes at her over the years. That was his default setting, but he'd never expected to get anywhere. The night of the wedding had taken him completely by surprise. The same with this deal. This was her idea.

"Calm down, Dylan. Benji is my co-worker. He's the one who showed me the site."

"Does *Benji* know all of the details here?"

"Yes he knows the details. What's the big deal?"

"I just feel like I'm not coming off too good in this story unless it's told right."

Her smile did that half-pity thing it had the morning after the wedding. "I promise I'm telling it right," she said, patting his hand. "But you're right, I shouldn't have told it at all. It's your business too. You don't have to worry about me telling Sonya or Cat or any of them. Trust me. The last thing we want is for everyone to know about this."

His jaw tightened another click. *Right.* He wasn't even the trophy bang in this situation. He was the dirty little secret.

Something age-old pricked at him. A feeling of unworthiness that he'd buried a long time ago.

Dani closed the cardboard container she'd been eating from. "I'm stuffed," she said. She stood and walked to the kitchen, tossing her leftovers in the fridge and rinsing out her beer bottle.

That was his cue, he supposed. "Yeah. I'd better get going." He lifted himself from the warm spot he'd made on her couch and pulled on his t-shirt. Then he collected his tie and belt, wrapping them both around his hand. "I guess I'll see you next weekend."

"Yeah." Dani toyed with the ends of her hair, her other hand on her hip. He knew that move. She wanted to make sure both hands were occupied when it was time for the goodbye.

Too bad. He was taking one more touch before he left. That was what he was getting from this deal, right? He snaked his hand around her waist and pulled her hard against his chest.

She landed with an *oomph.*

"Say goodbye to me right," he whispered against her ear. He felt her pulse thumping in her neck, and he dragged his lips across that soft patch of skin. All her muscles went loose in his embrace.

She caught herself, though. Her hands slid up his sides, coming to rest on either side of his neck, tugging him to look at her. Now instead of pounding angrily in his ear, his pulse rocketed. Damn, they were well-matched.

"Good night, Dylan," she breathed.

"Good night, Dani." He kissed her again, letting his teeth drag along her bottom lip. He felt her shiver and he didn't even try to hide his smirk.

Good luck, Mike.

Fifteen

"JOSHUA!" DYLAN LET HIMSELF INTO Josh's house, pushing open the door with his shoulder, his hands full of pizza and beer. It was Saturday night and he and Josh were going to spend it switching back and forth between the Red Sox game and the Orioles game on Josh's extended sports cable package.

Dylan was also going to spend the night trying to ignore the fact that while he was hanging out at Josh and Cat's house, Dani was at a romantic waterfront concert in the city. He wasn't sure why he'd felt the need to push Dani for those details. Having a picture in his head of who she'd be with, who'd be touching her after him, hadn't gone down as easy as he thought it would. It was nothing a few beers and trash-talking Josh's team wouldn't delete from his brain, though.

"Kit Cat?" He set the pizza on the kitchen island. The pre-game blared from the living room, but neither of them appeared.

Finally, after Dylan had helped himself to a

beer and pulled out some plates, Josh appeared from the hall to his bedroom.

"Did I interrupt something, bro?" He gave Josh a conspiratorial elbow to the ribs, but he didn't react.

"Nope. Cat will be out in a minute." Josh got a beer for himself, then he opened a can of ginger-ale, pouring it into a glass, and carried it all into the living room.

Dylan followed with three plates of pizza. He took the armchair, leaving the couch for the newlyweds. "So, we have to talk a little shop," he said.

He'd been dreading this conversation. He'd glossed over the whole job thing for Dani, some macho part of him not wanting to let her see how heavy his mind had been over it, but this was more than just a tough sale. Something about this client eluded him in a way he hadn't experienced before. Not only was every line he used met with a skepticism that he was starting to take personally, but he couldn't seem to get a handle on what exactly the Jansens were looking for so he could start tailoring his approach. For the first time ever, he felt out of his depth.

Of course, he wasn't going to say any of that to Dani. *I had a shitty meeting with a guy I need to impress. I'm scared I'm losing my touch, and it's kind of all I have.*

His forehead got damp just thinking about admitting that out loud.

"This doesn't sound good," Josh said.

Dylan cleared his throat and took a piece of pizza. "It's the Jansen building. I met with the owner, gave him my standard pitch, but this guy's tough." As he was explaining, Cat came out of the bedroom in a pair of pajama shorts and a baggy t-shirt, barefoot with no makeup. She looked like shit, which he had to admit was difficult for her to achieve.

"What happened to you?"

Instead of giving him her usual spunky reply, Cat's face fell and her eyes got all watery like she was about to burst into tears. He shot a *what the fuck* glance at Josh, who held his arm out to her.

"She doesn't feel well."

"Sorry, Kit Cat," he said, making a mental note to share this clue with Dani. "I got you extra veggies on your pizza, just like you like."

She wiped the corner of her eye with her t-shirt and took a plate from Josh. "Thanks, Dylan."

"So, anyway. Like I said, the guy is old-school. He's not exactly falling for my charming personality. He wants me to come to some big gala they're hosting there to woo the historical society, but I'm not getting a warm and fuzzy feel from him. I'm thinking I need to take a different approach."

"That invite sounds promising, though."

"Yeah, but it's this old dude and his wife. He's got grandkids. None of my usual topics of conversation are in this guy's wheelhouse." Usually he wined and dined his targets. He took them out on the town, and after a few scotch and sodas, gave them the Dylan Pierce closing argument. Not Jansen, though. This dude probably owned some of the swanky restaurants he used to impress clients.

"You're telling me you don't know how to sell a guy because he's a few years older than you and he's got kids?" Josh asked.

"I'm just saying he's stuffy." There was another piece, though. One Josh wasn't going to like. "At the end of the meeting, his wife told me to bring my girlfriend to the event and... I might not have corrected her and told her I didn't have one."

"Why not?"

"I don't know. I just got the sense she was feeling me out, seeing what kind of guy I was, and that it mattered."

Josh ran a hand over his chin, that line on his forehead reappearing. "What are you going to do now?"

Dylan glanced at Cat who picked at her slice of pizza, looking like she was being forced to eat garbage. It wasn't his best idea, but the only women he knew who would be able to hold their own at a thing like this were in the industry. He didn't want to tip his hand at how hard he was trying to win this job. "I thought maybe I could borrow Cat for the night," he said.

Josh laughed. "You thought what?"

"Just schmooze him with a pretty girl on my arm. One I know won't say anything stupid."

"Yeah, that's not gonna happen," Josh replied with enough amusement that Dylan felt a little jab of offense.

"Why not?"

"Because, asshole, if you win us this job, there's going to be a lot more meetings and events that I'll have to attend too. You're not borrowing my wife for the next year and a half while this project gets press."

Right. He hadn't really thought of that. Usually he got in and got out, but a building like this would require some extra face-time from both of them.

"Why don't you ask Dani?" Cat said.

"Dani?" Dylan coughed, nearly choking on his beer.

"I'm sure she would do you a favor," Cat said. "Free food and drinks. She likes getting dressed up. Plus she boosts peoples' images for a living. She'd be good at this. Want me to call her?"

"No!" The last thing he needed was Dani thinking he'd asked Cat to ask her. But Cat had a point. Why not? They were still friends even if they were the kind who were secretly sleeping together. Would he have thought twice about asking her if Cat had suggested it before? Probably not. Besides, he didn't hate the idea of spending the night with Dani in a pretty dress. This might be one of Cat's best ideas yet.

"Okay, Kit Cat. Thanks. I'll ask her."

Showing up to Sunday brunch hungover was another thing New Dani was determined to put in the past. After her wedding, Emma had instituted the once a month tradition to ensure that no matter what direction their lives went in, there would always be scheduled "girl time." Emma did stuff like that—scheduled fun and used terms like "girl time." Although, when Old Dani *had* been feeling a little under the weather on brunch days, she could admit she was glad that all she had to do was roll out of bed and show up to a perfectly-executed morning.

Today she was feeling great, having had a full eight hours of sleep after Mike had dropped her off at a respectable eleven-forty-five p.m. The date itself had only been so-so, the music was weird, and Mike turned out to be one of those guys who tried to sing along to all the songs to prove he knew the words. She hated that. That's what you're paying the band to do. But the fact that she had at least six more tries already guaranteed had kept her from finishing her night feeling like a failure. She'd even hydrated and taken off her makeup before bed. New Dani was so responsible.

"Bloody Marys?" Dani held up the drink special menu to the table when the waiter arrived. Sonya and Emma each held a finger up.

"I'll have cranberry juice, please," Cat said.

Oh right. This. "Why no Bloody Mary, Cat?" she asked in a perfectly pleasant, *I don't suspect anything* voice.

"This place uses too much horseradish."

"Why don't you have a mimosa, then?"

"Why don't you just drop it?" Cat snapped.

Woah. Dani's jaw dropped. Emma and Sonya exchanged a look. Cat wasn't one for snippiness. Her mood typically waffled between bubbly and sarcastic, but she was never downright bitchy.

"Forget I said anything," Dani said, holding her hands up.

"Sorry," Cat muttered, obviously embarrassed by her display. But it didn't really seem like remorse.

Dani changed the subject. "I had a date last night," she said, turning her attention to Sonya and Emma. "Mike. He's a freelance journalist."

"Oh!" Emma was her biggest audience when it came to dating stories. She'd been married the longest, so hearing about Dani's weekends was like taking an exotic vacation. "How did it go? Was there chemistry?"

"It wasn't terrible." She tried to picture Mike's face and pick out the best parts to share, but a flash of Dylan's bare, tattooed chest hovering above her manifested instead.

What the hell?

She chugged some ice water. "I mean, I'm not sure he's soulmate material, but we had fun. He took me to a concert downtown and dinner. It was romantic, I guess."

"And did you have your cheat night?" Sonya asked, her eyebrows raised.

Her cheeks flushed guiltily. She was sure Sonya noticed.

"What's that?" Emma instinctively turned her question to Cat for the answer, and Dani felt a stab of longing. For the first time in maybe ever, she and Cat were both keeping something from each other. She saw it on Cat's face too when she realized she was out of the loop and her cheeks pinked under Emma's gaze.

Between this weird tension with Cat and the feeling that she was skirting a line of betrayal talking about Dylan, anonymously as it may be, she started to feel as queasy as if she *had* had a wild night out.

Cat shrugged. "I have no idea what she's talking about."

"You didn't tell them?" Sonya asked.

Dani's phone buzzed with a text. She was grateful for the proverbial bell-save until she looked at the screen and saw it was from Dylan. If her face was red before, now her skin felt like it was on fire. She swiped the phone off the table and read.

Dylan: Saw Cat last night. She was twelve shades of green. Couldn't eat her dinner.

Dani's eyes bounced from the screen to Cat who drank her water in tiny little sips. *Perfect timing, Dylan.*

"I didn't *not* tell them," she said, looking pointedly at Cat. "I haven't seen either of you, and it wasn't a Facetime convo." Vindication coursed through her, but then her stomach sank when she remembered the conversation they'd all had about Cat. God, this brunch was the worst. "I joined a dating site and I can't have sex with the matches, so I have an, um, arrangement with a guy for the time I'm doing this. Something casual."

"A dating site?" Emma asked at the same time Cat asked, "Who's the guy?"

Heat crept up Dani's neck and she fiddled with the ends of her hair. Cat was smart, and they knew each other on a different level, but after examining the way she chewed on her straw casually, Dani could tell Cat didn't suspect anything. She was mad about being kept in the dark about the entire thing, though. That much was clear. Which was really rich coming from someone who was potentially hiding a whole baby.

Her phone buzzed again, but Dani shoved it in her purse without looking. "It's no one you know," she said. *Just your husband's best friend.*

Ugh. Her conscience came armed with a sledge-hammer today.

Luckily, the waiter arrived with their meals, including her cocktail and Cat's cranberry juice. Cat had skipped her usual eggs over easy and ordered french toast with an excessive amount of whipped cream instead. She obviously wasn't forgoing alcohol for the health benefits.

"I don't know why you're all of a sudden so concerned with finding your soulmate," Cat said, smothering her plate with syrup. "None of this seems like you."

Dani shrugged. "I'm turning over a new leaf." More buzzing from her purse. *For God's sake, Dylan. Not now.* She reached in and turned it to silent.

"Yeah, but why? It's like you made this timeline up in your head," Cat continued. She pushed around her soggy french toast with her fork. "Nothing has really changed. You just decided to put all of this pressure on yourself for no reason."

Were they fighting? Did she miss a memo? "That's easy for you to say, Cat. You've already found your person."

"You didn't even want a person before this."

"Do I need to remind you who you were when you met Josh?" Everyone just accepted Cat's transformation from bitter man-hater to lovey-dovey newlywed. But apparently they all thought

Dani was irredeemable based on the reactions she kept getting.

"Yeah, but I found someone who changed my mind," Cat said. "You changed your mind and now you're trying to find someone. It's backwards."

"So?"

"So what if it doesn't go like that? What if you make a plan and it doesn't come to fruition through no fault of your own? You'll be upset."

"I guess I might consider that point of view if I had any idea why you would bring this up when I'm two dates into this thing."

Cat's eyes narrowed. "To be fair, I'm just now hearing about it."

The table went silent. Dani swallowed her retort. It wasn't the same. Cat was making a conscious decision to keep something really, really important from her. She wouldn't feel the same guilt. She wouldn't feel any guilt at all. Maybe Cat was right. Maybe there would be consequences, but Cat's feelings about the whole thing didn't get to be one of those consequences. Not now.

"You're right, Cat," she said. "I should have told you. We've always told each other everything and I don't want that to change."

Cat looked chastened, but tears still burned behind Dani's eyes. The tension pushed on her chest, making it hard to breathe.

"I have to go to the bathroom," she said,

pushing her chair away from the table. "I'll be right back."

She slipped into the single-stall bathroom, taking a deep breath and letting the bright lights dry her eyes. She pulled her phone out of her purse to check her messages.

Dylan: I need a favor.

Dylan: A date for a work thing.

Dylan: Fake date, of course. Free food, open bar, fancy. I'll owe you.

Huh. She hadn't expected that, though she supposed it was a fair trade. And a break from the stressful string of first dates sounded good right about then.

Dani: What will you owe me?

Dylan: Dealer's choice.

Dani: I'm in. Text me the details. And thanks for the Cat info.

Dylan: You're welcome. Now delete this message and destroy your phone. Secret mission protocol.

A laugh burst from her lips, echoing off of the porcelain. She didn't feel like crying anymore at all.

Sixteen

"I APPRECIATE YOU DOING THIS, DANI-PIE." Dylan handed his keys to the valet, then offered Dani his arm, leading her into the old stone-front building that he hoped was his next big win. "I know I'm taking one of your soulmate date nights."

"There'll be more," she said. "Besides, dinner and drinks on Rideout and Pierce Architecture? Who would turn that down?"

He laughed. "So shrewd. I like that about you."

The building he'd been vying for for weeks had been built as a bank in the twenties. It still bore the original black and white checkered floor and grooved pillars. Gaudy chandeliers dropped from the ceiling like swooping birds, and a ten-foot-tall, round vault took up a large chunk of the back of the room, though someone had turned it into a walk-in service bar.

Over the last hundred years or so, it had housed a museum, a law firm, and a strip club, among other things. Now it sat empty with its next life in the hands of a couple with more money than God, and a vision Dylan was still trying to get a handle on so he could convince them to trust him with it.

"Just remember I warned you," he said, steering her over to a bar cart serving champagne. "This guy and his wife are total bores."

"And *I* am a master charmer. Remember me when I seal this deal for you. I like diamonds and shoes."

"So, a simple girl."

Dani smiled, all white teeth and red lipstick. She looked like a damn dream in a green dress that shimmered like some magical mermaid tail, her blonde hair pinned up in a complicated twist of curls. When he'd picked her up at her door, he'd nearly swallowed his tongue. It was one thing to see her all done up at the wedding, but to know she'd put that dress on for a date with him had his skin buzzing.

A fake date with him, of course.

"So, what do you think?" he asked.

Her heels put her almost at his eye level, and her black eyelashes and bright blue eyes sparkled as she took in the space. "It's gorgeous."

"Yeah?" He looked around again. He saw a cavernous room with out-of-date textiles and cracked veneers, dark corners that probably housed years of cobwebs. Easels were set up around the room with concept drawings of the revitalization the Jansens had planned, but he was still struggling to visualize it. It looked like the set of a haunted house movie, if you asked him.

Mrs. Jansen was across the room, speaking to a group of well-dressed older women. She was in her late seventies, plump from age and a good life. Her bright white hair was pinned back away from her remarkably unwrinkled face. When he'd first met her, he couldn't help but think of his mother, a decade younger and twice as aged.

She spotted him, waving a hand over her head.

"That's her?" Dani asked.

He nodded as she made her way over. "Dylan, darling. I'm so glad you came. I know you're here to sell my husband on your firm, but I wanted the opportunity to show you why this project is so important to us."

Her eyes slid to Dani and she beamed. *Bingo.*

"And who is this beautiful woman you brought with you?"

"This is Danica Petrillo." He wrapped an arm around Dani's waist. "Danica, this is Mrs. Juliette Jansen."

Dani shot him a look but didn't miss a beat. She reached a hand out to Mrs. Jansen. "You can call me Dani. It's a lovely building. I can see why you fell in love with it."

"Yes, it has so much history. And a little romance." The older woman winked at Dani, and she cooed appropriately.

Pride warmed Dylan's chest. Cat was right, Dani was superb at this. Having a beautiful woman on your arm never hurt when you were trying to win someone over, but Dani was more than arm candy. He could already feel the way she was studying Mrs. Jansen, trying to get a feel for this place. It was more than just her professional skills peeking out. She was helping him, and it was working.

He peeled his eyes off of her face just in time to see Mrs. Jansen attempt to pull her away. The woman clearly wanted a BFF for the night, but he wasn't ready to give Dani up.

"I was just about to get Danica a glass of champagne," he said, taking Dani's hand. "Can I get you one?"

"Oh, no. Sparkling water for me." She held up a glass. "Will you bring her out to the terrace when you're done? I'd love to show her the gardens."

"Of course."

Mrs. Jansen waltzed away and Dani stepped into his side. "Bring me out to the terrace, will you, *dahling*?"

Dylan laughed. "I told you she was old-fashioned. Imagine if I had shown up to all this romantic nostalgia alone."

"A playboy bachelor?" She covered her mouth in feigned horror. "No. She's sweet. I don't mind playing your adoring girlfriend for the night."

He tugged her closer, breathing in her perfume. "Because you secretly adore me?"

"No. And Danica? Really? How did you even know that?"

Both Jansens were across the room watching them and he whispered in her ear. "Cat's dad. At the wedding brunch, when you were pretending *not* to adore me."

She whispered back. "I wasn't pretending. You're just not nearly as adorable with your clothes on."

Dylan's jaw fell open. "You have such a wicked mouth, Danica."

"Oh, please. You love my mouth." She licked her bottom lip then pursed her lips and he remembered how much he did love it. He loved it when it was spitting fire at him, he loved it when it worked hard to hold back a giggle, and he really loved it when it was pressed against a certain part of his body.

He leaned in to taste those pretty red lips, but she turned her cheek.

"Careful," she whispered. "I can see your thoughts turning dirty, and you're supposed to be pretending to be a gentleman."

He took a deep breath and pressed a chaste kiss to her cheek. "Fine. Later?"

She narrowed her eyes—two little slits of ocean blue. "That isn't really part of our arrangement," she said.

"Neither was Minnie's birthday party." He was

171

trying to be smooth, but he really hoped she'd say yes. The night had just started and already he didn't want it to end. The way Dani carried herself, like she was the guest of honor and just waiting for everyone else to figure it out—it was hot as hell. He wanted to walk around this decrepit old building with her, pretend she was his for a while. He wanted to watch all these people stare at her because she was the most beautiful thing in the room, then he wanted to take her home and touch all the parts they couldn't see.

He really just wanted to keep hanging out with her as long as she'd let him. The hair on his neck stood up at that realization, but he ignored it and focused on the dip in the front of her dress while he waited for her answer.

Dani nodded, then pulled away. She fixed her smile to innocent, but her cheeks were flushed. "Later," she said. "Now get me a drink, and take me to the terrace."

The view from the terrace was spectacular. Attached to the back of the building, it jutted out over a garden trimmed with lanterns that illuminated hundreds of pink and red blooms. The stagers for this event had obviously wanted to highlight this secret oasis, and Dani could see why. The mid-August humidity was thick and heady, scented with rose and earth. Soft music drifted out through glass-paned double doors. Mrs. Jansen was right. This place had something to it that was hard to describe, but you could *feel* it in every square inch of the place.

Even Dylan looked impressed as he leaned against the railing, sipping champagne. Though she could see his thoughts running. She knew this was the job that had him stressed the other night and she could see it in his posture tonight. He was contemplating something in the moon-light. Something that made his shoulders tense.

She reached for his hand, half remember-ing her part, and half wanting to give him some encouragement. The rest of it might be pretend, but they were friends, and she cared about this for him.

"You okay?" she asked.

Dylan smiled, his eyes unexpectedly soft. "Of course."

He picked her hand up, brushing his lips over the inside of her wrist. It was sweet and intimate and it took her by surprise. Maybe he hadn't been brooding about the job.

"This is the romance I was talking about," Mrs. Jansen said. She'd found them again, ap-proaching their little corner with a knowing look. Dani blushed. "Did you know this building was used for political soirees in the twenties? After that, when it became a museum, people could still book the grand hall for weddings and other parties." She waved an arm across the gorgeous view. "Of course, like anything it's had some growing pains, phases it would like to forget, but you can almost feel the excitement of its heyday and the glamour of what it could be mixing together tonight. That's what we hope to keep alive when we restore it." She held a hand up and spoke in a whisper. "And what we hope to convince the city commissioners and historical society of tonight."

Dani could see it, the old dancing with the new. She got a little excited herself at the idea.

"It does have an ambiance," she said. "Will you continue to make it available to the public for those types of events?"

"Oh, yes. It's my goal to use the revenue from events to fund an expansion of the gardens. We'll offer indoor and outdoor space right here in the city. Whoever gets the job," she said, looking pointedly at Dylan, "will be tasked with keeping the vintage feel while expanding and upgrading the space into a premier event location."

"Sounds lovely."

"Doesn't it? Places like this are so important to people. I like to think that all of the happiness that occurs between four walls can be suspended and passed on if we preserve the place. That's why I love what we do."

Dani looked to Dylan, waiting for him to pick up on that opening. Give Josh a few beers and he could give a dissertation on the way people place value and significance to the places in our lives. She'd listened with interest to a few of his speeches, finding some common ground there with what she did—unearthing what's really important to people and presenting them the best version of it. For her, it was a brand or an image that reflected a person's dreams. For Josh, it was designing a space where they could grow it. That was what Dylan sold.

Unfortunately, Dylan didn't seem to have even heard. He was staring at her like she'd just shown up.

"She sounds like Josh, doesn't she?" Dani asked, nudging him back to life.

Mrs. Jansen's eyes lit up. "Oh?"

"Dylan's partner has a bit of an obsession with restorations like this. In fact, he and his wife just got married in a small chapel on the grounds of an old convent their firm worked on. Rideout and Pierce turned it into senior living, but they kept all of its historic charm."

"Ah. The Abbott Building. Our corporation bid for that job, but we lost. I did keep up with the press releases. Just beautiful work."

Dylan finally caught up. "It was one of our favorites," he said.

Mrs. Jansen gave him a playful, yet shrewd look. "This is a much smaller project. Why are you fighting so hard for it?"

"We've expanded recently," Dylan said. "We've hired on another full-time architect, and soon another salesperson, so that the principals, Josh and myself, can handpick the projects that we feel fit with the vision of our company. Like this one."

"Sounds like a good position to be in," Mrs. Jansen said. Her sharp eyes scraped appraisingly over Dylan, but he was in full-confidence mode now. Dani had never heard him give a pitch before. Being in the business herself, the effect only added to the cocktail of lust and affection this night was serving up. The lust she was used to, but the affection came on quietly.

She'd always admitted Dylan was handsome, always enjoyed looking at him. But tonight she noticed little details that had eluded her. The irises of his eyes were ringed in black, like a gate around the pools of green. He had dark freckles on his nose and cheeks, the kind that appear late summer when the sun has marked you for another year. He'd shaved tonight, exposing the beginnings of laugh lines that hugged his mouth.

Dylan put his hand on the small of her back, his thumb rubbing little circles that she felt all the way to her toes. Something deep in her chest fluttered and she had to remind herself again that this was Dylan—professional flirt. And she was doing him a favor pretending to find him adorable for the Jansens' sake. Though at the moment, it didn't feel all that much like pretending.

"Well," Mrs. Jansen said, watching them closely with a flicker of something in her eyes. "I look forward to hearing more about our similar paths in the near future. Tonight, you enjoy this little party with your beautiful date."

Dylan smiled down at her. "I plan on doing just that."

Seventeen

"YOU KNEW EXACTLY WHAT TO say in there," Dylan said. He tipped the valet and held the door open for Dani, helping her step into his low-riding sports car.

She grinned at his praise and a little at the chivalry. He really did have his moments.

"So did you," she said, letting him close her door.

He slid into the driver's seat, and she set her hand on his thigh. He covered it with his, and a smile tugged at the side of his mouth. "Thanks again for giving up one of your date nights."

Something in his tone pricked her attention. Almost as if he were testing out how sorry she'd been to spend the evening with him. She hadn't been. Not at all.

"It was nice to take a break."

"Yeah?"

"It's tiring, you know? Always being on your best behavior."

Dylan laughed, taking his hand back to shift. He steered toward her neighborhood, and she watched the lights flash by her window, briefly wondering if he would stay the night. They'd never done that before, but it was past midnight.

"I don't know if I would like you on your best behavior, Dani-pie," he said, his eyes on the road. "Your snark is my favorite part about you."

"Oh yeah? You have a favorite part about me, huh?"

"I wasn't counting the physical parts. I could never choose a favorite there."

He put his hand back on her thigh, his thumb nudging the fabric of her skirt up another inch. Whatever had come over him earlier was gone and he was back to the Dylan she knew. The one who smiled dangerously and pushed his luck. Her blood heated at the thought of that Dylan, and what he was about to do to her. She watched the traffic whoosh by, the summer air and the low growl of his engine making her feel warm and buzzed and free.

Maybe too free.

"Do you think this is a bad idea?" she asked, her voice suddenly thick.

"What?"

Me taking you home, letting myself feel whatever that was in my chest earlier.

"We've never really been friends who hang out alone. With Cat and Josh, sure. Or at some group event. But we're together a lot lately."

Dylan pulled his hand back, scraping it over

his face. "You're confusing the hell out of me, Dani."

"Me?"

"Yes, you. This whole idea of this was to get around some rule you didn't like, and now you're making more rules. Stop worrying so much and just let it happen."

Maybe she was worrying too much, but that comment certainly didn't help. Let what happen? What did Dylan think was *happening*? Because what should be happening is her focusing on finding her soulmate... or whatever. Honestly, she wasn't even sure what that looked like anymore. She'd now been on two scientifically-matched dates that should have given her this feeling in her belly, but none of them did. Dylan takes her out one night to a *work* event and her blood is hot and her head woozy. Was it the sexual tension they had? That wasn't a good sign for the way she was supposed to be finding her soulmate. Or was it that she had something broken in her brain that always found the wrong men exciting?

"Do you want me right now, Dani?" His blunt question startled her. He'd slowed to a stoplight and turned to pin her with his gaze. The low light of the dashboard made his features look sharper, more dangerous. Her heart raced.

"I—what?"

"Tell the truth."

Fire trickled down her neck and between her breasts. Low in her belly. "Yes. I want you."

He picked her hand up and brushed his lips over her knuckles, so sweetly that she almost swooned. "Did you have fun tonight?"

"Yes."

His cheek ticked up playfully, that flicker of danger going out in favor of his Good Boy smile. "Me too. So what's it matter what we said we were or weren't going to do?"

She had no answer to that. She was sure there was some sort of articulable reason why she and Dylan spending time together outside of their arrangement was wrong, but she didn't have it. Sonya would have it, maybe Cat, but she couldn't tell them. She'd promised. She was on her own. Just her and Dylan making decisions together.

They were utterly screwed.

"I should go." Dylan heard himself say the words, but his body made no attempt to make good on it. They hadn't bothered to turn on the lights when they'd come back to Dani's apartment, leaving a trail of formalwear from the front door to her bedroom, and it was too dark to see her expression, to tell if she was going to let him stay.

He put his hand on her back, feeling the way

it rose and fell smoothly like she was near sleep. It was early morning now, a few hours until dawn. As they'd made their way out of the city, the humid air had materialized into a soft, late summer drizzle. Now the steady sound of rain beat against the window. Fuck, he didn't want to move. Dani's naked body was like a furnace beside him. He wanted to curl up next to her, bury his face in her hair. Breathe her in while he gave in to sleep.

She was right, what she'd said in the car about them spending time like this together. He'd been thinking the same thing outside on the terrace—how nothing about tonight had felt like a part of their deal, or her doing him a favor by playing a part. It felt fun and easy. Listening to her have his back with Mrs. Jansen had sent a ripple of pleasure down his spine that he usually only got from sex.

And this, falling asleep beside her, this felt good too.

But neither one of them had any business exploring that if this arrangement was going to work, and he wasn't giving up the short time he had with Dani because she'd decided to go all analytical on him.

He smiled to himself at the way she'd been lying like dead weight beside him for half an hour, still in a daze. He was pretty sure he'd fixed that for now.

"Relax, Dylan," she said into her pillow. "I'm not going to kick you out."

"Isn't staying over against the rules?" Even as he pretended to argue, he closed his eyes in relief and pulled the sheet up around them.

"This is all against the rules."

He smiled, but something worried him on the heels of his victory. "I promise this wasn't what I was trying for when I asked you to go with me tonight." He let his lips brush the back of her shoulder. "I'll go if you want me to. No hard feelings."

"I don't want you to go."

The quickness of her answer settled it.

"All right, then. Let's get rid of the no cuddling rule too. Just for tonight."

She groaned a half-hearted protest as he wrapped his arm around her belly and tugged her back to his chest.

"Just for tonight," she breathed, a soft sigh escaping when he rested his chin on her head. "And then we go back to normal."

Eighteen

"Y OU, DANI-PIE, ARE MISSING OUT." Dylan took a bite of the ginormous sub he'd ordered, moaning dramatically as he chewed.

She scrunched her nose. "How can you eat all that salty meat?"

"Capicola, salami, prosciutto. This isn't just meat, it's the food of the gods."

She spread extra tzatziki sauce on her chicken gyro and pushed some lettuce back in that had fallen out onto the foil wrapper. "It's going to give you a stomachache."

It had been three weeks and two more of Dani's soulmate dates since the Jansen party, and sharing a meal on Friday nights had become part of their routine. Incredible sex on some surface in her condo, then a new takeout choice and a bad movie. They both had to eat, and eating across from Dani in a pair of tiny cotton shorts and a tank top with no bra was quickly becoming his favorite way to dine.

Tonight, her hair was up in a tight little knot

on the very top of her head, and her cheeks still glowed from exertion. It was adorable and hot as hell.

He took a pepperoncini from his sandwich and dropped it on the makeshift plate on her lap. She popped it into her mouth.

"So your family is Italian?" she asked after washing the pepper down with her wine.

"Yup. My mother's parents still spoke it when they were alive. We kept a lot of the tradition." He pulled off a piece of bread. "And by tradition, I mean carbs and cheese at every meal."

"If you tell me you can speak Italian, so much of your dating success will make sense."

Dylan laughed, then clutched his bare chest in fake offense. "You mean it's not my charming personality that makes all the women swoon?"

"Your personality is acceptable at best. It's that face that makes them swoon."

A grin pushed at his cheeks. Obviously Dani was attracted to him—she'd just spent an hour proving that—but that was the first time she'd admitted it out loud.

He took a slow sip of his beer, letting the compliment linger. "Well, I don't know any Italian," he finally said. "But you're making me realize a huge missed opportunity. All I picked up was a love for cured meats and some traditional cooking."

"My parents weren't much for tradition," she said, sighing. "Now, Cat's family? Going there was like going back in time. They had a ceremony for everything. Prayers before dinner. Some new saint celebrated every month."

"You spent a lot of time there, huh?"

"My mom and step-dad were always off doing their own thing. They didn't exactly relish the parenting gig. I saw my dad on weekends, but he was always pretty busy with work." She swallowed a gulp of wine and shook her head. "Not that they were neglectful. I had a perfectly sufficient childhood, but it was always clear their relationships came first. They always said they wanted me to be free. Which I realize now, just meant out of their hair."

"Huh."

"Luckily, Cat's house had so many people in and out of it, between her hundred or so cousins and her sisters' friends, they didn't mind one more. It was loud and chaotic, where my house was empty, like a museum."

He shifted his stool so their knees touched and nudged her with his foot. "You liked the attention?"

"Sure. I mean, I guess I felt a little left out at home. Carlos always had time for everyone. It was nice to be noticed, looked after. And of course, there was also the food." She stretched her legs out in front of her and pushed her flat stomach outward. "So. Much. Food."

He groaned. "I know that look. My mom was the same, always feeding everyone. Still is."

"Did you have siblings to share all of that food with?" She scrunched her nose. "It feels weird that I don't know that."

"I have a sister," he said. "Older."

"What's her name?" She asked it around a bite of chicken, juice wetting her lips, and he had to think for a beat.

"Katie. Her name's Katie."

"Are you close?"

He nearly laughed. They were three years apart, and because of when their birthdays fell, they'd never even gone to the same school, but you don't grow up like they did and not develop the bond of shared misery. That wasn't exactly light dinner conversation, though. "I don't see her that often," he said. "She's married, lives two hours away. But we text a lot."

"And your dad?"

"Non-factor."

Her forehead wrinkled. "What does that mean?"

"It means he left when I was thirteen, and he was never around before then anyway."

"Oh."

The easy smile Dani had been wearing thinned and her eyes softened. That was the danger of sharing your dirty laundry with women. All of a sudden, they'd get that doe-eyed *poor baby* look, like they were just dying to settle on the couch with a blanket and some popcorn while you spilled all of your childhood trauma. Dying to fix you. Girls used to do that shit to Josh all the time. The minute the subject of Josh's parents came up, it was like all the women in the room heard a dog whistle. Now Dylan had gone and brought it on himself.

His neck went hot at Dani's attention, still focused on him even though he'd stopped speaking, and something familiar kicked at him. "It's not an Afterschool Special, Dani. You don't need to feel bad."

"I don't feel bad," she said. "I just didn't know that."

"Anyway." He tipped his glass toward her. "You're definitely an only child."

She cocked her head adorably. "Is that so?"

"Oh yeah. You have that 'I never had to share' eye bat down pat."

Dani rolled her eyes, but it was all flirt. "Whatever. So it was just you and your mom and sister? That must have been interesting. Why aren't you more sensitive growing up in a house full of girls?"

An image of his father, callus and unattached, flashed in his mind. *Bad genes,* he thought. "I guess they couldn't corrupt me."

And you won't either, Dani-pie. No woman would.

He finished his sandwich and balled up the trash, effectively ending the meal and the conversation, then he stood to make a jump shot into her barrel across the room. She did the same, stretching her arms and pulling the fabric of that thin tank top tight across her chest.

She missed by a mile.

"You shoot like a girl," he said.

She shrugged. "I am a girl."

He laughed. "Yeah, but you're not like other girls."

She threw her head back and groaned. "For God's sake, Dylan. That is so sexist. Of course I'm not like every other girl. We're all different human beings. You just don't choose to look past our basic anatomy." She poked him hard in the ribs.

"Ow! Okay. I'm sorry." He grabbed her wrists and pulled her to his chest.

She struggled against him, but her lips twitched and her eyes danced.

"You know, given *your* basic anatomy, I thought you'd be stronger."

"That's it," she said. Before he could react, she dipped under his arm and twisted until his arms were locked and immobile. Then she brought her knee back.

He yelped preemptively, nervous and a little turned on. "Truce!"

She still had a hold of his forearms, her nails digging into his flesh while she smiled wickedly. If someone had offered him a million dollars right then not to kiss her, he would gladly work the rest of his life.

Dani released him, and he cupped her face,

kissing her softly. She opened easily, letting their tongues touch, and their heat mix. She smiled against his mouth, her eyes closed. He didn't usually get a round two with Dani on these little appointments, but they also didn't usually kiss once the clothes came back on. Maybe tonight. Or maybe he'd just take this—her being playful, sweet, so pretty.

She pulled away and her eyes darted nervously before she cleared her throat and walked to her couch. "What do you choose?" she asked while he willed himself to settle down enough to sit beside her on her couch.

"Comedy."

She groaned. "Of course."

"By 'of course' do you mean 'thank you, Dylan. I'm still sleeping with my lights on?'"

They had a deal; he chose the genre and she chose the movie. Usually he chose comedy, but last week he'd thrown her a curveball and picked horror. She'd put on some reality ghost hunting show. He'd actually felt bad when he'd gotten up to leave and she'd made him check all of the locks on her door. Because ghosts care about locks.

"I'll admit I was a little freaked out by that show. I'm not ashamed." She shrugged. "Fear saves lives."

"Yeah, no shame in being afraid of Casper." He flopped down on the couch, the belt he hadn't bothered to buckle again jingling, and pulled her into the spot beside him. The weather had gotten cooler and he wanted a Dani-sized blanket.

She tossed her bare legs over his lap and he rubbed his palms over her smooth, tan skin. Without thinking, he turned and pressed his lips to her apple-scented hair.

Something deep inside his brain whined like a fire alarm at the domestic gesture. That same alarm he'd heard the night of the Jansen party, before he'd quieted it by talking his way into her bed and doing what he did best.

He'd told himself not to analyze this, but it unnerved him how much he enjoyed these nights with her. If someone had told him two months ago that he'd be looking forward to spending Friday nights watching Netflix and cuddling, he would have laughed in their face, then planned some wild night out on the town to prove them wrong. But these Fridays were becoming his favorite. He hadn't had a night out since Kendra.

Dani had, though. She'd had plenty of them.

He looked down at her head resting on his shoulder and wondered if she was the same with her soulmate dates as she was with him. Snarky and sweet. Did she look at them the way she'd looked at him on that terrace? Did she tell them stories about her childhood, the things she'd just shared with him?

Of course she did. She should.

Even as he told himself that, he tightened his

arm around her, a weird possessiveness nipping at him out of nowhere.

What the hell? He didn't possess her and he didn't want to. Not like she was looking for.

He buried that thought and turned his attention to the television. Dani had clicked on an old episode of *The Office.*

"This is the one where Ryan sets off the fire alarm," he said, laughing preemptively.

"That's my date tomorrow night's name," she said. "Ryan. Hope he has better cooking skills."

Dylan's jaw clenched, annoyance rippling through him. For fuck's sake, he'd been inside her less than two hours ago. He grunted a reply and pulled his arm back, shifting into the corner of the couch.

Her head popped up. "What?"

"I just could have gone without that info, thanks."

She raised an eyebrow. "You asked for pictures the first night, Dylan. Now you don't even want to know a guy's name?"

She had a point but the wolf stirring in his chest didn't care. It snarled and spit. "I'm just saying, save the girl-talk for Cat. This isn't that kind of slumber party."

Dani's lips pursed, but not in that *get ready to be chewed out* way, it was more confusion. Maybe a little hurt feelings. *Fucking hell.*

"Sorry," he mumbled.

By the time the opening theme song had

ended, the tension over his little outburst had turned into another presence and wedged itself into the sliver of space between them. Dani's legs had gone stiff on his lap, her hands folded politely in her own. His muscles were whining from holding perfectly still, afraid of an accidental brush or caress.

He eyed his shirt across the room, his skin itching with the need to cover himself up. Actually, he was itching to get off of that couch altogether.

He reached down to fasten his belt, giving her a reason to move her legs. "You know what, I'm not really feeling like TV tonight."

She fiddled with the hem of her tank. "All of a sudden?"

"Yeah. You were right. All that meat gave me a stomachache. I should go."

"Dylan—"

He held up a hand at the pity in her voice. "No, it's fine. Things have been getting kinda weird, right? Should probably rein it in a little."

She nodded her head slowly, and her lower lip pushed out, torturing him. "I'm sorry," she said. "I guess I didn't know the rules."

He huffed out a laugh and even he heard the edge in it. The total lack of humor. "Right," he said. "The rules. I think you know they were always yours, Dani."

Nineteen

"DANI. HEY." SOULMATE DATE NUMBER five leaned in to kiss her cheek, a day's worth of soft scruff brushing her jaw. Spicy cologne filled her nostrils, warming her against the early September air.

Ryan Tulci. Tall, dark-blond hair, cut like a statue. Also, the highest scorer yet of all her matches. He'd messaged her a few weeks ago, but she'd had the Jansen party with Dylan. This was the first night they could fit in both of their planners. It felt good having a high score for date number five. She was more than halfway through this, and she needed her odds to increase. And looking at Ryan, it seemed that increase they did.

"You look gorgeous," he said, appraising her but stopping short of ogling.

"Thank you."

Ryan let his hand fall to her lower back, leading her down the sidewalk. "I hope you like Italian food. I made a reservation, but we can change it if you'd rather something else."

Something annoying buzzed in her brain at the cuisine choice, but the last thing she needed was a bratty outburst of Dylan's ruining an entire genre of food. Or this date.

She'd been thinking about it all day—the way Dylan had spoken to her. Maybe he was right. Maybe they needed to rein things in. She supposed he had a point about her talking about other guys while they cuddled on the couch. And maybe if she really dug down deep, she might admit she'd said it *because* they'd been cuddling on the couch.

Things were getting messy and she knew it. She'd known it since the night of the Jansen party when Dylan had asked if he should leave, and her heart had sunk at the thought. She'd *wanted* him to stay. She'd been wanting him to stay more and more. It scared her, so she'd thrown Ryan's name out there to see what would happen. And then *that* happened. And it caught her completely off guard.

Ryan stopped in front of a restaurant and turned to her, waiting for her response.

Enough. Dylan and whatever had happened last night couldn't interfere with this date. This one had promise.

"Italian is great," she said.

"Great." Ryan's shirtsleeves were rolled up, and his veiny forearms flexed as he held the door open for her. They were the arms of a man who lifted heavy things for fun. His picture on his profile showed him wearing a track jacket with the logo of a local gym on the chest. She'd actually been a little surprised when he'd shown up in a dress shirt and slacks, expensive shoes. He wore wire-rimmed glasses like Benji's and his hair flopped casually at the top. He looked sort of like a body-builder librarian.

"I'm glad we could do this," Ryan said after they'd taken a corner table and got their drinks.

"Me too."

"I actually just moved here a couple of months ago from New Hampshire. I'm still getting used to the city, but I've been wanting to come to this restaurant. It's obviously better with you."

Normally she would have rolled her eyes at a line like that, but his smile was so the opposite of cocky, she instantly believed him.

"I'm glad we could do it too. I'm sorry again that it was so difficult to schedule."

Ryan sipped from a lowball glass of bourbon, the low light bouncing off of each cut of the glass like a prism. "I have a theory about that, actually."

"Oh, really?"

"It's not exactly my theory, but something along the lines of good things come to those who wait."

The flirtatious comment slid down her body like molasses. He was smooth, this one. But somehow he pulled it off without even a hint of smug. Maybe it was the glasses or the way all his teeth showed when he smiled, but Ryan's brand was genuineness and he seemed to wear it proudly. Unlike *some* people who make you wade through innuendo and jokes for a glimpse of the real them. Or who can't even express themselves without getting irrationally upset and letting it out in an outburst.

She lifted her drink to her lips, letting her eyes wander around Ryan's face. "I've definitely heard that theory before," she said, leaning closer and pushing out the thought of that other particular someone. "And I'm interested to test it myself."

The afternoon after her date with Ryan, Dani stood in Cat's kitchen, filling a plate with football snacks. The house was full, everyone gathered around the television for what was apparently an important game for the guys' alma mater. She hadn't planned on coming over, given how awkward things were between her and Cat, and the fact that she didn't give a damn about college football, but she knew Dylan was coming and she wanted a chance to clear the air with him after Friday night.

She hadn't spoken to him since he'd left, not even a comment on one of her social media posts or a Not Safe For Work meme. She'd thought a lot about it after Ryan had dropped her off, and whatever she and Dylan had been slipping into needed to stop. She'd let it happen, some part of her wanting to explore the way he was when they were alone—different, surprisingly sweet. But she needed to focus on the dates she was supposed to be going on. The ones like Ryan who had potential. The little twinges of attachment she was starting to feel for Dylan were just her old habits coming back to haunt her. The ones Benji warned her against.

As for today, there would be no kissing at a group event, no weird heart-thumps or cuddling on the couch. No chance of anything getting confusing. They could get back to their easy way of being around each other. Whenever Dylan decided to show. Normally, he would be the first one there since he lived right down the road, but it was past kick-off and he still hadn't shown up.

"You want some chicken, Dani?" Josh held out a platter of wings, and she nodded. He put some on her plate, and she followed behind him into the living room.

Shawn and Minnie were there. Someone had drawn orange stripes on their son's face. Shawn's Hokies t-shirt, that he'd proudly informed them was the one he got at freshman orientation, struggled against his not-so-eighteen-year-old-frame. Josh had on his old, ripped V-tech sweatshirt that she'd only ever seen on Cat.

Cat poked Dani's arm as she took the seat beside her on the couch. "Josh put garlic sauce on that chicken," she said with a mouthful of potato chips.

Dani's face fell and Cat snickered. At Spring Fling their senior year, Dani had consumed a few too many Bahama Mama wine coolers before she and Cat had ended the night with a large order of garlic knots from Stavros. The combo was less than enticing on the way back up. Even now, the flavor made her gag reflex kick.

"You married a monster."

Cat let out another half-laugh, half-snort, and a smile tugged at Dani's cheeks. She missed that snort. This was a good idea to come today, even if Cat was pretending it wasn't odd for her to be sipping ginger-ale instead of gin.

Before she could let that thought fester and become unpleasant, the front door swung open and she heard Dylan's voice. *Finally.*

Dani casually scooted closer to Cat, making room for him on the couch. But when Shawn moved his big body out of her line of vision, it wasn't Dylan she saw. It was a woman she didn't recognize.

A woman with her arm linked through Dylan's, smiling as Dylan introduced her to Shawn and Minnie in the foyer.

Oh.

Dylan entered the living room and bumped his fist against Josh's. He had on a baseball cap, and he nudged the brim up to give Cat a kiss on the cheek.

She'd never seen someone do a double-take in real life—an actual, turn away and whip back of their eyes—but when Dylan pulled up from Cat's embrace, and their eyes met, that's exactly what he did.

She watched the muscles in his throat move as he swallowed, his lips parting on a greeting that wasn't materializing. Hers wasn't coming either, just blinking and an internal repeating of the words: *What. The. Fuck.*

The brunette who'd come in with him stepped to his side. She wore a thin, paisley maxi dress, and her long hair draped over one shoulder in a loose fishtail braid. It was very hippy-soft. Not Dyan's type at all.

She aimed a smile at Dylan, waiting to be introduced.

Dylan tugged on the brim of his baseball cap nervously. "Um. Cat, Dani, this is Cassidy."

Cat was all smiles, and Dani felt a completely ludicrous stab of betrayal. The back of her nose burned and a lump that tasted salty and bitter formed in her throat. *What. The. Fuck.*

"So nice to meet y'all," Cassidy said with a thick, Southern Belle accent.

Dani set down her plate, suddenly not hungry in the least. In fact, her stomach rolled and she cursed Josh and his stupid garlic chicken. Why else would she feel so queasy?

She took a deep breath through her nose and

held her hand out, heat sweeping her cheeks when Cassidy shook it.

This was ridiculous. She should be used to this. How many times had Dylan shown up with a new woman on his arm?

Not any time recently. He'd been conspicuously alone on the Fourth of July. Again at Minnie's party. The night she'd run into him when she was out with Nick was the last time she'd seen him with another woman. The thought pricked something in her brain but she shoved it away. He'd been in a slump, that was all. Before that, it was a hundred times. This was no big deal. This was *him.* This was why she'd picked him. Everything was *fine.*

Dylan asked Cassidy what she wanted to drink then disappeared—escaped, really—while Cassidy took the seat beside Dani. The one she'd been stupidly saving for Dylan.

"How do you and Dylan know each other?" Dani asked, forcing her face to smile through her queasiness.

"We work together." Cassidy smiled back and the sunlight from the windows sparkled on her perfectly-highlighted face. She had good cheekbones—Dani would give her that.

"Cass is the interior designer on that new medical office building we're doing," Josh supplied, his eyes on the television.

Which would explain why Dylan didn't have

to introduce her to Josh. She wondered if Cat had heard of *Cass* before now.

But Cat didn't seem affected in any way, ignoring everyone to steal chips off of Josh's plate.

"That's great." Dani turned her eyes back to the TV to give her fake smile muscles a rest.

Dylan came back in and perched himself on the arm of the couch beside Cass, handing her a bottle and taking a long sip from his. He kept his eyes on the television, but the muscles in his neck flexed like his teeth were scraping back and forth, grinding like he sometimes did.

Josh and Shawn both yelled at something that happened on the TV, and Cass clapped her hands daintily like she was at the ballet. *For God's sake.*

"Are you a fan too, Cassidy?" Dani asked, gesturing to Shawn and Josh's orange-wear.

Cassidy gave a pretty, feminine laugh. "Oh. No. I just like good sportsing." It was self-deprecating adorableness and Shawn belly-laughed. *Jerk.*

"Ha," Dani said dryly, forcing her eyes not to roll. Christ. She was annoying herself with how snarky her voice sounded. Cat raised a suspicious eyebrow over the burger she was biting into. Even Josh had an amused *WTF* look on his face.

Dylan's jaw continued to twitch.

"I'm going to grab a beer." Dani turned to Cat to ask if she wanted one, then remembered the other secret elephant in the room. That bitterness in her throat was back with a vengeance. She needed to get out of that space. She pushed off the couch and walked to the kitchen, but when she turned the corner, a hand wrapped around her wrist.

Twenty

$\mathcal{D}$YLAN PULLED DANI INTO THE bathroom, closing the door with a tiny click, then pushed the lever on the faucet to full-force. "You said you weren't coming," he hissed.

She tilted her chin at him, her badass face. He wasn't falling for it this time.

"My plans changed," she said. "And I didn't realize you were asking because you were bringing a date."

"I wasn't when I first asked. But, again, you said you weren't coming."

Dani crossed her arms and leaned against the sink. "Whether I'm here or not, we have rules."

"And I'm not breaking any of them."

Dani scoffed. "You're not sleeping with her?"

"Not at the moment."

"What does that mean?"

Dylan shoved a hand in his hair and growled. This was infuriating. How was she going to stand there and throw one rule in his face when they'd broken all of the rest? Besides, he had no intention of sleeping with Cass, and he was already trying to deal with that realization himself.

"It means, Dani, you could find your soulmate tomorrow, so yeah, I'm keeping some options available."

"That's so romantic, Dylan. She's a lucky gal."

"Why do you care? You're being a jerk to her."

"I'm not trying to be, but she's making it difficult. Does she even speak in full sentences?"

The cut in her tone was enough to make him take a step back. "Wow, Dans."

Crimson slashed across her cheeks. Dani wasn't a Mean Girl. A comment like that was completely out of character, and he was starting to understand the real reason she was spitting verbal darts at him. Dani wasn't mad about some stupid rule. She was jealous.

Of all the hypocritical B.S.

He stepped in front of her, trapping her against the sink. "She's pretty though, right?"

Dani's jaw clenched.

"I mean, who knows, maybe she's my soulmate."

She clucked her tongue. "Please."

"Hey, you never know when you're going to meet the one. Cass could be it."

"She's not."

He took a step closer. "How do you know?"

"She's too sweet for you. You'll walk all over her."

Another dart. He mentally plucked it from his skin and tossed it aside. "That's what you think of me?"

"You're a shark, Dylan. And you're swimming with a minnow."

"What does that make you?" He tilted his head and dragged his eyes over her face, stopping on her mouth. "Huh, Dani-pie?"

Dani tilted too, her lips parting, but no answer came out. "I..."

His pulse ticked up and the back of his neck went hot. Flustered. Speechless. If he thought he liked Firecracker Dani, this was a whole new kink. *Fuck.* He was half hard.

She licked her bottom lip and tipped her chin, but instead of taking that pretty mouth like he wanted to, and he really fucking wanted to, he pressed his thumb onto her bottom lip and dragged it down.

"I'm not going to kiss you when I'm here with someone else," he said, letting his breath tickle her ear. "I do have some morals."

Dani snapped her mouth closed and swallowed. The lingering pink in her cheeks deepened. "Good," she said, her voice raspy. He watched her let out a slow and steady breath, then square her shoulders. "I think we need another rule."

"Oh yeah?"

"Events like this, don't bring someone."

"Ha. And why's that?"

"It's just common courtesy."

"No. See, the no sleeping with other people rule I understand. It's a health thing, I get it. But this seems like it's coming from a different place."

"What place?"

He huffed out a laugh. Her clueless act was starting to piss him off. "Why can't you just admit that you're jealous, Dani?"

"That's the second time you've accused me of that." She pushed her finger into his chest. "Maybe you're projecting."

"Maybe I am!" Exasperation raised his voice dangerously and he dragged a hand over his mouth, reminding himself they were a wall away from all of their friends. A wall away from the show they were putting on for everyone—the one where he didn't know the little sounds she made when he touched her, or the way her hair looked like a tornado had hit when she woke up in the morning. The one where he didn't think about her the whole weekend.

And he did. As much as he tried to chalk it up to a natural possessiveness over someone he considered a friend, he'd spent more and more time stalking Dani's social media accounts for glimpses of the guys she was seeing, signs that she was enjoying herself. Hoping she wasn't, so she'd be forced to continue this arrangement.

"Look, like I said, I'm not going to kiss you

when I'm here with someone, but Cass and I took different cars. She has plans after this. I don't."

"What's your point?"

"My point is you're already in town. Why not stay?" He trailed a finger down the length of her neck, over the ridge of her collarbone. He wasn't going to kiss her, but standing this close and not having his hands on her required more willpower than he had on him at the moment. "I missed you Friday night after I left."

Her eyelashes fluttered. "You missed me?"

"I did." He was tired of denying he enjoyed her company. Not getting to finish that show with her had jabbed in his side like a thorn, rubbing at him the rest of the weekend. He'd stewed over it. Tortured himself over the thought of her having dinner and God knows what else with some guy Saturday night after he'd acted like an asshole. He'd only called Cass to ease some of the irritation arguing with Dani had caused him.

Cass wanted him. She was an easy smile, a stroke to his ego, and yet the second she'd sat down next to Dani on that couch, the comparisons started. She was too sweet, too easy to please. He didn't have to be any better than when he woke up that morning in order to impress Cass. He didn't know when the hell *easy* became a point against a woman, but there it was. And he had no idea what to do about it. But he did know one thing.

"I'm going home alone, Dani," he said. "You should meet me there."

"I don't know why I'm here." Dani kicked her shoes off at the door and followed Dylan over to his couch. She'd stayed at Cat's for a full hour after Dylan and Cassidy had left. She'd wanted him to wait, wonder. She wasn't sure herself if she'd go. But as soon as she'd gotten in her car to leave, she had this overwhelming need to be the last woman Dylan touched today. The last one to touch him.

"Do you need a reason?" he asked, unfazed. He'd lost that growly tone he'd used with her earlier. Now he was back to being charming. Smooth. She wasn't sure which was more dangerous.

"I also don't know if I'm staying."

"Fair enough. Do you want something to eat? A drink?"

"A drink would be good."

Dylan handed her a glass of wine and took the seat beside her. "One and done if you're really driving home."

Her stomach knotted with indecision. She'd never slept there before. She wanted to stay and sniff his sheets and pillows like a weirdo, but she also kind of wanted to smack herself upside the head. This was a mess.

"Convince me," she said, taking a slow sip.

"To stay?"

"Yep."

Expecting a dirty suggestion or his hands wandering, she watched him curiously as he leaned down and took her foot into his hands, pulling her into a half-reclined position. He pressed his thumb into her arch and a moan slipped out of her mouth before she could stop it.

"What's this?"

"I'm convincing you."

"With a foot rub? I'm not saying it's not working, it's just a new tactic from you."

"I'm not trying to convince you to sleep with me. I'm trying to convince you to stay here." He lifted her foot and kissed the top of it. "Sleep in my bed. Wake up next to me. Maybe have coffee before you take off."

"So not have sex?"

"Of course have sex." His face fell. "I mean, if you want to. But the other stuff too."

The other stuff. They'd been doing a lot of that lately. Without realizing it, they'd been breaking rule after rule, and breaking them was a lot more fun than keeping them. It was all fine and good until her belly started flipping and her heart fluttering.

She didn't appreciate those little knee-jerk reactions from her other organs. She was doing just fine. She had it under control. Whatever that stupid little fit was over Cass was a fluke.

Dylan was a fun time. He was a summer night, and she had this overwhelming feeling that fall was setting in her life and she was so afraid to end up alone when the air cooled and that beach bonfire went out. And that's all it was, the fluttering she kept getting. Like Dylan's chemical reaction spiel, that's all it was. Loneliness and proximity conspiring to trick her into seeing something that wasn't there.

And yet, she wasn't going to leave. She was going to let herself sleep in Dylan's bed and she was going to warm herself with his fire, and she certainly wasn't going to think about the way he'd accused her of being jealous of Cassidy.

Or how painfully, devastatingly jealous she'd been of Cassidy.

Dylan's lips turned up in that Good Boy grin, eyes like emeralds. His hair was flat from the baseball cap he'd been wearing. She ran her fingers through it, spiking it back up, and his eyes slipped closed, the weight of his head settling in her palm.

He pressed his lips to her wrist. "Stay with me tonight."

She closed her eyes too, shutting out the feeling of free fall that had come over her in favor of soaking in that tiny touch of lips on skin. "Okay, Dylan."

Twenty-one

Dylan: I left my tie at your place last weekend. When you're done smelling it before bed, can I have it back?

Dani: Ha. Ha. I think I sent it home with someone else by accident.

YLAN SMILED. THAT WICKED MOUTH would be the death of him.

He and Dani hadn't spoken about the whole Cassidy thing—what he'd admitted in Josh's bathroom. Or what Dani'd admitted by sleeping in his bed that night. She'd stayed longer, they'd had coffee in their underwear and shared a shower, and neither of them said a word about it. As soon as she'd left the next morning, he'd moved Cass's number from his personal to his professional contacts list.

Then last weekend, he'd gone to Dani's house Friday night, stayed for the entire movie, and talked himself into her bed for the night. Any time he'd wondered if she had a date the next night, he shoved it away. He certainly wasn't going to torture himself with details again.

> **Dylan: That was an expensive tie. I guess you'll have to owe me something in return.**

> **Dani: Let's call it even since you drank half of my gourmet coffee before you left.**

> **Dylan: That coffee wasn't even that good. I only left you two stars on Yelp.**

"What are you doing?"

Dylan looked up from his phone at the smirk in Josh's voice. He'd pulled up to a red light and was staring at Dylan over the center console of his Jeep, his head cocked.

Dylan considered his options. Lie or bend the truth. Bending was a lot easier.

"Texting a woman."

"Really?" Josh laughed.

"What?"

"Nothing. I've just never seen you do that with that look on your face before."

His neck went hot. "I don't have a look on my face."

"You do." Josh laughed again.

"I don't think so."

"Trust me. You have a look."

Jesus Christ. *Now* he did. He put the phone

in his pocket and turned away, irritated at the way his skin burned. "I think you might have just forgotten what the look I had meant, Joshua. Married sex must be getting pretty boring by now."

The light turned green, and Josh stepped on the gas. "Yeah, I don't think so."

Dylan chuckled. The best way to piss Josh off was to call into question the institution of monogamy that he felt so strongly about, and getting Josh riled up was a good way to deflect the attention off of whatever "look" Josh thought he'd seen. A dirty trick by some people's standards, but not Dylan's.

"You saying you're still hitting it like you used to now that you're married up?"

"I'm saying that's none of your business, but if it were, there's only one of us who has a woman in his bed every night."

That serve was begging to be spiked back, but after his fit over Dani's overshare with some guy named Benji whom Dylan had never even met, he figured he should shut his mouth. Besides, Josh still had him beat. Until a few weeks ago, Dylan only had Dani in *her* bed—sometimes her couch—and only on Fridays.

Great. The good mood his flirty texts with Dani had put him in just disintegrated into an unproductive rivalry over something he didn't want in the first place. Was he really competing with Josh over who had to share their bed? The joys of someone stealing your covers and snoring? No thanks.

Okay, he did sort of like sharing a bed with Dani. The way she sprawled out over half the mattress, her arm thrown over his stomach in an aggressive-even-in-her-sleep embrace was adorable. He caught himself smiling at the memory, but quickly rearranged his face before Josh saw him. "Whatever, man. Let's drop it."

"So you're not going to tell me who she is?"

"I'm not."

Josh shrugged. "Your call. I'm sure she won't be around long anyway. Unless you're bringing her camping?"

In a couple of weeks, they were spending two nights tenting oceanfront for Shawn's birthday. Dylan had been counting down to it all month. He could practically feel his muscles relax in anticipation of doing nothing but enjoying the water and the fall air for the whole weekend. He'd already scoped out some hiking trails, and knowing Shawn and Minnie, the food was going to be fantastic. It was just the kind of re-charge weekend he needed.

"First of all, a weekend away with a bunch of married couples isn't anything I would invite a woman to. Second of all, have fun killing scary bugs and listening to Cat whine about not being able to blow dry her hair the whole weekend. I'll be fishing and paddleboarding. Working on my tan."

"Cat doesn't whine, and it's not just couples. Sonya is coming without Marcus, and I don't think Dani is bringing anyone."

Dylan's head snapped up. Dani had better not be bringing anyone after that little tantrum she'd pulled at Josh's. His mood took another nose-dive at the thought of some jerk killing scary bugs for Dani. They might not be going on this trip together, but he would be killing Dani's big scary bugs, thank-you-very-much.

Oh, for Christ's sake. Did he really just have that thought? Josh was breaking his brain. What he should be thinking about is how to get Dani into his tent after everyone went to bed.

"I guess we'll see who has the better time, Joshua," he said. He'd lay bets it would be him.

Twenty-two

ECAUSE HER SUV POSITIONED HER as the driver for most road trips over the years, Sonya had begun enacting what she called Sonya Says—a set of rules that applied when she was shuttling a group of them to a long-distance destination.

One bathroom break per two hours on the road. Use it or lose it. (Otherwise known as the Emma rule.)

Do not, under any circumstances, connect your phone to her Bluetooth and attempt to hijack the playlist because she "will cut a bitch".

Hands and feet inside the vehicle at all times. (That rule was mostly for Cat.)

If you attempt to navigate from the backseat, she *will* pull over and you *will* walk. (This rule was added the first time Dylan rode with them on a trip to Ocean City for the weekend.)

"It's like Josh wants to be married to an amputee," Sonya said, shaking her head and pointing to Cat's arm hanging out the window of Josh's Jeep in front of them.

Dani shrugged and took another sip of her twenty-ounce iced coffee. The sun was far too bright for this early in the morning. Considering they were about to spend two nights in a tent, she should be glad for the good weather, but at the moment all it was doing was exacerbating her pounding headache.

She glanced in the mirror through her thick, black sunglasses, to see Dylan stretched out across the back seat, his head on his backpack, and his own aviators hiding the fact that he was most definitely asleep.

She sensed an internal struggle brewing in Sonya's mind between the importance of seatbelt safety and the peace and quiet that a sleeping Dylan afforded her, but that would be determined when she updated the rules.

The right-hand blinker on Josh's Jeep flicked on, and Sonya slowed to follow him. The dirt road they'd pulled onto was lined with maples on either side, the edges of their late-September leaves red and yellow and gold. Dani lifted her sunglasses and rolled down her window to look at them without a filter. The scent of ocean air and dried leaves mixed together and rushed her airways.

Minnie had picked this place. She and Shawn had been here a few times before Mattie was born, and both Dylan and Josh had jumped at the idea of oceanfront camping. Neither one of them could stand to be too far inland.

Because Marcus was out of town, Dani and Sonya were sharing a tent, which was basically the only reason Dani had agreed to attend this trip. It wasn't that she was nature-averse, not entirely, but she liked her nature in small doses—an afternoon hike followed by a warm bath and a glass of wine; a trip to the botanical gardens where she could enjoy the flora in heels and a sundress. Sleeping on the ground and wearing hiking boots and socks that put her at risk for an awkward tan line was not exactly something she would have chosen. But birthdays were a big deal, and Shawn, *Mr. Craft Beer,* had come along on the wine cruise they'd all taken for her last birthday, so she wasn't going to be a spoilsport.

Josh pulled to a stop in front of a little hut labeled "Main Office", and he and Shawn got out. Sonya parked behind him. "I'll check-in," she offered. "You stay with the snoring cargo."

With an evil smile, she slammed the door when she got out. Dylan bolted upright.

"We're here," Dani sang.

"That didn't take too long."

"You slept the whole way."

Dylan's lip curled up, baring that pointy canine tooth of his—the one that made him look a little bit like a wolf. "Someone wore me out last night."

"You're old. Besides, I'm sure you went right back to sleep after I left this morning."

Against her better judgment, she'd slept at

Dylan's the night before. Then, because they were both supposed to be at Cat and Josh's house at eight a.m. sharp, and it made the most sense for Dani to ride with Sonya, *and* she couldn't exactly tell Sonya she was already down the road, she'd had to get up at the crack of dawn to drive home, change, and jump in Sonya's car to make the trip right back where she'd started. The things they did for this lie.

Though, last night had nothing to do with their arrangement. Neither had the last time he was at her place. They'd been together three times since their fight at Josh and Cat's house, and she'd had a grand total of zero soulmate dates. Not that Dylan knew that.

The whole thing just seemed so exhausting after fighting with Dylan in Cat's bathroom. Her emotions were all over the place. One minute her finger was hovering over the accept button on her newest match requests, the next, she was texting Dylan instead, inviting him over and hoping he'd stay the night. It was starting to hit her that she had three more dates to schedule and then she was supposed to stop all of this. Presumably because she'd find some perfect match. Someone *else*. Maybe Dylan would be fine with that. That was why she'd picked him, right? Because he was supposed to be fine with that? Though, after what he'd said in Cat's bathroom, she doubted it.

It was a lot to consider, and going to Dylan's

last night, having sex in his pool, then sleeping in his bed, that just seemed like a better way to spend her weekend.

"I didn't go back to bed, actually," Dylan said. "I got up and went for a run on the beach."

Dani downed some more caffeine just thinking about that. "Ambitious."

"The cold spot you left in my bed was too sad. I couldn't sleep without you, Dani."

Dani's head whipped around to see what kind of facial expression accompanied that very loaded statement, but Sonya came back, swinging a key chain around her finger.

"Got a map and a key to the showers," she said. "Let's go!"

Sonya was a glutton for punishment when it came to manual labor. Insinuate something was man's work, and Sonya made it her mission to master it. As a supportive friend and fellow feminist, Dani allowed her to prove her skills by only doing the bare minimum required to help set up their campsite. She did manage to break a sweat in the hot sun, though, so after she'd unrolled her sleeping bag and stashed her bag, she headed down the dirt path to the beach for a quick swim before dinner.

When she got to the shore, Dylan was at the edge of the water, steadying his paddleboard with one foot. His tan legs were squared off and his abs flexed as he tugged his t-shirt over his head. He tipped his head to the sun and pulled in a deep breath like he was refilling his soul.

"Leaving so soon?" she asked, admiring that tan line peeking out from his shorts. The one she'd had her tongue on just that morning.

Dylan pushed his sunglasses into his hair and smiled. He'd skipped the hair product this morning. The longer pieces on top, usually meticulously arranged, flopped into a School Picture Day side-part, giving him an air of innocence she happened to know he didn't deserve.

"Just going to take a spin around the inlet," he said.

"Have fun." She laid out the towel she'd brought, pulling a magazine out of her bag.

"You want a lesson?"

She gave him a look, wandering over to the water's edge to eye the board. "Why would I want to exert that much effort when I could just lay here?"

Dylan leaned in behind her, his fingers brushing her hip. "I can give you a ride if you want."

She startled at his lips on her neck. Minnie's playful laughter easily breached the thin line of trees and rocks that separated them from the campsites, and she didn't actually know where Cat and Josh were at the moment. They hardly alone, and she didn't add two hours to her morning routine just to get caught now. Still, the scent of sunscreen and sweat replaced his usual cologne and it was too new not to explore. She tipped her head back and he stole her lips for a quick, affectionate kiss.

"I don't think that's a good idea," she said, pulling away.

"That's not what you said last night."

Her jaw dropped and she kicked a wave of water at him. Dylan dodged it easily, reaching for her again, but the crunching of footsteps froze them both.

Cat and Josh emerged from the wooded path, both in their bathing suits. Josh had one hand on Cat's back, a red plastic cup in his other. Cat sipped coconut water.

Dylan took a step back, steadying his board. "Look who it is."

"You going out?" Josh asked, nodding toward the inlet.

"Yeah. Figured I'd explore before dinner." Dylan tossed a secret look at Dani. "You want a beer, Kit Cat?" He tipped his chin in the direction of the cooler he'd wedged in the sand.

Cat shook her head. "No thanks. I'm saving room for dinner."

LI-AR!

"Okie doke," Dylan said, interrupting the look Josh was giving Cat. It was unfamiliar on his face, like maybe they'd just been arguing instead of gazing dreamily into one another's eyes. They weren't touching or flirting. Josh had taken a step toward Dylan, turning his back to Cat completely while they chatted about tides.

Dani's hair stood up. Something was weird. She tried to make eye-contact with Cat, attempting to ask her with one of their best friend facial expressions if she was fighting with Josh, but she wouldn't look up. She smoothed her blanket on the sand, obviously avoiding Dani's gaze.

Dani's shoulders fell. For the first time ever, Cat's business didn't feel like her business.

That thought wormed through her brain, leaving knots of hurt and confusion. She turned to Dylan and set her hands on her hips. "You know, I think I will go with you."

Dylan grinned, licking the moisture from his upper lip, and swept a hand toward the front of the board. "Hop on, Dani-pie."

Sure, Dylan had given Josh shit about having to entertain a woman all weekend, but taking Dani on his paddleboard trip wasn't the same. It wasn't like he was in charge of making sure Dani had a good time, or worried about whether he was paying enough attention to her. That was Josh's weekend. That was probably why he'd had that look on his face when he and Cat had come down to the water. Things like this were just more fun when you didn't have someone else to worry about.

But taking Dani for a spin around the inlet was different. Having a passenger meant a better workout, and with her perched cross-legged on the front of his board, he had a perfect view down the front of her halter bikini top while he soaked up the peace and quiet.

Except *this* quiet—her staring out at the water not saying a word—felt off. He didn't like it.

"So this is fun, right?" he asked. "I can't believe you and Cat have never camped out."

Dani leaned back on her arms, scooting her butt closer to the edge of his board. She let one leg dangle in the water. "We're city girls, Dylan. Our version of camping was making a fort on Cat's four-poster bed and sneaking *Cosmo* to read by flashlight."

"Maybe you two can have a slumber party tonight. Make Josh sleep alone. You can braid each other's hair or whatever." He nudged her with his foot. "I could help."

She shook her head. "One: you're ridiculous, and two: she would never."

"Braid your hair?"

"Make Josh sleep alone."

He chuckled. "True. You want me to ask Josh to have a sleepover with me? I can be your slumber party wing-man."

She turned over her shoulder to glare at him,

but a laugh burst out instead. His own smile exploded.

"That's a kind offer," she said, still laughing. "You sure you're doing it for me?"

"You caught me. I just can't live without him." He flicked water at her with his oar. "Really, though. You all right?"

Her face fell and she turned back to the water. "I'm fine."

He knew that line. Usually that was his free pass to end a conversation he didn't want to have, but this was Dani and he did want to have it. He honestly wanted to know why she and Cat hadn't said a word to each other just then on the beach, and why Dani had that sulky look on her face.

He pushed his oar into the water, steering them in a wide arc that followed the shoreline. "How'd you and Kit Cat meet?"

She gave him a look that said he wasn't being smooth, but she answered anyway. "We both had Ms. Curtis in fifth grade. We were seated alphabetically."

"That's it?"

"That's it. The best friendship of my life started because my last name started with P and hers started with R."

Dylan huffed out a laugh.

"Okay, but something had to make it stick, right? Sixth grade comes and you're not side by side anymore, but you're still tight."

Dani cocked her head. "What made it stick for you?"

He shrugged. "Josh is my business partner, and Shawn has an Xbox." She groaned and he knew he'd have to do better than that. How do you explain why someone is your best friend? Family is decided for you, and love is a cocktail of hormones, but what makes the kind of friendship he had with Josh and Shawn?

One memory did come to mind. "When my dad died," he said, "I hadn't been in touch with him for years. Still, it felt like a bomb had exploded. Josh and Shawn took me out that night, just a couple bars near campus, and I started some shit with a guy. Typical twenty-something shit. I was pissed at the world and this guy was nearby. Turned out, so were his friends."

"Ouch."

"Yeah, ouch. But not for me. Shawn, you know he's a big guy, he pins me to the bar with one hand like the fucking Hulk. But Josh goes and puts himself right in the middle of it, squares off with this dude, ready to take a punch that I deserved. Luckily the guy decided not to bust up his pretty face."

He laughed and Dani rolled her eyes.

"Anyway, he never said a word about it the next day. Never once held it over my head. Josh and Shawn are two of the most loyal people you'll ever meet."

Dani nodded, turning back to the water.

"Back to you," he said, splashing her again. "What makes you and Cat as close as you are?"

"No one thing, I guess. Cat's neurotic and her own worst enemy sometimes, but she holds the people in her life to a high standard. You don't get away with excuses with Cat, but she'll fight for you like no one else will."

"Sounds like a good person to have as a best friend."

"You're trying to make me forget she's lying to me."

"I'm not trying to do anything." *Except maybe get a couple more of those smiles.*

"Good." She pushed her sunglasses up her nose and sighed. "Thanks for taking me out here."

"Anytime, Dani-pie." He smiled, already hoping she'd want to go again tomorrow.

Dani might not have any camping experience, but she was pretty sure the feast Shawn and Minnie had prepared for dinner wasn't standard roughing-it fare. She filled her plate with a second serving of Pinterest-worthy pasta salad, enjoying the way spending the afternoon on the water had loosened her shoulders and dulled the little ache she'd been carrying around about Cat.

She'd kind of hoped she and Cat could reconnect on this trip—bond over their shared lack of desire to get dirty. But if Cat was going to be weird, Dani didn't hate spending the afternoon with Dylan. He definitely had a way of cheering her up. It was hard to maintain a good self-pity huff when Dylan was around. When he'd joked about her and Cat having a slumber party, she'd wanted to scowl. She'd really wanted to cross her arms and tell him to shut up, that jokes about her and Cat's strained friendship weren't funny, but instead, a bubble had burst inside her chest and she'd laughed until she snorted at the image of Dylan and Josh sharing an air mattress and reading *Surfer's Digest* by lantern light.

Then she'd looked up at him and found his eyes were sober, like he might really find a way to make that happen if she asked. There was a comfort in that that appeared out of nowhere and squeezed her chest.

Now, he was hovering beside her at the buffet, in a pair of board shorts and a t-shirt with a hole in the collar, popping the cap off of a beer.

"Thanks," she said, plucking it from his hand.

He laughed and grabbed another. "Slow down, babe. That's your third one of the night and we just finished dinner."

"Don't call me babe," she said. "And why are you counting my drinks?"

He leaned in and set his hand dangerously on her hip. "I don't want to have to carry you over my shoulder into my tent later."

She stifled a laugh, pressing a finger into his

chest. She was getting ready to tell him that's the only way she'd be there, but she caught Sonya staring at the two of them curiously. The same way Shawn had when they'd come up the path together for dinner after stowing Dylan's paddleboard.

She jumped away, letting Dylan's hand fall.

That was way too close.

"We're not," she said quietly.

"Okay," he whispered back, adding a wink.

She headed to the picnic table, taking a safe seat beside Minnie. "This is the last thing I'm eating," she said. "I swear."

Dylan followed. "Until dessert."

Sonya gasped and jumped from her seat. "I almost forgot. Catia, look what I made for you." Sonya went to the table and lifted the lid off of a Tupperware cake holder like she was revealing a rabbit in a hat. "Your favorite. Mocha coffee poke cake."

"Oh my God. Yum!" Minnie said.

"Well, I guess it's for Shawn since it's his birthday," Sonya said. "But I know Cat's going to eat most of it."

"Not if I can help it," Shawn said, rubbing his belly.

Sonya walked the platter over to where Cat was sitting, but Cat pulled her knees up to her chest like a shield, shaking her head. "I'm full," she said, but the way she said it was like she couldn't open her mouth all the way.

Sonya scrunched her nose. "Really? You barely ate anything. It's *coffee!*"

Cat put the back of her hand to her mouth and—Dani wouldn't have believed it if she didn't see it—actually started gagging.

Josh noticed too. He set his plate on the ground and turned in Cat's direction just as she scrambled up from her chair and darted through the trees to her own campsite. Josh took off after her, and the sound of what Dani assumed was Cat emptying her dinner onto the sand mixed with the peepers croaking and waves lapping.

"Is she okay?" Minnie asked the group who were all sitting there half stunned, half grossed out.

Sonya shoved the cake at Minnie and disappeared down the path Cat and Josh had taken.

Dani should go too. She knew that. But her brain was too busy accepting that there was no other explanation after what she had just witnessed. Anger and disbelief coursed through her. It was a selfish reaction, given the fact that she could still hear Cat retching, but she couldn't stop it. Unless she had some sort of months-long stomach bug, Cat was definitely pregnant, and for whatever reason, had kept it from her.

She turned to see Dylan watching her, waiting for the reaction only he knew she would have. Tears pricked her eyes. She couldn't explain it, but every cell in her body wanted to climb into his lap and bawl.

"So, can we eat this or..." Shawn held up a stack of plates.

Dylan jumped to his feet. "I'll take a piece. Dani? You want some?"

She shook her head.

Sonya came trudging back up the path. "Josh said they'd be back in a minute," she said with a tight grin that screamed: I have a secret.

Dani's stomach twisted harder, preparing herself to put on a show. She'd have to pretend to be thrilled, hand out congratulatory hugs before she could sneak away. If she kept her eyes off of Dylan's sympathetic ones, she might be able to pull it off.

Everyone had finished a piece of the offending cake by the time Josh came back. His mouth was straight and serious, but his eyes were dancing with a happiness he was trying to contain. He shoved his hands in the pockets of his shorts, his gaze stopping on Dani's for an extra second. He swallowed hard. Guiltily. "So, Cat's pregnant."

"What?" Minnie jumped up, nearly spilling her plate. "Oh my God, Joshy. Yay!"

"Well, that took about five seconds," Shawn said. "Congrats, man." He stood to shake Josh's hand, and Dylan did too, slapping Josh on the back then giving him a tight hug. The kind she should be giving Cat.

Dani stayed glued to her chair.

"She's been sick," Josh said, rubbing a hand down his face. "It's been a rough few months."

"Months?" Minnie's eyes widened. "How many?"

"Almost five."

Josh looked down at the ground, the guilt that felt so personal to Dani laid bare. Dani did the math. Just like she thought, they'd been keeping this from them since before the wedding.

Dylan's eyes darted to her again, watching her carefully like he was afraid she was about to lose it. She felt her face getting blotchy from holding back tears.

"Shut up," Minnie said, the glee that should be Dani's shining on her face. "I just saw her in a bathing suit! She is not five months along."

"Almost five. And she's been sick, so she hasn't gained much." He looked over his shoulder toward their tent. "We were hoping it would end once she hit her second trimester, but so far, she hasn't gotten a break."

The details and Josh's excuses faded out, and Dani's chest expanded like a balloon of irritation and sadness. Did Cat really think she couldn't tell her? Okay, maybe the condolence card she sent Sonya for her engagement was a bit over the top, but this was Cat! And a baby Cat! Baby JoshCat. She was there when Cat met Josh. She was there when they had their first fight. Bachelorette party, maid of honor at her wedding, now all of a sudden she was being shut out. *Why?*

She chewed on her lip to keep her tears from spilling over. As much shit as she liked to give her, Cat being happy was all she wanted and instead of being really, really happy like she should be, Dani just felt really, really sad.

Dylan reached around her and tugged her ponytail, probably to remind her that she hadn't said anything remotely congratulatory yet.

She cleared her throat and turned to Josh. "Is Cat okay?"

Josh nodded. "Yeah. It was just the cake. She hasn't even been able to smell coffee without getting nauseous."

"Poor Cat," Sonya groaned. If there was one thing Cat loved as much as she loved Josh, it was coffee. She must have been miserable.

The sound of leaves crunching whipped everyone's head toward the footpath, and Cat appeared wearing a new shirt, her hair tied up.

Dylan slid his hand onto Dani's shoulder, giving her a comforting squeeze. She let herself lean into it. No one was paying attention to them anyway.

"Cat." Minnie rushed to hug her. "Congratulations, sweetie."

Cat's face twisted in an uncomfortable expression. "Thanks."

Minnie let her go, and Cat and Josh had a little tiff with their eyes. Cat looked like she was going to burst into tears, and for some reason, Josh looked unhappy with her.

Cat rubbed her arms. "I just came back to say thanks for dinner and sorry for puking in front of your cake. I'm going to turn in."

Dylan nudged Dani's shoulder, and she stepped toward Cat. She was pissed, and Cat still smelled like puke, but she gave her a hug anyway. "Congratulations, Kit Cat," she whispered. "I hope you feel better." She braced herself for a wooden hug, to feel the disappointment of their distance up close, but instead, Cat squeezed her back. It was tight and needy, and Dani had the sudden urge to wave everyone else off and pull Cat somewhere quiet and talk this out.

But Cat broke away and headed to her tent. Alone.

Twenty-three

"YOU KNOW, THERE'S A DECK of cards and a bottle of gin just through those trees," Dylan said. "You don't have to drink alone." He dropped into the chair beside Dani and crossed his arms over his chest, studying her face.

After Cat had left and they'd cleaned up from dinner, Dani had claimed she needed a sweat-shirt from her tent. Thirty minutes later, he'd begun to doubt the cover story. He'd seen her shoulders fall when Josh told everyone about Cat. As much as he'd tried to keep it light, use it to cheer her up, their "secret mission" game was real life to Dani. He hadn't missed the way her eyes were shining when she gave them that sweatshirt story.

Sure enough, he'd found her sitting in a camp chair at her own site, sulking over a beer.

"I can't play drinking games with Shawn and Josh," she said. "I'll die of alcohol poisoning."

"What about me?"

"I can beat you."

He laughed, her biting comeback easing his worry a little. But her voice was still flat, plaintive. Seeing her usual spark dim made a place inside his rib cage ache. He wanted to take it away, and since he couldn't go back in time and fix whatever girl drama was happening between her and Cat, all he had left was distraction.

"Come on, Dani-pie. Don't be sad."

"I'm not."

He poked her side and she batted his hand away. "Then don't be mad. Let's go for a swim."

"It's like fifty degrees out."

"Yeah, but the water in the inlet stays warm from the sun. It'll be like a hot tub."

She narrowed her eyes.

"I swear. Please?" The sound of Minnie and Sonya laughing echoing off of the rocks and trees seemed to worsen her mood.

She didn't answer, just picked at the label on her bottle of beer with her thumbnail.

Time for the big guns. He stood up and scooped her from the camp chair, and she squealed, pounding her fist into his bicep.

"Shhh." He laughed at her weak little assault. "Enough of this. You can either change into your bathing suit or go naked, but you're swimming. It's a beautiful night, there's a full moon and everyone up there"—he jutted his chin toward the next campsite over—"is hammered. No one will even know we're gone."

Dani stopped hitting him and her face twisted

into a scowl that he had to fight really hard not to kiss.

"Bathing suit?" he asked.

Dani's scowl wavered and twisted, then turned upward into a devilish smile. "No bathing suit."

"There she is."

She did insist on a towel, and after grabbing those and two more beers, he took her hand, tugging her the whole way down the bumpy path to the water. He had the overwhelming sense that this was his job right now, to force Fun Dani back to life. Lucky for her, fun was his forte.

The inlet was a sheet of glass, the huge autumn moon spilling light over the surface to illuminate the empty patch of sand. Dylan dropped the towels and popped open one beer, keeping the other hostage.

"Strip," he said when she went to reach for it.

Her jaw tightened but her eyes flashed hungrily, betraying her.

So complicated, Dani.

He rolled his hand impatiently, and Dani fixed her face into a seductive, open-mouthed expression that made him swallow hard. She unzipped the sweatshirt she was wearing, keeping her eyes on his the whole way, and let it fall onto the sand. When her tongue peeked out and skated across her bottom lip, he almost tossed the beer on the ground and took over undressing her.

Luckily, he maintained his patience because the image of her tugging her t-shirt slowly over her head, her blonde ponytail swinging, was something he was going to store for future use—whenever she got bored of him and moved on.

Dani flicked open the button on her shorts, revealing some black lace boy shorts that should have been the death of him, but his train of thought had snagged.

That was what was going to happen, wasn't it? One day he'd show up and find an expired notice on his all-access pass to Dani.

When she finds her match.

The thought unexpectedly punched at his sternum. He chugged another sip of his beer, while she kicked the shorts off her legs. He was starting to realize that he hadn't fully thought this deal through. He'd been so quick to accept any offer that got him back into Dani's bed, but in typical Dylan fashion, he hadn't planned his end game. After what had happened with Cassidy, and the rest of that night, that suddenly seemed like a major miscalculation. What would it be like for this to just end? To have to see Dani with whoever she chose when they hung out with their mutual friends?

"Can I have my beer now?" she asked. "I'm freezing."

"Right. Yeah." He handed both beers to her, then ripped off his t-shirt and shorts as quickly as he could.

Dani dragged her eyes down his body, and he felt something push against his ribs. It was warm and soft and unfamiliar and... needy. His shoulders straightened under her appraisal.

She gave a pointed gaze to his crotch. "I told you it was cold."

His breath whooshed out in a laugh. "You're a she-devil."

She laughed for the first time in hours, and that pushing nearly shoved him off his feet.

"This better be as warm as you say." Dani stuck the bottom of her bottle in the sand and took a few cautious steps into the water. Goose-bumps spread down the back of her thighs, and he took a slow sip of his beer as he studied her long tan legs and little waist. Those narrow hips that fit just right in his hands. Even in those lace panties, she looked small and cute like she had the morning after Josh's wedding. The side of her that was usually dolled and painted and fluffed was naked again, and it was doing strange things to him.

Her hips disappeared under the water, and he ditched his bottle and jogged to her, wrapping his arms around her middle. She laughed as he picked her up, her legs hooking easily around his waist as he walked them further in. The water warmed them like he promised it would.

A few stray clouds crossed over the silver dollar moon, and the weakened light made the beach feel more secluded. Now he could just make out Dani's features; her blue eyes glowing, her pink lips still turned downward. The ends of her ponytail started to curl as they splashed.

"Do you think Cat and Josh are fighting?" she asked.

The question surprised him since he thought they were there because *she* and Cat were fighting. "No. I don't."

"They're not stuck together at the moment, and earlier, on the beach, he seemed irritated at her."

Dylan huffed out a laugh, knowing the level at which Josh's irritation maxed out. It was a three at best on a scale of Dylan's typical eleven. Maybe even a one-point-five when it was directed at Cat. "I think if he was, he'll be over it by the time he stumbles into their tent for the night."

Dani pulled a lip between her teeth and chewed. "I'm pissed at her, but I'd hate it if they were fighting." Her face crumpled again, and it sent an ache through his chest.

"Tell me why you're taking this so hard, Dani."

"I don't know."

He let go of one ass cheek and tipped her chin toward him, what little light there was catching in the moisture in her eyes. "You do."

A rush of air left her lungs, like she'd been waiting for someone to come along and uncork it. "I just don't understand how she could keep this from me. It just...it feels like a judgment."

"What do you mean? Why would it be a judgment?"

"It's like she got married and now we don't have anything in common anymore. Like silly Dani wouldn't care about babies. Maybe I was less than into the wedding details, that's Emma's thing, but this is her child. My best friend is spawning a little replica of herself and she didn't think I would be excited about that?"

Dylan chuckled and shifted her weight. "Look, I don't know why she chose to keep it to herself, but I don't think she feels that way. You're a good friend, Dani. That's like your thing. You're everyone's cheerleader even if it's a long shot. Like with the Jansens. I wasn't sure I was going to pull that one off, but you were. You were so damn confident in me, like you were personally invested in some building you'd never even heard of. Cat has to know you'd be the same about this."

Dani took a minute, still chewing her lip, then she tightened her arms around his neck, bringing them closer. She laid her head on his shoulder, and a sigh escaped from deep in his chest. He liked it way too much, holding her like this.

"Thank you," she whispered.

"For what?"

"You're the only one who hasn't made me feel crazy for feeling like this."

He couldn't see her pretty eyes anymore, but her voice sounded genuinely relieved. He squeezed her tighter. "Look, I get it. I'm kind of disappointed Josh didn't tell me."

"You are?"

"Sure. He and I have been through a lot. But since I know it was Cat's decision, I'm gonna let it slide."

"Do you ever feel like things are different between you two since him and Cat?"

"Nah. Josh has always been a few steps ahead in life. He's got like a sixth sense, feels the weather changing, so to speak, and makes the adjustments before I even feel the rain."

"The weather changing?"

"Yeah, like junior year in college he started partying less, nose to the grindstone. It was time to grow up and so he did. And then I did. After that, when he'd been working at the firm he was at for a while, he knew it was time to go out on his own. Convinced me to come along. He bought a house and then kicked me out, so I bought a house. Josh is like a human barometer. He senses the little pressure changes, knows when it's time to head for higher ground. But it's never been a problem—him there, me here."

"What about his first marriage?" she asked. "You didn't follow him down that path."

Damn right. Even science has a margin of error. "That was different."

"How?"

"I knew him marrying Sarah was a terrible idea," he explained. "And I knew he was doing it for the wrong reasons. That was the one time in his life Josh didn't have a clue what he was doing."

Dani pushed her hand into his hair, stroking absently. They'd gotten used to the warmth of the water now and her fingers felt hot on his exposed skin.

"Maybe you're the barometer sometimes too," she said quietly.

The idea burrowed into his brain. He'd never thought of it that way. People had their roles in friendships that long, and he knew his, but maybe she was right. Maybe there had been a time or two where he'd been on the other side.

Her finger stopped moving, and she sighed. "With Cat, it feels like she's moved to a different universe, and maybe I'm so mad because she likes it better there, whether I'm there or not."

"Do you want to be in that universe?"

She shrugged. "Maybe. If I found the right guy."

The right guy. The distinction sliced at him. Who was the right guy for Dani? Someone who would sweet talk her? Hold her hand and stare longingly into her eyes? He doubted it. Maybe it was his competitive side, but that little ache in his chest from before and the multiple beers he'd consumed stirred together and made him wish he could just say it. *Why not me?*

But he couldn't. He couldn't say it, and he couldn't be it. That wasn't him. He'd never been the right guy.

He sniffed and refocused his gaze over her

shoulder. "Hey, at least you know what you don't want, right?" he said, nodding through the trees to Josh and Cat's tent.

She followed his gaze, then her eyes dipped to his. "Maybe I do, though," she said, pinning him with two beams of electric blue. "Maybe I want that."

He felt that look like a punch to his solar plexus—the question she was asking with her eyes. Part of him wanted to dive for cover, run back up the beach and forget he'd ever started this conversation. Maybe if she wasn't wrapped around him, molded to him so perfectly with her breath coming in shallow little spurts like she was holding it just for him, he might have.

Regardless of what he would blame it on later, though—too much to drink, the atmosphere—he didn't shut up. He didn't run.

"Yeah," he said, his blood pumping dangerously. "Maybe I do too."

Dani's eyes darted over his face, her mouth dropping open before easing over his in the kind of kiss that they hadn't shared yet. The kind that traveled from his mouth to his groin but stopped somewhere in the middle and made his gut flip. Maybe he hadn't shared a kiss like that with anyone before.

He bent his knees, taking them deeper into the water so he could use the buoyancy to hold her up while he touched every bare inch of skin he could find.

Her fingers clutched his hair, then darted to

his chest, tracing the lines of his muscles. She touched him like it was the first time, like she wasn't already intimately acquainted with every part of him. And it sort of felt like the first time. Like one last piece of clothing had been removed and now they could finally see each other. They'd admitted something to each other after Cassidy, and then they'd both run from it. But here it was again, pulsing between them in hot heavy breaths.

He broke their kiss, both of them rushing to pull in air. He caught her eye in the moonlight, and in a way they'd gotten very comfortable communicating, she lifted an eyebrow.

He looked between them, disappointment surging. "I don't have anything," he said. "In my tent..."

He started to walk them out of the water, but she shook her head. "I'm on the pill, remember."

"You're sure?"

Dani bit her lip and nodded. "I trust you."

"You can." His fingers were already pulling aside the wet fabric that separated them.

It was probably just the lingering emotion of the thing with Cat, but the sound she made when she sank down onto him was different, vulnerable. Despite himself and the rawness he felt at his own exposure, he leaned into it, testing out what he'd just suggested—the idea that maybe he could want something he'd never allowed himself to ponder before.

It felt better than he could have imagined.

Twenty-four

*D*YLAN'S PHONE BUZZING ACROSS HIS chest snapped his head up from the arm of the couch. He'd fallen asleep there sometime after dinner, exhausted from a long week of being back at work. He rubbed his eyes, letting them adjust, then fought a smile when he saw the caller ID. He'd been waiting for this call.

"Hey, Dani-pie. Thinking about me again so soon?"

She huffed a chuckle into the receiver. "Something like that."

He was dying to play the *did you miss me* game with her, but a fit of nerves he was unacquainted with sparked in his chest, making him pause.

After that moment in the water, when he'd gone and admitted something that felt monumental, things with Dani were largely the same. They'd kissed goodbye in secret when Sonya wasn't paying attention, shared almost daily texts back and forth during the week, now she was calling to invite him over for their usual

Friday night hookup. It was their normal weekly routine, but he felt different. He felt edgy, irritated like he sometimes did when he'd gone too long without coffee. His whole body felt tight and restless. He'd passed out on his couch because he'd barely slept all week.

Knowing Dani might have a date with someone else Saturday night was eating away at him. "What time do you want me to come over tomorrow?" he asked, needing to start an official countdown.

"Actually, I need to cancel tomorrow night."

Dylan turned down the volume on *Thursday Night Football* and sat up quickly, the remote clattering to the floor. "What do you mean?"

"I will not be requiring your services this week, Mr. Pierce." She was joking but his stomach dropped. Was this the day his Dani card finally got declined? With a phone call? Thanks for the good times, see you around? It wasn't even twenty-four hours notice. Okay, it wasn't an appointment for maintenance on his car, but still. He wasn't ready.

"Just all of a sudden?" he asked, trying to sound unaffected. "What, did you end up liking one of them?"

"One of what?"

"Your dates." He cleared his throat. "Did you meet your soulmate or whatever?"

Dani laughed, sweet and girlish, and a spot

in the center of his chest cracked open like an egg. What the fuck had she done to him?

"I didn't meet my soulmate, Dylan. I just... have an early visitor."

What did that mean? *Fuck.* Was she seeing some other guy on *their* day? "I can come later," he said, refusing to think about how that would feel, to swoop in after someone else left her wanting. That was worse than being the opening act. It was a low point even for him, but he was panicking.

Dani groaned dramatically. "Ugh. Dylan. I got my period early, okay? You really don't know how to take a hint."

A hard laugh rushed out of him, pure relief bubbling out of the smile that split his face. He felt like he'd just missed getting hit by a bus. "Jeez, Dani. Why didn't you just say that?"

But then a fresh wave of distaste appeared in his mouth. They were supposed to spend Friday night together and now he wasn't going to get to see her.

"I'm going to be in the city anyway." That was a lie, but he could reschedule some stuff in the morning. "I can still come by."

"Dylan. Did you hear what I said?"

"Yeah." He shoved a fist in his hair and tugged, thankful that this wasn't a video call. "I just figured if you were going to stay in anyway... Were you?" His heart thumped against his rib cage. It felt like that time he went base jumping in Arizona when he was supposed to be at a sales conference, the way his hands shook unexpectedly when he'd clicked that harness in place. It was probably safe, but how could he really know?

"Yes, but I was planning on eating ice cream and watching Netflix in my sweatpants."

He smiled at that mental picture. "What were you planning to wear on top?"

"Oh my God. The rattiest oversized t-shirt I can find."

"I'll bring you one. Look," he said, "it's a Friday night and it's too late to fill the spot on my dance card, Dani-pie. I'm coming anyway and you're going to entertain me with your shining personality. I'll bring the ice cream."

"Fine."

"Fine."

She paused. "Cookies and cream."

"You got it, babe."

"Don't call me babe."

He chuckled and the line went silent for a beat, her soft breathing the only sound between them.

When she spoke again, her voice went quiet. "I don't know what you're doing, Dylan. But I'll see you tomorrow."

She hung up and Dylan ran a hand over his face. He didn't know what he was doing either, and yet, here he was doing it anyway.

There's nothing like your uterus seizing up to kill any sexual tension between you and your Friend With Benefits. When Dylan arrived on Friday night, he might as well have been her elderly neighbor Mr. Cravits. She took one look at his mischief-eyes—the ones that usually tied her stomach in knots—and felt nothing but bloated and bitchy.

"That had better be cookies and cream," she said, pointing to the paper bag he held in one hand. He had something that looked like a flat pillow tucked under his other arm.

"I told you, I got you. Wine and Doritos too. I brought you a whole buffet." He nudged her out of the way and walked to her kitchen, setting the bag down. "And I brought you something else." He put the pillow-looking thing down on the counter and took something out of the bag that was definitely not edible. Shaking it out, he held up his faux-vintage Rolling Stones t-shirt—the one with the mouth and the big tongue.

"That's my favorite shirt of yours."

"I know what you like." He tossed it to her and she held it up.

"It's not ratty, though. I said I was going to slob out on you."

"Mmm. True." He came around the island and kissed her on the head before unpacking the rest of his bag. "But, I also know how much you like the tongue and since I can't give it to you tonight, this is the next best thing."

"Oh my God. Do you just say whatever comes into your head?"

He shrugged and she couldn't even roll her eyes at him. He was being cute. She'd allow him a few raunchy comments.

After he'd put the ice cream in the freezer and sorted the rest of the menagerie of snacks, he turned to her and put his hands on his hips. "Aren't you going to put it on?"

She didn't have a bra on under the t-shirt she was currently wearing but it felt a little silly to leave the room to change after his intimate all-too-true tongue comment. She turned away from him and lifted her shirt over her head. She could feel Dylan's eyes on her naked back, hear him breathing, but he stayed put.

When she was done, she turned around and held her arms out, his shirt billowing around her like a sail. If the nausea and bloating didn't kill any misguided hopes on his part, that was sure to do it.

Though, for some reason, he looked... smitten.

"What are we watching?" she asked, turning away from that soft smile.

"You're the patient."

"I have my period, Dylan. I'm not injured."

"I guess you won't need my magic heating pad then?"

He lifted the pillow thing up and she eyed it curiously. "What makes it magic?"

"I don't know, but I wrenched my back pretty bad one summer on a bad wave. Bought this thing online. I was back on the board by the next weekend."

Dani examined the heating pad, then unfolded it, popping it into the microwave according to the instructions. "That was kind of you to think of this."

"Yeah, well. I'm not that bad once you get to know me." He was smiling, playing it off, but his eyes were searching. He did that all the time now—looked at her like he was sending her some esoteric smoke signal he was praying she'd see.

She'd felt something in that inlet last weekend. He was different.

It had felt so different that she'd considered whether she should stop all of this. Dylan was supposed to be consequence-free. She wasn't naive enough to think she couldn't form some sort of attachment through this whole ordeal, so she'd picked the one guy who she was sure would never form one back. Someone who, if she even looked at him wrong, would stomp that budding spark of intrigue with a heavy foot. But now she got the impression he'd taken his boots off.

"Go pick out something to watch, Dani-pie,"

he said when she'd been studying him for too long. "I'll get you some ice cream."

"What's going on, Dylan?"

"I'm feeding you comfort food. You demanded it, remember?"

"No. I mean what are we doing? We're breaking every rule we set at the start of this thing. First you started staying over, now we're doing this without sex. And camping..."

"What about camping?" Discomfort rolled over his features and he leaned against the counter, his fingers curling around the edge like he needed it for support.

"Dylan, please." She couldn't go on making herself crazy. Ever since that day at Cat's house, she'd felt like she was sliding down a hill, clutching at the earth to keep from landing somewhere that would hurt. Or at the very least, would leave her a muddy mess. But looking at those eyes, tortured with whatever he wasn't saying, but still utterly mesmerizing, she got the distinct feeling she was definitely in hurt territory. God, how did she get here?

"Look, Dans," he said, squeezing the back of his neck. "I'll be honest. I have no fucking idea what's going on. I just know I wanted to be here tonight. When you said you had to cancel, I was disappointed. I didn't want to spend the night without you. I guess I was kinda hoping you felt the same way." Dylan raised his eyebrows and the hopefulness, that Good Boy grin, sent a shiver through her shoulders.

She did feel the same way. She wanted him there too, whatever that meant.

She twisted his shirt between her fingers. "You really just want to hang out?"

"Yes."

"By ourselves, with our clothes on?"

"Completely."

He smiled, all honesty and vulnerability, and she knew exactly what it meant.

They'd put on a movie after their ice cream and Dani had fallen asleep on his chest almost immediately. Her little cupid mouth puffed tiny staccato breaths of air while he watched her dream—her eyelids fluttering, her feet twitching under the blanket.

He reached around her for the remote to shut off the television and she pulled her legs into her tummy and whined. "Was I snoring?" she asked when he laughed beneath her cheek.

"No. Just drooling."

She shot up and wiped her mouth with the back of her hand, finding it dry. "Jerk."

"You missed the end of the movie." Dylan stretched too, groaning in a way that he knew showed his age. "It was the mother the whole time."

"Obviously."

"Oh. You knew that, huh?" He poked her arm.

She groaned. "I should have known you wouldn't have figured it out since I had to explain the ending of *Shutter Island* to you twice."

He cracked up. It was his favorite part about her, the way she had no mercy when it came to his ego. He banded an arm around her waist and held her in place. "Be nice," he said, his fingers creeping along her sides.

"Tickling a woman with cramps is a good way to get a broken nose."

"Aw. You still have a tummy ache, Dani-pie?" He let his tickle threat fade into a hug, tugging her onto his lap and bending to set his chin on her shoulder. She made a little sigh that wormed its way straight into his bloodstream.

"I feel better actually," she said, snuggling closer. "Your heating pad might actually be magic. Sorry if I was snippy."

"You weren't."

She nuzzled her face into his neck, slipping her arms around his back in a hug that was so affectionate it made his chest tight. A wave of longing washed over him. The same one he'd felt in the water last weekend. He had her in his lap, her flesh beneath his fingertips, but it wasn't enough.

"Dani?" he whispered.

"Mmm?"

"Can I stay tonight?"

"Yes," she said, snuggling closer. "I want you to stay."

He nodded. Everything felt tense. He couldn't pull in enough air, like the room itself was holding its breath, waiting for him to figure out where he was going to take this. Dani was right. Something had happened in the water last weekend. Something had *been* happening.

He squeezed her tighter, every cell in his body screaming at the idea that she was only halfway his and only in secret.

He couldn't take it anymore. How could some website say she was supposed to be with someone else when he was the one who knew all of her little secrets? The way she'd toss her hair and push her lips into a pout when she didn't think she was getting enough attention. How just before she fell asleep, she'd flop onto her stomach and kick one leg out of the covers. That bringing her coffee in bed was the best way to convince her to share a shower. *He* was the one who knew all of the spots that made her scream his name, and he was the one who'd made her laugh when she was heartbroken. Maybe he'd never been "the right guy" before, but he also wasn't the guy who let something he wanted stay just outside his reach. And God damn it, fuck it, he wanted Dani.

All of her.

He cleared his throat, his heart hammering.

"Do you ever think that maybe this whole soul-mate thing might just be a fairytale?" he asked.

"What do you mean?"

"I mean of all the people in this world, you're supposed to be out there looking for one match?"

Her brow furrowed. "You don't believe there's one person for everyone?"

"I think it's a self-fulfilling prophecy."

She leaned her head on his shoulder, her breath on his neck. "Explain."

"Take Josh. He's had too much shit go down in his life to chalk it up to chaos or chance. It would be too hard to wrap his head around, so he believes there's a plan, and Cat is it. He'll spend the rest of his life dedicated to that. Even if there was someone else out there, he'd never see her." Dani gave a tiny nod. "Me on the other hand, I hate the thought of some predetermined plan for me. What's the fucking point of living if I don't have a chance to make some choices?"

"I get that," she said, "but the thought of choices like that, the big ones, in my hands only? It's terrifying. Look at all the ways I could mess up my life. I like to think there are some safety features on this ride—someone making sure it doesn't go off the rails."

"What about people like my mother?" he asked. "Who was supposed to buckle her seat-belt?" A little voice told him to shut up, leave his dirty laundry out of this, but something about talking to Dani always made that little voice sound further away.

"My father was a monster," he said. "Treated her like shit, and then left her to work the rest of her life for his mistakes. Was that sad life her destiny? Or did they both make choices that put them there?" He tipped her chin with his fingers, looking her in the eye. "You met Josh the same night as Cat. You met him first. He's a good looking guy, you're a beautiful woman. What if Cat wasn't there that night? Maybe you two'd be married right now."

A laugh bubbled out of her, shaking her shoulders. "No way."

"Why not?"

"Look, I love Josh. He's a great guy and I couldn't ask for anyone better for my best friend, but he's a saint. Cat needs a man like that. She has more trust issues than I can count. She needs a guy who'll never make her guess. Me? I'd be bored that way."

"Okay, well then who's to say us meeting on that beach wasn't just as important? Destiny or chaos, who knows? Josh was looking for fate and so he found it, but maybe you and I just happened to meet and get to know each other. Maybe there's plenty of other options for both of us, but I've already made the decision, the *choice*, that I want to see where this thing goes with you."

Dani's body went still. "Is that what you're saying?"

It was. Whether it was fate or not, he wanted so badly for her to tell him her version of the "right guy" was six foot one, dark hair, green eyes, had a joke to interrupt every sentimental moment, and thanks to his dad's genes, had a better than fifty-percent chance of ruining a relationship before he even started one. "I'm saying, Dani-pie, it doesn't have to be some lightning striking, angels singing moment. Sometimes two people just enjoy each other's company. Then they start to see how the other person would make their life better, and it grows from there."

Surprise washed across her face. "Like us?"

"Yeah. Like us." His mouth went dry. If she didn't feel the same way, he'd have a front-row seat when she met the guy who *was* good enough. That image burned in the back of his throat, but he kept going. Her took her face in his hands. "I don't want to be the warm-up anymore, Dani. Don't go out with any more matches. Cancel them. Go out with me instead."

Anticipation bubbled in his veins. There'd been only a handful of moments in his life when he'd been so dependent on what someone else was going to say. Almost always with work, and never staring into the eyes of a woman.

"Okay," she said.

"Okay?"

"Did you think you were going to have to convince me?"

"I guess I did."

She laughed quietly, nervously. "I don't even have a date planned tomorrow. I told myself I wasn't scheduling them because I was too busy, but that wasn't true. I think I just didn't want to see anyone else."

He forced his voice out around his heart sitting in his throat. "How come?"

She pressed her mouth to his chest, her breath escaping in a hot whoosh. "Because I want to see where this thing goes too. It's already gone somewhere, I think."

The way his stomach did a somersault told him she was right. It had gone somewhere he wasn't sure he'd ever find his way back from.

Twenty-five

"**Y**OU'RE STARING," DANI SAID, SIPPING a gin and tonic that a guy with a man-bun and a flannel shirt had dropped off in front of her. They'd just finished dinner in a dimly-lit dive not far from her condo. The floor was concrete and the decor consisted of neon signs advertising beer in cans, and a Little League team picture from 1996 thanking the owner for their sponsorship.

He'd told her to pick anywhere she'd wanted to go for their first dinner together off of her couch. He hadn't expected this.

He smiled around a sip of scotch—bottom shelf, the one brand they had. "I was thinking about how much time you spent getting pretty for me tonight."

She snorted. "Oh my God. You should teach a class on male chauvinism."

"Maybe."

She reached for an olive left on the plate of nachos they'd shared, and her sweater fell off of one shoulder. He wanted to press his lips to her skin, warm it with his mouth. She was right. He'd been staring since he picked her up.

"You do look pretty, though," he said, catching her hand on the table.

Dani's little cherub cheeks turned pink. "Thank you."

He turned his palm over, letting their fingers lace. It was a move he'd practiced. Women loved it, but tonight he just wanted everyone in the room to know she was his. Even if it was just the bartender and a couple of old guys playing cards at the bar.

"So is this a common soulmate date spot for you?"

She laughed. "God no. One guy took me to a place that we could only get into because his boss's sister was the chef. It was completely over the top."

He laughed with her but then his smile fell. "I'm an idiot," he said.

She gave him an amused look. "Usually. But, why this time?"

When he'd told her to pick the place, he was trying to make her happy. He thought she'd like that. He didn't give a damn what they did as long as she was with him instead of one of her soulmate dates, but he couldn't help thinking about all of the women he'd dropped a small fortune on just to take them home. Now he was finally with Dani and he'd bought her chips and cheese. Shit. Was he already fucking this up?

"This is our first date. I should be wining and dining you."

"No," she said, so firmly it startled him. "I don't want to be Dylan Pierced. That's not why this works."

He was only fifty-percent sure she wasn't playing off some hidden disappointment, but hell, they'd been sharing Chinese from a sketchy takeout joint for weeks. It would be kind of weird to start now with fancy wine lists. But then, she'd also enjoyed the hell out of that night they'd spent with the Jansen's.

Shit. He wanted to get this right more than he thought possible.

"Why does it work, Dani?" he asked, stroking her hand with his thumb.

"It works because you're my friend. Look, dating sucks. There's so much pretense. Good impressions, extra effort. Then you get to this part, where you're not pretending to be some- one else anymore, where you're wearing baggy clothes and shoveling ice cream into your mouth because you have cramps, and you start to feel like some magic slipped away." She took a breath and his heartbeat echoed in his ears. "But I think that was the magic part. That was my favorite night in a long time. I don't want you to play pretend for me and I don't want to lie to you. This is good, Dylan. I'm happy."

"I'm happy too." The feeling was like seeing a face that's familiar but you can't place it. It had been a long time since he'd felt happy. He'd enjoyed himself, sure. He'd had fun, been content with his life. But right now, looking at her smiling, he remembered how it felt to be more than content. "It's not going to be all takeout and dives, though," he said. "You deserve the fancy nights too. Like the Jansens' party. You're coming to all of that stuff with me."

"Already planning the second date, huh?"

He grinned. "You got me."

"Well, I'm in for that too. As long as those future fancy nights end like that one did."

"You might be perfect," he said.

She tipped her chin and batted her eyelashes at him. "Took you long enough to figure that out."

"Nah. I knew it from the start." He just didn't think perfect was his style.

He raised his hand and signaled the bartender for the check. "Come on," he said. "I want to take you somewhere else."

Dylan pulled up his GPS app on his phone and typed in an address that he wouldn't let her see.

"Where're we going?" Dani stepped gingerly over a crooked cobblestone, the high heel of her boot twisting.

He offered his arm and pivoted to cross the busy street. "A place I know."

A few blocks later, they were walking down a set of concrete stairs. Dylan handed some cash to the big guy in a black t-shirt who guarded the door. When he let them pass into the basement bar, a wall of thick, damp heat hit her face, and she had to blink a few times to adjust her eyes to the darkness.

Dylan held tight to her hand, guiding them through a sea of people, over to the bar. There was a band on the small stage at the far end of the room where people were dancing, and the music was too loud for her to hear what he ordered. The little hairs at the nape of her neck, the ones too short to fit in her ponytail, curled and stuck to her skin in the humidity.

She took a seat on a barstool, and Dylan sidled up beside her, his front pressed to her back. He handed her a lowball glass with something pink inside, then dipped his head and brushed her temple with his lips. The atmosphere in this place was pure sex and that little touch of his mouth shot a lightning bolt deep in her belly. Maybe she did want to get Dylan Pierced.

"How'd you find this place?"

"A date took me here," he answered, sipping his drink.

That warm, heady feeling started to deflate, like a slow leak in a balloon. But then he leaned closer and pressed his lips to her ear. "You texted me in the middle of it and I spent the rest of the night thinking about you. I've been wanting to take you here ever since."

Her heart jumped. "When was this?"

"One week into your soulmate search."

"One week?" she asked, her voice almost too quiet to reach him over the band.

He shrugged, giving a shy smile that looked strange on his face. Strange, but beautiful. He was beautiful. How could she not have seen this coming? It was like a veil had been lifted and she realized how stupid she was to think she could look at this face, touch every part of this man and not end up wanting to keep him. *Destiny or chaos? How could they ever know*, he'd said, but looking at him now, it felt like maybe that chemistry they'd always had was a tether keeping them connected until they were ready to follow the string and find each other. Maybe she hadn't veered from that soulmate search after all.

She gulped her drink and turned to set the glass on the bar. "Dance with me."

Dylan didn't miss a beat. He swept an arm around her middle, lifting her off the stool and setting her on her feet. Her steps swayed as she followed him through a crowd of people—too many drinks, too many thoughts making her skin hot. Her hair curled around her temples, and she felt her mascara turning to liquid. She could only imagine what she looked like, melting under the heat and the dawn of all of these revelations.

But if the way Dylan stared at her as he pulled her close was any indication, maybe it wasn't as bad as she thought.

He found the rhythm of the music immediately, keeping it through every turn they took. It surprised her not one iota. There are certain things you can tell about a person by the way they carry themselves, the places that their eyes linger. Dylan had her movements mapped out before she made them. It was intimate, erotic, this way he moved against her. The bass thumped in her ears and she flattened her palm on his chest to feel it thumping in his body too.

His skin was damp, moisture bleeding through the cotton of his button-down shirt. The heat between them felt luxurious. Like a tropical vacation, considering it was unseasonably cold out on the street. She pushed closer, stepping wider until his knee wedged between her legs. Dancing like this, letting him kiss her shoulder in front of all of these people the way he did in the mornings when they woke up together, tangled and sore, it felt both exhilarating and like not nearly enough.

Suddenly, all of these people, all of these clothes, needed to be gone. Whatever this new way between them would be, it was time they took it back to her place and explored the hell out of it.

Twenty-six

*D*ANI'S BACK COLLIDED WITH THE door to her condo, and she let out a half laugh, half yelp.

"Shit. Sorry." Dylan broke their kiss, panting. He'd carried her up the stoop to her landing, swearing under his breath about her shoes and not being able to wait another second.

"I'm fine," she said, her voice breathy. "In the little pocket."

He shifted her weight, propping his knee under her ass and holding her against the door with his chest while he dug through her purse.

"How do you find anything in here?" His exasperation was adorable, but seriously, he had about two seconds to find that key or her neighbors were going to get a show.

She tightened her legs around his waist and let go of his neck to help him search.

"Here." She found it and shoved it into his hand.

Dylan pushed it in the lock and the door

swung open. They tumbled into her living room, giggling into each other's mouths.

"Shit, Dani. I thought I was going to have to take you in the hallway."

"I was going to let you."

His eyes flashed dangerously and it occurred to her that neither of them was kidding. Goose-bumps swept the still-wet skin on her neck where his mouth had been.

He walked her backward into her bedroom, his mouth glued to hers, until the back of her knees hit the edge of the bed. His hands darted under her sweater like he was afraid she'd disap-pear before he touched everywhere he wanted to.

"Take this off," he said, pulling at her clothes while he nipped at her neck. But she couldn't move, frozen from the feel of his tongue on her skin and the tone of his voice. It was urgent, more serious than he'd ever been. Command-ing. Stern. Every time they'd done this before there was laughter in his eyes and behind his words. He was playful, easy. But tonight his fin-gers were clumsy as he unclasped her bra, and they trembled as they glided down her sides and hooked into the top of her jeans, pulling them down over her hips. His breath came in heavy puffs, fanning over the moisture that formed on her skin.

She swallowed against a tightness in her throat, and dropped onto the bed. Her strapless bra had fallen to the floor and when she slipped her sweater over her head, his dark eyes rolled closed and his head tipped back. "Beautiful," he whispered to the ceiling, then he fell to his knees in front of her, pressing his mouth to her stomach.

"You too," she said, tugging at the collar of his shirt. He sat back and unbuttoned it while she kicked her jeans off her feet. When he'd stripped out of his pants, he sat down beside her and pulled her onto his lap, their chests rising and falling together.

"Why does this feel so different?" she asked.

"I don't know." His voice was strained, and her heart felt like it would burst as she watched him fight some sort of emotion washing over his expression.

This was the first time they'd been together since he'd said those things. Since she'd said them back. Knowing that tenderness was in there all along, and touching him again with that knowledge, it felt like walking a high wire. The fall would be disastrous, but if she could stay upright, God, it felt like flying.

She leaned back to look at him, and his hand came behind her back, holding her steady. The only light in the room was the city shining through her bedroom windows, but it was bright enough to see the tiny freckles on his chest, matching the ones on his cheeks. She trailed a shaky finger over them, letting him feel what she was thinking: *This is unexpected, but I like it.*

He sucked in a hard breath, watching her move over his skin. He liked this, being explored. Last week Dylan had finally given her a door into himself, and tonight it was wide open again. Tonight she wanted to touch all the places she'd neglected.

She dragged her nail over his tattoo, tracing the circle. North, then South. East, then West. Like an optical illusion, the ink turned a deep indigo where before she'd only seen black. She pressed her lips to it. The word "layers" flashed across her thoughts.

His breathing turned ragged and his hands came up to wrap around her arms, stopping her fingers. He dipped his head in the dark. "I need you."

"Take me."

His eyes flashed and he flipped her onto her back, sliding over her to part her legs with his knee. He kissed a trail between her breasts, down to her stomach, then pressed a sloppy, sucking kiss to her center. It was enough to make her back arch and her breath catch. Every thought dancing around her head flopped over dead.

Dylan tugged her panties down her legs and watched her—eyes wild, breath rushed. Usually they took turns, giving, taking, leading, following, but tonight she wanted him to take whatever it was he wanted. She was useless to herself anyway, caught up in this weird spell of discovering Dylan.

He stretched his body over hers, then seemed to remember something. He moved to push off the bed, but she caught his arm. "Don't," she said. "I want to feel all of you."

Without a second thought, he wrapped his hand around the back of her thigh, dropping it over his waist, and pushed inside of her, groaning like a man who'd been walking for miles and finally found a place to rest. When he was buried as close as he could be—their bodies pressed against each other, fingers interlaced above her head—his face finally broke out into that sweet, dimpled smile she loved so much. Her heart swelled.

Afterward, they laid in the dark of her bedroom, their breathing slow and spent. Dani pressed her nail into the center of the compass on his chest and twisted it. She'd been resting like that, her head on his shoulder, her weight draped over his torso, for fifteen minutes now. He'd only been counting because it wasn't like her to linger. Usually, she'd jump up and throw her hair in a bun, find something to cover up all of that pretty, golden skin. Usually, they were on her couch, or in her kitchen—that kitchen island shouldn't be used for food prep—but tonight they were in her bed and she was still in his arms.

"I like this," she said, still tracing.

"I could tell earlier."

She flattened her palm, the light slap echoing in her silent bedroom. Even the traffic sounds had petered out by now. "Tell me again why you got it."

She'd asked him this when they first met. She and Sonya were on the back of his jet ski while Josh was falling in love with Cat on another. That day, he'd given her his standard line about freedom and self-direction. The one that made him sound like some philosophical adventurer. That line always worked.

"It's the direction I never had as a kid," he said now. He felt her shift ever so slightly and she could feel her eyes on his chin. He swallowed hard. He'd never told anyone this, but there were a lot of things he'd never done until her. "The night my father left, he screamed at my mother till he was hoarse, packing his shit in this big dramatic scene. He always wanted it to look like he was wronged, you know? Make her believe somehow she, or we, were responsible for the things he did. Anyway, right before he walked out the door, he looked me in the eye and he said 'you're on your own, kid.' It was the truest thing he'd ever said to me."

He cleared his throat and shifted her body in his arms. "Then he was gone. My mother could barely keep herself afloat, so I had to figure out how to navigate that. That's when I realized I needed to depend on me. The compass reminds me to be my own guide, find my own way."

He glanced down at the top of her head to see her reaction, wondering if he would see disgust or pity. But she just tightened her arm around his waist and nodded.

"I felt that way too as a kid," she said. "Like I was flying alone."

"Is that why you have that little bird on the back of your neck?"

She reached back and touched the ink, nodding. "But it's got a branch underneath it. Stability. Somewhere solid to land. That's the difference between me and my mother. She wanted me to fly, but I just wanted a nest."

A nest. He supposed that's what he'd wanted too when he was a kid. But then he'd grown up and realized that only a tiny percentage of people saw that side of life. And the ones who did, put up with a lot of heartbreak to get it. It was better to fly than to settle in a nest made of straw where it's one strong breeze and you're falling.

Though, if this was somewhere solid to land, being warm and wrapped around Dani in this bed, maybe he could just point his compass this way for a while and see what happened.

Twenty-seven

"THANK YOU FOR MEETING ME here," Mrs. Jansen said. Her white hair was pinned haphazardly around her head, and she was wearing a pair of overalls splattered in paint. Dylan followed her up the curved stairway to the top floor of the old bank, out to the balcony where Dani had won them this job.

She walked straight to the railing and leaned over.

"So you said you wanted to make an adjustment?"

"Yes." She swept an arm over the view. "The sketches Josh sent were wonderful. I was hoping he might be able to add a water feature here, right in the center of the garden. Do you think that's possible?"

He pulled a pen from his bag, and popped off the cap with his teeth. These types of questions could really be done over email. The job being theirs and all, it was time to hand meetings like this over to Josh, but he'd grown kind of fond of Mrs. Jansen and he hadn't minded the trip into the city. Besides, Josh was presenting a course at a conference in a few weeks and he'd been handing everything he could off to the new guy so he could prepare for it. Dylan wasn't sending a rookie to this building. He'd worked too hard to close them.

"I'm sure I can make that happen," he said. He tried not to look at his watch as he jotted down her ideas. He was hoping to finagle lunch with Dani since he was there. "Let me get this back to Josh and have him email you a new file."

"Thank you, darling. Listen, I know you're done pitching us, and you probably have weekends full, but I wanted to invite you to another event. We've only just begun to put an exploratory committee together, but there's a hotel downtown we're thinking of bidding on. Another historical renovation. Of course, if we get it, you get it, and I'd love to have your input from the beginning." She turned to make her way back inside, and Dylan followed. "There's an auction there next month. My husband and I have made a donation and plan to attend. We want to use the evening to discuss the possibilities, along with the dinner and dancing. Will you and Josh join us?"

Dylan did a mental fist pump. He was already typing a text to Josh in his head to relay what she'd just said. "If we get it, you get it." It wasn't a signed contract, but he had a feeling Mrs. Jansen's word was just as good.

"Absolutely," he said. "Anything you need."

"Excellent. I'll send you the details. And bring Dani."

Damn right. He couldn't wait to tell her.

After a quick goodbye, he hustled back to his car to get out of the wind. The cold had come early. It felt like it could snow any second and it wasn't even November.

He dialed Josh as he started the engine, blasting the heat, but he only got voicemail. "Call me back, bro. Got some Jansen news. And tell that little bun in Cat's oven, Uncle Dylan just paid for its nursery or whatever babies want." He hung up the phone, slightly disappointed that he'd had to put off that announcement, but he still had another call to make. He swept his thumb over the number and transferred to hands-free.

"Hey, Danica."

Her sigh crackled over the line. "I'm gonna let that slide since you sound like you're in a good mood. What's up?"

"You eat yet?"

"No."

"I'm in town. I'm coming to get you for a celebratory lunch."

"What are we celebrat—"

"See you in ten." He hung up and pulled away from the curb, his face stuck in a grin.

"Scratch off my lunch order," Dani said.

Benji raised an eyebrow curiously from his desk. "You get a better offer on that phone call?"

"Maybe."

"Oh, really? Is this one of the matches?" Now he was rolling his chair across the office, lunch order forgotten.

Shoot. She wiggled uncomfortably in her seat. She hadn't mentioned any of this to Benji, but to be fair, it had just happened.

"So, I actually have some news."

He clapped his hands together like a circus seal, and she rolled her eyes.

"It's not the app, but I have been seeing someone."

"How the hell did you manage to see someone else while you were trying to fit in eight soulmate dates? I swear your social calendar is life goals."

Dani pulled a lipstick out of her bag and touched up in the mirror on her desk. "You might not say that when you hear my story."

"Regale me."

"So, remember when we were talking about the 'fine print' and how I didn't think I could make it all those weeks..."

"Yesss. And I gave you my most supportive side-eye?"

"And I told you I found a little work-around. Well... I kinda sorta started dating him for real."

"Kinda sorta?"

"Yes, and you know what?" She squared her

shoulders, preemptive indignance bubbling in her chest. "This just proves that rule was a terrible idea because, trust me, if I wasn't sleeping with Dylan, this never would have happened. Clearly sex was a crucial component in our compatibility which goes against everything—"

"Woah, Nelly," Benji said, waving a finger at her. "*Dylan*? Cat's husband's best friend is the freebie?"

Dani felt her cheeks burn. "That same one."

"The one you've known for years and who, by the way, I've been saying you had something with for years?"

"Yes. Him. Why does everyone feel the need to clarify so many times? Geesh."

"Because you specifically said, and I quote—"

Luckily for her, Benji's court stenographer act was cut short when the man himself rapped his knuckles on her office door. Dylan leaned on the frame, crossing his legs at the ankles and gave her his Good Boy smile. She was butter.

Apparently so was Benji. Dani shot her officemate a look, and he pulled his chin off the ground.

"Dylan, hey."

"Hey, babe. You ready?"

Benji mouthed the word "babe" in her direction as he turned and rolled back to his desk.

She ignored him. "Yeah. Just let me shut down my laptop. This is my friend Benji, by the way."

Dylan's eyebrows jumped in recognition. "Benji," he said, drawing the word out. "Nice to meet you. He crossed the room to shake Benji's hand and Benji gave him a "you too" that sounded like he had a mouthful of marbles from holding in a laugh. When she got back from this lunch, they were officially fighting.

"Let's go, Dylan. Benj, I'll see you in an hour."

"I'll be right in this very spot," he said.

"So why the midday celebration?" she asked when they were alone in the elevator.

"Uh uh. First, say hello to me right." Dylan wrapped an arm around her waist and tugged until she stumbled against his chest. He kissed her long and slow, his other hand caressing her cheek with a wide, affection-filled swoop of his thumb.

Her face flushed hot. It was familiar, that heat, but she was still getting used to the *caressing*. There was a sweetness to it that, when mixed with the roughness of the way he held her, felt almost... secret. Like maybe she was the first person to experience the side of Dylan that thumb-swooped.

He let her go, and she straightened her dress while she composed herself from the wreckage that was that thought. "Well, that certainly felt like a good news kiss."

Dylan smiled at her, wiping her lipstick from his bottom lip with the back of his hand. All the other times he'd made that motion flashed in her head and now more than her face was hot.

"Looks like Mrs. Jansen is coming through like Josh and I hoped," he said. "She's got another building they're eyeing. Wants us in from the beginning. It's unbillable hours until they actually win the bid, but they want to win it with us already in place."

"Wow," she said, feeling a rush of pride and second-hand excitement. "You did it. This is what you were shooting for."

"Yup." Dylan's smile stretched for miles. She'd never seen him so pleased, and she'd be lying if she didn't like how eager he was to tell her. He shoved his hands in his trouser pockets and lifted onto his toes like a kid waiting for a pat on the head.

Even better, she stepped into his chest and tugged on his tie. "I'm proud of you. You nailed it, *babe.*"

"I did, didn't I?"

"I never once thought you couldn't."

His cocky smile dropped, and his eyes turned serious. Serious enough to make her breath still. "I know you didn't," he said. Then he kissed her again, hungrier than the last time but still that *affection.*

The elevator dinged and he knew enough to let her go when the doors opened to the lobby of her building.

"You know what?" she said, her heartbeat in

her ears from that fabulous kiss. "I think this deserves more than lunch. Do you have another appointment?"

"Nope."

She put a little sway in her hips as she stepped off the elevator, looking at him over her shoulder. "I could call it a half-day. Finish up some stuff from home tonight."

Dylan's expression turned dirty. "Yeah?"

"What's the point of being the boss if you can't quit at lunch on a Friday?"

"That's the philosophy I built my career on."

"Looks like it's about to pay off."

Just like at the hotel the first night they'd slept together, Dylan woke to Dani's golden brown tan popping against white sheets. He curled his fingers in her mess of blonde curls and gathered them off her neck, leaning in to nuzzle her shoulder.

She murmured something into the pillow that sounded like an insult and he chuckled. Dani was not a morning person when she wasn't escaping hotel rooms.

"I need coffee, Dani-pie. You want some?"

"Don't call me that," she slurred, her eyes still closed.

"Too late. It's stuck. Two sugars, one cream?"

Dani rolled over dramatically, causing the

sheet to tug down to her waist. Maybe he didn't need coffee that badly after all. He tossed on his side to follow her, but before he landed where he was headed, he caught a glimpse of the clock on her bedside table.

Damn it. He didn't have much time. When he'd picked her up for lunch the day before, he'd been hoping to bring her back to his house. But after a quick, celebratory meal that turned into mid-day drinks, it had seemed urgent that they get to the nearest bed available to continue the celebrating. That was Dani's condo, and considering this was the first morning he'd actually wanted to linger in a woman's bed, he cursed himself for making plans.

"I have to head out soon," he said, kissing her shoulder. "I'm supposed to meet Josh to go surfing. I don't even have any clothes with me."

"Mmm. I have brunch with Cat. It's their one day a month apart."

He leaned down to kiss her stomach, rethinking the entire day. "You wanna blow them both off and go for round... four?"

She giggled and swatted at him. "No. Go make coffee."

After coffee and a shower, Dylan sat on the edge of Dani's bed, buttoning his shirt from the day before and watching Dani prance around in her underwear while she searched for something to wear after her shower.

"So, you're having brunch with Cat, huh?" He

gave her a sly smile. "Does this mean you're not mad anymore?"

Dani slipped a cotton t-shirt dress off of a hanger and popped it over her head, smoothing the skirt with her palms. "It's with everyone, actually, and the scheduling predates me being mad."

"Still. You didn't cancel it."

Dani made a huff and plopped down beside him. She pushed his hand away and took over his buttoning. "I haven't spoken to her since we went camping." She sighed. "I can't remember a time we've gone weeks without speaking." Dani's lower lip jutted out in the saddest of pouts, and something twisted in his chest. "I guess I'd rather be mad with her than without her."

"I saw her a few days ago," he offered. "She came into the office."

Her eyes shot up to his. "How'd she look?"

"Fat."

Dani reached under the shirt she was buttoning and pinched his skin.

"Ow! I mean like cute fat, like she's supposed to."

She finished with his shirt and smoothed down his collar. "Still sick?"

"Josh said she's a little better." He caught her hand and brought it to his lips. "So listen, I'm gonna spend the whole day with Josh, and I need to know. Are we still keeping this a secret?"

Her eyebrows jumped. "You want to tell him?"

Want wasn't the right word. It wasn't that he had some burning desire to gossip about this new thing between them. In fact, having Dani without the "will he or won't he fuck it up" spotlight was nice. But not telling Josh that he was dating Cat's best friend felt like a big omission. "I feel bad lying," he said.

"Like they did about Cat being pregnant."

"That's your fight, babe. I get how you feel, why you're mad, but that's not something between me and Josh. This is starting to be." He gestured between them. "Dani, if we're going to do this, let's do it. We're all going to be in the same room at some point, and I'm not pretending." He thought of the game at Josh's house, their fight in the bathroom. It had turned into a good night for both of them, but he'd bet she didn't like the feeling of it either—lying to everyone they loved. "Either we keep this secret and never go to a group get together again, or we come clean."

"It's going to get a lot harder once everyone knows."

Fuck if he didn't know that. "I don't care."

She pulled her lip between her teeth and studied him. "You really don't, do you?"

"I really don't." Hell, he'd woken up that morning with both the job and the girl. Keeping it to himself was sucking some of the glory out of that.

"Okay," she said, one shoulder lifting. "Tell him."

"Are you going to tell Cat?"

"I haven't decided yet, but either way, after today she'll know."

Twenty-eight

"*D*ANI, DANI?" JOSH HEFTED HIS surfboard onto the top of his Jeep, clicking it into the Thule rack, then reached for Dylan's.

"As in the only one we know."

"Bullshit."

"I'd never get away with lying about that." Dylan had waited until they'd gotten a good few hours of surfing in before broaching the subject. When he'd picked Josh up, he still had that stress line on his forehead, but Dylan knew the salt water would put him in a better mood.

It worked. Josh was surprised, but he didn't seem pissed.

Josh squinted at the October sun glinting off of his Jeep. "Is this official, or are you two just screwing around?"

"Official, I guess." Dylan went to the opposite side of the vehicle and helped with the straps. "I mean, we're not just screwing around."

"How'd this happen?"

"I don't know. It just... did." Dylan avoided

Josh's stare as he unzipped his wetsuit and pulled a fleece zip-up over the goosebumps that rushed his salty skin.

Josh did the same, throwing on a beat-up sweatshirt and hopping from foot to foot on the freezing sand until he could get his sneakers on.

They jumped in the cabin of the Jeep and Josh blasted the heat. "When?"

"First time? After your wedding."

"This has been going on for five months?"

"Almost as long as your little secret baby." He'd meant what he said about it not being a thing between them, but if Josh was going to bring it up...

Josh spun his baseball cap forward, pulling the brim down low. "It wasn't a secret," he muttered. "Cat just—it's not the same thing."

One could argue it wasn't even close and Josh had way more to apologize for, but Dylan wasn't in an arguing mood. "Maybe not," he said. "It wasn't *official* then, it happened a few more times in between. But then—" he let out a long puff of air, watched it turn to mist. "She was still seeing other guys, and I realized I didn't want her to."

"Because you weren't doing the same? This isn't some irresponsible reaction to one of your slumps, is it? Cause that would be—"

Dylan put a hand up. "It's not."

"Okay." Josh put the Jeep in gear and turned back to the road.

"I didn't want her seeing other guys because I like her. She's fun and easy to hang with, the sex is phenomenal. We just sort of grew into it."

And maybe he wanted to grow too. Usually, when Dylan met women like Dani and Cat and their friends, he stepped aside, let the grown-ups like Josh do their thing. He'd spent his childhood having to be a man so young—taking care of his mother, looking out for his sister—that whenever he was expected to be one it felt stifling.

He didn't want to be like that anymore. There had to be a balance.

"How did you know?" he asked. "With Cat, I mean."

"I don't know," Josh said. He lifted a shoulder and took a beat, his brow furrowed. "When I met Cat, I guess something about her just felt like mine."

That was how he felt, like Dani was his. Like none of those other guys had a right to her the way he did. He just wanted to live up to that right.

"You got any advice for me?" Dylan scratched at the back of his neck, his voice sounding unnaturally weak to his own ear.

Josh ran a hand through his wet hair, silently digesting the conversation as he was prone to do. Dylan caught himself holding his breath.

Finally, Josh nodded. "My advice is, if it scares you this much, it's probably good for you. And also don't be stupid."

Dylan's breath whooshed from his lungs, and he turned away to watch the beige and blue beach disappear from sight through the passenger window. For once, he actually had no intention of it.

"Oh my goodness! Look at you!" Emma hopped off of the stool at their usual high-top table by the window and rushed to fawn and squeal over Cat. It had been three weeks since their camping trip, and Dylan was right, the tight sweater and leggings she was wearing revealed a perfect little baby bump. The back of Dani's throat burned. It was a good thing Cat had been forced into telling her secret because there was no way she was hiding that.

Dani took a sip of her mimosa as Emma continued to *ooh* and *ah*. She wanted to be happy for Cat. She was happy for her, and she did look so damn adorable with her little belly. But there was a wall between them, something that had never been there before, and she didn't know how to get past it. If she didn't have that kind of access to Cat, then she was alone.

An annoying little gnat of a thought buzzed around her head reminding her that she was doing the same thing keeping her new relationship with Dylan secret. That was different though, right? Cat was growing a human in her body.

Dani was supposed to be bringing Cat pickles and ice cream and listening to all the gross pregnant body stories Cat would never tell Josh, like peeing her pants or not being able to shave her bikini line.

Cat hoisted herself up onto the stool next to Emma and sighed. "It's a good thing it's leggings season," she said. "I'm officially out of pants that fit."

"You look gorgeous," Emma said, beaming.

Sonya nodded, her hand flat on her heart. "You do, Cat."

"So tell us everything! When did you find out? How did you tell Josh?"

Cat's expression went flat like it had at the campsite. She looked uncomfortable, maybe even guilty. Good. So she did know it was terrible to keep this from everyone. She was showing and they hadn't even heard the story of how she found out yet.

"Oh, you know," Cat said. "I just... told him." She shot Dani a glance. The kind that said: *subject change?*

Dani focused on her orange juice and champagne. If Cat was looking for help from her, she wasn't getting it today.

"Was he out of his mind?" Emma asked. "He must have been so happy."

"He was. He is."

"So," Sonya said, picking up the menus and handing them around the table. "Elephant in the room—you were pregnant at the wedding, weren't you?"

"Yes, but I didn't know." Cat sighed like telling this story was physically paining her. She sent Dani another look, and Dani started to feel guilty. Why was this so difficult? Was telling her best friends in the world about her baby horning in on some private moment between her and Josh?

"Luckily, we found out on the second day of our honeymoon," Cat said. "Before I could take advantage of the eight swim-up bars at the resort."

Emma sighed. "You must have been so happy, Cat. It's so romantic."

Cat picked up the glass of water at her place setting and drank instead of answering. Her forehead was shiny and damp like she was either going to puke again or she really did need a lifeline out of this conversation.

Seventeen years of friendship twisted in Dani's chest. She supposed if she was going to make her own announcement, she could throw Cat a line in the process. She chugged the last of her champagne like it was a Bud Light at a frat party and cleared her throat. "Well, I have some news."

"Oh!" Emma said, shimmying on her stool. "Dani Story time. This will be good."

"It is." Though, she might be the only one to think it. "I've been seeing someone."

"And?" Emma clapped her hands.

"It's been great. Some of the best nights I've had in a long time." She twisted her fingers to stop her hands from shaking. This was harder than she thought and now her drink was gone.

Emma cooed. "That's great! Who's the guy?"

"It's Dylan."

Cat choked on her ice water.

Sonya peeled her eyes away from her menu, her jaw hanging open. "*Dylan* Dylan?"

Dani's cheeks flamed. "That's the one."

"Dylan Pierce?"

"Yes, Sonya. Dylan Pierce. Josh's best friend."

"What in the hell?"

"Um..." Emma twisted a napkin in her hand, clearly unsure if she should let her shock show.

"It's okay," Dani said. "You can say it. If I wasn't there I wouldn't have believed it myself."

Sonya slapped her palm on the table, her silverware jangling. "I knew you two were acting weird on that camping trip! You were standing too close, touching. You went swimming that night. It was different. How the hell—" She ran a hand over her mouth. "Oh my God. He was the freebie, wasn't he? Oh my God. I will not take responsibility for this, Danica!"

"What's a freebie?" Emma asked.

"It started out like that," Dani explained. "But then things... changed."

"Bullshit," Sonya said. "We *know* Dylan. He

doesn't change! He's... he's... *Dylan* for God's sake. "

Emma's eyes bounced frantically for a face to land on. Between Sonya's disbelief and Cat's confusion, she was clearly at a loss as to how to react. Apparently she decided to go with diplomat. "Dylan's always been very nice, Sonya."

"Dylan?" Cat repeated, her eyes blinking rapidly. Her pregnant brain was probably short-circuiting. "You're sleeping with Dylan?"

"I'm dating Dylan."

Sonya pointed at Cat. "And how did *you* not know?"

Cat's eyes turned glassy as she sputtered. "What...I... How could you not tell me?"

"Really?" Dani said. Cat snapped her mouth shut. They would hash that out later. Right now her apprehension had turned to indignation. She hadn't expected an intervention. She'd expected... well, she didn't know what she'd expected, but not this. "I didn't tell you to get your advice. It's already happening. I removed my profile from the dating site. Dylan and I are good together. We have fun."

"Oh, I bet it's fun." Sonya shook her head. "I want to be happy for you, Dans. It's just that it was only a couple months ago we were sitting at this same restaurant and you were telling us you were ready for something real. And now Dylan? I don't want to see you disappointed when you realize he's not it."

"Maybe he is." They all turned to look at Cat who had apparently broken out of her spell. "Maybe Dylan is ready for it too. Maybe Dani made him ready."

Dani chewed on the inside of her cheek, caught between her lingering resentment and being grateful for the help. Cat knew Dylan better than all of them. Her support would hold some weight.

Sonya shook her head. "I don't know, Catia."

"Look, I'm not saying Dylan is a choir boy all of a sudden," Dani said, "but he told me he wants this to be more. I want this to be more. So we're trying it." She looked at Cat. "It's been really good."

Cat nodded. "Then we're happy." She smiled, and Dani felt a tiny thaw.

When they'd finished their meals, Emma and Sonya passed out parting hugs.

"I'm sorry if I was harsh," Sonya said, squeezing Dani's shoulders. "If you're happy, then I'm happy."

"Same," Emma said.

Sonya turned to hug Cat, then gave Dani one last look. "I just hope Dylan knows that I'll kill him if he screws this up."

"You'll have back up," Cat said. She didn't move to get off her stool and Dani stayed glued to hers too. It was time to have a long-overdue conversation.

"Cat," Emma said, "you stay healthy. Dani, you stay happy. We love you both."

Sonya waved Emma off. "Don't speak for me, Em. They're both on my shit list. Secret babies and secret boyfriends. "

Dani watched them leave, Sonya still ranting, and the little bell over the door signaled play time was over. She gulped the last of her newest mimosa and spun in her stool to face Cat, a hundred different opening arguments lining up on her tongue.

But Cat beat her to the punch. "Why didn't you tell me about Dylan?"

Here we go. Nerves swarmed in Dani's belly, but she squared her shoulders. "Why didn't you tell me you were pregnant?"

"What?"

Her voice cracked as she pointed to Cat's belly. "This right here, Cat. You know, the child growing inside of you!" They were actually going to have a real fight about this. One of only a handful in their long friendship. But it felt like the pin on a grenade had been pulled weeks ago and they'd both been watching in slow motion, waiting for the explosion to finally put them out of their misery.

Cat's mouth dropped open. "I did tell you!"

Dani huffed at Cat's indignance. "Actually, Josh told me—all of us—and five months late.

You never said a word." She crossed her arms over her chest, mentally checking off a point on her board.

But then Cat's lower lip started to tremble, and her nose scrunched. "I'm sorry," she said, her voice shaking with corked emotion. "I didn't know Josh was going to say anything. I would have done it myself, he just—"

Dani held a hand up. "I mean why didn't you tell me when it happened, Cat? Why did you wait until you were picking out maternity clothes before you shared that with me? We share everything. When things with you and Josh were rough, it was me you came to. When you got engaged, you called me before you even called your mom. Every single big moment in my life, breakups or ups and downs with my career, you've been there for it. This is the most important thing that has ever happened to one of us and you kept it from me. Are we in such different stages of life that you didn't think I'd be happy for you?"

Cat's brow knitted. "No. Of course not."

"You thought I would send you a condolence card? I was joking with Sonya!"

Cat was silent for a moment, her lip still quivering. "I knew you'd be happy," she whispered.

"Then what the hell, Cat?" Dani could hear the desperation in her own voice, and she thought of Dylan's little arm punch of encouragement. The way he'd gotten her to admit that all of her anger wasn't directed at Cat, but at something inside of herself that she was still working out. She sucked in a breath to calm herself. "Just tell me why."

Cat's face crumbled, her answer coming out as a sob. "I didn't tell anyone because I didn't feel like celebrating."

Dani's jaw fell open, confusion bubbling up in her belly and boiling over into a hot flush on her cheeks and neck as she watched tears stream down Cat's face. "What do you mean?"

"We didn't plan it," she said, choking on another sob. "It was an accident. I think the weekend of Josh's birthday party. I don't know. We went away—I might have forgotten to take my pill that morning. There were a bunch of last-minute things to do and I got up late. I can't remember." Cat sputtered like a beat-up engine. She rambled when she was nervous. It had always been her tell, no matter how tough she was trying to be. "I *just* got here in my career," she said. "Josh has all these plans to expand his business. This wasn't supposed to be for a few years." She dropped her face into her hands, groaning. "Dani, I was pregnant at my wedding."

Dani blinked, all of her best friend replies fleeing her brain. This was the type of thing that would knock Cat's whole world off-kilter—clearly—but she was married to the love of her life. All the rules about how life's supposed to go are predicated on that one thing. She had to know it wasn't that bad.

"At least you didn't get married by a priest," Dani said, giving Cat a playful punch. Josh's divorce had made that impossible which, of course, he'd felt awful about. Maybe everything really did happen for a reason because Cat would have damned herself to hell over that.

Cat huffed out a tiny laugh and sniffed. "My parents haven't done the math yet."

"Oh, Cat." Dani's mind was spinning. She'd been obsessed with catching up to this imaginary timeline for months now, and here Cat was, terrified because she'd arrived too early. What the hell did that mean? She'd made a lot of decisions in the last few months based on this comparison, and it turned out she was comparing herself to a reluctant model.

More importantly, she'd been feeling sorry for herself about being kept out of the loop while Cat was dealing with something huge. She'd come here to have it out with her best friend when really it was her who should be apologizing.

"Come on, Kit Cat." Dani brushed Cat's hair off of her forehead. "You always knew you and Josh would have kids. He can't have been upset about this."

Cat shook her head.

"Oh." Dani's heart squeezed again. She'd seen the look on Josh's face when he'd made the announcement. He was ecstatic, and if Cat wasn't, it had to be more than a little uncomfortable for them. Uncomfortable enough to be the source of the tension she'd picked up between them. Dani spent a lot of time being jealous of Josh, but now she was mentally hugging him too.

"I was upset, and he was upset with me for being upset. I nearly ruined our honeymoon crying over it." Cat sniffled and pulled in a deep breath. "But I couldn't do that to him, you know? This is everything he's ever wanted, and I was acting like my life was over. I forced myself to pretend it was okay for him, but telling everyone else, letting people gush about it? I wasn't ready for that."

"But Josh knows you way better than that."

"So do you, I guess."

Dani forced a smile. "Don't forget it."

Cat smiled too, dabbing at her eyes with the little square napkin from under her water glass.

"Anyway, then we got home and I could not stop puking. None of it felt celebratory. I just didn't want to face it. I told Josh we should keep it to ourselves for the first three months, like you're supposed to, even from you all. But then it became four, then five…"

"What about now?" Dani asked, her voice cracking. "Are you happy now?"

Cat bobbed her head, one more tear spilling over before she tipped her head to the ceiling. "I am. And of course, Josh is still so happy. He convinced me that everything was going to be okay, and I know you would have done that too, Dani. I'm sorry I didn't tell you and let you say it. You're my best friend. I was stupid to try to go through this without you."

Dani reached across the table and pulled Cat into a hug. "It's okay. I'm sorry I made it about me. It's just..."

Cat sniffed. "What?"

"I thought you'd given up being this neurotic."

Cat laughed and another tear escaped, weaving through her freckles. "I fell off the wagon for a while, but I'm back. Totally zen. See?" She pressed her hands beneath her chin in a prayer pose and hummed.

"Until you have to pop that baby out..."

"Okay, one crisis at a time." She wiped at her smudged mascara. "And speaking of crises. I meant what I said. Sonya's wrong."

Dani's pulse ticked up. The warm glow of the spotlight turned in her direction, and she shifted uncomfortably in it. "About Dylan?"

"Yes. I mean she's *right*, but she's also wrong. Whatever you see in him, I think it's really there. For what it's worth, I don't think it's a mistake."

Dani's shoulders felt like they'd shed a fifty-pound weight. As much as she'd told herself she didn't feel bad for keeping her and Dylan a secret from Cat, what she really needed was her friend's blessing. For the person she'd known longest and best to tell her she wasn't crazy for believing in this. Now that she had it, she allowed herself a little bit of giddiness that she'd been holding back. Whether soulmates were a thing or not, she'd found the person she wanted to spend the foreseeable future with. Her smile pulled so wide she could feel her muscles stretching. "Thanks, Kit Cat. It's worth everything."

Twenty-nine

"WHAT DO YOU THINK? SAGE?" Dani held up a picture on her phone and made a face. "Or minty-green?"

Dylan flicked his eyes away from the road to see the options and shrugged. They both looked exactly the same. "I think you ought to call Emma and get her opinion, Dani-pie."

"You're no help. I know you like planning parties, Dylan. I've been to plenty of them. You can't hide from me."

"Baby showers aren't in my wheelhouse. Find me when it's Superbowl time." Though he had to say, listening to Dani chatter on happily about hors d'oeuvres and napkin colors was worth it to see her and Cat back on good terms. It was like someone had upped the wattage on Dani's whole personality, and he liked a good strong dose of her.

She waved him off and stretched her legs out in front of her. His eyes ran the length of them. The winter leggings she had on for their run were distracting to say the least.

"Fine. Don't help. You and Shawn should do something for Josh, though. Whatever guys do."

"We mostly just let it happen and don't make a big thing."

"It is a big thing. What did you do for Shawn when he had Mattie?"

"Um. I don't remember. He was in the Navy. We didn't even see Mattie much till he was about three or four. Josh probably sent him a gift."

"Well, Josh is here. Take him out for drinks or something. Buy him some dorky World's Greatest Dad t-shirt."

"Ok. You got it. I'll tell Shawn to get on that."

She huffed just like he knew she would, and he smiled at the side of her face. He'd probably take her advice, though.

He pulled into the turnoff to the beach trail, letting his car idle for the heat while he gathered his things. "You ready for this? It's gonna be cold."

They'd been adding a run into their weekend routine—Dani's idea to offset all of the take-out—and he'd convinced her to run on the beach today. When they'd woken up and he noted the late fall temperature, he'd contemplated ditching out, but forced himself to follow through. He wasn't usually this lazy on the weekends but something about Dani in a pair of his boxer shorts made him reluctant to suggest anything that required clothing. Still, having a running partner who looked that good in her winter gear was good motivation.

Dani tightened the laces on her sneaker and tossed him a sideways smirk. "I'm ready to embarrass you if that's what you mean."

Competition and lust mixed in his blood, warming it, making it pump. "Oh, are we racing? I can get down with that. What's the prize?"

"Winner gets to pick dinner."

He smiled at the subtle indication she'd be staying another night. "You're on." He stepped out of the car and the coastal air froze his windpipe. Once their breathing turned heavy, this would be uncomfortable. Dani bounced on her toes at the front of the car and he wrapped his arms around her, blowing on her ear as he spoke. "There's an old lighthouse foundation down the beach. First step onto the sand is go. First one to get to the stone foundation wins."

"This isn't some secret place I'm not going to be able to find, is it?"

"Of course not. It's plain as day on the sand. Straight shot."

"Okay." She shrugged off his hug and stretched her arms over her head. "Let's go, Rocky."

"You know Rocky was a boxer not a— Hey!" She was off before he could finish. "We were supposed to start at the sand," he called, the first long pull of cold air burning his airways.

She shrugged without breaking her stride.

He found his footing and fell into a steady pace behind her, biding his time. More than once, the sight of Dani's ass bouncing in those running tights caused him to stumble. He was like a salivating dog being led by a piece of meat. Pathetic, but not surprising. He should have taken that into account when he challenged her.

Even with the distraction, though, he gained on her easily.

She tossed a look over her shoulder and pumped her arms, pulling away again. She was quick, but running on sand was his regular training routine. Not exactly the same as the hard-packed soil of the running trails in the city she usually took to. Plus he had the advantage of recognizing the finish line before she did, knowing when to give it his final push.

And there it was.

His footfalls grew heavier as he blew past her. She made a sound that was surprise and anger and stretched her stride, but her legs were too short. She'd never catch him. He looked over his shoulder to gloat just as her knee went out to one side and she fell flat on her ass.

"You okay?" He pivoted and rushed the few steps he'd gained on her, dropping to his knees in the sand. Shit. Maybe racing on unfamiliar terrain was a bad idea. "Did you hurt your ankle?"

"No." She shook her head, breathing heavily. "I'm fine."

"You sure?" He went to reach for her foot, but she swung it out of his reach and pulled to her hands and knees, doing some weird bear crawl for a few steps until she could get her top half upright. She jumped the last yard to the old crumbling cement finish line while he sat, his ass and thighs in the cold sand.

"Really?" he huffed.

Dani bent at her waist, her hands on her knees, and caught her breath. "What? I said I was fine. Shoulda believed me."

Dylan pulled himself to his feet and walked to her. "Should have left you sitting on the sand and made a break for it, huh?"

She shrugged again, panting. She was in good shape, but the cold wind off of the water would take anyone's breath. It whipped her ponytail, tossing it around her head wildly. He reached a hand out to capture the blonde strands, pulling until her head tipped up to his. "That was dirty."

A little smirk tugged at her lips, but she held his gaze. "What are you going to do about it?"

A variety of punishments flashed through his mind, all of them more explicit than the last, but when her fierce face broke and she started giggling, those x-rated thoughts drained from his brain like the surf pulling away from the shore. He laughed too, his shoulders shaking with the sheer enjoyment of playing with her like this. He pulled her down onto the sand and she landed on his chest, laughing. Instead of thinking about spanking that tight little ass, all he wanted to do was press his mouth to hers while she giggled against his lips.

Either he'd gone soft, or Dani Petrillo was just that intoxicating.

After making out in the sand for way longer than was appropriate, they walked back to the car to add another layer, then down the access road to the part of the beach reserved for swimming. Even this late in the season, a few food trucks put in lunchtime hours in the parking lot. Mostly for hardcore surfers and fishermen. He bought Dani a crab cake and himself a burger and they found a log on the beach to sit on.

"Hey, remember that fancy dinner I promised you on our first date?" he said.

She wiped mayonnaise from her chin and grinned. "I do remember that promise. I figured this was it."

He pinched her thigh, glad for her joke making what he was about to ask feel a little easier. "Well, um, it's not black tie or anything, but I always take my mom out for dinner on her birthday. Somewhere fancy."

"Sounds like you."

"Yeah. Anyway, you wanna maybe come with me?"

Dani's perfectly-shaped eyebrows shot to her

hair. "You're asking me to come to your mom's birthday?"

His heart beat harder against his cold chest, and he forced a shrug, hoping his face didn't scream *please, I need you there.* Lately, spending time with his mom was wearing on him. The comparisons, the foolish comments. The ghosts she seemed to like to keep around. He needed a break, a buffer. Dani made things easier.

"You've already met, so it isn't weird, right? I can't take too much of my mom and her..." *complete disconnect from reality* "... drama. You were great with the Jansens. Come charm her so I don't have to."

"I mean, I guess I could." She pulled her lip between her teeth. "You really want me to?"

"You'd be doing me a favor."

"Is this going to be a habit, me getting you out of talking to people?"

"Maybe." He gave her that smile that always worked—his *close the deal* smile. This was a big one. "Look," he said, Dani's shyness about the whole thing giving him the courage he'd been lacking. "She likes you and we're doing this, so let's do it."

He watched her swallow, her eyes darting around his face like she was searching for a lie. That being her first inclination twisted in his gut, but then she smiled. "Okay."

The breath he'd been holding rushed from his lungs, fogging on the cold air. "Okay."

Thirty

"**H**ERE'S TWO MORE," HIS MOTHER said, dropping two white envelopes on the table in front of him. Dylan tore one open, examining it. A letter from her dentist about a payment plan for her last cleaning. His mother let out a long-suffering sigh. "I just don't know where they all come from."

"From the businesses where you buy stuff, Ma. Cable company. Credit cards." He shook his head. His father had been useless when it came to managing money, mostly because they didn't have any, but maybe she deserved some of the blame. The woman couldn't balance a checkbook for the life of her, and she was from the generation that still used those.

He entered the amounts of the last two bills into her online bill pay and wrote "paid" on the front of each of them, then put the dentist letter in his pocket. He'd take care of that one. He stacked them with the others, handing them over for her "filing system".

"Thank you, Dylan." Her smile was genuine

and he felt guilty for his irritation. She was doing her best. She always had.

"No problem."

"So," she said, turning back to her oven. "What's new? Have you found a nice girl yet?"

He almost laughed at the standard grilling, thinking of Dani in the shower last weekend, and how not nice she could be. He bit the inside of his lip to suppress a grin. He could tell her about it (well, not that part) or he could just let Dani show up to her birthday dinner and shock her properly. He was looking forward to the shocking. The shocking would be good. And if he examined a little further, he was just looking forward to her being there. Dani wasn't one to turn things like this into milestones. And this wasn't one. It was a simple favor. She would help him get through it and she wouldn't overanalyze it. Since she'd said yes, he'd started to let himself imagine her being there for all of the things like that in life. Work stuff, times when he couldn't deal with his mother. Partners in crime. Maybe this was why people took chances on other people.

"Oh you know me, Ma," he said. "I know lots of nice girls." She swatted him with her dish towel and he didn't even bother dodging. "Anyway, did you decide where you want to go to dinner for your birthday?"

"You know I don't care where we go, Dylan," she said. "Just as long as I get to see you." Italian Catholic guilt lilted her voice and he rolled his eyes.

I'm. Sitting. Right. Here.

"How about Parkers?"

She waved a hand at him. "That's a bit much, don't you think?"

"No, I don't think." She always did this, acted like a nice meal might put him into financial ruin. His shoes cost more than the once a year dinner would run him.

"You know I'm not comfortable in those types of places," she said.

He ran a hand over his face. Must they play this game every time? "How about The Hills? We went there for Mother's Day."

His mom sighed. "The year you were born, your father took me to Mother's Day brunch at a restaurant on the water. We had champagne and eggs and an ocean view while you sat so quietly in your little baby seat. It's one of my favorite memories."

Dylan stopped scrolling through his phone and peered at her, a cold chill prickling the skin on his arms. No way was that a true story. Was she actually losing it now? Did she see that on one of her soaps and imagine it to be her own memory? Or had she switched from twisting the truth to outright lying? He wasn't sure whether to rage or start googling symptoms of psychosis.

He watched her putter around her sink, wiping up crumbs from the cookie she'd just eaten.

She looked normal enough. "Can we not with the trip down memory lane today, Ma?" *Or crazy town highway, as it may be.*

"The man is half of you, Dylan. You can't pretend he didn't exist."

"Thanks for the reminder. You're the only half that mattered."

Something flashed over her face. Gratitude and embarrassment at the same time. "He worked very hard," she said. "He could be unpleasant, but that was because he wore himself out providing for us."

Dylan huffed out a sardonic laugh. He'd been letting sleeping dogs lie for too long now. "Ma, that's bullshit and you know it."

"Dylan..."

"No, come on. 'Worked very hard.' He worked hard at wearing a groove in that bar stool down the road. At being a tyrannical dickhead when he was awake and a lazy, good for nothing bum when he was passed out drunk. And then he took off and *you* worked very hard. You did that. Not him. How can you have any sort of kind feelings left for him? He left you with two kids to raise and you still smile and get all heart-eyed when you say his name. For Fuck's sake."

Her mouth turned up into a grin like she hadn't heard a thing he said. What the hell was happening?

She brushed her hands over her pants. "There were a lot of good things too, Dylan. And maybe I smile because I see a lot of those good things in you."

Pressure exploded behind his eyes and he had to clench his teeth to keep from screaming. How could she say that to him? How could she dig out the deepest-seated fear that he had inside him and stab him with it like a deranged Mommy Dearest while still looking like the tired, prematurely-aged woman who'd given him all of the affection he'd ever received?

If the good parts of his father were in him, then so were the bad parts. It was ludicrous that she didn't see how that made him seethe.

And panic.

He pushed his chair away from the table and grabbed his coat from the hall. *Just go.* That's what his gut always told him in times like these. Leave before you say something awful and make her cry. Then he'd really be like his father.

"Where are you going?" She scrambled toward him. "You don't want to eat?"

"I have plans." With Dani, and he really didn't need his night ruined by one of these arguments.

"Okay then." Her face tightened in defiance and he wondered once again how much of this was an act and how much was honest to God delusion. Today was not the day he was going to find out.

He leaned down and gave her a stiff kiss on the cheek, then pushed out into the cold evening to his car. His hands shook as he turned the key and took the scenic route home to clear his head.

He should call his sister. Katie would understand. She knew why this kind of bullshit made his head explode. After all the struggle, the working two jobs, the money they never had, the *crying*, his mother still made those eyes when she talked about his father. And then she had the nerve to compare him to the bastard, reminding him of the genetic material he was forced to carry around.

It wasn't like he could forget. Dark hair, green eyes, tall enough to be intimidating to his wife and kids. But Dylan had never felt that urge to impose his will over people who loved him. He'd never accepted someone's trust and smashed it just for fun.

Or maybe he'd just never accepted anyone's trust in the first place. He knew he wasn't his father, but he sure as hell didn't want to be put in a position to be proven wrong.

"Fuck you, Vince," he said aloud. "I'm not you, God damn it."

This bubbly feeling in her belly was ridiculous. Dani pulled into Dylan's driveway just after dark. It was Friday night. They'd spent almost every Friday night together since the Fourth of July. Now it was November and she had butterflies. It was silly, really. The thought bounced around in her head as she dabbed at her lipstick in her car mirror, then made her way to his front door and into his living room.

"Dylan?" She dropped her things on his couch and peeked up the spiral staircase to the loft where he had his office set up. "Dylan?"

Finally she heard the slider in his kitchen open and close and he appeared from the back yard, dressed in jeans and a black sweater, a tumbler of some dark liquor in his hand.

"Hey, Dani-pie."

A smile bigger than she could tame spread across her face, but he didn't return it. He seemed distracted, moody. Waves of irritation flowed off of him, crossing the empty space that was still between them and stinging her skin.

"What's wrong?"

He downed the rest of whatever he was drinking and pushed past her to set the glass down on the kitchen island. "Nothing's wrong. You ready?"

Emma was having a dinner party tonight and everyone was going to be there. It would be their first time showing up somewhere *together.* He'd said he wanted to do this. He'd seemed excited. Now her pulse ticked up and the giddiness she'd just been chiding herself over disappeared on the wind of this new mood. "Dylan."

He turned toward her and pushed a smile onto his face, but it had no mirth. He still hadn't kissed her. Was he having second thoughts about this whole coming out to their friends thing? Did he suddenly remember that what they were doing was as non-Dylan as it gets?

Swallowing the acid that crept into her throat at the thought, she crossed the kitchen and stood in front of him, crossing her arms.

Dylan sighed. "What, Dani?"

"Do you want to skip tonight?" she asked. She forced herself to be direct. She wasn't going to wonder or leave things up to over-analysis. Not with Dylan. And not anymore. "If this is too much too soon, I—"

"It was my idea to tell everyone."

"I know, it's just, you seem..."

"I'm not having second thoughts, Dani. For Christ's sake, let's just go."

Okay. She might be nervous to pull on the thread they'd built this whole thing on, but she sure wasn't going to take that. "Hold up." She put a hand on his chest, something flaring inside her. "First of all, don't bark at me."

Dylan's jaw twitched, but he looked chastened.

"Second of all, fine, I believe you. But if it's not that, I still want to know what's wrong."

Dylan stood there blinking for a few moments, his jaw set, then his shoulders fell and he stepped toward her. "I'm sorry," he said. "Let's start over." He took her face in his hands and kissed her mouth, then her forehead. "I'm glad you're here. Tonight is going to be fun."

"Okay," she said, letting herself melt into his chest. That was weird, but she'd let it go for the sake of not going into this already weird night with any extra weirdness. "Let's reserve judgment on 'fun,' though. It could be completely obnoxious."

Even Cranky Dylan had to laugh at that, his chest shaking. She was delighted at the sound of it. "I'll give you that. Are you ready?"

"As I'll ever be."

Thirty-one

DANI WAS RIGHT. THIS PARTY was completely obnoxious.

Dylan had always liked Emma, but sometimes she could go a little overboard. Usually it was just the Christmas-themed events that he'd felt he had to show up for, but Dani had to go to all of them. She'd warned him on the way over, but he still wasn't quite prepared for the signature cocktail or the menu written in script on a chalkboard.

None of this was Dani's scene either and he wished he could just take her back to his house, take those jeans off of her, laugh and play with her in bed.

He popped the cap off of a beer, forgoing the homemade wassail in Mason jars. The bottle was cool against his sweaty palms, and he tapped it to Dani's while she made conversation with a friend of Emma's he didn't know. Dani winked and made a face like she was about to fall asleep. He cracked a tiny smile.

He just wasn't in the mood for it. There were

too many people, too many elbow nudges and puzzled looks. He knew it would be awkward the first time they did this, but after the day he'd had, he really wasn't up for the scrutiny.

The conversation with his mother had been breathing down the back of his neck all night, but for Dani's sake, he'd tried to put it out of his head. He hadn't meant to take it out on her, and he certainly didn't want her thinking he had some issue with walking into a room with her on his arm, no matter who was in that room. Fuck, walking around with Dani was maybe the best thing he'd accomplished in his life, and everyone here seemed to agree, given how they'd all been looking at him like the whole thing had to be a practical joke—Dani and him *together.*

When they'd arrived, Emma's husband, Adam, had opened the door and visibly startled at the sight of Dani's hand in his. Emma had rushed to the door, waving them in. "I forgot to tell you," she'd whispered to Adam who stood there silent and wide-eyed. Then she'd announced them to the room in a weird, high-pitched sing-song voice. "Dylan and Dani are here." Wink, wink.

It occurred to him now, while Sonya studied him from across the room with her arms crossed and her expression vaguely disapproving, that maybe the weirdness was more than just everyone getting used to him and Dani being a thing. Maybe not everyone was as convinced as he was that he could do this. Maybe everyone here was thinking: Here comes Vinnie Pierce's kid to ruin our friend. He hadn't expected that, though he probably should have.

The doorbell rang and Emma went to answer it, squealing like she did every time anyone new arrived. Josh and Cat were finally here. *Thank God.*

Cat walked into the kitchen and immediately grabbed a handful of crackers. She shoved them in her mouth, her cheeks popped out like a chipmunk, and walked straight toward him. His muscles tightened like he was preparing for an incoming assault, but instead she gave him the first genuine smile of the night.

He leaned down to hug her, Josh's soon-to-be son or daughter barely fitting between them. Out of nowhere, a weird mix of affection and envy rushed him. The kind that he had no place feeling on the heels of that sharp reminder his mother had given him. "You look cute, Kit Cat," he said.

Josh shot him a knowing look while he made himself a drink. He'd been the new boyfriend here years ago, but somehow Dylan doubted he got the same reception.

Emma waved everyone into the dining room and he followed behind Dani. "You okay?" she whispered when he pulled out her chair.

He put on his most convincing smile and reminded himself that no one here knew him as Vinnie Pierce's kid. He was overreacting.

"Of course," he said. He pressed a kiss to her temple, his neck going hot when he saw Sonya watching him again.

"So this is really happening?" Sonya took the seat across from him and gestured between him and Dani. The table went quiet and he felt a sweat break out at his temples.

"Yes, it is really happening," Dani said. "And I think Emma had some games planned after dinner, Sonya, so you don't need to treat us like the entertainment for the night."

Cat slapped a hand over her mouth to keep from laughing. Sonya rolled her lips inward but her eyes softened. Everyone else studied their place settings. Dylan drained the rest of his beer. This party was definitely obnoxious.

After dinner, Cat hooked her arm through Dani's and tugged her down the hall to Emma's bathroom. "Sorry we were late," she said. "That was freaking intense."

"No kidding. Are you puking or peeing?" Dani asked.

"Peeing. I haven't puked in three whole weeks." She shut the door behind them and hiked down her tights.

Dani turned to the vanity, picking up a little

mermaid figurine that held Emma's hair ties. "Sexy," she mused, running a finger over its cleavage.

Cat giggled.

"You're really feeling better?"

"I'm good. Second-trimester endorphins finally kicked in. I'm happy."

Dani bounced her eyebrows. "Your man is beaming. Were you sharing those endorphins before you came?"

"Pleading the fifth." Cat flushed then pushed Dani out of the way to wash her hands. "So, this is kind of weird, seeing you and Dylan together in person." Her lips pulled into a smirk in the mirror. "You two sure are awfully touchy-feely."

She shrugged. "I like touching him. He's very firm."

Cat snorted a laugh. "Perv."

"You're the one who went there."

"Anyway," Cat groaned. "You're happy, though? "

"I'm happy." Sure, Dylan had been a little moody tonight, and despite swearing up and down he wanted to do this with the whole group, he'd seemed more than a little uncomfortable, but it was rough in there. Sonya had been watching her like a hawk, like she was going to miss some sort of secret SOS. Emma had gone completely in the other direction, smiling and elbow-nudging anytime Dani and Dylan spoke to each other. She wasn't sure which was more painful. Dylan had looked like he was having a tooth extracted the entire night, but he was here doing it. She had a feeling it was more than most people expected from him. Protectiveness rippled through her. Sonya and Adam were going to get an earful later.

Cat studied the scowl that had made its way to Dani's face. "You're being pessimistic," she said.

She shook her head. "Actually, I'm not even being realistic. For once, I actually have high hopes. I'm just letting it happen and it's *fun*."

Cat smiled. "That's what you've been looking for."

"Who would have thought?"

"Never in a million years."

They came out of the bathroom and found Josh and Dylan outside. Emma's deck was one of those meticulously crafted "outdoor living spaces" that belonged in a decorating magazine. The coffee table had a gas fire pit built in, and string lights that looked like miniature lanterns hung from a pergola above a full sofa set. Built-in speakers made sure you didn't lose the party's playlist when you stepped out for fresh air. Dani thought it was possible that Adam had built this space specifically for when guests needed a break from Emma's Pinterest-inspired parties.

Clearly Dylan already needed one of those breaks.

Cat lowered herself onto Josh's knee and he

handed her a plate with a slice of the pie Emma had made for dessert. It was the size of her face.

Dani flopped down next to Dylan. He wrapped an arm around her and pulled her against his side, sharing his warmth in the chilly night. He seemed less tense out here, just the four of them. "It's good to see you eating again, Cat."

"She's still underweight," Josh said. His hand wrapped around her belly, and Cat covered it with hers, linking their fingers. All of the tension between them seemed to be gone. It was good to see that too.

"I've gained enough to buy a new dress for that auction." Cat looked at Dylan. "Congratulations, by the way."

Dylan smiled that grin that made the corner of his eyes crinkle and gave away his secret craving for validation. Dani always wanted to wrap him in a big hug when he smiled like that.

"Thanks, Kit Cat," he said, tipping his beer to her. "Dani's coming to that too."

"I am?"

Cat beamed. "Good! We can go shopping." She took another bite of pie, then handed it to Josh, declaring that she needed an iced tea refill.

Josh moved to stand, but Dylan beat him to it. "Come on, Kit Cat. I need another beer. I'll waddle in with you." Dylan held out his arm, helping Cat off the couch, and then Dani was alone with Josh.

Unusual awkwardness prickled at her.

Though her fight had never been with him, there was something unsaid lingering in the quiet that fell over them. "I don't think I've said congratulations yet."

Josh gave her a smile over his beer that said she didn't need to apologize. "It was weird," he said. "How it all went down."

Understatement. "A little. But things are good?"

"Things are very good."

His smile warmed her heart. Without the din of her one-sided competition with Josh for Cat's attention, she found herself less annoyed by those little smiles.

"And things are good with you?" he gestured in the direction where Dylan and Cat had just taken off, and Dani's eyes went wide. *Oh.* They were going to have that talk too.

"Um. You know. It's tough dating someone who's always dressed better than me, but it's going well."

Josh laughed, breaking a piece of crust off of Cat's pie and popping it in his mouth. "You know why he does that, right?"

Her cheeks warmed. She was a little embarrassed at how much she wanted to know these things. She'd never really wondered if there was a reason behind any of the things Dylan did, but now she wanted to know everything about him. Especially the stuff he kept secret.

She cast her eyes to the fire pit, watching

the flames jumping between them, trying to look casual. "You mean why he's always dressed like he has somewhere better to go later? I always assumed it was part of his ladies' man persona."

Josh finished chewing, letting her dangle in her intrigue. "His dad drank more than he worked, couldn't hold down a job. He let them struggle. All the expensive stuff—his car, his designer clothes—it's Dylan's way of sending a big fuck you to his old man. Proving he's better than his roots."

She wasn't expecting that. She remembered Dylan's *Afterschool Special* comment and the bitterness in his voice when he'd made it. It was the kind that said stop prying, so she had. Now she wished she'd asked more. She hated to think of him keeping that in. She wanted to be the person that he told that stuff to.

The air felt thick with that realization and she thought of his mood earlier. How she hadn't pushed. Just like with Cat, she'd assumed it was about her and left it alone.

She looked up at Josh who didn't seem fazed at all by what he'd just revealed. "Isn't it against some bro code for you to tell me that?"

One of Josh's cheeks lifted. "It would be against the code to let you think he was just a superficial douche."

She laughed. "You're a good friend, Joshy."

"You are too, Dani."

Thirty-two

DYLAN WOKE ALONE SUNDAY MORNING to the smell of French roast coffee wafting into his bedroom. He stretched and threw on a pair of sweatpants, not bothering with a shirt, and followed the sound of Dani humming. He found her puttering around his kitchen, equally undressed. She'd put on one of his t-shirts, the lacy blue underwear she'd worn the night before peeking out from the hem.

"Hey, lazy." She spun around to look at him and the haphazard way she'd tied her hair up caused a piece to fall across her eyes. He brushed it aside and his chest filled up like a balloon. That party had been torture, and it took the whole next day to shake off his mood, but *this* was worth it. She was drinking from his Rideout and Pierce coffee mug, her face dewy without any makeup on. When was the last time he lounged around with a woman on a Sunday morning? Now it was a regular occurrence—her in his house or him in hers. Coffee, sometimes a meal, sometimes a repeat of the night before.

He rounded the kitchen island and pulled her toward him, pressing his lips to her neck. "Morning. Did you make coffee?"

"I did. And I put bagels in the toaster. That's the extent of me impressing you with my breakfast skills."

"Something tells me I'm going to enjoy breakfast very much this morning." His hands were like heat-seeking missiles, sliding up her sides and searching out the softest parts of her, but his brain wasn't actually thinking about sex. He was thinking about whether or not she was going to stay and prance around his house like that for a little while longer. If maybe they'd go for another run, or take a nap on the couch together later. If he could get her to stay the night again, even though she had work the next day.

"I have to go soon," she said.

The little domestic picture he'd drawn disappeared and he felt his shoulders slump. "Why?"

"Cat and I have plans."

"Mmm," he muttered into her neck. "I think I liked it better when you two were fighting."

Dani squirmed out of his embrace to take a sip of coffee. "We weren't *fighting*, and no you didn't."

"I guess not."

"What are you going to do today?"

Dylan fixed himself a cup and leaned on the counter, watching her blow into her mug, her pretty lips pursed. Okay, now he was thinking about sex.

"I have to work on the Jansen job," he said. She lifted her palm for a high five and he grinned like an idiot. "You sure you have to rush off?"

"I do. But I have time for a shower."

"Now you're talking. Hey, so I know I never actually asked you if you wanted to go to that auction. But what do you say, think you can stand another double date? This time you won't have to lie to poor old Mrs. Jansen about being my girlfriend."

"Is that what I am?"

He froze, his mug halfway to his mouth. *Shit.* Had he just stumbled into a "moment"? He'd heard the "what are we" line before, but he'd never been the one doing the asking.

He scratched at his head, suddenly nervous. "I guess I just sort of figured—"

Dani stepped to him and pushed up on her toes, pressing a finger to his mouth. "Whatever you're about to say, I'm in. And I'm in for the auction. We both know you need me there." She smacked his ass, then blew him a kiss over her shoulder as she headed toward his shower.

This girl.

He'd failed at his mission to keep Dani longer than just their shower, but he eventually got over it. She'd be back, and he really did have work to do. Maybe next time she came for the week-end he would slyly suggest she bring her work with her, just in case. Maybe he could clear out some space for her to keep some clothes there. Then he could sell her on the idea of weeknight sleepovers.

He zipped a sweatshirt up over his still-damp chest and plopped down on the couch with his laptop, flicking on the television for company.

Before he could even open the spreadsheet he'd been working on, his phone rang. He reached for it, knowing it was one of two Pierce women calling for their weekend check-in.

"Hello, Katherine," he said, seeing his sister's name.

"Hey, Dill Pickle."

He pushed his work aside and leaned back on the couch. "You are absolute shit at nicknames. You know this, right?"

"Yeah, they always were your thing, but you still couldn't come up with one for me."

He shrugged. "It's not my fault Mom gave you the most boring name in the world."

"Excuses."

"What's up?"

"I have good news. Kevin and I are going to drive down for Mom's birthday dinner."

He sat up straight, his throat going dry. "I thought Kev was out of town."

"His trip got canceled and I've missed the last

two years. His parents are going to watch the kids, so we can make it."

"Oh." The back of his neck started to sweat. This wasn't good.

"You sound disappointed."

To see his sister? No. But he'd invited Dani to that dinner and it was about to become an entirely different thing. In the seventeen years since he'd left home, he'd *never* introduced Katie to a woman he was seeing. Showing up with a date to dinner would make his mother's day but he could easily play it off. She'd deluded herself into thinking he wasn't settling down because he was still sowing wild oats at thirty-five. Not because he was terrified of becoming one or both of his parents. But Katie would see right through him. His palms were already damp just thinking about the interrogation, the analysis, what Katie would think this means.

He wasn't about to try to explain it to Katie before he knew himself. What he was trying to do with Dani was too new for that. And he really was trying. He wanted to be the person he was with Dani, but when it came down to it, he wasn't ready to own that out loud. Not to his sister who knew all too well how far he was reaching with a woman like Dani, and how likely he was to fail. It wasn't happening.

"I'm not disappointed," he said. "Not at all. But, ah, you sure? I know Fridays are tough.

You'll have to rush. I won't be offended if you want to set up a separate time with her."

"No, silly. I want to see you too. I need to make sure you're not turning all grey and wrinkled before you finally find a woman."

And there it was. "Yeah, well, you know I love to disappoint both you and Mom at the same time."

"Whatever. Besides, Kevin's mom is coming to our house to watch the kids and she retired in May. She doesn't mind what time we get back."

How convenient.

"Okay. Cool," he said. "I guess I'll see you then."

"Yeah… cool. I can tell you're excited."

"You know I love you, Katie Caboodle. I'll see you then."

Dylan tossed his phone onto the sofa and ran a hand over his face. He couldn't show up with Dani if Katie was going to be there. He just couldn't. He'd make it up to Dani. He'd take her somewhere even better another night, anywhere she wanted. But he had to get out of this.

"Oh no. That's terrible," Dani said into the Bluetooth speaker in her Mazda. She was on her way to pizza and ginger-ale with Cat when Dylan had called with the news that his mother had come down with conjunctivitis.

"Yeah," Dylan said. "Doctor said she'd be contagious for at least a week, so dinner is off."

Dani pouted, surprised at how disappointed she was. She shouldn't be. It was a meal with Dylan's mom. It was bound to be awkward, despite Dylan's insistence that it was no big deal. But for some reason, she'd been looking forward to the awkward. Awkward meant real and if Dylan was uncomfortable in the least, she would be able to tell, and then she'd know it was hard and he did it anyway. That was a meaningful choice. Healthy or not, she had planned to analyze the hell out of the entire interaction.

"Are you going to reschedule?"

"Um, maybe," he said. "She's got a pretty busy schedule."

"Oh."

"Are you on your way to see Cat?"

"I am."

"You could come back after," he said. "I'll wait up and give you dessert."

She could just picture his expression and she suppressed a smile. "Mmm. Tempting, but it's going to be late and I have to go into the office tomorrow."

"All right. I'll see you in a couple days. Have a good time, Dani-pie.

"Bye, Dylan." She clicked off the call feeling oddly deflated.

Thirty-three

AFTER ALL OF THE BACK and forth, the restaurant Dylan's mother had finally chosen was fancy enough to warrant a tie and he'd been tugging at it all afternoon. He wasn't sure if it was the silk or the lie he'd told that felt like a noose tightening every time he breathed.

"I think I'm going to have the prime rib," Irene said, folding her menu onto the table. Dylan shot a look at Katie which she returned. He was never sure if his mother did things like ordering his father's favorite food on purpose or if it was more of a well-hidden dysfunction, the kind she didn't even know she had.

"So tell us about work, Dylan." Katie's husband Kevin was a land developer, so their fields crossed paths from time to time.

"Work's good. Just closed a big deal that promises to lead to more." One that Dani had helped him win and he was repaying her by lying to her. He took a sip of his water and tugged on his tie again.

"Excellent. Things are looking bright."

Katie tipped her glass at him. "Now he just needs to meet a woman."

For fuck's sake. "You know, Katie, could we go one dinner without making it about me and my relationship status?"

"You mean your lack of?"

He sawed his teeth back and forth. Maybe he should just tell them, watch their heads explode. *Actually, I have a relationship. She's way out of my league and I think I might actually be in—*

His mental outburst was cut off by his mother poking his arm. "Dylan, isn't that Cat's friend? Danielle?"

He turned over his shoulder and he nearly choked on a bite of bread.

Dani was standing at the bar with the guy she worked with, Benji. Benji handed his credit card to the host and laughed at something Dani said.

No, no, no. This could not be happening. Why was Dani even in this part of town? A cold sweat sprung on his brow. Fuck. Did it even matter?

He glanced around for the restroom sign, considering making a break for it, but he knew he couldn't stop his mother from approaching her herself. Maybe he could cut Dani off at the bar, lie and say he was here on business, steer her back outside and pray she didn't see his family sitting there. For the first time, the thought of lying to a woman to avoid an awkward situation came with more than just a guilty conscience.

This was real fear—the kind you feel deep in your bones.

Because it wasn't just some woman. It was Dani. And he had way more to lose.

He remembered the way her lip had trembled that night in the water over her fight with Cat. How the sight of her hurt feelings had wrapped around his chest and squeezed until he felt physical pain. What would it be like to see that expression aimed at him? He couldn't take it.

Christ. His heart hammered in his chest, his brow cold and damp. He felt like he was going to hurl right there on the fancy white tablecloth.

"Are you going to say hi?" His mother swatted his arm. "Dylan, that's Danielle, right?"

"It's Danica," he said as he shoved his chair away from the table.

He made his way through a sea of tables, bumping into coats and chairs and mumbling apologies. She hadn't seen him yet. The vision of what her face would look like when she did stabbed at his ribs like a physical blow. Those pretty, always-red lips would part in surprise, then her eyes would pop. She'd give him that smile that she saved just for him, probably hug him hello. Then she'd realize.

She laughed at something Benji said, her head tipped back, her hair glowing like a halo under the light from the bar.

Angels singing. That was it. He finally knew

what that felt like, except he was sure he was about to get struck by lightning.

"Dylan?"

He swallowed hard as she spotted him, discreetly wiping at his temples. He was sweating like a pig now, his dress shirt stuck to his back.

"Hey, babe. What are you doing here?" He gave her a cool smile but didn't touch her, aware of his family's eyes on him. *Christ.* He couldn't decide which story he was protecting here.

His. He was only protecting himself.

Dani smiled and gestured to the bar. "Benji won us a big account today. We're getting cocktails to celebrate. What are you doing here?"

"Dani!" Irene waved frantically from her seat. "Yoohoo. Over here. Come."

Dani's face scrunched in confusion, and his throat tightened. Time screeched to a stop. She held a finger up to Benji and walked with wooden posture over to the table he'd just left, his empty seat still askew from where he'd bolted.

Dylan rushed to follow.

"Hi, Irene," Dani said, so calmly he thought maybe he was imagining the entire thing. "It's so nice to see you again."

"You too!" His mother looked back at the bar where Benji was gaping at them. "Is that your boyfriend? Bring him over."

Damn it, Mom. He felt like his knees might buckle.

Dylan watched the muscles in Dani's neck

as she swallowed. Her hands balled at her sides. "No." She finally met his eyes. Hers were wet, and he felt his stomach lurch. "I don't have a boyfriend."

The words stuck in his chest like a knife.

"And I'm sorry I can't stay. It was lovely running into you."

"Dani..." His throat squeezed around her name, sounding like a choke. He touched her wrist but she yanked it away and waved over her shoulder. A hole ripped right through his chest— he felt it as vividly as if his heart lay bleeding on the carpet.

"I'll be right back," he said to the table. Three confused faces nodded back at him and he rushed to the door Dani had just escaped through. She was half a block away and he picked up his pace, his heart stampeding.

"Dani. Wait."

He expected her to keep walking, but she spun on him, her eyes pure fire. "What the hell, Dylan?" He skidded to a stop in front of her, and she slammed a finger into his chest. "Why would you lie about this?"

He shoved his hand in his hair, his mouth dry. "I'm sorry, Dani. Really. I didn't mean to hurt your feelings."

"Hurt my feelings? You mean lie to my face? Make me look like an idiot?" She glanced over her shoulder at Benji who had mercifully tucked himself into an alcove. He was just out of hearing range, but close enough to be there if she needed him. Needed him to protect her. Protect her from him.

He hung his head as that realization tore through him. "I'm the idiot, Dani."

"That's a fact." Tears gathered in the corners of her eyes, and the sight twisted in his chest. "You really only care about yourself, don't you? I bought a dress, Dylan. I was excited about this for who knows why."

And there it was. The sharpest tip of his guilt started to calcify and crumble into indignance. Dani had put some hope on his shoulders that he didn't even know about. He'd told her this wasn't a big deal, but she'd made it one in her head. How was he supposed to be responsible for that? This was exactly why things like this always ended in someone getting disappointed. "Look, Dani. I'm sorry. I'm just no good at this."

"That's a cop-out, Dylan. Treating other people well isn't something you're good or bad at. It's a choice you make."

"So is trusting other people to make you happy." He felt his fingers curl into fists, that place that Dani had softened over the last six months turning back into a stone-cold wall. Maybe it was a choice or maybe he had something running through his veins that he just couldn't deny. God knows he'd tried this time and he'd still found a way to disappoint her. This was why he didn't try.

"Look," he said. "If you start pinning your happiness on other people, you're going to be severely disappointed. Buy a dress for you if you want one. I didn't ask you to do that."

"Yeah, well, thanks for the fucking life lesson." She sniffed loudly and blinked back the tears, not letting one fall. "I'll see you around, Dylan. Don't call."

She turned on her heel and his hand was on her wrist before he'd even made the choice. He didn't mean any of that. Why couldn't he *do* this? "Wait, Dani. Please? I'm sorry."

"Fuck off." She wrenched her arm out of his grip and took off down the sidewalk, her middle finger above her head.

Dylan watched her go, an ache ripping through his body. He felt frantic, his pulse thundered in his ears. His chest heaved with the urge to scream. He had to get himself together. He still had to go back in there and explain this all away to his family. *God damn it!* He wiped his hand down his face and spun on his heel.

And nearly crashed into his sister.

"Dylan?" Katie rubbed her arms against the chill. "Who was that?"

"No one." He wrapped an arm around his sister's shoulder. "Let's go back inside."

Katie looked past him down the sidewalk, but Dani was out of sight. "You sure you're okay?"

He forced his mouth into a grin, even though

he felt like his chest was caving in. "Of course," he said. "When am I not okay?"

Katie narrowed her eyes, but kept walking. If he could sell his sister, maybe he could sell himself.

"Screw you, Dylan Pierce!" Dani growled. Her knuckles blanched as she clutched the bathroom counter, staring at herself in the mirror. Benji had dropped her off at the curb. She'd assured him she was going to be fine and didn't need a babysitter, but he'd already sent her four texts since he'd left. She swiped the latest one away and used a washcloth to wipe away the trail of black mascara that stained her cheeks.

Screw Dylan for making her cry over him. Screw him for being so goddamn predictable. And yet, she really hadn't seen it coming. She'd believed him, believed *in* him. People had layers, like Cat had said. She'd been pulling his back without even thinking, and he let her. She thought she'd found something special the deeper she went, but she had worse judgment than she thought.

Another sob darted up her windpipe but she bit it off. Instead of dissipating, it expanded in her chest, aching and trembling until she let it out. This always happened with the men she dated. Things started out great—chemistry, fun—then reality hit. The slap in the face that reminded her that when it came to a deeper connection, she didn't get that. It was the same thing with Dylan, she just hadn't realized it was happening because it stretched out for months. Months! When was the last time she gave a guy months to break her heart? She'd been pulled into some spell by the idea of soulmates and perfect matches and all that bullshit, but maybe that wasn't in the cards for her after all.

Her knees buckled and she lowered herself to the floor, bawling. She stayed there for what seemed like hours, sobbing and wiping at her nose until finally her breath steadied.

She rinsed off the rest of her makeup and pulled her hair up into a ponytail. She'd already changed into her pajamas and there was a pint of ice cream with her name on it, but she was done crying. Screw Dylan and his smug face and stupid green eyes and every goddamned sweet thing he'd ever lied. She'd cop to having trusted him when she shouldn't have, but she wasn't blaming herself for this mess. They were friends. That was why this was supposed to work, but friends didn't do this to each other. They didn't lie to each other's faces—humiliate each other in front of a room full of people. And they certainly didn't pretend to be falling for one another.

No. She and Dylan weren't friends. They weren't anything at all.

Thirty-four

"**H**OW ARE YOU?" CAT ASKED, pulling Dani into a tight hug. Well, as tight as she could with the little bowling ball between them.

Dani kissed her fingertips then pressed them to Cat's belly. After she'd finished her ice cream last weekend, she'd broken down and called Cat, telling her the whole story. At least Cat wouldn't give her an "I told you so." She'd believed Dylan too.

"I'm fine," she said. "And I don't want to talk about it."

Cat rolled her eyes. "Do you really think that's smart?"

"I do actually. Aren't you freezing?"

The sky spit barely-there snowflakes as they walked down the sidewalk to the shopping area, but instead of boots and a coat, Cat had on a cropped cardigan and ballet flats.

Cat tossed her dark ponytail over her shoulder. "I'm actually in a constant flop sweat. It's really attractive. And my winter coat wouldn't zip, anyway. I've been wearing one of Josh's coats, but I'm already sick of looking like a troll. Thanks for coming shopping with me."

"You have an excuse to buy a whole new wardrobe! Of course I'm here."

"You just think it's fun because it's not your pants that won't button. And don't change the subject. Are you really okay?"

"Of course. It wasn't a big deal to begin with, so no sense in crying over spilled milk." Her throat tightened around the words, but she tried to make herself feel them, tried to make herself forget that her eyes were bloodshot and her throat was hoarse from crying for forty-eight hours straight. God, she was such a liar.

And Cat was having none of it. "Dani. It's okay if you're upset. I'm upset. He came over to see Josh yesterday and I couldn't even look at him."

Dani's shoulders fell. "Look, thanks for the second-hand anger, Cat. I really do appreciate it. But Dylan wasn't going to change and I learned that pretty early on. I should be relieved." That was her mantra and she was sticking to it. Even if she had to cry it into her pillow for a little while longer.

She opened the door to the baby store and tugged on Cat's arm. "Now please, let's stop talking about Dylan because this is much more fun."

"Okay," Cat relented.

"Oh my God. Look at this!" Dani lifted a pair

of grey knit booties the size of her palm and squealed. "How do they even make them this small?"

Cat took them from her and her eyes started to mist.

"Don't cry. But definitely buy these."

"Okay." She tossed them in her shopping basket. "But we're supposed to be looking at maternity clothes. I can't buy all the baby stuff yet."

Dani ignored her, plucking a little pink tutu off of a hanger. "When are you going to find out the sex?"

"We're not, actually."

Dani scrunched her nose. "What? How will you plan?"

"Thank you!" Cat exclaimed. "You get it! It was Josh's idea, but you know I can't stand uncertainty."

"You're a saint to agree to that."

"I've been kind of a brat. It's the least I could do."

"You've also been sick as a dog. You've earned one of those little gender reveal party things. Emma could plan the hell out of that."

"True. But I promised. And it was a rough few months, but things are back to normal." She looked down at her round belly. "Well, as normal as they can be."

It seemed nothing was normal anymore. And just when Dani was starting to get used to the new version.

"Come on. Let's find you some clothes. Maybe we can find some maternity lingerie." She winked and watched Cat's cheeks flush pink.

"Let's start with elastic waist pants."

An hour later, Cat had enough empire waist dresses for a full week of work and a new winter coat. She also had the grey booties Dani had picked out and two sets of footed pajamas—neutral green—with tiny ducks on them.

"Where are we eating? Any particular cravings?"

Cat shook her head and looked at her phone as they walked. "Can we stop into Josh's office on the way? I want to show him the booties."

Dani froze, a wave of anxiety washing over her.

"Dylan isn't there," Cat said. "I checked."

Great. Now she had to call ahead before she went places. Dani supposed this was the kind of awkwardness they'd been risking when they decided to give this a go. They'd always known whatever fall out came from this would be on display for the entire group to witness and she wasn't about to let Dylan keep her from going to certain places, seeing certain people. "Fine," she said. "Let's go show Josh the baby booties."

Rideout and Pierce Architecture was on the seventh floor of a narrow row house turned office

348

building. The other businesses on site included a social media start-up, a realtor, and a private practice psychologist that Dani considered taking a detour toward on the way up. She could stand a clinical analysis after this Dylan debacle.

Dylan and Josh's office space in the city was barely big enough for the third desk they'd added when they hired the new guy, but they really only needed the address. They both worked from home the majority of the time. In order to expand, though, they'd wanted the downtown location on their business cards and the ability to entertain clients in a more central location. Dylan had explained the entire five-year projection to her one night over drinks. She tried not to let that memory stick while she took in the space for the first time.

Cat stepped off the elevator and Josh spotted them through the glass door, jumping up to open it for them. "Hey." He kissed Cat on the forehead, then gave Dani a smile that dripped with guilt by association.

"Don't look at me like that," she said, reaching up to give him a hug. He smelled vaguely of sunscreen, the way Dylan always did even under his expensive cologne, and she pulled away, angry at herself for the way her stomach tightened painfully.

"No look," he said, his hands up in surrender. "What are you two up to?"

Cat stepped into his side, smiling up at him.

"I took a long lunch to buy some new clothes," she said. "Dani helped me."

"I sure did. Wait until you see the lacy little maternity nighty I picked out for her."

Cat's eyes went wide. "Dani!"

"Dani. Hey."

Dani spun around to see Ryan Tucci leaning in the doorway of the office across the hall. He had a stack of folders tucked under his arm, standing there in his fashionably fitted dress shirt and tie. Her belly fluttered in remembrance of their romantic date, right before Dylan had shown up to Cat's with Cassidy and tricked her into thinking he gave a damn.

"Hey," she said. He stepped in to hug her, his solid arms squeezing her shoulders.

"It's good to see you again."

"You too," she said, hoping her face wasn't bright red. "Do you work here?"

"I do. My office is upstairs." He shifted the folders he was holding under his arm and took a sip of his paper to-go cup of coffee. "Can we talk?"

"Of course." She waved Cat and Josh along and they disappeared into his office. Ryan led her to a bench beside a window looking out over the city, and she smoothed her damp palms on her jeans. "How's city life treating you these days?"

He smiled, clearly pleased that she remembered he was new here. "I'm finally getting the hang of it, just in time for the snow."

"Are you going home for Thanksgiving?"

"I am. For a week, actually. Things slow to a stop around the holiday and I haven't seen my parents in months."

She nodded, suddenly nervous as the small talk went on. "Well, here's hoping for good weather."

"Thanks. Hey, can I ask you something?"

"Shoot."

Ryan rubbed at the back of his neck and dipped his head nervously. "I wanted to contact you again after our date," he said. "But I was out of town for awhile for work, and then when I came back, I saw you'd deleted your profile."

Dani's cheeks warmed remembering lying in bed, Dylan's scent still on her skin, his obnoxious singing coming from her shower as she'd hit that little delete button, officially retiring the soulmate search. God, she was an idiot. "Right," she said. "You know, it was just bad timing. I had some things come up."

"So it wasn't because you didn't want me to contact you again?"

"No! Not at all. Um. I mean, kind of. I started dating someone, and I didn't think it would be appropriate to keep my profile. Anyway, it didn't work out. I actually put it back up a couple of days ago."

"Oh." He grinned. "So, what happens now? Do you start all over? Eight more dates?"

Dani laughed. "I have no idea. I kind of did

it on a whim." Another memory nudged her. A bottle of wine, her credit card, the *unfollow* button on Dylan's Instagram. "Maybe more like a fit."

His smile tipped knowingly. "I get it. What do you say I take you out again then? Before you find out if it's against the rules."

"That sounds great."

"I have these tickets to a river cruise this Friday—there's a live band, fireworks. You probably have plans, but..."

"I don't have plans." She was supposed to be at the Jansen fundraiser this Friday, sharing an expensive meal with Dylan and Josh and Cat. She'd been racking her brain to come up with an equally extravagant night to distract her from where she was supposed to be. Hopefully, she'd just found it.

"Would you like to go with me?"

"I'd love to."

"Love to what?" Cat asked, appearing back in the hallway.

"Ryan invited me on a river cruise this weekend."

"Oh." Cat's mouth dropped open, but she thought better of whatever she was going to say and pivoted. "That's great. You've been wanting to do that."

"I have."

Ryan smiled, his decidedly not-green eyes twinkling.

"We should go eat before we have to get back," Cat said. Her tone was full of "we'll talk about this later" but for once she bit her tongue.

"I'll call you then," Ryan said.

"Great."

Cat tugged on her arm, and Dani let herself be pulled toward the elevator.

"Who's the librarian gym rat?" she asked.

Dani laughed. It was *so* good to have her back. "That was Ryan. One of my pre-Dylan dates from the website."

Cat scrunched her nose.

"What?"

"Did you know he worked in this building? Don't you think that's kind of awkward? What if he and Dylan know each other?"

"Yeah, well, this thing has already made awkward an understatement. Besides, if it wasn't for Dylan and his piss-poor attempt at being an adult, maybe Ryan and I would have done this a long time ago. It's not fair that I should have to ruin that chance when Dylan and I barely had a thing." Her voice caught, but she cleared her throat to hide it. "I need to move on."

Cat's brow creased. "I understand that. I do. But I don't think he thought of it that way. He was completely the asshole here, but I don't think Dylan thinks what you had was barely a thing."

Dani's chest felt that familiar tightness. It traveled up her neck and tingled at the back of her throat. It didn't matter what was or wasn't. Dylan made his bed. Now she was moving on to Ryan's. "Well, I do."

"Okay," Cat said. "Whatever you need to do, I support you. Listen, Josh is going out of town soon for a conference he's presenting. Maybe we can get Sonya and Emma together and do something fun."

"Oh! Movies and pizza?"

"Uh...*yes!*"

Dani smiled, curbing the urge to smother Cat with a huge bear hug. Her love life might be a disaster, but she had the best friends in the world.

Thirty-five

APPARENTLY CAT WASN'T SPEAKING TO Dylan either.

Dylan climbed out of the back of Josh's new Grand Cherokee—the baby-friendly version of his old ride—and Josh handed the keys to the valet. Cat hadn't said a word since they'd left the island, making for an extremely uncomfortable hour ride into the city, now she had her back turned to him while she waited for Josh.

Dylan opened the door for her, and she brushed past him without even looking.

She looked so innocent in her little black maternity dress, her hair in one of those buns ballerinas wear. With her flat shoes, she barely made it past his shoulder, but Cat could shoot daggers just like Dani, and right now, Dylan was dodging them all around.

Josh patted his shoulder and gave Dylan a *she'll come around* look as they entered behind her.

"Dylan!" Mrs. Jansen spotted him immediately, waving a heavily-ringed hand across the lobby. Her heels clunked on the floor as she came to greet them. "And Josh. So good to see you both." She turned to Cat after dousing them both with perfumed air kisses. "And who's this?"

"This is my wife, Catia," Josh said. "Cat, this is Mrs. Jansen."

"How lovely to meet you," Mrs. Jansen said. Her eyes dropped to the basketball Cat had grown over the last few weeks. "And a future Rideout, I see."

"Yes, ma'am," Josh said, smiling at Cat's face.

Mrs. Jansen looked like she was going to cry as she clutched the actual pearls she wore. *For fuck's sake.*

Behind his annoyance, though, was a pain he hadn't felt since he was a kid—the kind that comes from wanting something you can't have. This... this optimism. He'd felt it with Dani, and then like a kid's balloon, it had popped. Now what was he in for? What was the future of Pierce? Dylan, old and grey-haired, running the business with Josh's brood of offspring after Josh took off with Cat to some retirement paradise? He'd keep working because what else was he going to do? He'd be alone. Maybe he'd take a couple weeks vacation a year and travel. Alone. Or maybe he'd pick up some old person hobby... alone.

He'd play favorite uncle to Shawn and Josh's kids. Mattie loved him. Josh and Cat's kids would be the same. Unless Cat still wasn't speaking to him ten years from now. What if they had an army of mini-Cats to hate him? Josh would eventually be overpowered and he'd hate Dylan too. Whatever guy Dani ended up with would be their new favorite uncle, while Dylan clung to what? Freedom? Whatever it was, he'd get it alone.

He needed a fucking drink.

"Dylan, love, where's Dani tonight?" Mrs. Jansen turned her sights on him now and his stomach lurched. Hadn't he come up with a cover story for this? He couldn't remember it for the life of him. All three sets of eyes bore into his face and he opened his mouth to reply. "Ah..." was all that came out.

"She had another commitment," Cat said. It was half save, half dig as she emphasized the word commitment like it was in a foreign language.

Mrs. Jansen smiled and patted Dylan's arm. "Too bad. I was looking forward to seeing her again. You all must be so close," she said to Cat. "With Dylan and Josh being business partners."

"Yes," Cat said. "We're very close. Dani and I have actually known each other since we were kids. Long before we met these two. She's my best friend in the world." Another dagger flew by his head.

"Oh, what an interesting story! You'll have to tell me all about it over dinner."

"Of course."

With the pleasantries over, Josh launched into Twenty Questions regarding the project timeline and vision. Josh was playing both parts tonight with Dylan having forgotten everything he was there to do and anything he might have to say. He'd have to thank Josh later.

He was still spacing out thinking about his future of solitude when Cat placed her hand on the inside of his arm.

He looked down at her red fingernails digging into his jacket, then at her face. It wasn't smiling. "Can we dance?" she asked, tightening her grip.

"Um." Dylan glanced at Josh who seemed to have the job conversation under control. "Is this a trick?"

"It's not a trick."

"Okay."

Cat brushed her fingers over Josh's chest and they had one of their silent conversations, then she linked her arm through Dylan's and tugged him toward the ballroom.

There were a handful of people dancing. The gold and white tiles of the dance floor were glitzy and over the top and everyone around them had a look of elation on their faces like they were extras in a movie.

He took Cat's hand, letting her settle into his arms. He was thankful for the distance her pregnant belly forced them, as he had a nagging fear she just wanted to get him close enough to kick him in the balls. "You look adorable, Kit Cat," he said. He meant it, even if he had a motive. The color had returned to her cheeks and her belly was a perfectly round little bump.

"Don't flatter me, Dylan. I'm mad as hell at you."

So it *was* a trick. "Okay."

"Just explain something to me," she said. "Why Dani? Why my best friend?"

Dylan let out a sigh. "Cat—"

"I mean you could have picked anyone else to practice being in a relationship."

He huffed. "I've had other relationships. Monogamous ones."

"Monogamous doesn't mean committed. Monogamous means you're not fucking anyone else at the moment. Committed means you don't want to."

"I didn't want to," he pleaded. "I wasn't. I'm not now. It was never about anyone else."

Cat narrowed her eyes, making the dark freckles on her cheeks pop. She looked like a terrifying little doll. "I went to bat for you," she said. "Sonya was all: 'Dylan will never change', but I stuck up for you. I said you could." She poked her finger into his chest and Dylan glanced around, wondering if the other guests were watching. He did actually have to be professional here. "Dani believed you were better than what you show the rest of the world. I believed it too."

That one hit its mark. His shoulders sagged,

and Cat pulled her hand away from his chest and pressed it to her belly, a grimace crossing her face.

"You all right?"

"Yes." She looked over her shoulder at Josh. "I need to eat something, and I'm very, very mad."

"If I take you over to the hors d'oeuvres, can we knock it down to just one very?"

"Dylan—" She took a deep breath through her nose, and her face softened as she let it back out. "We can take it down to one very. I think you should call her."

Dylan steered Cat toward one of the waiters, and Cat used his hand as a plate, arranging canapes on a napkin on his flattened palm. "I left her a voicemail last week," he said. "It wasn't the first."

"You did?" Cat's eyes popped in surprise, but she quickly recovered. "Well, I'm sure she'll consider whatever you had to say. I hope it was good."

Cat had turned on her lawyer voice, and his sounded unsteady in comparison. "She hasn't called back, or answered any of my texts."

Cat chewed a bite-sized cracker and went back for more. "I'm not sure she will, Dylan. Dani is stubborn. But..." She sighed and patted his chest. "You are too, I suppose. If you could get on the same page, I think you'd make a great match. You could be stubborn for each other. Hey, baby."

Josh appeared at Cat's shoulder and plucked a bacon-wrapped scallop from Dylan's hand. He pretended to eat it but held it to Cat's mouth at the last minute. She giggled, batting her eyes. Instead of the vague sense of nausea Dylan usually got when he witnesses those little moments, his chest felt tight with longing. The entire world had flipped.

"Everything okay over here?" Josh asked, his gaze bouncing back and forth.

Dylan handed Josh Cat's napkin-plate and leaned over to kiss the top of Cat's head. "Everything is fine. I'm going to get some air."

He left them on the dance floor and crossed the marble floor to a set of patio doors. The frosty air hit him in the chest but he was grateful for the pain of it. He'd been numb for weeks now, going about his days with nothing but a lingering sense of dread to prove he was still breathing.

Cat had been surprised to hear he'd been calling Dani. He saw the way she'd hesitated. She must have been under the impression that he'd given up, which meant Dani hadn't found his begging to be particularly important information in the story of them. Maybe because it wasn't. Maybe Dani didn't have any of that dread. He knew she'd signed back up for that dating app. One night, after a few too many beers, he'd entered his credit card number and made himself a profile before he'd even decided to do it. And he'd found her. His Dani, still searching for her soulmate.

He felt that tightening in his chest again. He'd had it—the thing he was envying. The genuine laughs, the secret looks. He'd had his own version, and he'd ruined it.

He pulled his phone from his jacket pocket, thinking about what he would say this time. He'd been riding on impulse since Dani left, unable to put together a rational plan of action. Texts in the early hours of the morning, slurred voicemails after he'd drank away his inhibitions. Like an insane person, he kept expecting a different outcome from repeating his actions, but this whole thing was out of his wheelhouse. He'd never cared about losing a woman before. He'd lost plenty, but when Dani had walked away he'd felt a desperation that scared the hell out of him. All his life he'd been worried about becoming his father, callous and cruel; or like his mother, foolish and pathetic. Now he was a combination of all of those things.

He dialed Dani's number again. He would say it again. He would say it a million times until she listened. Her voicemail picked up, like he knew it would, and he tightened his fingers around his phone to keep from chucking it.

"Hey, Dani. I'm standing out on the patio at this hotel, wearing a suit and holding a glass of champagne. It's like a fucking Gatsby party. You would love it." He paused, the back of his throat burning. "Anyway, I wish you were here. You were supposed to be my date for these things. Partners in crime. I know I fucked all of that up. I miss you, Dani-pie. Fuck, I don't think I've ever missed anyone. I know I screwed this all up. I know I did that. I just... I need another chance. Please call me back. I miss my friend."

"I can't believe I've lived in D.C. my whole life and I've never taken a river cruise." Dani sipped from a glass of champagne and looked out over the harbor lights rippling over the glassy water. She had to hold her pashmina closed to keep from shivering. Maybe she should have planned her first river cruise in the warmer months.

But Ryan stepped closer, running his hands down her arms, and the cold air turned romantic. "I can't believe I've lived here less than a year and I'm the first one to take you. I'm glad we could make this happen."

"Me too."

He lowered his voice, leaning into her ear. "Whoever it was that didn't work out, I hope he knows it's my gain."

Dani's throat tightened. It was supposed to be a compliment, but the place in her heart where Dylan had wrenched himself from was still so raw. "I'm not sure he does," she whispered. She tipped her head to see Ryan smiling down at her, and the understanding in his eyes made an ache flare in her chest—the one she'd been trying to ignore all night with reminders of how perfect Ryan was. The candle-lit dinner, the slow-dancing, the way he opened doors and pulled out chairs; he was checking all of the grown-up boxes and yet here she was longing for a beer and a dirty joke.

"Should we try and get higher for the fireworks?" Ryan nodded toward the upper deck and checked his watch.

"Let's."

With his hand on the small of her back, Dani climbed the boat's staircase, the wind winding around her bare legs. When she reached the top, the view caught her breath. Ryan's tie fluttered in the breeze and he reached out and pulled her shawl tighter around her shoulders. "Here's a spot," he said. They leaned against the cold metal railing and Dani breathed in the scent of the river. She felt Ryan's arm wrap around her shoulders. He smiled out at the night, looking handsome and content, but for some reason she couldn't bring herself to care.

What was wrong with her? This man was gorgeous and obviously into her. He was reliable, sweet, and looking for all of the same things she was, but when she drew a mental picture of her future, it wasn't him beside her at some stupid scary movie night Cat organized or one of Emma's Christmas and Cocktails events. Ryan was exactly who she'd been trying to find when she'd signed up for that website and yet...

She felt her clutch vibrate with an incoming message. It would be rude to check it, but she needed a distraction. "Sorry," she said. "Just give me a second."

Missed Call: Dylan

A bitter laugh bubbled in her chest, falling out of her mouth like a choking sound. "Fucking perfect," she muttered, touching a fingertip to the corner of her eye to keep it from leaking.

"Everything okay?"

Before she could answer, the sky erupted in color. A bit of spray from a bottle of champagne being popped misted the back of her arm. Ryan turned toward her, his hands landing on her cheeks. He smiled and he really was beautiful, blond hair and bright eyes, a smile that was all good intentions and reliability. When he kissed her she wanted so badly to melt, to flutter, to *something*. But instead the corners of her eyes burned and she had to clench them shut to keep from crying.

Thirty-six

FRIDAY AFTERNOON, DYLAN PULLED INTO his driveway just as the clock hit three p.m. His last appointment had canceled due to the snow that had been falling all day long, and with Josh gone to a conference all week, he'd worked enough to call a half-day good. He knew the trip was important if they wanted to push up their expansion plans, which seemed increasingly important with each inch Cat's stomach grew, but working side by side with the new guy was a testament to Dylan's strength of character if there ever was one. When he'd complained about it, though, Josh had shot back with the fact that he was leaving his pregnant wife alone for the week and Dylan's low tolerance for training employees was last on his list of give-a-shits.

Fine. Maybe he had a point. But either way, he'd earned a half-day. He scuffed the snow off his shoes and opened the door, dropping his laptop bag and coat in the foyer, then headed to the bedroom to change into jeans. He would make a snack, then catch up on emails in front of *Sportscenter*. Perfect Friday afternoon.

No. Perfect Friday afternoons were the ones he used to have. The ones he spent with Dani.

He piled some meat and cheese onto a bulky roll, slathered it with mayonnaise, and booted up his laptop. He was halfway through his meal when his phone rang. Hoping it wasn't Josh, or the new guy, or his mother, he fished the phone out of a pile of job packets he'd set on the couch and saw the name Kit Cat flash across his screen.

He sighed, rolling his shoulders for strength. After the dance they'd shared the weekend before, he'd thought he'd felt a little thaw, but Mrs. Jansen had extracted that story of Cat and Dani's childhood friendship at dinner. Telling it seemed to remind Cat how much she hated him, and she'd gone right back to Ice Queen Mode on the ride home. She was probably calling to give him another piece of her mind. Like he wasn't already torturing himself.

"What is it, Cat?" he asked, feeling preemptively annoyed.

"Hey, Dylan. Are you in town?" Her voice sounded weak, a little breathless, and he sat up straighter.

"I'm home. What's up?"

"I can't get a hold of Josh."

"Yeah, he probably won't have service until

he gets back to the hotel. The convention center is on the top of a damn mountain."

"I know, he told me." He heard what sounded like a shaky gasp. "I just... I'm having some pain and I think maybe I need to go to the hospital, and I really need to talk to him."

A cold chill slithered down Dylan's spine. Cat wasn't one to overreact. He'd deny it if anyone ever quoted him, but Cat might be the toughest chick he knew. If she said she was in pain, it was probably pretty bad. "Are you in labor?" he asked, praying she said no. This was way too early.

"I don't know."

Shit. Shit. Shit. He could tell it was an effort for her to answer him. This wasn't good. Josh would—

He didn't want to think about it. He needed to handle it.

"I'll be there in five minutes, okay?"

"Okay. Thank you."

He threw on a coat and boots and grabbed his car keys from the counter where he'd tossed them. Josh and Cat's house was right around the corner, but he still burned rubber the whole way there, skidding to an icy stop in their driveway.

The door was unlocked, but when he let himself in he didn't see her. "Cat?"

"I'm in here."

Dylan followed her voice toward the master bedroom and found her bent over the mattress, the duvet clutched in two tight fists. Her hair fell around her face, her brow damp. She was breathing heavily. The sight made his blood stop. *Shit.* He wasn't qualified for this. Maybe he should call Shawn and Minnie, Sonya, or even Dani. But by the looks of things, he should probably just get her to the hospital.

Cat breathed out through her teeth and relaxed back onto her heels, the pain seemingly subsiding. "Thank you for coming."

"Can you make it to my car?"

She nodded, and a few tears slid down her cheek. Dylan's pulse quickened, his mind going to the worst place.

"It's gonna be okay, Kit Cat." He put his arm out and she took it. "It's snowing. Where's your coat?"

"In the closet by the door."

Dylan got her things and kneeled to help her put on her boots, then he carefully led her down the snowy steps and into the passenger seat of his car.

"How long do you think it will be until Josh is back at his hotel?" she asked once he was on the road. She gripped the arm rest, her breathing coming in little spurts. Dylan stepped on the gas a little harder. *Please don't have a baby in the car, Cat. And please, whatever saint is in charge of these things, please don't let anything go wrong while Josh isn't here.*

"Let me make a couple calls," he said. "I know

some other guys that are there. Maybe one of them can find him, get him on the phone."

That seemed to soothe her. She bobbed her head in agreement, then went back to closing her eyes and breathing weird.

"It's going to be okay, Kit Cat."

It had to be.

The OB ward was waiting for Cat when they arrived. The nurses checked her in and got her changed into a gown. One of them talked her through the pain she was experiencing, typing everything she said into a computer. Dylan stepped just outside of the exam room to stare at his phone, close enough that he could hear her if she needed him, but alone so he could answer it the second Josh called.

The whole way there, Cat's face had wavered between terrified and the kind of exhaustion that comes from real pain. He was almost thankful Josh wasn't there. He didn't know how Josh would cope with seeing Cat like that. He wasn't coping so well himself.

"Dylan!"

He looked up from his phone to see Dani jogging down the hospital corridor in a red pea coat and boots, snow in her hair. His heart jumped to his throat. "Dani."

"Is she okay?" She stopped to catch her breath, her cheeks pink from the cold.

Dylan gestured over his shoulder to the exam room door. "She's in there."

"I was in a meeting. I just got her voicemail. Did you bring her here?"

"Yeah."

Dani nodded, then pushed through the door. He followed.

When Cat saw Dani, she burst into tears.

"Oh my God, Kit Cat. I'm so sorry I missed your call. Are you okay? Is Josh on his way?"

"I can't get a hold of him."

Dani reached around the spider web of wires hooked to Cat's belly and gathered her in a hug. Then she turned to Dylan. Both of their pleading eyes on him sent heat surging up his neck.

"I've got people on it," he said. He scraped a hand over his jaw, finding his skin clammy. He would handle it. He wouldn't let them down. He'd already let Dani down enough and Cat was the most important thing in the world to his best friend. He would take care of her.

"Dylan will get Josh on the phone," Dani said, the confidence in her tone pricking some dormant need for validation.

The doctor cleared her throat, and Dani tore her eyes away from Cat to listen. "So, I was explaining to Cat that she's experiencing preterm labor. She's thirty-one weeks which is too early for comfort in my opinion. We're going to try to stop your labor, but if we're unsuccessful, there's going to have to be some quick decisions made."

"I need to talk to Josh," Cat said again.

"It's okay, Cat," Dani said, smoothing her hair.

Dani shot Dylan a glance that was no hate and all commiseration, and the knots in his muscles loosened. He shouldn't take pleasure in the way it felt to meet her eyes again, to have her express confidence in him he wasn't sure he deserved. Given the circumstances, he shouldn't be happy about a forced moment with Dani, but after weeks of not speaking, he'd take what he could get.

The doctor was listing off some medications and their uses when Dylan's phone buzzed in his hand.

Finally. He held a finger up to Dani and stepped into the hallway to answer.

"Is she okay?" Josh asked as soon as Dylan connected the call.

"The doctor said she's in preterm labor. They're going to try to stop it. How soon can you get here?"

"I'm pulling out of the hotel now. Two hours max." He sounded like he was out of breath.

Dylan's heart was racing. He could *not* give Josh bad news over the phone if it came to that. He prayed to every saint his mother taught him that it wouldn't, but Josh needed to get here and he also needed to stay calm. "Okay. Listen, Josh, drive carefully. Everything is under control right now. Just trust me and get here safe."

"Dylan..."

"Trust me, man. It's under control."

"How are you doing, sweety?" Dani reached out to hold Cat's hand, listening to the monitors beep all around them. Cat's fingers were cold and clammy, and Dani pulled her chair closer and tucked the blanket around her belly.

Cat let out a breath that shook and shuddered. "I'm scared."

"I know. Josh will get back here, and everything will be just fine." The doctor had given Cat a cocktail of meds in her IV. With the pain easing, the adrenaline had deserted her, leaving her looking exhausted and emotionally wrecked.

"What if this is my punishment?" Cat whispered. She slipped a hand under the sheet and cradled her stomach, her already puffy eyes spilling again. "What if this is what I deserve?"

Dani's heart sank. "For what, Cat?"

"For not wanting this. For crying over it. For not celebrating the way I should have. I said it was a mistake." Her words trailed off into a sob and Dani's eyes burned.

"Cat. No."

"That was only a few months ago and now

the thought of not having her is ripping my heart out."

Dani climbed onto the bed and laid her head on the pillow beside Cat. "Priorities change really quickly sometimes. Sometimes you wake up one day and something you'd never even considered becomes a reality, and it feels like a smack in the face. It's okay to be sad that it didn't go the way you planned, and it's okay to admit you were wrong and that the new plan brings you a joy you hadn't expected."

Cat sniffed and rubbed her belly again. "She does bring me joy."

"Well, there you go. It doesn't matter if you planned her or fate gave you a little shove in the right direction. You love her just the same."

"I do."

"Wait!" Dani's head snapped up. "*She*? You know?"

Cat's pale, sweaty face actually pinked. "Yes," she admitted. "Don't be mad I didn't tell you. I was thinking about what you said, and at my last appointment, I asked the tech to tell me. Josh doesn't know."

"So I know something before Prince Charming?"

Cat chuckled through her tears. "Yup. Congratulations. It's our secret."

Dani clapped her hands together. She was happier than she should be in the current situation, but she never claimed to be magnanimous.

She moved her face to Cat's belly, whispering around the monitors. "Aunt Dani's going to spoil you rotten, little girl. But you have to stay in there a little longer, okay? I have too much shopping to do."

Cat smiled and leaned back into her pillow, finally letting her eyes close. "She's the luckiest little girl already. She has so many aunties and uncles."

Dani looked at the exam room door, still ajar from when Dylan had left for a coffee run.

So many people who loved her.

Thirty-seven

*C*AT WAS SNORING PEACEFULLY. WITH her contractions stopped, all of the commotion and pain must have finally caught up to her because she'd passed out hard.

Dani glanced at Dylan, stretched out in a too-small wooden chair, his boots on the rolling stool the doctor had used and his eyes closed. With things having calmed down for the moment, the awkwardness of seeing him began to seep back into the room. No. Awkward wasn't accurate. It hurt.

But she needed to focus on Cat now, not think about how Dylan's green eyes were red-rimmed. How he'd looked scared when she found him in the hallway. How she'd been scared too, and she'd wanted so badly to fall into his arms and let him hold her. Now, with Cat asleep and stable, she felt that urge again. She wanted one of his hugs—the slightly-too-tight kind. She wanted it so badly she could feel the ghost of it in her limbs. She wanted him to say something completely inappropriate and laugh away this tightness in her chest. She'd been surprised at how much comfort she'd taken in him when things weren't right with Cat, and a part of her still wanted to cross the room and curl up in his lap and have a good cry over the fact that her best friend was in the hospital. Maybe she was imagining it, but he looked like he could use it too.

They didn't do that anymore, though. He'd ruined it. That fact that she couldn't go to him now felt like a new wound. Like he was betraying her all over again.

"You can take off," she said, trying to sound indifferent. His presence was superfluous at this point. She was there now to watch over Cat. He could go back to whatever it was he was doing before breaking her heart again. "I'll stay with her until Josh gets here."

Dylan looked exhausted, his eyelids heavy as he slumped in the small chair, but his expression told her he had no intention of leaving. He tipped his head back and closed his eyes.

Maybe he thought he owed it to Josh to stay.

"She's in good hands, Dylan. It's not like you're leaving her alone."

"I'm not worried about Cat. The nurse said she was stable, and she's asleep." He looked like he was going to say something, then stopped himself and pivoted. "I just want to be here."

"Fine." They might have to share the room, but they didn't need to keep each other company. She pulled out her phone and found the group chat she'd been using to keep Sonya and Emma updated. It was an old one that didn't include Cat because they'd started it to plan her bachelorette party. Cat would kill them if she ever read through this exchange. Mostly she'd kill Dani. A different death for each time she'd brought up the idea of male strippers.

She held in a laugh as she read through the old messages, but it only had the effect of forcing fresh tears to burst from the corners of her eyes. She sniffed and wiped them away. Dylan opened his eyes again, looking at her like a lost little puppy, but she ignored it.

A new message from Sonya popped up. She and Emma had been waiting for an update. Dani told them Cat and the baby were fine, and she didn't even tell them that the baby was a girl because she was working hard on her self-control. It was the same reason she hadn't taken a picture of Cat snoring in her hospital gown.

She glanced at Cat again—her mouth was open and her hair was half out of her ponytail.

Okay, fine. Everyone was safe and she couldn't change who she was. She snapped a quick picture and sent it to the group chat.

Levity. If they didn't need it now, when did they?

Emma: Evil.

Sonya: Tell her we love her.

Dani: I promise.

Dylan's breathing had turned into a tiny snore and she watched his chest rise and fall. In addition to holding onto the baby detail, she also didn't mention that she was stuck in the room with Dylan because A) she really didn't need anymore checking in on her emotional state, and B) she didn't feel like giving him the credit he might deserve for taking care of Cat. They could hate him a little while longer.

Except they didn't hate him. Both Emma and Sonya had given her the "you knew what to expect, Dani" speech. Cat was the only one who had joined in her Screw You, Dylan Pierce party. But she supposed after today he was going to be back in her good graces.

An ache stirred in her chest. Maybe it should be enough for her good graces too. At least enough for her to drop the silent treatment. He'd really stepped up today, been that guy she knew he was. If it weren't for him, who knows what would have happened to Cat or the baby.

She stole another look at him. His thick eyelashes fluttering while he dozed, his mouth pulled into a frown. She racked her brain for something to say that would unfreeze the room but not sound too friendly. She was still trying out opening lines when the sound of dress shoes running on tile snagged her attention.

Dylan's eyes popped open and he sprung up

from his chair. He caught Josh with a hand to his chest as he barreled through the door. "Hey, man." Dylan put a finger to his lips to say be quiet, but Josh wasn't seeing him. He just stared at Cat, his eyes glassy. He didn't look like he was breathing in regular intervals.

What the hell?

"Josh?" Dani stood up, half afraid she was going to have to get the nurse for him. She'd never seen Josh anything but laid-back and smiling. This was weird.

Dylan took a step closer, grabbing him by the shoulders. "They gave Cat something to help her sleep. She's fine. Hey, you hear me, man?"

Josh was making her nervous, but whatever was going on with him, Dylan seemed to have anticipated it. Had he done this before?

"Josh. Look at me." Dylan tapped his fingers on Josh's cheek. "She's fine. The baby's fine. Okay?"

Josh nodded, finally meeting his eyes. "You're sure?" Josh's voice cracked, and a sob tried to rush out of Dani's mouth, but she clapped a hand over her lips.

"You're not losing anyone today, bro."

Josh's whole body seemed to loosen at that. His eyes rolled closed and he let Dylan wrap him in a hug. They stayed there for a minute, talking too low for her to hear. Dani watched them, fascinated by this dynamic, until finally Josh looked up and noticed she was there.

"Hey, Dani," he said, crossing the room to hug her. It was tight and shaky, and she clutched the back of his jacket.

"Hey, Joshy. Cat's going to be so happy to see you."

He ran his hand through his hair and sniffed. "Thank you for being here."

"Of course."

As soon as she let him go, Josh shrugged off his jacket and crossed the room, climbing onto the edge of Cat's bed.

Dylan watched him, his feet planted and his arms folded across his chest like a soldier on guard until Josh, carefully avoiding the monitors on her belly, wrapped his arms around Cat and pressed his face into her hair.

Only then did Dylan gather his coat and head for the door. Dani followed him out of the room in silence and when the door shut behind them, she told herself to just keep walking, but the image of Dylan talking Josh down like that was too jarring to ignore.

"Hey," she said as Dylan zipped his fleece jacket.

He looked at her in askance, his face tired and a little sad.

"Is that why you wanted to stay? You knew he was freaking out?"

Dylan looked away and ran a hand over the scruff on his chin. He seemed uncomfortable with the subject, but he blew out a breath and spoke in a half-whisper. "Josh wasn't home when his parents died. He was away at a friend's house. He found out the next day." Dylan rubbed at the corner of his eye, then gave her his full gaze, his eyes hard. "He and I were out of town on a ski trip senior year in college when he got the call about his grandfather passing. You get what I'm saying?"

She nodded, swallowing hard.

"I've only seen him like that once, but I had a hunch, with the similarities, he wasn't going to deal with it well. I wanted to be here just in case."

She'd only heard a brief rundown of Josh's past from Cat. These extra details made her throat tight. She used to wonder why Josh and Dylan were so close—Josh being the mature one, the trustworthy one, the one who had his shit together. She'd come to realize Dylan had that in him too.

But what started out as a thawing between them, suddenly calcified and pricked at her brain. "So much for your 'you can't count on other people' excuse," she said.

His forehead scrunched. "What?"

"Josh can count on you. Maybe it was just me. Either way, you'll just have to come up with another one, because that one is obviously bullshit. "

Dylan winced then nodded, turning away.

"Wait," she said, touching his sleeve. "Dylan.

Listen, I know you were helping Josh out, but Cat's my best friend, so thank you for taking care of her."

"I didn't just do it for Josh. I love Kit Cat."

Her face softened into a smile. "Everybody does."

"Yeah."

"And everybody loves you too."

"Not everybody."

She dropped her eyes to the green and white tiled floor, scuffing her winter boot. What could she say to that? She'd tried. She'd wanted to.

When Dylan spoke again his voice was raw. "Seeing them just now, it made me think about a lot of stuff, Dani. Josh would do anything to get back here. To be where Cat needed him. I always thought of it as a huge ask—being responsible for someone like that. But maybe when it's the right person, it's not that hard." His voice dropped to a whisper and his eyes were pleading. "I can do better, Dani."

"Dylan—"

She took a step back, but he followed. "Wait, Dani, please. Can we just talk?"

"I'm sorry. I can't. I have to go." She buttoned her own coat, ignoring the way his face was lined in pain. She wasn't here to do this with him. What could he possibly say to erase what she'd seen with her own eyes? He'd lied once before, and she wasn't going to stand here outside of her friend's hospital room and listen to it again.

But before she walked away she needed him to know something. "You were really good today, Dylan. You're better than you think you are."

His shoulders fell and he nodded. "Thanks, Dani-pie."

Thirty-eight

"**O**KAY. SERIOUSLY, JOSH, GO!" DANI kicked the back of Josh's leg as he stood by Cat's bedside, fussing over her, *still.* He'd had his coat on and had been "headed out the door" for the last fifteen minutes.

Cat had been ordered to bed rest, and Josh hadn't left her side for two weeks. She'd stopped by twice with freezer meals from Sonya and Emma (since she didn't cook, she'd offered to deliver) and both times she'd found him with his computer and job packets spread out over their bed while Cat slept beside him. He had a whole office on the second floor of their house, but after hearing Dylan's story, she was less inclined to roll her eyes at him.

Today he had a meeting he couldn't get out of, though. Dani had taken the day off to hang with her, but even so, she could tell Josh was nervous to leave the house. She hip-checked him out of the way and plopped down on the bed beside Cat with a pint of ice cream and two spoons.

"I got this," she told him sincerely. "Now please leave so we can talk about you."

"Okay," he said, his hands up in surrender. "Call me if you need *anything*." He leaned over her to kiss Cat one more time, then patted Dani on the head. "Thank you."

"You're very welcome, see ya, bye."

"Bye, baby," Cat said. The two of them shared some obnoxious silent eye conversation, and then he left.

"Finally," Dani said.

"Shut up. Give me a spoon." She handed one over and Cat took a huge bite of mint chocolate chip. "So what's new? I'm bored out of my mind here. Got any gossip?"

"Ha. I wish. Unless you count Emma's new pots and pans set and Sonya's real estate woes. Everyone is so boring now."

"What about Ryan?"

Dani shrugged, hesitant to admit that, despite their near-perfect date, she hadn't had any desire to see Ryan again. Every memory she had of him was tied up with one of Dylan. It was completely unfair that Dylan had to go and ruin that too, but there it was.

"Nothing new there," she said safely. "I'm starting over with eight new dates. The first one is tonight."

Cat shoved another spoonful of ice cream in her mouth, giving Dani one of her meaningfully silent replies.

Dani rolled her eyes. "Use your words, Cat."

"What about Dylan?"

Well, that couldn't have been more blunt. "What about him?"

"I'm just wondering why you're willing to give the dating app another chance but not him?"

Dani pulled the ice cream container back and scooped her own bite. "Mostly because the app never lied to my face about wanting a relationship."

Cat sighed. "Dani."

"What? I thought you were on my side."

"I am! But maybe taking sides at all was premature."

Dani jammed the spoon into the ice cream and picked at a loose string on her jeans. The only explanation for Cat's change of heart toward Dylan was the last one she wanted to hear. "Because he's Josh's best friend, right?"

"No," Cat said firmly. "Because you're *my* best friend. And because I know a thing or two about misunderstandings and making bad choices with good intentions."

That was true. It was easy to forget with the way they were now, but Cat had messed up big time once with Josh. Maybe even more than Dylan had. But Dani wasn't Josh. She didn't forgive and forget so easily.

"Look, Dani," Cat said. "When I first met Josh, I was scared and I was stupid. It took breaking my own heart to finally understand what was at stake. I guess I just see the same fear in Dylan. Sometimes we tell ourselves we don't want certain things because we're afraid we can't have them."

Dani's throat was tight again. Cat was lucky she was stuck in this room because this was the kind of conversation that usually had Dani frantically looking for an escape hatch. She'd done all of the deep emotional analysis she was going to do over Dylan. She'd gotten a little attention and mistaken it for something it wasn't. End of story. It was the Catch 22 Benji had warned her about. Her repeated downfall. "It's not the same," she said.

"How is it not?"

"Because you fought for Josh. Dylan has sent me a total of two *drunken* voicemails and some texts. That's not exactly a committed approach to wanting a second chance."

Cat shrugged, going back for more ice cream. "He has no idea what he's doing, Dani. He has a lot of growing up to do, but that's part of why he's so fun. Dylan is the kind of guy who will stay out all night partying with you while I'm changing diapers and Emma is redesigning her kitchen again."

"But that's just it, Cat. I want more than that. Maybe not right now, but someday I'd like to have diapers and kitchens of my own."

"And you don't think Dylan does?"

Maybe I do want that. He'd said he did, but how could she trust anything he said now?

As crazy as it would have sounded to her six months ago, she and Dylan could have been great together. They may have arrived there via different routes, but what they wanted out of life was nearly identical. Not to mention their chemistry. He'd hit every one of her buttons on practically the first try, and then, slowly, when she'd felt like everyone who knew her best had moved to another planet, he'd shown her how great their friendship could be. That had turned to an intimacy she rarely experienced with men, filled with vulnerable moments that felt like revelations. But he had to go and ruin everything by being... him.

"I don't know, Cat," Dani said, forcing her voice to stay steady. "I don't know if he's capable of it, whether he wants it or not."

Dylan let himself into Josh's house, scraping the snow off of his boots before going to the kitchen and pulling out a casserole that Emma had made. He checked his phone for the instructions Josh had sent him, then heated the oven. After he'd set a timer, he walked down the hall on his toes, hoping not to wake Cat.

Josh was tied up in a meeting that ran late, and he'd asked Dylan to check on her on his way home to make sure she didn't have to get up to make dinner; and to make sure she ate it or to make her something else; and to check the temperature of the house and light a fire if it was too cold. It was a whole list. Cat was allowed to get out of bed for short periods of time, but he wasn't about to remind Josh of that. Besides, he was pretty desperate to get back in everyone's good graces.

"Kit Cat?" He tapped on her bedroom door.

"Hey, Dylan." Cat sat up and rubbed her eyes like she'd been fast asleep, despite it being five-thirty in the evening. Sympathy rippled through him. It must be lonely and mind-numbing to be stuck in this room all day. "Did Josh send you to check on me?"

"I offered. He's going to be late tonight."

"I know. He called. I'm sorry you had to go out of your way."

Dylan flipped on the lamp on her bedside table and took Cat's water glass to the bathroom, refilling it with fresh water. "It's right on my way, actually," he said. He tried a smile to put her mind at ease, but his heart wasn't in it.

Cat took a long drink of the water. "How are you doing?"

"I think I'm supposed to ask you that."

"I'm fine as long as I'm laying in this bed. You're the one who's still walking around looking like your dog ran away."

He ignored that, moving to close the curtains

on her bedroom window. "I put some dinner on for you. It should only be a few minutes."

"Thank you. You didn't have to do that."

The meekness of her voice weighed his shoulders even heavier, like she'd all but given up on him. "Cat, look. I know I messed up with Dani, and I know it's a lot to ask, but can you and I get back to cool? Please? I'm running low on friends at the moment."

Cat pulled a long breath through her nose, then pointed across the room to her dresser. "Can you get me that hair elastic?"

He found it and handed it to her, waiting while she gathered her mess of dark hair on the top of her head.

She patted the bed beside her and he fell heavily on top of the duvet, his muscles sighing in relief. She was right. He *was* walking around like his dog had run away and it was exhausting.

"I want us to be cool too, Dylan. But why didn't you think about this before you broke my best friend's heart?"

"I didn't mean to."

"But you did."

If only he had the balls to admit he'd broken his own heart too. "Cat. You have to believe I didn't want this. I *don't* want this."

"I do believe that, but she's so *sad*, Dylan."

His heart cracked again and he could barely get his voice to work. "I joined the site. Eight Dates or whatever. I tried to answer every question the way I thought Dani would so it would match us, but it's been weeks and nothing. I know she's moving on."

"Oh, Dylan."

"She won't even talk to me."

Cat was quiet for so long, he thought maybe she'd fallen back to sleep. Finally she whispered, "Do you love her?"

"Cat…"

"Do you? Yes or no?"

"I don't know what that means, Cat. What it feels like. I've never even been close."

Cat frowned. Either she felt bad for him or she knew he was full of shit.

"I know I miss her," he said. "I know I'm happier when she's in the room."

She sighed, pushing herself up against the pillow. "Okay then," she said. "Think about the worst thing that's ever happened to you."

"What?"

"Just do it. Put yourself in the memory and feel it."

Dylan didn't know where Cat was going with this, but he was willing to try anything if it helped him figure out what to say to get Dani back. He closed his eyes again and sat on the old brown couch in the den of his childhood home. The buttons of his father's plaid shirt strained against his middle, round from indulgence, and his stringy, sparse hair fell over his eyes as he stormed around the house, shouting—something about being done with them, with all of it. All of what, Dylan had always wondered. What was it he ever gave any of them in the first place?

Dylan's mother was crying at the kitchen table. He felt like crying, salt burning the corners of his eyes, his forehead damp with the exertion of holding it in, but he wouldn't let himself be weak like her.

"You're on your own, kid."

"What about it?" he asked now, the memory squeezing his throat until his voice sounded like sandpaper.

"When you think about that moment, who do you wish was there to hold your hand? Who do you want to tell about that moment and let them hold you and tell you it's going to be okay?"

Dylan's vision went blurry and a bitter acid burned at the back of his throat. He visited that memory often, using it like kindling to stoke whatever fire he needed at the moment. Sympathy to deal with his mother. Motivation to succeed in his work. But he never let himself feel it fully, never went all the way there. He brought a hand to his hairline and scrubbed it back and forth over his brow, then let his head drop to Cat's shoulder. There was only one person he'd ever told about that moment. Not even Josh or Shawn. He'd held Dani's warm, naked body, and spilled like a geyser from the deepest part of himself. But there were other parts he still wasn't sure he could ever give. The part where he was desperately afraid of being that man in the plaid shirt, disappointing everyone who ever trusted him. But he was also afraid of being his mother. Loving someone so much it made you a fool.

"I don't know if I can do it," he said. His voice sounded like an old rusty hinge. "Love, marriage. All that soulmate shit. I don't know if I even want it."

How could he when the only example he had was one person sucking the life out of another? Are some people just born knowing how to sort that out? How to separate your past from your future? His sister had done it. Somehow she had, but whenever he thought of love, he thought of disappointing someone or being disappointed every day for the rest of your life until love and hate felt the same.

"So what do you want then?" Cat asked.

Pain spread through his chest and his eyes burned. Why was she making him boil this down? Distill it into specifics instead of just this abstract idea that he could easily dismiss as not for him?

Why was she making him *say* it?

"I just want someone to look at me the way you look at Josh. Like you trust him with your life and he's worthy of it."

"He is."

Dylan nodded, her bluntness chastising him into a whisper. "And I want to look at someone the way Josh looks at you. With all that hope written right on his fucking face for everyone to see." He laughed humorlessly. "I've been giving him shit for that for so long. That blind faith. I felt it, you know? With Dani—that hope. I just never let it hit my face." His voice cracked, and he felt like his heart was being crushed like a tin can.

But Cat wasn't giving him an inch. "That's a choice," she said. "You and I both know Josh has every reason in the world to doubt the future. We all have reasons if we want to dwell on them. He chooses to be all in every day. It's terrifying and I don't know how he does it."

"I want to choose that with Dani." His chest ached with how much he wanted it. When he'd watched Dani walk away from him, it felt like someone had blotted out the sun. He'd ruined it, just like he'd always suspected he would if he ever decided to go down that road with a woman—the one where he tried to be something he wasn't sure he had in him. But he hadn't expected the way needing to fix it would over-shadow any sort of indignance he could claim for being right about love.

But he wasn't right.

He opened his eyes to see Cat's left hand moving slowly over her belly, Josh's mother's ring shining in the dim light of the bedroom. His parents weren't the only example he had. Maybe he'd spent so much time giving Josh shit for his all-in, optimistic version of love because he was afraid to see it for what it was—proof that his excuses were bullshit. He had examples all around him now—good men, being adults, being responsible. So far it hadn't killed any of them.

Love wasn't about disappointing someone. That happened no matter what you called it. Love was about trying your hardest not to disappoint them, and showing up to fix it when you failed. It was about sticking around and promising to do better next time. He wanted so badly to make things better with Dani and that could only mean one thing. His stomach turned. What a thing to realize too late.

"If you want to choose that, Dylan, why are you here instead of there?"

"I can't get in touch with her. She won't take my calls. Besides, Josh pretty much ordered me to be here to make you food, so..."

Cat laughed, then she put her hand over his and her laugh turned to sniffling. "Shit."

Dylan's head sprung from her shoulder. "What? Are you okay?"

"Yes. I'm fine. It's just..." she wiped at her eyes. "God, I'm too pregnant for this. She's going to Bartucci's. On Main and Tenth. Damn it. She's going to kill me. She's going there tonight with someone from the app. A new guy."

"What time?"

Cat rolled her lips inward like she was about to pivot.

"I'll wait there all night if you don't tell me."

"Ugh! Seven."

An idea hit him and he shot up to his knees, cupping Cat's face and pecking the top of her head. "You're an angel, Kit Cat." He hopped off the bed. "I'll get your dinner."

Thirty-nine

THE DECEMBER TEMPERATURE HAD DROPPED below average with the sunset, leaving a dusting of frost on the ground. The sound of Dylan's boots crunched loudly in his ear as he trudged toward Bartucci's. Inside, the warm orange light from a stone fireplace shone through the glass front. He could see the back of Dani's head at a tall pub table in the corner, a glass of wine in front of her as she fiddled with the bracelet on her wrist.

Emotion punched at his chest. He knew the language of her body now, knew her tells—she was nervous. What he couldn't tell from the way she kept lifting her glass then putting it down without taking a sip, using her fingers to smooth her ponytail, was why. Did she already like this guy? Enough to have first date jitters? Was she anticipating a bad time? Did she somehow know he was about to swoop in there and make a scene?

It occurred to him then that he had no idea what this guy he was there to intercept looked like. That was a minor detail that might prove to be a problem for his brilliant plan. But how many single guys in a certain age range could be showing up to this very date-like restaurant?

It turned out more than a handful. "Hey, man," he said, catching a guy in a leather jacket on the sleeve as he passed.

"I don't have any change," the guy said, his eyes straight ahead.

Really? Dylan looked down at his pressed white button-up and dark wash jeans, his fucking two-hundred dollar shoes, and gaped at the guy. At least the dude who thought he was a pimp had looked him in the eye.

"No, I was wondering if you're here to meet a woman named Dani."

"Sorry. No." The guy brushed off his grip and kept walking into Bartucci's.

Dylan leaned against the brick wall of the building and pulled his phone out to occupy him while he waited.

Katie: Where the hell are you, D-bag? I didn't drive two hours to wait all night for you. Pick an outfit and get over here.

He swiped away the third and most exasperated message from his sister without answering. One step at a time. He'd pulled up his Instagram looking at Dani's last post—her in a backless dress winking over her shoulder. She held a glass of champagne up for the camera.

Dylan smoothed a thumb over his screen, enlarging the picture. He should have been there, wherever that picture was taken. It should have been him. Tonight it might not be champagne and little black dresses, but it would be him. He had to make sure.

Another guy approached—mid-thirties, beard, dress shirt— and Dylan stashed his phone. "Hey. Excuse me."

"Yeah?"

Dylan ran a hand over the back of his head. "Are you here to see a woman named Dani by any chance?"

"Who are you?" The guy took a step back, clearly caught off-guard. This had to be him.

Dylan put his hands up to say no harm meant and cleared his throat. "I'm Dylan." He held his hand out and the guy reluctantly shook it.

"Jake."

"Listen, Jake, I'm a friend of hers." He stopped. "More than a friend. Or I used to be. I know this is weird, but I'm going to appeal to you, man to man. I blew it with her. I know you don't know her yet, but trust me, it was a big mistake. I need another chance." He straightened, tugging at his shirt hem. "I'm here to ask you to let me take this date from you."

Jake laughed, and not in an *I totally get it, dude* way. More in a *this guy is insane* way.

"I know it sounds crazy," Dylan said. "But you don't understand—"

"First of all," Jake said, holding up a hand, "what the fuck?"

His shoulders sagged. "I know."

"Second of all, how do I know you're not some creepy ex-boyfriend she doesn't want to see? Or a stalker or something? I let you go in there and she ends up in the trunk of your car."

"No. Look, it's nothing like that—"

"Of course, you wouldn't tell me if it was."

"You've got a point." Dylan nodded, giving Jake his best normal dude smile. "You're right. You're a good guy, Jake. Give me two minutes." He pulled his phone out again, swiping away another message from Katie, and dialed a video call.

A couple of rings later, Cat appeared on his screen. She was in her pajamas, the hem of her tank top riding up to show her round belly. She looked adorable. *Perfect.*

"What did you do?" she asked.

Jesus, Cat. Not helpful. "Hey, Kit Cat. I'm here with Jake."

She threw a hand up like she had no idea what he was talking about. *So Dani hasn't even told Cat this guy's name. Good sign.*

"Jake, very rightfully, is just a little concerned about letting me go on this date with Dani instead of him."

"Oh my God. This is your plan? You couldn't just call her?"

He gave Jake another innocent smile, then pulled the phone to his ear and whispered. "I did. She sent me to voicemail. Please? Just tell him I'm not a threat."

Her growl was loud enough to get to Jake, and he pulled his lips inward, glancing through the window. Jake was about to run out of patience, which in turn would lead to him going in there and telling Dani about this immediately.

Dylan was putting all of his trust in Cat right now, trust he didn't deserve, but it was his last shot. He switched back to video and held the screen up to Jake.

"She's pregnant," he said. "Did you see that?"

"I saw."

"Hi, Jake," Cat said flatly. She could have feigned a little more enthusiasm but at least she was doing it. "I'm Cat, Dani's best friend. That's our friend Dylan. This is so rude, and he's way out of line—"

"What the hell, Cat?"

"But!" she shouted. "He really is a good guy and Dani will not be upset to see him once she hears what he has to say. He owes you for your time, so please accept dinner and a drink from him in exchange for him ruining your evening, but know you'll be doing a good thing."

Dylan nodded like a Bobblehead doll at Cat's speech, praying it was convincing enough. Jake crossed his arms over his chest. Inside, Dani looked over her shoulder again, probably thinking she was being stood up. "Please, man," Dylan said. He held the phone away and lowered his voice. "I love her. I think she might love me too. She shouldn't be here."

Jake let out an exasperated sigh. "You're all insane."

"Totally," Dylan agreed. "But not criminally. I promise."

"All right. Shoot your shot, man. Honestly, this is some crazy shit, but I get the feeling I should split and let it play out."

"Thank you." Dylan held out his hand again, relief pouring through him as Jake shook it. "And Cat's right. Go in, order at the bar. It's on me."

"Forget it," Jake said, waving him off. "If this works, maybe the karma will help me out on my next date."

"I hope so, man. Thank you."

Jake slapped Dylan's shoulder and nodded, heading back the way he came.

Dylan pulled the phone back to his face to see Cat still waiting.

"Psycho," she said, her arms crossed on top of her belly.

He grinned. "Thank you. I owe you one."

"Consider us even if you don't screw this up."

"I won't, Cat. I promise."

By the time Dylan pushed into the restaurant, his fingers were like ice. His cheeks burned when the warm air hit him and he took a breath to steady himself before crossing the room to where Dani sat, still fiddling. She had her phone out now, hopefully not calling Cat to tell her about how her date didn't show. Poor Jake. Dylan would clear his name as soon as he could. Jake was a great guy. Jake was a fucking saint.

He stepped to her table and cleared his throat. "Dani?"

Her head popped up, her ponytail bouncing. "What the hell, Dylan?" she hissed. "I'm meeting someone." She did another scan of the room. "Shit. Don't tell me you're here on a date too. Why does everything have to be so complicated?"

"Dani. Wait. Look—" He stumbled for his next words. He'd rehearsed his plea to whatever guy showed up tonight, but maybe he hadn't even really believed it would work himself, since he hadn't planned this any further. He swallowed and ran a hand over his hair. "Jake, right?"

"Oh great," she said, tossing her phone on the table. "Even better. You know him?"

Her head was still on swivel and guilt started to eat at him. He needed to spit this out. "We just met. Um, I convinced him to let me take his place."

"*What?*"

Okay, maybe he'd misjudged the romantic gesture angle with her. "Let me explain."

"How did you even know where I—"

"Cat. Don't be mad. Dani, please. I fucked up. Bad. I never meant to hurt you, but you never even gave me a chance to explain or apologize. You said we were friends. We have way more history than the few weeks you let me be with you, so I guess I'm just calling on that history and asking you to let me tell you what was going through my head when I called off the dinner. I can't promise it will be what you want to hear, but I can promise it will be the truth."

Dani's red lips parted, her eyes darting around his face. If she sent him away now, he didn't know what he would do. This was his last shot, his last desperate plea, and the first time he'd ever done desperate.

Finally, she snapped her mouth shut and held a hand out for him to sit.

Dylan's heart rushed. "Thank you." He pulled up onto the stool and tugged at the damp collar of his shirt. In the span of five minutes, he'd gone from freezing his ass off, to sweat beading around his temples and the back of his neck. *Don't blow this, Pierce.*

"When I asked you to go with me to that dinner with my mom, I meant it. I wanted you there and everything that came with that. But I was taking a flying leap and I hadn't given two thoughts as to how I was going to land. I was just focusing on, you know, the rush of it all, the way it felt to have you beside me, supporting me. Taking some of the pressure that's always there. Like the Jansens that night."

Dani's eyes were unmoved, but he continued.

"I had every intention of telling my mom about us. Being all in with you. Hell, I was even looking forward to the shock on her face. But then my sister called and said she and her husband were coming. It turned into this whole thing and I panicked. I was about to show up to a Pierce Family event with a girlfriend. You have to understand, I've *never* done that before. Instead of a meal with my mom, it felt like a statement I wasn't ready to make." He paused, his heart hammering. "God, it sounds stupid coming out of my mouth, Dani. I know how stupid it sounds. But there's a difference." His voice cracked and he looked at the ceiling. How could he make her understand this?

"Tell me," she said quietly. He met her eyes again and she gave an almost imperceptible nod. Enough to put some air back into his lungs to finish.

"I know it doesn't sound like a big difference, two extra guests, but my sister is not my mother. My mom has typical mother expectations but she doesn't understand why it's so fucking hard. She's blissfully ignorant to what our dad leaving did to us. She needs to be, maybe. And explaining it to her feels ungrateful for how hard she worked to make us feel like a normal family. How can I tell her that she worked two jobs and volunteered for all our school shit and ran herself ragged all those years and we still ended up fucked up? So I let her think I'm just some player who doesn't want anything real—no correlation to my father and the blood that runs through my veins. I lie to her every day. I lie to everyone, every fucking day."

Shit, it felt so good to say it. Like a dam breaking, the water rushing over him, making him clean.

"I can't lie to my sister like that," he went on. "She lived what I did. She knows what it means for me to put that aside and choose to be with someone. Be with you. It's a choice to make a stand and say that I'm not him. I didn't know if I could do it. What if I fucked it up, you know? What if I made that stand and then I found out I was wrong? It was easier just to hide for a little while longer where things felt easy. You and me, we felt easy before all of this. I liked it there, Dani. I want to go back. But I also want to make the stand."

Dani blinked, her dark eyelashes fluttering. "Dylan."

"I know it's a shitty excuse."

"No," she said, touching the corner of her eye. "It's not. But you didn't have to lie. I would have understood."

Dylan laughed humorlessly. "That might be the worst part about it. I know you would have. I just didn't want you to know. I've spent my whole life trying not to let that part of me show. The part that came from him. But Cat said something to me earlier. She asked me to think of my worst day and then tell her who I wished was by my side when it happened. I've never thought of how it would feel to let someone see it. To lean on someone else. But when I imagined it, it was you."

He paused and took a deep breath through his nose. This was his chance to man up, embrace what he'd been afraid to.

"Somewhere between wanting to get in your pants and wanting to be your friend, I fell in love with you, Dani-pie."

Dani laughed, a tear spilling over her cheek. "Thank God. I was afraid the real Dylan got lost somewhere, but you're still in there."

Dylan's smile nudged its way in. "I'm always going to be me, unfortunately. But I'm going to try so hard to be the me that you liked for the last few months."

"I've always liked you, Dylan. Friends, remember?"

A lump formed in his throat. Had he just confessed he was in love with her, just to get the same friend speech they'd started with?

But her tears fell faster now, and she pressed

her fingers to her temples. "Damn it, Dylan. I hate crying."

"I'm sorry."

"No. Don't be sorry. I've been waiting my whole life for someone to tell me something that real. To think of me as more than just a fun time. I more than like you. I love how you can't let a sappy moment stand without throwing a joke in. I love how loyal you are to your friends. I love how you make any event more fun just by walking in. And I love that stupid grin of yours when you know you've made me melt over something you've said. Like right now."

She pointed at him and he realized he was smiling again.

"That one," she said. "I love that face. I've missed it so much. God, I didn't know it until right now, but I love you too."

Dylan launched himself across the table, nearly knocking Dani's glass of wine onto the marble floor. She caught it though, pushing it aside while he cupped her face and kissed her. He pulled her bottom lip between his teeth, biting gently, and she made a little whimper of a noise.

"Let's go," he said. "I want to take you somewhere."

"Can we eat there, because I was supposed to be having a fancy antipasto salad right now."

"We can definitely eat there, and no salad. You don't even like salad."

"I hate salad."

"Good. I'm going to feed you." He reached into his wallet and threw a twenty on the table to cover her wine and the waiter's time. Then he grabbed her hand and pulled her down from the stool, into his arms. Her chest pressed against his, molding to him like she was supposed to. "For the record, Jake wasn't the type of guy who would want you to get a salad you hated. He was a stand-up dude."

"Good to know. I'll keep his number in case you ever make me cry again."

"Fuck that," Dylan said. He dipped her into a kiss that was much more tongue than appropriate for the setting. "I lied. He was an asshole."

Dani's cheeks turned five shades of pink and she giggled into his chest. "Let's go before we get kicked out."

Forty

"SO HOW MUCH TROUBLE SHOULD Cat be in?" Dani asked as Dylan led her up a concrete walkway. He'd pulled the car in front of a brick ranch with white shutters and a mismatch of potted flowers crowding the small set of front steps.

"She should wear a crown, actually. I think I'll get one made for her."

Dani laughed, butterflies darting around in her belly. Dylan hadn't said it outright, but she had a feeling she knew whose house this was. When they stopped under the yellow light from the replica lantern above the door, he cupped her elbows and stared down at her. "I was serious about making that stand."

"Where are we?"

"Pierce family game night. It's the absolute worst, but these are the things you're going to have to do now. I hope you understand."

Dani could feel herself beaming. "I'll make the sacrifice. But you did promise me food."

"Lucky for you, my mother could probably

Lauren H. Mae

put that fancy Italian restaurant out of business if she were so inclined."

"Looks like my night turned out well, then."

"Don't speak too soon. You ready?"

Dylan didn't wait for an answer. He pushed open the front door and wrapped an arm around her waist, ushering her into a small foyer off of the kitchen. When he kicked off his boots, she reached down to slip off the heels she'd worn with her navy blue sleeveless dress. She was quickly reminded she was probably way over-dressed for game night, but Dylan was perpetu-ally over-dressed so she pushed that aside.

Dylan slid his fingers into hers and tugged. He kept his eyes on her as he navigated into the living room, like he was worried she might flee if he stopped to look where he was going.

"Dylan!" Irene jumped up from the couch and took two steps before flattening a palm over her chest dramatically. "Dani. From the wedding."

Dani felt Dylan's palm getting moist but he didn't let go. "Hi, Irene," she said, offering her free hand. Irene brushed it away and went in for a hug, forcing Dylan to drop his grip. Over Irene's shoulder, a slender woman with straight black hair just like Dylan's got to her feet. She'd been sitting cross-legged on the carpet with two young boys who were also now staring.

"Dylan. You've been ignoring my texts. We weren't sure if you were coming."

"Hey, Katie. I wasn't sure if Dani was com-ing," he said, capturing Dani's hand again as soon as Irene released her. "Didn't want to come without her."

Katie looked Dani up and down, but it wasn't appraisingly. It was more uncertainty as to whether she should greet Dani, or if she might disappear into thin air any minute.

"I'm Kate," she said, apparently deciding to chance it. "Dylan's sister."

"Hi, Kate. I'm Dani." She plopped a period at the end of that sentence, giving Dylan a break, but he didn't hesitate.

"Dani's my girlfriend," he said.

Dani watched Kate's eyes widen before she caught hold of her expression and smiled. "I'm very glad to meet you."

"I'm glad to meet you too."

Kate opened her arm to usher them into Irene's living room, since Dylan's mother had apparently gone still with confusion. Happy confusion, it seemed. This was all very happily confusing. Dylan ruffled his nephews' hair and chose an armchair, tugging Dani onto his lap. Irene snapped back to the room, rushing to offer Dani a glass of wine.

"Get her some food, Ma. Will you? I sort of stole her dinner."

"Dylan! Why would you..." Irene threw her hands in the air and headed to the kitchen. "I'll be back with a plate and a napkin to cover that pretty dress, Dani."

Dylan squeezed her tighter. "Call her Danica," he said with a smirk.

Dani smiled. "Go ahead."

Forty-one

DANI PEELED BACK HER WARM sheets and craned her neck to see the time. Since he'd been staying over every other weekend, Dylan had claimed the side of the bed with the nightstand so he could take off his watch and charge his phone. She peered over his bare shoulder and squinted at her clock.

"We should get up," she mumbled half-heartedly. It was early, but the grumbling in her stomach didn't care. "I need food. And coffee." A dull throbbing in her head that she'd been mildly aware of picked up tempo, knocking out a morse code plea for caffeine.

Dylan rolled to his back and stretched his arms above his head. She watched his biceps flex and his abs tighten, the sight zinging electricity between her legs. "This is a first," he said through a yawn. "You trying to wake me up instead of the other way around."

She smiled at the way his eyes scrunched against the light. He looked so innocent in the mornings. Utter deception.

"Call it a New Year's resolution." Actually her hunger had just pushed past ignorable and she was a little afraid that if she didn't eat, she might puke.

They were both on vacation from work for the holiday, and after spending a quiet Christmas day at Dylan's mom's house, Dylan had come back to the city and stayed the whole week. Last night, they'd stayed out far too late, ringing in the New Year at a white-tablecloth restaurant, then dancing at an exclusive club that the Jansens owned a share in. Cat was still on bedrest and Sonya was spending the holiday in Fiji with Marcus—his annual travel gift to her for being gone half the year. This was the first time in a long time that they hadn't all been together on New Year's Eve. Instead of lamenting that things had changed, she smiled at all of the ways spending all night with just Dylan had been perfect.

All night might have been too late this time, though. Even Dylan's mouth on her neck couldn't beat out her need for liquid sustenance. She tried to push out of the bed, but Dylan tugged her back with a big hand across her belly. He was so warm and naked and hard. Her lower half battled against her brain. "Mmm. Stop," she whispered, tugging at his hair. "I promise if you give me coffee, I'll be much nicer to you."

"I kind of like it when you're not nice to me," he said, running his tongue under her ear, leaving a trail of goosebumps.

"Well, then I'll be mean. But first, coffee."

Dylan laughed and rolled away, stealing the covers from her. She whined, but after he pulled on a pair of sweatpants that he kept permanently balled up on her chair, he tucked her back in. "I'll make the coffee. You stay here all warm and cozy, Dani-pie."

She snuggled back into the pillow, taking a deep breath of his cologne still lingering on the sheets as she watched him pad barefoot and bare-chested out of the room. He looked good at her place, surrounded by her stuff. And she couldn't complain about the service. "I feel like a princess right now."

"Get used to it," he called over his shoulder. "This is what dating Dylan Pierce is like."

"I never would have guessed," she whispered. Her eyes closed and she listened to him singing some song from the club last night while he opened cabinets and fiddled with her coffee maker. Her return to sleep was interrupted, though, by the loud buzzing of her cell beside Dylan's.

"That has to be Emma," she grumbled as she reached around blindly for the phone. No one else would call this early after the biggest party night of the year.

But just before she answered it with some snarky line, she caught Josh's name on her caller ID. Her heart skipped nervously.

"Why is Emma up so early?" Dylan called to her.

"No," she said. "It's Josh." She answered it. "Hey. Is Cat okay?"

"Cat is perfect."

"Oh," she said. She pressed a hand to her chest. "You scared me with the early morning call. What's up?"

"I know you're probably sleeping in today, but we can't hold her family off for too long, and Cat really wants you to be the first one to meet the baby."

"Baby?" Dani threw the covers off of her legs and sprung to her feet.

"Last night," Josh said, laughing. "It's a girl. New Year's Eve baby."

He sounded like a kid on Christmas and she wished she could reach through the phone and squeeze him.

Dylan wandered in with a mug of coffee, tipping his head curiously while she bounced on her toes.

"Congratulations, Josh. And everything is okay? It's still early."

"Everything's fine. She's tiny and she's going to have to stay at the hospital a little longer than normal, but no complications. Cat had a C-section, so more bed rest."

She heard some of his joy slip at that. "She'll be absolutely fine, Josh. She must be ecstatic." She looked up at Dylan and mouthed: *baby.* His face lit up, emerald eyes and dimples shining. "Dylan's here."

"I was hoping he was," Josh said. "Can you both come?"

A tiny cry sounded over the phone and tears blurred Dani's vision. Everything that had seemed so big over the last few months suddenly felt as small as that cry. "Of course. Yes! We'll be there right away."

"Great. Thanks, Dani. I'll see you soon."

"See you soon, Joshy."

"It's a girl?" Dylan asked when she tossed her phone on the mattress.

Dani nodded, wiping at the corner of her eye and sniffing. Her heart felt too full for her chest. "We've got to go." She took a mug from him and gulped, then shoved it back into his hands. She grabbed a towel and her robe and headed down the hall.

"Wait," Dylan called, laughing. "What's her name?"

"Oh! I didn't ask."

"Catia, you really picked another name that your poor husband can't pronounce?" Dylan ran a finger along the seam of the swaddle blanket, watching it expand with each breath the baby took. She was so tiny. So warm. Her little eyelids fluttered as he bounced her gently in one arm. This was worth the early morning ride, hungover and still uncaffeinated.

Josh looked about as good as Dylan felt, his head tipped back in the wooden chair, his clothes wrinkled from sleeping in them. Or not sleeping in them. He didn't even open his eyes to fight back. "It was my mother's name, dick head. I know how to say it. It's Lucia." He pronounced the "C" with a "Shh" and Dylan shook his head.

"Lu-chee-ah," Dylan said. "Your mother was Italian. Say it right."

Dani and Cat shared a look from Cat's bed.

"I'm gonna call her Lulu."

Josh grinded his teeth. "You do that."

Even in his wrinkled jeans with bags under his eyes, fatherhood already looked good on his best friend. The thought burst into Dylan's head and he wasn't sure where to put it. It was strange looking at Josh and knowing he'd be something Dylan's father had never wanted to be—that he would take this responsibility and treasure it. Like all of a sudden, fatherhood itself had a new face.

Dani nudged his shoulder from her spot sitting on Cat's bed. "I need another turn." She held out her arms, and Dylan twisted to pass the baby to Dani. Their gaze caught over Lucia's tiny pink hat. Dani's eyes were wet, her mascara smudged in the corners. She was hungover and wearing sweats and so, so happy. The joy on her face hit him square in the chest. This scene they'd found themselves in together was something she wanted one day. He'd made the choice to be there with her knowing that. Today it felt dangerous in a thrill-ride kind of way instead of a dread kind of way.

Dani settled next to Cat and they cooed together over the baby while Josh sat slouched in the chair, half-asleep. Dylan kicked his foot. "Let's get some coffee."

Josh pulled himself out of the wooden chair, lumbering over to Cat like he might actually be sleepwalking. He leaned down and with one hand on the back of his daughter's tiny head, kissed his wife. It was closed-mouthed and lazy, but it felt so intimate that Dylan turned his head away.

"So this is life now?" Dylan asked as they walked the long hospital corridor, toward the cafeteria. "Diapers and spit up."

A goofy grin spread across Josh's face. "Weird, huh?"

Dylan nodded. It was weird, but it also felt like the natural order of things; another one of those pressure changes in action.

They found a coffee cart in the hospital lobby and took a seat at a cafe table. "So, how's it feel?"

Josh ran a hand over his face, yawning. "Like I'm never going to sleep again."

"Yeah, I hear babies will do that to you."

"I guess so." He took a long sip of his coffee, gazing out the glass doors of the lobby. "I don't mean the diaper changes and feedings, though. I mean so much could go wrong. I don't know how I'll ever sleep thinking about it."

Suddenly Dylan saw the exhaustion on Josh's face wasn't only from lack of sleep. He didn't know much about birth, but he knew Lucia was early, and a C-section wasn't part of the plan. Even though everyone was all smiles today, the night had probably been stressful, scary.

"Yeah," he said, following Josh's gaze to the bright winter morning. "It didn't go wrong, though. Cat and Lucia are fine. This is all you've ever wanted, man. You can't be afraid to have it now."

Josh nodded, a resilience Dylan had always envied seeping back into his expression. "What about you?" Josh asked around another sip of coffee. "You seem different with Dani. More regular Dylan, less Dylan Pierce, International Playboy."

Dylan laughed. "I haven't gone international in a while."

"You know what I mean. Where do you see it going? What is it *you* want?"

"I don't know," he said, a cool, easy shrug lifting his shoulders out of habit. But that felt like a lie. He looked again at Josh—eyes bloodshot, scared shitless but not even a hint of turning tail in his steady posture.

"Would it be crazy to say I want it to go here?" He looked around the lobby. "Or, you know, somewhere in this general direction?"

He braced himself for Josh to laugh, or tell him to lower his expectations, but he didn't. He just kept staring out the window. "No, man. I don't think it would be crazy at all."

Forty-two

Three months later

"WHERE DID YOU DECIDE ON?" Dani thumbed two pages of notes written in Cat's bubbly cursive while Cat checked the temperature of a bottle for the fifth time. In addition to feeding times, she'd written out the exact location of every baby-related item, including a hand-drawn sketch of the nursery. She was so neurotic.

"The Jetty is open for the season," Cat said. "We're just going to get dinner. We won't be long."

Dani stepped behind Cat while she gathered her coat and purse, attempting to herd her toward the door. "Take as long as you want. It's under control." She pointed to the living room where Dylan had Lucia pressed to his shoulder, bouncing his knees to the music playing from a pink and yellow bouncy-seat.

Dani shared a smile with Cat, knowing full well hers was sappy as hell. Dylan with a baby was up there with the most adorable things she'd ever encountered. It was possible, even if this entire soulmate search hadn't happened, Dani might have fallen in love with Dylan anyway. The first time she'd seen him play peek-a-boo with Lucia, her heart would have been his.

She was glad they took the long road, though. It was rougher, more battle-tested. It meant when Dylan was less adorable, she didn't feel the need to question things. She had her moments too. With personalities like theirs, sparks flew more often than not. It was just a matter of keeping the good ones flamed and stomping on the bad ones. They were doing okay at that.

Dylan looked up and made a face at the fact that Cat still hadn't finished getting ready.

Dani laughed and mimed strangling Cat when her back was turned. They were doing more than okay.

"You're sure you know how to warm the breast milk?" Cat asked, nearly catching her.

"I'm sure."

"Catia," Josh said quietly. He'd been standing at the door patiently, his coat on, his keys in his hand.

Cat took a deep breath. "Okay." She turned to hug Dani, squeezing hard. "Thank you for doing this."

"Are you kidding? We're going to have so much fun." She crossed the room and took Lucia from Dylan, nuzzling her warm baby-scented skin. "Aren't we, Lulu?"

Josh kissed the top of Lucia's head, then swept Cat out of the house like he was afraid she might turn into a pumpkin.

When the door closed, Dylan fell onto the couch with a tired sigh. "Ridiculous," he said.

"I don't know. They're kind of cute." Dani laid the baby on her lap, fussing with her pink onesie.

Dylan cupped her head in his big palm. "This one is kind of cute."

"She's the cutest. And I got to watch her before Emma or Sonya."

Dylan laughed from his belly, and Lucia pulled a tiny baby half-smile at the sound. "You're always running a race, Dani-pie. That's why I love you."

The declaration warmed her cheeks. It still surprised her how free Dylan was with his affection. It was like he'd been storing it up for so long that he couldn't help but say things like that every chance he got. And he did—Friday nights when they'd turn off a movie early and fall into bed; Saturday nights when he was dressed in a shirt and tie and they were at some trendy new restaurant; Sunday mornings that turned into Sunday afternoons in bed. His bed, usually, which was new. With Cat and Josh, and now Lucia, right down the road, she didn't spend much time at her condo. She'd always liked this little town they all called home. Maybe she'd call it home someday too. But there was plenty of time for that.

"I think I'm done running races, actually," she said. She leaned into Dylan's side and smiled down at Lucia. "At least about the important things."

He smoothed his thumb over Lucia's cheek. "Things have changed a lot, haven't they?"

"I think so. But I think that's the whole point. Maybe I missed that before."

"Yeah?"

"Yeah. Stasis is death, right? Life moves forward whether you're ready for it or not."

Dylan raised an eyebrow. "You thinking about doing this whole song and dance, Dani? The babies and the diapers and the family?"

Shit. She hadn't meant to imply anything. Sure, she'd let herself think about it, what that would look like with Dylan. And she'd caught him more than once, watching Josh with Lulu. He did the same with Shawn and Mattie now too, his eyes intense like he was studying for an exam. She knew he was taking it all in, these examples of a world he thought he lived outside of. She knew because she was taking them in too. The two of them were finding their own way, but it never hurt to have an idea of the terrain.

The last thing she wanted to do was push, though. "I didn't mean it like that," she said.

Dylan's lip twitched, his dimples sneaking out.

"Really, Dylan. I wasn't trying to—"

He interrupted her with a kiss, laughing against her mouth. "All right, Dani-pie. Just say when."

Did you enjoy The Rules?

Reviews help indie authors
get our books noticed!

If you liked this book, you can
leave a review on Amazon.

Or leave a review on Goodreads.

If you haven't read book one in the
Summer Nights Series, check out
Josh and Catia's story, *The Catch*

Acknowledgements

I'm one of the lucky ones who have never found myself writing in a vacuum. From the beginning of this series and before, I've had a group of writers who I can bounce things off of and whine to when the writing gets tough. I'll never stop crediting them with making me make this happen. Through all of the ups and downs of starting a career like this, your support has been immeasurable. As always, this book is for The Chat.

One thing I didn't fully understand when I released The Catch out into the world, was how many women like me I would meet through writing this book. Romance lovers, shippers, fierce seekers of HEA's, those who know that love really does make the world go round and proudly fill their bookshelves with stories about it. Meeting you has been the most fun, and your support for The Catch and anticipation of The Rules keeps me going. Critique partners, beta readers, other romance writers, Bookstagrammers, and romance readers—if I have one wish it would be to keep making new connections through these stories that encompass so many real life emotions and experiences. I think that's what writing and reading is all about—finding common ground with real people through fictional stories. Thank you for loving my characters as much as I do. Thank you for caring about their worlds because they look a little bit like yours and thank you for telling me about those little pieces that you connected with. It means everything.

As always, to my husband and boys, thank you for weekends spent at this computer when the state of the world took my weekday writing time. Thank you for giving me the time to pursue my dreams. And thank you for being my dream.

Don't miss the next book
by
Lauren H. Mae

Follow me on Twitter: @lhmae_me
Facebook and Instagram: @laurenhmaeauthor
Or subscribe to my website for
updates, release info, and cover reveals.
www.laurenhmae.com

Epilogue for The Catch

JOSH REACHED FOR HIS PHONE in the dark to silence his alarm. He swiped his thumb over the screen, his eyes lingering on the lock screen photo—a blurry selfie he'd taken right after Cat had said yes to his proposal. It was night when he took it, and their faces looked shiny and flushed in the flash, an ocean breeze blew her hair over one eye. His lips were pressed to her temple and she smiled like the sun. It was his favorite picture.

He rolled over to look at his wife, face down in her pillow, her dark hair like a typhoon around her head. One arm dangled over the side of the bed—a sign she'd fallen asleep rocking the bassinet beside her. He wanted to ignore the time, curl up and steal another few minutes of sleep with her, but he'd gotten a four hour stretch—a record lately—so he couldn't complain.

Leaning over Cat, he brushed a thumb over his daughter's cheek, then flattened his palm on her warm belly, watching it rise and fall with tiny little puffs. Lucia was a mini Cat—the same dark hair, the same brown skin, only slightly lightened by his genes. They even snored in tandem. Quiet vibrations that barely broke the silence. Yeah, it was hell leaving this every morning.

Luckily, today he didn't have to, but he did have to get out of bed.

When he came back into the room after his shower, their record stretch had ended. Cat was sitting up, the baby in her arms, milk-drunk and—he swore he wasn't imagining it—smiling. "She missed you," Cat said.

He kissed the top of Lucia's head, then turned to his wife. "I missed *you*." He leaned in to nuzzle her neck, knowing she'd dodge him if he tried for a kiss. Even after the time he'd washed puke out of hair in a public bathroom during a particularly violent bout of morning sickness, Cat still wouldn't let him kiss her before she brushed her teeth.

She did thread her fingers into his hair and snuggle back, though, letting out a quiet hum of contentment that made his body warm. Her skin still smelled like coconut, but now the scent mixed with baby lotion and milk. He opened his mouth and breathed her in. The mornings when he got to stick around were the best.

"You should shower," he said, straightening and lifting Lucia out of her arms. "We don't want to be late." Today was Easter Sunday and they were celebrating Lucia's baptism, something Cat's mother had been planning since the birth.

Another yawn and she swung her legs off of the bed. He shifted Lucia to one arm and wrapped a hand around Cat's elbow, helping her stand. She was fully-healed from the C-section now, but he couldn't break the habit. Catia, for all of her toughness and independence, let him do it. She always acquiesced to him. Only him.

Cat's parent's house overflowed with family, all eating and celebrating after Mass. Her mother had insisted on hosting the party with her annual Easter Brunch, and Cat was glad to be able to relax and rest. And eat.

She set her empty dessert plate aside and leaned her head back in her father's arm chair, listening to the sound of Josh's laughter—rich and happy. She used to worry that the chaos of Roday family holidays would wear on him: aunts and uncles and cousins all swarming him like locusts, her mother always trying to feed him. But that laugh was content. It had been almost three years since she'd first heard it, and that laugh still warmed her belly, still made her heart race and her legs squeeze together. That laugh was home.

At his bar, her father held court with all of his sons-in-law—a favorite pastime. Today he mixed mimosas there, something Cat was sure was a concession to her mother's strict holiday menu planning. Cat noted that for the silent little act of love that it was. She saw them everywhere now, drawn in each person's individual style. The way in a room full of people, Dylan turned to Dani first whenever he made a joke. The way Dani laughed louder than anyone else. Every. Single. Time. The way her mother put tomatoes in everything she cooked because Carlos loved them, then picked them all out one by one because she hated them. The way Josh, always braver than everyone else, had held her face in his hands and cried like a baby when Lucia was born.

Love.

Speaking of little acts of love, Josh's pale blue dress shirt had a growing wet spot on the shoulder, his salmon-colored tie wrinkled between Lucia's tiny fingers. She watched him press his lips to their daughter's head casually as he chatted, and that warmth in her belly ignited into a roaring bonfire. If she thought she was hopelessly in love before, watching Josh with their daughter had unleashed a whole new level of infatuation for her husband.

"You look adorable, Catia," her sister Olivia said, gesturing to her flowered dress. It matched LuLu's tights and Josh's tie because as much as she hated to admit it, she was *that* mom.

"Thank you. It took three months, but I finally fit in my clothes again."

Olivia bounced her toddler on her knee while she handed Cat a bunny-shaped cookie. The boy grabbed at the frosted shortcake, and Cat broke off a piece in aunty solidarity. Taryn smiled, getting frosting on his nose.

"Is Lucia sleeping well?"

Cat touched a fingertip to the bags under her eyes. "Not exactly."

"It gets better," Olivia said, her eyes sympathetic.

Cat glanced again at Josh. The scruff on his jaw was days old, and his normally bright eyes were tinged with the pink of exhaustion. Lucia's eyelids fluttered too, her head now resting on Josh's collarbone, her other hand clutching her pacifier. The bonfire in her belly roared. How could it get any better than this?

After lunch, Carlos and Cynthia's house was quieter, the more distant relatives having left. Josh's eyelids and shoulders felt heavy. A day like this was a lot on such little sleep. He wondered how Cat was holding up on even less.

"Looks good on you," Carlos said, gesturing to Lulu, asleep on Josh's chest. He was alone with Cat's father now, the others having heeded Cynthia's last call for dessert.

"You mean the spit up?"

Carlos laughed, his hand on his belly. "I mean the family."

Josh nodded, letting that thought flavor the air around him. "Feels pretty good too."

Carlos took a sip of his drink—a scotch and soda he'd made for them in lieu of the mimosas. When he spoke again, his voice was low, thoughtful. "Something occurred to me today, Josh. I realized that if I don't say something to you, you may never hear it."

"What's that?"

"I think you should know we're very happy you're part of this family. I mean no disrespect to the family who raised you, but I think of you as a son now, and if I may say it, I think your parents would be very proud of you."

Emotion tightened the back of Josh's throat. It was hard not to think about his own childhood now that he was a father. He *had* wondered from time to time what his parents would think of this life he'd made. But it was the other words that got him in the gut. He remembered the first time he'd met Carlos, visited this house. He'd known right away he wanted to belong here, and now he did. Sometimes he had to remind himself that all of this was real—that in the span of a few years, he'd acquired his life's fortune.

"Thank you, sir. For saying that." It was all he could get out, but maybe all the moment needed from him.

Carlos slapped a big hand on Josh's shoulder and tapped his glass. Then he headed toward the sound of Cynthia's voice.

Josh went to find Catia.

"Maria is driving me crazy," she said, when he'd settled next to her on the couch and placed Lucia in her outstretched arms. "She just asked me if I really thought I should be lifting Lucia's diaper bag. The *diaper bag!* It weighs like eight pounds."

He smiled and wrapped an arm around her. "Let them take care of you, Catia. You deserve it." It had been a difficult pregnancy, a complicated birth. If he thought for a second she'd allow it, he'd still be waiting on her hand and foot.

She rolled her eyes. "It's been over three months."

"Don't be a tough girl." Now she pushed her elbow into his side, but her big brown eyes captured his and held on.

"Kiss me and I'll stop," she said.

He took her face in his hands and kissed her like he had the first time, with everything he wanted her to know right on the edge of it.

Thank you. I love you. I'll never get over this feeling.

She kissed him back, the same sentiment flowing back to him in the way her lower lip trembled between his. The kiss lingered a little longer than he'd intended and he felt something familiar spark through the haze of exhaustion and the sappy, chest-achy kind of love he'd been in lately. Something he should probably tone down since they were sitting in her parents' living room.

"I want to go home," she whispered, reading his mind. Her fingers walked up his chest and tugged his wrinkled tie.

At the front door, he could see Dylan and Dani getting ready to leave. Dylan held Dani's coat out for her, and Cynthia had a stack of Tupperware she was waiting to hand them. Shawn and Minnie had already left. It was definitely time to escape.

He brushed Cat's hair aside and whispered in her ear. "Oh, I'm going to take you home. I'm going to feed you some leftover cake, then put on a movie and let you sleep so hard."

She giggled. "I love it when you talk dirty."

"I love you."

"I know that you do."

He kissed her again. She had no idea.